BERYL MATTHEWS was born in London but now lives in a small village in Hampshire. As a young girl her ambition was to become a professional singer, but the need to earn a wage drove her into an office, where she worked her way up from tea girl to credit controller. She grew up in a family who loved reading, and books have always been an important part of her life. She had always weaved stories in her head, but never written them down. After retiring she joined a Writers' Circle in hopes of fulfilling her dream of becoming a published author. With her first book published at the age of seventy-one, she has since written sixteen novels.

By Beryl Matthews

Hold on to Your Dreams
The Forgotten Family
Battles Lost and Won
Diamonds in the Dust
A Flight of Golden Wings
The Uncertain Years

Hold on to Your Dreams

BERYL MATTHEWS

Allison & Busby Limited
12 Fitzroy Mews
London W1T 6DW
allisonandbusby.com

First published in 2009.
This paperback edition published by Allison & Busby in 2015.

A CIP catalogue record for this book is available from
the British Library.

10 9 8 7 6 5 4 3 2 1

ISBN 978-0-7490-1803-0

Typeset in 10.55/15.55 pt Sabon by
Allison & Busby Ltd.

The paper used for this Allison & Busby publication
has been produced from trees that have been legally sourced
from well-managed and credibly certified forests.

Printed and bound by
CPI Group (UK) Ltd, Croydon, CR0 4YY

Chapter One

London, December 1899

Sensing that she was being stared at, Gertrude Melrose glanced up from the book she was reading. When she saw her brother standing just inside the door with an expression on his face she was becoming far too familiar with, she drew in an irritated breath. 'No, Edward!'

He leant against the door; already immaculately dressed for the New Year's Eve party they were to attend that evening. 'You don't even know what I am going to ask for yet.'

'Yes I do, and the answer is still the same. You've squandered grandfather's inheritance at the gaming tables, and you cannot do the same with mine! Grandfather left me that money so that I should have a degree of independence.'

'Oh, come on, Gertie, it's only a loan. I'll pay you

back.' He pushed away from the door, smiling in his most engaging way.

She wasn't fooled. 'Do you think I'm soft in the head, Edward? You know I'll never see it again. I'm your sister, remember, and know you too well. Anyway, you're forgetting something. Father has control of my money until I reach the age of twenty-one, or I marry.'

The affable, good-natured mask dropped from his face. 'You're twenty now and Father would let you have some of it. You only have to ask. I don't see why you're making such a fuss about it. Once you marry it will all go to your husband, so you might as well let me have some of it now.'

'It most certainly will not! Father has tied it up so only I can draw on it. Even he can't touch it without my signature as well as his. It's a great shame they didn't do that with yours!' She placed the book on the table beside her and studied her brother, sadness in her eyes. She hated refusing him, but he had to see the error of his ways. 'You're with a disreputable crowd, and you must break away from them and stop gambling. They can afford to lose money – you can't.'

'I know you don't like my friends, but it's just high spirits, and I don't always lose.'

'They are not friends!' Now she was exasperated. Why couldn't he see them for what they were – idle wasters and good-for-nothings. 'You've only ever had one true friend. And where is David these days? We haven't seen him for ages.'

Her brother snorted in disgust. 'He doesn't know how to enjoy himself. We've asked him to join us, but he's refused.'

'Then he has good sense.' She picked up her book again, hoping to end this distasteful conversation. She loved her brother, but it hurt her to see how much he had changed of late. He was only two years older than she was and they had always been close, until he got a taste for gambling.

'What about that diamond necklace Aunt Hanna gave you? Let me have that. You never wear it.'

She slammed down the book and surged to her feet, her violet eyes wide with concern. 'What kind of trouble are you in? It must be bad if you want to start selling my jewellery!'

'Don't get upset.' His smile was back in place, trying to make light of his plight. 'I just need a little cash to see me through until the New Year comes in. It will be 1900 – a new century, and things will change then. You'll see.'

She sighed, not able to stay angry with him for long. 'I do hope so.' She reached for her purse and tipped out the money. 'I only have one guinea, but you are welcome to that.'

'That won't get me far!'

'What's going on here?' Their father walked into the room. 'The entire household can hear your raised voices.'

'I'm sorry, Father. Edward was teasing me again, and I didn't find it amusing.'

'And that was all?' Sutton Melrose cast his son an enquiring glance.

'Yes, sir.' He gave an easy smile. 'I keep forgetting that my sister doesn't have a sense of humour.'

'And what was this . . . teasing . . . about?'

'I merely said it wouldn't be long before she found

a suitable husband.' He bent and kissed her cheek, whispering his thanks for not giving him away. 'I'm sorry, Gertie. I didn't intend to upset you.'

'I know you didn't.'

Edward straightened up and turned to his father. 'If you will excuse me, sir, I'll see you at the party. Save a dance for me, Gertie,' he called as he left them.

Her father was frowning, then his expression cleared and he smiled at her. 'You should be ready by now, my dear.'

'Do I have to come? You know how I dislike these affairs.'

'We cannot always do the things we like,' he chided gently. 'This is not only New Year's Eve, but also the turn of the century. The Harcourts have been kind enough to invite us, and your mother is looking forward to the evening.'

She couldn't stop the grimace forming. 'But the year 1900 will be there in the morning. I don't see why we have to gather in a crowded room to watch the clock tick past midnight. And I suppose Mr Glendale will be there and I shall have to spend my time avoiding him.'

Her father chuckled. 'Alexander has not tried to hide his admiration for you, and he's not a man to be turned away by your snubs. It will only make him all the more determined.'

'I don't understand why he is set on me. He makes me uneasy.' She gave a puzzled shrug. 'I don't know why I dislike him so.'

'Perhaps you should give yourself time to get to know him better? I only want you to be happy, my dear.'

Gertrude actually shuddered at the prospect of spending time with the man. Every time she saw him, she wanted to run. And she wasn't a coward! At least, she'd never thought she was. She studied her father thoughtfully, and then asked, 'Are you happy, Father?'

'That's a difficult question to answer.'

'Would you try, please?'

His frown deepened. 'You have been asking questions from the moment you could speak, always searching for answers about life. I believed you would grow out of it, but you haven't. I'll do my best with this one, but happiness means different things to different people.'

'I realise that, but I'd like to know what happiness means to you.'

After pausing for a moment to gather his thoughts, he began to speak. 'I have enjoyed building up the business and seeing the quality of the furniture we make. That has been satisfying, and yes, that makes me happy. When I look at my wife, I am content. We didn't know each other well before our marriage, but respect and affection have grown over the years. When I look at my son, I am disappointed that he has shown no sign of following me into the business. The only interest he appears to have is to enjoy himself.' He drew in a deep breath, and a gentle smile appeared. 'But when I look at my daughter, I am happy.'

She gazed at him with affection. He was tall, straight and still a handsome man. 'Oh, Mother is so lucky. If I could find someone like you I would be pleased to marry.'

He laughed, a quiet rumbling sound. 'I think we've

paid each other enough compliments. Will you now agree to come to this tedious celebration?'

'Ah!' she declared triumphantly. 'You don't want to go either.'

'As I've said many times, we can't always do what we want to. But give me the pleasure of escorting two charming ladies to the ball.'

She rushed over, standing on tiptoe to kiss his cheek. 'How can I refuse?'

'Gertrude!' Her mother bustled into the room. 'You will make us late. Do hurry and get ready. I'll send Annie to help you put your hair up. It looks so much more elegant that way.'

Gertrude cast her father an impish wink. His expression remained unchanged, except for a slight twitch at the corners of his mouth. Oh, how she loved him!

'Come, Sutton.' Florence urged her husband out of the room. 'Leave Gertrude alone or we shall never get to the celebration. Everyone we know will be attending, and it is an honour to be invited. Edward has already left and will meet us there.'

Her mood dipped as the door closed behind her parents. She prayed her brother had not headed for the gaming tables again. She didn't know how aware her parents were about their son's gambling, but from the way he had been pressuring her for money of late she guessed that he must be in debt. She thought a great deal of her brother, but was not blind to his faults. On several occasions she had urged him to tell their father and ask for a loan to pay off what he owed, but he always laughed and said it wasn't that desperate. That worried her even more, because to her way of thinking, that made him afraid to face their father because his debts were worse than he said. Of course, she just might be imagining it.

Annie arrived then and Gertrude pushed away her concerns. It was no good delaying the inevitable. She had to go to this party!

The celebration was being held at the impressive Harcourt house in Knightsbridge. They had a large ballroom and it was already full to overflowing. Gertrude only just managed to stop a groan escaping from her. How she disliked crowds.

'Courage, my dear,' her father said softly, slipping his hand through her arm. 'Smile. It's quite easy. All you have to do is turn up the corners of your mouth.'

Tipping her head back and looking up at his face, she did as he said.

'Perfect.'

They were both laughing when Florence said, 'I can't see Edward. Can you, Sutton?'

'It will be difficult to see anyone in this crowd, my dear. He'll find us eventually. Now, let us find you a seat where you can see the room clearly, and then I'll get you a cool drink. It's already stifling in here and the evening has only just begun.'

'Thank you.' Florence smiled fondly at her husband, and then turned to her daughter. 'You look very beautiful tonight and will be in demand. I shall expect to see you dancing.'

'Of course. And I've never seen you looking more elegant. You outshine all the other ladies here. Doesn't she, Father?'

'Indeed. I have already told her so.'

The compliments were received with obvious pleasure. 'This is an important occasion and we all look our best. I am proud of my family.'

'Here we are, my dear.' Sutton led them over to a vacant seat right by the dance floor. 'You'll be able to see everything from here.'

As her father made his way through the crowd in search of drinks, Gertrude noticed the large column behind her mother's seat. It was festooned with white flowers and would make an excellent hiding place. At the first opportunity she would slide behind it and hope to remain unnoticed for part of the evening anyway. But first she must find her brother. It was usual in these large houses to set aside a room for the men to smoke in and play cards. That was probably where her brother was and would have to be dragged away.

When her father returned he had a young man with him. Gertrude smiled with genuine pleasure as he greeted her mother first, before turning to her. 'Hello, David. How lovely to see you here.'

He bowed slightly, making a strand of fair hair fall forward. He brushed it back, his grey eyes glinting with a smile. 'May I have the pleasure of this dance, Gertie?'

'Of course.'

'Have you seen Edward?' her mother asked David. 'He came before us, but I can't see him anywhere.'

'No I haven't, but if I bump into him I'll tell him you have arrived and are looking for him.'

Once they were dancing, she looked up at David. 'Do you know where my brother is?'

Nodding his head and sighing deeply, David said softly, 'He's been here for some time and is in the card room with his disreputable companions.'

'Gambling?' When he nodded again she was furious. 'The fool!'

'I'm sorry, I've tried to make him come to his senses, but he won't even speak to me now.'

'Show me where this room is, and I'll get him out of there.'

'Ladies are not allowed in the card room tonight. It has been delegated as a retreat for men only.'

'I'm not a lady! You ought to know that by now, David.'

The corners of his mouth turned up in amusement. 'I have often thought you should have been the boy. Except you are far too lovely to be anything but a girl.'

'Flattery won't stop me doing what has to be done,' she declared. 'Now, take me to this room.'

Without protesting further, he guided her along a passage until they reached a closed door. 'This is it, but I'd better come in with you.'

'No!' She touched his arm. 'I won't have him accusing you of interfering.'

'I am *not* leaving you,' he declared firmly.

'Well, wait in the room opposite. If I need you, I'll scream.'

He gazed up at the ceiling and muttered, 'Dear Lord, Gertrude Melrose has been nothing but trouble from the moment she could toddle. What can we do with her?'

She gave him a playful push. 'Disappear, and stop your nonsense. When have I ever been trouble?'

'When haven't you,' he said, and then beat a hasty retreat to the other room.

Opening the door, she stepped inside. The room was full of smoke, and she peered through the haze. Eight tables had been set up and all were occupied. She spotted her brother on the far side of the room.

'Ladies are not allowed in here,' a man told her, looking up from his cards.

She ignored him and marched over to Edward, laying a hand on his shoulder. 'There you are. Mother and Father are looking for you.'

He glanced up and scowled. 'I'll come when I'm ready. And you shouldn't be in here.'

It was time for her little girl act. 'Oh you men, always playing your silly game of cards.'

'Get her out of here,' one of her brother's companions growled irritably. 'She ought to know better than to come in here disturbing men at their cards!'

Every eye in the room was now fixed on her, but it didn't worry her. She bent down until her mouth was level with Edward's ear, and her fingers dug into his shoulder. 'I'm not leaving unless you come with me. I'll make a scene if I have to.'

'You've already made one!' he muttered, tossing down

his cards and surging to his feet. 'Excuse me, gentlemen, while I get rid of this nuisance!'

Propelling his sister from the room, he slammed the door behind them, then turned on her, absolutely furious at being disturbed. 'What the blazes do you think you're doing? I had a winning hand!'

'No you didn't. The man opposite had a Royal Flush, and that was too good for the hand you were holding.'

He stared at her in amazement. 'How do you know about cards? I've never seen you playing.'

'I read it in a book.' She took hold of his arm. 'Now wipe that scowl from your face and smile for Mother.'

'You and your bloody books!' he muttered, as they made their way back to the ballroom.

She merely smiled, satisfied that she had stopped him losing any more money. For the moment, anyway!

Chapter Two

Now was a good time to fade into the background. Her father was busy talking to a crowd of men. Her mother was sitting with her friends and content to have her son with her. Gertrude made her escape and slid behind the column, intent on staying out of the way. If she could remain unnoticed until supper was served, then the evening would be half over, and she would consider that a success.

'Where's your daughter?' she heard a woman ask her mother.

'I don't know.' Florence sighed. 'I took my eyes off her for a moment and she disappeared. I dare say she has found herself a place away from the crowds. A young girl should be enjoying functions like this, but she just isn't interested. I don't know what we are going to do with her, Lillian. All she is concerned about are her books.'

'Hmm. She is a clever girl.'

'Too clever,' her mother exclaimed. 'I found her stretched out on the floor the other day with her grandfather's clock in pieces. When I asked her what she was doing, do you know what she said?'

'Do tell.' There was a hint of laughter in Lillian's voice.

'She told me she wanted to see how it worked! Did you ever hear such a thing? I told her to collect all the pieces and we would send it to the clock repairer. She simply declared that she would put it back together herself.'

'And did she?'

'Yes, and it keeps perfect time.'

She could picture her mother shaking her head, completely at a loss to understand her daughter.

'Men do not like clever women and Gertrude makes no attempt to hide her intelligence. It will not be easy to find a husband for her.'

'Glendale appears to be quite interested in her,' observed Lillian.

'But she doesn't like him and does her best to avoid him. I really can't understand it. He is a man of good standing and well-respected.'

'And wealthy.'

'I'm afraid that doesn't impress Gertrude. She told us that the only thing to consider is a man's character, but she won't even give herself a chance to get to know him.'

'I've noticed she does her best to avoid him,' Lillian said. 'Has he declared his interest?'

'He's spoken to Sutton, but he made it clear we would never force our daughter to do anything she didn't want to. Seriously though, I wish she could be more like her brother. Edward knows how to enjoy life. He's out every evening with his friends, but Gertrude seems content with her own company.'

'I shouldn't worry about that. I had similar worries with my two, but they're both married now and have settled nicely. I shall be a grandmother in another month.'

'Congratulations. How marvellous for you, Lillian.'

'Caught you! And you shouldn't be eavesdropping. It's rude.'

Gertrude jumped when someone spoke softly in her ear. 'David! Don't creep up on me like that. I can hardly help hearing their conversation. And how did you find me?'

'I just looked for a suitable hiding place.'

She pulled a face. 'You know me too well.'

'Indeed I do, and I will not allow you to shirk your duty tonight. Your father asked me to find you and bring you out into the open. He wishes to dance with you, and so do I.'

'Of course.' She made to move away from the column when David placed a hand on her arm, his expression serious. 'Has Edward said much to you about his gambling?'

'No, but he's asked me for money several times. I can't give him any without going to Father, and he will want to know what I need it for. When I ask him how much he owes, he just smiles and says it isn't much. But I'm worried. Will he talk to you, do you think?'

David's eyes clouded with concern. 'We have been friends since childhood, and I would help him in any way I could. I am not wealthy, as you know, but I would give him whatever money I have if it would get him out of trouble.'

'Trouble?' she said in alarm. 'Do you believe his debts are large?'

'I have no proof. He will have nothing to do with me, as you know, but he's running with a bad crowd. They are all from immensely rich families. He can't possibly keep up with them, and I feel he could be in deep.' When he noticed her distress, he smiled. 'But I'm probably wrong. It's hard to see an old friend go astray, and I expect I'm allowing my imagination to paint a dark picture. Let's dance and forget all about it. Edward is intelligent, and will eventually see what he's doing and sort himself out.'

'You're right, of course, but let's hope it's soon.' She allowed him to escort her to the dance floor. She enjoyed his company and relaxed. Because they both cared very much for Edward, it was easy to let their imaginations run riot.

When the dance ended, David escorted her back to their seats. Her father was also there now, and she smiled broadly at him, then whispered, 'Did you find somewhere to hide as well?'

He shook his head, amused. 'I had some business to attend to.'

'Ah.' The music began again, and she was about to claim her dance with her father, when she saw Mr Glendale heading for them. She didn't even try to stifle a groan.

He gave a perfunctory bow to her parents, which irritated Gertrude. Arrogant men considered themselves superior, and it showed. Well, in her opinion, her family were the superior ones. Their comfortable lifestyle was the result of skill and honest labour, and she doubted if Mr Glendale had ever done a useful day's work in his life. What did he have to strive for when everything he owned had been handed down from his ancestors?

'Will you have the next dance with me, Miss Melrose?'

There was no way she could refuse, and he knew it! She saw his eyebrows rise as she scowled at him. She had been looking forward to a dance with her father.

'You go ahead, Gertrude,' her father said, reading her mind accurately, his eyes alight with amusement. 'We can dance later.'

She was trapped, and would have words with her father later for not rescuing her. But for some odd reason her parents liked this man. Her mother was smiling at him with obvious pleasure.

'Will you join us at supper, Mr Glendale?' Florence asked.

'I'm afraid I am already committed, Mrs Melrose, but I thank you for the invitation.'

Gertrude allowed him to lead her to the dance floor. She knew she should make polite conversation, but she couldn't think of a thing to say, and that was not like her.

'You dance very well,' he said, breaking the silence. 'And you don't talk endlessly about nothing. That's a refreshing and rare quality, Miss Melrose.'

She looked up then, sure his tone had a sarcastic ring to it. 'I'm not sure if I have just been insulted?'

A slight smile touched his mouth. 'I assure you it was meant as a compliment. So many young girls appear to have nothing in their heads except gowns and the need to find a husband.'

'I'm interested in neither.' She gave a parody of a smile. 'And you appear to have successfully avoided those seeking marriage.'

'Now I have just been insulted!' A deep laugh rumbled through him. 'I think we should finish our dance in silence, don't you?'

'By far the best thing,' she agreed, enjoying herself now. At least he had a sense of humour and did not easily take offence. But one good quality was not enough to make her like him.

When the music ended he returned her to her parents, bowed to them and said, 'I shall call upon you, Miss Melrose.'

Before she could answer he had melted back into the crowd, leaving her bristling with indignation. The cheek of the man! He didn't even have the good manners to ask if he could call. I'll make sure I'm not at home!

Supper was then served, and Gertrude was relieved when her brother joined them. At least he hadn't returned to the card tables, but he appeared distracted. He sampled very little of the sumptuous buffet, and as soon as the music began again he was on his feet.

'It is only an hour to midnight. I'll join you then so we can welcome in the new century together.'

'Of course, Edward.' Florence smiled indulgently at her beloved son. 'You go and enjoy yourself.'

Much to Gertrude's relief, Mr Glendale didn't come near her again. She danced with her father, several young men, and David twice. She almost managed to find some pleasure in the noisy evening.

On the stroke of twelve everyone cheered, clapped, and wished each other a Happy New Year. As Gertrude hugged her parents and her brother, she was overcome with a sense of foreboding. Something was telling her that there would be difficult times ahead. She was sure the new century was ushering in change for the Melrose family.

No matter how sternly she told herself to stop being so silly, the feeling would not leave her.

Chapter Three

'Are you going out again, Gertrude?'

'Yes, Mother. The threat of snow has passed so I thought I'd make the most of a fine day.'

'But I heard Mr Glendale say he would call on you. He'll be disappointed if you're not at home.'

'That was a week ago. He didn't say when.' She tried to keep the irritation she felt out of her voice but without success. 'Am I to remain a prisoner in my own home till he decides to grace us with his presence?'

'Don't be sarcastic,' her mother told her sharply. 'I fail to understand what you have against him. He is a presentable man – many consider him handsome – he is wealthy and much in demand.'

'I agree, but he is also arrogant and old.'

'Old!' Florence exclaimed. 'Hanna told me he's twenty-nine, and that's the perfect age for a man to settle down with a wife and family. And he's quite taken with you, my dear. Many girls would like to be in your position.'

'I expect they would.' She pulled on her gloves. 'But there's something about him I don't like. He makes me uneasy and it's a feeling I can't dismiss.'

'You and your feelings.' Florence shook her head. 'I don't know how we managed to have such a strong-minded daughter. I can't think who you take after.'

Gertrude grinned. 'Aunt Hanna?'

'Oh, good gracious! Don't become too much like her for all our sakes.'

'I'll try,' she said. 'But I don't know why you look so horrified when Aunt Hanna's mentioned. You know you like Father's sister.'

'That just shows you what a foolish woman I am.' She couldn't remain serious as her daughter burst into laughter. 'Where are you going?'

'To the bookshop in Wandsworth.'

Florence sighed. 'Why don't you find a local bookshop that sells *new* books? You've no idea where those awful soiled books have been.'

'New books are not as interesting as the second-hand ones. I can find all sorts of treasures on the shelves of Mr Partridge's dingy old shop.'

'You are a mystery to me.' Her mother kissed her cheek. 'Off you go and take a carriage both ways. Do you have enough money with you?'

'Yes, Mother. I will only be about two hours.'

'I'll tell Mr Glendale that if he calls.'

A look of devilment crossed Gertrude's face. 'You could also tell him that I spend my time in dusty second-hand bookshops and I'm not the kind of person he should associate with.'

'I'm sure he'd find you even more intriguing if I did,' her mother teased.

'Heaven forbid!' She heard her mother laughing as she left the house.

The bell on the door jangled when Gertrude entered the shop. Instead of sounding a clear musical tone it was dreadfully out of tune. It always made her wince and wonder why on earth the shopkeeper didn't replace it. Still, it was all part of the character of the place.

She took a deep breath. There was nothing so evocative as the smell of old books. It was like the finest perfume to her and she adored it. The usual tingle of anticipation ran through her as she wondered what she would find today.

She was completely lost in browsing when discordant voices came from behind another bookshelf.

''Ere. I've told you not to come in my shop. Clear off!'

'I'm only looking. You're a mean old bugger!'

The voice was female and young by the sound of it. Unable to resist the temptation to see what was going on, she walked around the shelf. The owner was glaring at a girl of around fifteen or sixteen, Gertrude guessed. She was scruffy and holding a book in her hands.

'I wasn't going to pinch it. I ain't a thief.'

'Maybe, but you ain't got no money either. You can't

just creep in here and read the books without buying them. I've told you that time and time again.'

The look of longing on the young girl's face as she put the book back on the shelf tore at Gertrude's heart. She knew just how she was feeling.

Stepping forward, she said, 'Hello, my name's Gertrude. What were you reading?'

'Er . . .'

'Miss Melrose.' The shopkeeper smiled. 'I didn't know you was here. Nice to see you again.'

'Thank you, Mr Partridge. I love your shop, as I'm sure this young girl does.' She smiled at the girl, who was standing transfixed, not taking her eyes off the posh girl in front of her. 'Will you show me what you were interested in?'

'Er . . .' She glanced anxiously at the shopkeeper.

'Show Miss Melrose,' he snapped irritably.

A grubby hand snaked out and whisked a book from the shelf. It was thrust towards Gertrude. 'I'm saving up to buy this one, but I wanted to see if it was still here. I'm afraid someone might buy it before I've got enough money. It's four pence.' She gazed at the book and sighed. 'Takes a lot of saving, that does.'

Gertrude was absolutely astonished when she saw the title. 'Shakespeare?'

'What's wrong with that?' The girl bristled with indignation. 'I can read proper. And I like to learn about kings and stuff.'

'I wasn't implying that it was above your intelligence,' she said hastily. 'What else do you read?'

She shrugged. 'Anything really. I got favourites though. Dickens. I like him.'

'So do I. Have you read anything by Jane Austen?'

She shook her head. 'Good, is she?'

'Very.' Gertrude turned to Mr Partridge. 'Do you have one of her books?'

Muttering under his breath, the owner disappeared behind a shelf.

'What's your name?' Gertrude asked the girl while they waited.

'Millie.'

At that moment the door opened cautiously. A hand reached up to stop the bell from ringing, then a face peered in. 'Is it safe, Millie?'

'Come in Fred. I'm talking to this lady and he won't chuck us out yet.'

A painfully thin, gangling youth slid in. He looked slightly older than Millie and his dark eyes shone with intelligence. Sadness swept through Gertrude and she studied the two scruffy, under-nourished youngsters. They were obviously bright, but desperately poor.

'Do you like to read as well?' she asked him.

Fred was studying her intently. His dark eyes were taking in every inch of her elegant outfit. He nodded. 'I don't like the kind of stuff Millie reads, but he's got some smashing books in here about military battles and . . . birds, and things like that.' He finished in a rush, looking slightly embarrassed.

'Go and find a couple and let me see them.'

'Er . . .' Fred gave Millie a puzzled glance.

'Go on.' She gave him a shove. 'Show the lady what you like.'

At that moment the owner appeared and glared at the boy. 'Not you as well.' He managed a smile as he handed Gertrude *Emma* by Jane Austen. 'This is the only one I've got at the moment.'

'Splendid.' When she held it out to Millie it was almost snatched out of her hand.

The first page was devoured quickly and a smile appeared on Millie's face. 'Cor, this looks good. I ain't never heard of her before.'

The longing in her pale blue eyes was there again as she handed the book back to Gertrude. How terrible to be deprived of the pleasure of books because you couldn't afford them. Gertrude handed Mr Partridge the Shakespeare book and Jane Austen. 'Wrap these for Millie, please.'

Fred appeared clutching two books, one of which was already open. 'Look at this, Miss. Have you ever seen anything like it?' He was pointing at a picture of a peacock with its wings displayed in all their glory. 'I draw from pictures and then carve them in wood, but one day I'm gonna draw the real thing. We're gonna get out of the slums and live in the country.'

Millie nodded in agreement.

He looked Gertrude straight in the eyes. 'We got dreams, and one day we'll make them come true.'

'I'm sure you will.' There was a lump in her throat as she took both books from Fred. The other one was *King Solomon's Mines* by H. Rider Haggard.

'You got a dream? Everyone should have a dream.'

'I've never thought about it, but you're quite right,' she replied, handing the books to the bemused owner. 'Wrap these for Fred, please.'

'Er . . .' Millie looked worried. 'We ain't got no money.'

'I know, but I have. Wait for me.'

Mr Partridge brightened up when he realised he was going to get a lucrative sale. The books were quickly wrapped and the money put in his till. He was smiling when he handed Gertrude the parcels.

She thanked him and went over to the youngsters, who were waiting by the door for her. 'Here you are. You must tell me what you think of them the next time we meet.'

'Gosh,' Millie said, her eyes shining. 'You're a real kind lady.'

'We won't forget this,' Fred told her. 'If there's anything we can ever do for you, you just ask.'

'Thank you, Fred. Now, there's a nice little teashop along the road. I'd like you to join me for some refreshments.'

Millie spluttered. 'You mean that posh place with the blue tablecloths?'

'Yes, that's the one.'

'Oh, they won't let us in there!'

'They will today. You're my guests. Whatever you have will be paid for, and that makes you just as good as anyone else in there. My Aunt Hanna says you can walk in anywhere, no matter how elegant, if you have enough money in your purse.'

The girl grinned. 'I like the sound of your aunt.'

'She's a very unusual woman.'

'So are you, Miss. There ain't many of your class who'd

29

take notice of the likes of us.' Fred stopped at the door of the cafe and peered in. 'They ain't gonna be happy about you taking us in there.'

'They won't object.' Her mouth set in a firm line. 'My mother says I'm just like my Aunt Hanna.'

That brought giggles from the youngsters and they were all smiling when they walked in.

A look of horror appeared on the face of the owner and he tried to block the entrance, but Gertrude had been in the cafe many times and spoke with authority. 'They are my guests. We'd like a table by the window.'

It was obvious the last thing the owner wanted was to have two scruffy youngsters sitting in full view of the public. She didn't give him a chance to object as she guided them towards a table in a prime position. As soon as they were seated, she smiled at the owner who was still hovering uncertainly. 'We'd like a selection of sandwiches and cakes, please.'

'Of course, Miss Melrose.' A look of resignation crossed his face. He couldn't refuse such a valued customer.

They were served speedily and she watched as the hungry youngsters devoured every scrap of food.

'Ain't you eating?' Millie asked, as she collected up the crumbs from her plate. 'The grub's smashing. What was that orange stuff in the bread? I ain't never had that before.'

'That was salmon. Did you enjoy it?'

Millie nodded and turned to Fred. 'What ones did you like the best?'

'All of them,' he said, gazing longingly at the empty plates.

Gertrude called the waitress. 'We'll have another pot of tea and some more cakes, please.'

'Yes, Miss.'

The waitress was about to turn away when Gertrude touched her arm. 'Prepare two parcels of food to take away.'

'At once, Miss.'

Millie leant forward eagerly. 'Could I have some of that salmon stuff? My mum would like that. I bet she ain't never had anything like that before.'

'Of course.' The waitress smiled and stooped down slightly as she spoke to Millie. 'What cake did you like the best?'

'Chocolate!'

'And what about the young gentleman?'

Fred looked behind to see who the waitress was talking to, and seeing no one, turned back. 'Blimey, I ain't never been called that before!'

Millie giggled. 'And am I a young lady?'

'You're both with Miss Melrose so you must be,' the waitress joked, giving them a sly wink. 'Now, sir, what would you like?'

'Everything.' His smile couldn't get any brighter.

Watching the exchange, Gertrude decided that she must leave an extra generous tip today. A visit to the teashop was an ordinary part of her life, but for Millie and Fred it was an exciting adventure. It brought home to her how important it was not to take the good things in life for granted.

'Tell me about yourself, Millie,' she said as they worked their way through another plate of cakes. The poor little things must be starving. 'Are you still at school?'

Millie shook her head, and swallowed a mouthful of cake. 'Wish I was. They chucked me out when I was thirteen. I've been working in a factory, but that's closed now. I'm trying to get another job, but it ain't easy.'

'Millie's ever so clever.' Fred gave his friend an admiring glance. 'You ought to see her writing. Real beautiful it is.'

'That's interesting. And what about you, Fred?'

'Me? Oh I ain't brainy like Millie, but I'm good with my hands. I like making things, and drawing of course.'

'Fred made me a shelf to put my things on. It's got pretty flowers on it. Carved it all himself.'

Gertrude was now more than interested. 'Would you meet me here at the same time next week and bring a sample of your work with you? I'd love to see your writing, Millie, and something you've made in wood, Fred.'

They both nodded. 'Yes, Miss.'

'Don't forget now. If you can't make it for any reason leave a message with the bookshop owner.'

'We'll be here,' Fred told her.

The waitress appeared and handed the youngsters a parcel each.

'Oh, thanks!' Their eyes were wide with excitement.

She paid the bill, and once outside said goodbye to Millie and Fred. She watched them running up the road clutching their parcels. It had been an interesting and worthwhile morning. It was only when she was on her way home that she realised she hadn't bought a book for herself. Never mind, she'd find one next time she came.

* * *

Later that night Gertrude couldn't sleep as every detail of her meeting with the youngsters kept running through her mind. Fred's declaration that everyone should have a dream wouldn't leave her thoughts. They had a dream of living in the country, away from the hardship and squalor of the slums. But what dreams did she have?

This took some thought as she considered what she hoped for in life. The most pressing desire was to see her brother stop gambling and start to do something useful with his life. And she would like to marry one day. But it would need to be a man of her choice – someone she loved and who loved her.

Turning over to try and get some sleep, she pulled a face. There didn't seem much point in having an impossible dream, but that didn't stop Millie and Fred. They nurtured the hope that things would be better for them in the future, and she was touched by their optimism and courage. There were many who could learn from them. She wished her brother had some of their inner strength.

Sadness swept through her as she thought about her dear brother. She would be happy to see him back to the person he used to be. That was the most important thing in her life at the moment.

Chapter Four

'Sutton's late tonight.' Florence stood in front of the clock on the mantelpiece. 'Cook will be annoyed if the dinner is spoilt.'

Edward stood up and poured himself a drink. 'He's only half an hour late.'

At that moment they heard the front door open and close and Gertrude smiled at her mother. 'Here he is.'

When he came into the room they gasped in horror. One of his eyes was swollen shut, his top lip was split and he was clutching his side. Florence was the first to reach his side. 'Oh my dear, what's happened? Have you had an accident? Gertrude, ask one of the servants to go for the doctor.'

'Not yet.' Sutton walked over to his son. 'I have made the acquaintance of some of your friends, who have persuaded me it's time your debts were honoured.'

All the colour drained from Edward's face. When he

tried to speak, his father thrust a sheet of paper in front of him. 'I am told that this is the amount you owe. Is it correct?'

Edward read it and could not look his father in the eyes. 'Yes it is. I'm sorry—'

'It is too late to be sorry! After giving me a beating to impress upon me the urgency of the matter, they have threatened to harm your sister. The full amount must be paid within a week.'

'I'll go and see them, Father—'

'Don't ever call me that again.' Sutton spoke with quiet fury. 'You are no longer my son. We have given you every advantage in life. I had hoped you would come into the business and take over after me, but that wasn't good enough for you, was it? You have put your family in jeopardy and tarnished our good name.'

'I'll never gamble again. I promise.' Edward was shaking, hardly able to stand upright.

'I don't care what you do!' Sutton rounded on his son. 'I'll pay the debt in full, and that is the last thing I will ever do for you. You have an hour to pack your things and leave this house, never to set foot in it again.' Then he turned his back on his son. 'Go now before I give you the thrashing you deserve.'

A cry of distress came from Florence as her son left the room. 'Oh, Sutton, please don't do this. What is to become of him?'

'I won't have him under this roof. He must learn to fend for himself.' He sat down heavily, his brow wet with perspiration.

Seeing the distress her father was in, Gertrude ran to the servants and sent one of them for the doctor, then she hurried back. She was horrified by what had just taken place, and as worried as she was for her brother, she was more concerned for her father. She hadn't been able to catch sight of the paper, but Edward's debt must be enormous for her father to disown his son.

Florence was holding her husband's hand and crying uncontrollably.

Gertrude put her arms around her mother and reached out to touch her father's shoulder. 'I've sent for the doctor.'

'Thank you, my dear. It feels as if those thugs have cracked my ribs.'

'Sit very still.' Gertrude moved to the other side of her father and wiped his face with her clean handkerchief. Then she asked gently, 'How much does Edward owe?'

'Over three thousand guineas.'

Florence gasped, and Gertrude felt as if the floor had shifted beneath her feet. How could her brother have lost so much? Had he no thought for his family?

'We can't find that much,' Florence whispered, hardly able to speak. 'All our money is tied up in the business.'

'You must use my inheritance,' Gertrude insisted.

'No, my child. It would not even cover a fraction of the debt, but I'll find the money, have no fear.'

'I'm not afraid for myself. I expect the threat to me was to frighten you into paying the debt.'

'Maybe, but I will not take that risk.' He placed both hands across his ribs, obviously in great pain.

'Where's that doctor?' Florence turned her whole

attention to her injured husband. 'Go and find out, Gertrude.'

Before she could reach the door it swung open and the doctor strode in. He took one look at Sutton and turned to the maid. 'Find me a male servant. I'll need his help. The ladies can leave.'

'I'm staying with my husband. You do not order me around in my own home!' Florence was determined and nothing would move her.

Gertrude spoke quietly in her father's ear. 'May I have your permission to see Edward before he leaves?'

He gave a slight nod.

'Thank you. I'll see you again when the doctor's made you comfortable.'

As soon as she was out of the room she ran up the stairs and along the passage to her brother's room. She burst in without knocking. Edward had his back to her and was packing a case.

'Where will you go?' Her voice trembled with emotion.

When he turned his face was grey, anguish etched on every feature. He appeared to be incapable of speech. She reached out to touch him but he backed away. 'Go to David. He'll help you.'

He shook his head and stood there, a picture of dejection. 'How's Father?' he managed to say.

'We don't know yet. The doctor's with him.'

'I'm so sorry. Oh God, I'm so sorry . . .' Tears tumbled down his face. 'I'll never gamble again for as long as I live. Somehow I'll repay him. I swear it. Take care of Mother for me, Gertie.'

He picked up his case and walked towards the door.

'Tell me where you're going,' she pleaded. 'Aunt Hanna will take you in.'

'I am no longer a member of this family. And that is right, for I don't deserve to be. Goodbye.'

'Take care of yourself,' she whispered as he closed the door behind him.

Edward Melrose was under no illusions about the seriousness of the situation he had left his family to deal with. But no matter how bleak the outlook, he would not go to David or Hanna. He only had himself to blame. He found it unbelievable that he had allowed himself to be dragged into gambling. It had become an obsession and he hadn't been able to stop. He must be a very weak man! His father's words had cut him like a dagger and it had been as if a curtain had disintegrated before his eyes. He saw exactly what he had become, and that filled him with self-loathing and disgust. He hated himself. But if it took him the rest of his life, he would somehow right the terrible wrong he had done his family. Not only had he placed them in danger, but he'd also ruined them financially.

He had been walking aimlessly for about an hour when it started to rain. He was hungry and wet, and shame weighed on him, making him stumble on the wet pavement. Stopping for a moment he saw that he was in a poorer part of town. Well, that was all right. It was where he belonged now. A notice in one of the windows offering rooms caught his attention. Without hesitation he knocked on the door and went inside. It was none too clean, but it was cheap so he took a room for the night. This would give him time to rest, because tomorrow he would have to find work, and that wasn't going to be easy. He had no skills, but he was strong and would dig ditches if he had to.

Stretching out on the bed he ignored his hunger, allowing his mind to drift back over the last year. When Charles Hayworth had drawn him into their exclusive circle he had been flattered. At first the stakes had been low, but they'd slowly increased, and by then he'd been in too deep to back out. If he did win, which wasn't often, it was when there was little on the table. He could see it all now. He won when they allowed him to, and that meant they had been manipulating the games. Charles always sat opposite his brother, Howard, so they could make eye contact. He recalled the coughs, fingers moving on the table, and other subtle signals. They must be cheats to keep winning like they did, but it would be impossible to prove. No one would be brave enough to speak out against them.

Edward clenched his hands into tight fists. He had allowed their flattery and friendly attitude to blind him to what was really happening. What a weak, pathetic man he was!

But no more. One day he would redeem himself in the eyes of his family. And that wasn't an idle dream. From now on it would be the focus of his life.

Gertrude stayed in her brother's room while the doctor carried out his examination and they moved her father into his bedroom. It was some time before her mother appeared in the doorway. Florence had aged in that short time.

'Is Father all right?'

'The doctor says he has cracked ribs and is badly bruised, but he will be fine after a long rest.' Her mother gazed around the empty room, silent tears running down her cheeks. 'I never got the chance to say goodbye. What is to become of him, Gertrude?'

'I advised him to go to David or Aunt Hanna.'

'I hope he does. I'm so frightened for him. I've begged your father to reconsider, but he won't hear of it.'

She put her arms around her mother, trying to comfort, but she was just as distraught. 'I'll find him so we can keep an eye on him.'

'Thank you, my dear. I know your father has disowned him, and in the circumstances no one could blame him, but Edward is my son. I gave birth to him and cannot turn my back on him.'

'I know.' Gertrude's eyes were brimming with tears, but she fought them back. This terrible disaster was upon them and it had to be faced. She had to be brave for both her parents' sakes. 'May I see Father now?'

Florence nodded. 'Don't stay too long. He's very tired.'

Her father was propped up on a heap of pillows to keep him in a comfortable position. His eyes were closed and deep lines of pain were etched on his face. She knew the pain wasn't only coming from his injuries. Disowning his son would have been the hardest thing he'd ever had to do. Walking to the bed, she knelt down and took his hand in hers. Not wanting to disturb him, she remained silent.

After a while he turned his head and opened his eyes. 'Did you know he was gambling?' he asked.

'Yes,' she had to admit. 'He has been asking me for money just lately, but I had no idea things were so bad. Honestly.'

'You should have told me.'

'I know that now, and I'm sorry.' The tears of remorse would not stop now and they poured down her face.

'Don't cry, my dear. I'll pay the debt. I won't let anything happen to you.'

'I am not concerned for myself. I am sad for all of us. You have been brutally attacked, Edward is lost to us, and he is now alone in the world. It is hard to bear.'

'The future for us will be hard. I can't find that kind of money without making drastic changes to our lives. I want you to promise me something.'

'Anything.'

'Support and comfort your mother. There are dark days ahead of us.' His eyes closed and he gently squeezed her hand. 'Leave me now. I must sleep, for there is much to do tomorrow.'

She stood up. 'I'll help you. Just tell me what you want me to do.'

He shook his head. 'I don't want you or your mother involved in this unpleasant business. I will do what has to be done. Don't hate me for the actions I'm forced to take.'

'We'd never do that,' she said forcefully. 'You have our support.'

'Thank you. That is a comfort.'

As she left the room, Gertrude knew their lives were about to change. Only her father knew exactly what those changes would be, but the carefree, happy life she had known was no more.

She found her mother downstairs in the sitting room. 'He's asleep now,' she told her.

'Good.' Florence looked exhausted. 'I want you to go and stay with Hanna for a while.'

'No, Mother!' She wasn't going to be sent away. She would not let them face this alone. 'Father said he will pay the debt. They won't carry out their threat to harm me. I'm quite safe.'

Her mother sighed deeply. 'I wish it were that easy. Have you given any thought to how we are to raise such a large amount? I am not a fool. We are ruined. But I will not see Sutton lose the business. It has been in his family for three generations.'

'I am not a fool either, Mother. Whatever is to come we can face it together. Don't send me away. Please let me stay. I'll be strong. I promise.'

Florence considered her daughter for a few moments, then stood up. 'Very well. Thank you, my dear. I wish your brother had more of your strength of character. It's painful to realise he's so weak. Now we should try to get some rest. Cook will bring you food if you wish.'

'I couldn't eat.' The thought of food made Gertrude's stomach heave.

'Neither could I.'

She watched her mother leave the room, walking as if every step were an effort. Then she whispered, 'With such

42

courageous parents Edward can't be weak. He lost his way for a while. Now he must find the strength to fight back, or he will not survive.' She prayed he had it in him to make it out there alone.

She was distressed for the family she loved.

Chapter Five

The next two days were worrying, as Florence and Gertrude watched the man they loved struggle to raise the money. He was grey with pain from his injuries, but he did not shrink from the task ahead of him. In an effort to raise the money, paintings were removed from the walls and several items of furniture went. This was particularly upsetting for Florence because they had been in her family for a long time, but she watched them go and said nothing. But they were still a long way from the amount needed.

Gertrude could not bear to see her father suffer any longer. 'Mother, I have several pieces of jewellery. We can sell those, and we must use the money Grandfather left me.'

'I agree, and I have also gathered together the best of my jewellery. Come, let us persuade your father.'

They went into the library and Sutton glanced up. He looked near to collapse.

'We have come to help, my dear.' Florence sat beside her husband. 'You cannot shoulder this burden alone.'

He ran a hand over his eyes. 'I am desperately sorry to be stripping our home, but I'm afraid it is to no avail. I shall have to sell the business.'

'No!' Gertrude and Florence spoke together.

'I will not allow you to do that, Sutton,' Florence told him. 'You may sell everything in this house, but not your business.'

He sat back, admiration showing in his tired eyes. 'This is your home. You have always loved it.'

'That is true,' she said gently, 'but I love you more. Let us get this debt paid, and then we can start again. We will have little chance of doing that if you sell the business. That is our future, my darling. You must hold on to it whatever the cost. Gertrude and I have some pieces of jewellery. They can be sold.'

Gertrude spoke for the first time. 'And I insist you use my money, Father.'

He studied them both intently for some moments, then said, 'I have been blessed with two of the most unselfish women a man could wish for. I might be forced to use your inheritance, Gertie, but I'll try not to. Keep your jewellery though. I will find another way.'

Florence leant across to look at the figures her husband was working on and shook her head. 'We may have to sell this house. Hanna will take us in. I've already told her and she has offered us a home with her.'

Sutton groaned. 'Dear Lord, what a mess that boy has landed us in. You do realise this can't be kept secret. News that we are selling possessions at great speed will already be circulating.'

'I don't care what people are saying.' Florence sat up straight, a determined glint in her eyes. She managed a grim smile. 'Let the truth be known. And a name or two should be mentioned. Carefully, of course. We don't want those thugs paying us another visit. But it will alert society to those men, and hopefully make other young men wary of associating with them.'

'That is a splendid idea,' Gertrude agreed, her admiration for her mother growing all the time. 'I could do that quite easily. After all, I am the daughter and naturally distraught about the situation. It's understandable that I cannot hide my distress.'

'Very understandable,' Sutton said dryly, seeming more relaxed knowing he had the support of his family. He sat back. 'The three of us will pull together, and we'll get through this.'

'Of course we will!' Hanna strode into the library and placed a purse in front of her brother. 'There are fifty guineas in there. It is all I could raise at short notice. If you lose this house then you may all move in as soon as you please.'

'Thank you, Hanna.' Florence greeted her sister-in-law with a kiss on the cheek. 'That is very generous of you, and I fear it may come to that.'

Hanna studied her brother. 'Don't look so grim, Sutton. Florence is right. You must keep the business. Everything else can go. And if I see Edward I shall take a stick to him. Which is something you should have done a long time ago.'

'Spoiling him was my fault.' Florence couldn't stop her voice shaking. 'I am responsible for this disaster.'

'No, my dear, you have no reason to feel like that,' Sutton declared. 'We treated both of our children in the same way and our daughter has never let us down. There's a weakness in Edward we failed to see.' He glared at his sister. 'You will watch what you say, Hanna. I will not have you upsetting Florence.'

'I had no intention of doing that. Please accept my apologies, Florence. This is a terrible time for you and I'm sure my sharp manner is unwelcome. But you know me. I speak my mind without thinking.'

'There is nothing to forgive,' Florence told her. 'You are quite right. We have been too lenient with Edward and now we are paying for that mistake.'

Gertrude watched in silence, upset by the pain so obvious in their faces. They were suffering, and the home they had built together with love was being disposed of because of the son they had thought the world of. He had betrayed them, and that was causing them incredible pain. She knew that betrayed was a harsh word to use, but it was how she saw it at this moment. She'd been told about titled men who had lost their homes and estates at the gaming tables, unable to stop, and believing that the next hand would win it all back. But it never did, and it was like a sickness some men caught. Even though she had begun to be concerned about her brother's gambling, she hadn't allowed herself to believe it was this serious. But in the midst of this crisis she didn't love her brother any the less. Her fear for him was constantly with her. She would search for him, but at this moment it was her parents who needed her support.

The door opened and David was shown in. He went straight to Sutton. 'I have been hearing dreadful news, sir. Is it true Edward has massive debts and you have been – persuaded – to pay them?'

'That is true, David.'

'Forgive me if you think I am prying into your personal affairs, but I have always had great affection for your family. Can you raise the money?'

'With difficulty. I've been over and over the figures, and until this house is sold I cannot pay in full. I will need more time than these men have given me.'

'Sell your home?' David's face drained of all colour. 'It can't be that bad, surely! Edward wouldn't have been that foolish.'

'I'm afraid he has.' Sutton grimaced in pain as he stood. 'It was kind of you to come and see us.'

'You are badly hurt!' David spun around to face Gertrude. 'This is appalling. Where is Edward? I will tell him what I think of his behaviour.'

'He isn't here,' she told him.

'I turned him out.' Sutton sat down again, anguish written on every line of his face. 'He is no longer my son and can never return.'

David glanced at each stricken face in horror. 'Dear

God,' he murmured. 'Let me help you. I should be able to raise some money for you.'

'No, no,' Sutton said firmly. 'That is generous of you, but this is our problem. We will deal with it.'

Their friend would not be stopped. 'You say you cannot raise all the money at once so I am assuming you will have to ask for more time.'

'I shall approach them tomorrow.'

Gertrude took a quick step forward. 'But you are not well enough. Tell me where to find them and I'll go.'

'I will *not* allow you near them!' her father said. 'Have you forgotten they have threatened to harm you?'

'What?' David glared at her. 'Do you wish to cause your father more grief, Gertie? What are you thinking?'

'Don't you question my thinking!' she said, furious. 'We need more time. Father is injured and cannot go. Who else is there?'

'I'll meet the men.'

Her anger faded. 'Oh, David, you're a good friend, but it must be a member of the Melrose family. Don't you see that?'

'You are right about that, my dear.' Sutton sighed deeply. 'But I will not place you in such danger. I am the one who must go.'

'You will not, Sutton. I'll represent the Melrose family and David will come with me as protection. And don't you dare argue about it.' All eyes fixed on Hanna, who was examining the ivory lion's head on her walking stick. Then she looked up and smiled. 'I shall take this silence as an agreement.'

Sutton covered his eyes with his hands, head bowed, then he looked up. 'This is impossible, Hanna.'

'Of course it isn't. They are hardly likely to become violent when faced with a frail, elderly lady.'

The tension in the room was great, but Gertrude was unable to stop herself from shrieking with laughter, albeit rather hysterical. Her aunt was not even fifty yet, and anything but frail. If anyone attacked her, she would give a good account of herself.

'Stop this, Hanna. You're younger than me – and I suspect – stronger. You just like a fight. Admit it.'

'Ah, you know me too well, brother dear, but nothing will stop me from doing this.'

'Very well, but I am the one to go. You may come and support me. I cannot do this alone and if I turned up with another man they would take it as a threat.'

'Exactly. A woman will appear harmless.'

'Little do they know,' he murmured as he turned to David. 'I thank you for your courageous offer, but I would never be able to forgive myself if you suffered harm.'

David was clearly disappointed. 'I do understand, sir. If you need help at any time I hope you will call on me.'

'We'll be grateful for your support.' Sutton reached out and shook his hand.

'With your permission, I'll call tomorrow evening to see how the meeting went.'

'You're always welcome here. Don't concern yourself too much. We'll sort this mess out.'

'I know you will.' He smiled sadly at Gertrude, holding out his hand. 'Will you walk with me to the door?'

Once away from the others she said, 'I need your help.'

'Anything,' he replied without hesitation. 'We've known each other from the age of five. You and Edward are like brother and sister to me. I can't stand by and do nothing. Seeing the family I love and respect being ruined is hard to take. Tell me what you need and it shall be done.'

'Find Edward for me. He's out there alone and destitute. I need to know where he is and what he's doing. I suggested that he go to Aunt Hanna or you, but he's done neither. He can't rely on those so-called friends of his, for they are pressing for the debt to be paid. Mother's desperately worried, though she is doing her best to hide it. She's giving Father her complete support but I know she's suffering. Edward's conduct has devastated her.'

'Leave it with me. I'll do everything I can to find him.'

She squeezed his hand. 'Thank you. We'll keep this between the two of us, please.'

'Of course. You can trust me.'

'I know, and bless you.'

'That's what friends are for.' He squeezed her hand. 'You call if you need me.'

She watched him leave, grateful to have such a good friend. As she turned to return to the library she heard a slight sound coming from the drawing room. The sight that met her when she opened the door tore at her heart. Her mother was standing by the fireplace with her hands clasped over her mouth to stifle the sobs.

'Oh, Mother.' Gertrude placed her arms around her. 'We'll get through this.'

'I know, but it's so hard. Not only have we lost our

beloved son, but also everything we've worked for has gone. Your father will have to work like a slave to pull us out of this disaster. And that isn't right.'

'No, it isn't. But he'll do it.'

Florence nodded and dried her eyes. 'Don't tell him I broke down. He has enough to worry about. I don't want him to know how weak I am.'

'You're not weak!' Gertrude protested. 'I saw you agreeing to the sale of this house and you didn't even flinch. That took great courage, Mother, so don't you dare belittle yourself like that. I am proud of you. I am proud of both of you.'

'Thank you, darling. You are a great comfort to us. I'm frantic about Edward. If only we knew where he'd gone.'

'I've asked David to find him for us, just to put our minds at rest.'

'Oh, that was good of you. He's a fine boy and will do his best to find Edward.'

Gertrude felt helpless. If only she could save this house. It had always been a beautiful home. Her father would be ashamed he could no longer provide for his family. It wasn't his fault and he had no reason to blame himself. But he would. She knew him so well.

If only there was something she could do, but the situation was hopeless.

Taking a deep breath she silently asked her brother the question, 'Do you know what you've done to your family, Edward?'

Chapter Six

The tension was unbearable as they waited for her father and aunt to return from their meeting with the debt collectors. Sutton had refused to tell them anything about the meeting place, or the men, saying it was for their own protection, but this just made the waiting harder. Florence and Gertrude rushed to meet them as they came in, but all they would say was that the men had agreed to give them another ten days to find the rest of the money. Even her aunt remained silent on the subject, and this was unusual. Every effort was being made to sell the house, but without success so far. And more bad news was that David had been unable to trace Edward. He had disappeared. The only news bringing relief was that the debt collectors had given them more time.

The day after, Gertrude was wandering aimlessly around the house, not able to settle to anything.

'Why don't you go to your bookshop?' her mother suggested. 'There isn't anything you can do here.'

'I was intending to meet two young people there today.' She was doubtful about leaving her mother, even for a couple of hours.

'Then you must go, my dear. It will do you good to browse through your beloved books for a while.'

'The youngsters will be disappointed if I don't turn up.' She studied her mother's face, but she seemed quite calm. 'If you don't mind, I would like to go.'

'Go along then. You mustn't keep your friends waiting.' Florence hesitated for a moment. 'On your way back, will you call on David and see if he has any news?'

'Of course.' She rushed upstairs for her coat and purse, eager to be on her way. Standing around doing nothing was against her nature.

Millie and Fred were standing outside the bookshop when she arrived, stamping their feet against the biting wind. Their clothes were inadequate for such weather and Gertrude decided she would bring them something warmer to wear next time she came. 'You should have waited in the warm,' she admonished. 'You're shivering with the cold.'

'We tried,' Fred told her. 'But he chucked us out.'

She opened the door and ushered them inside, annoyed they should be treated so badly. 'Please don't turn my friends out in the cold, Mr Partridge. They were waiting for me and I'm a good customer.'

'Sorry, Miss Melrose. I didn't believe them and I know they haven't got any money.' He gave the youngsters a suspicious glare. 'And I have to be careful. Books have a habit of disappearing.'

''Ere!' Millie was indignant. 'We're poor, but we ain't thieves. My mum says that if a thing don't rightly belong to you then you shouldn't have it, and it wouldn't do you no good if you took it. I ain't never pinched nothing in my life!'

'Nor me!' Fred said forcefully. 'Being poor ain't a crime, and just because we ain't got two farthings between us don't mean we can't be trusted.'

'Quite right.' Gertrude nodded in agreement. She placed a hand on each of their shoulders. Fred's words about it not being a crime to be poor echoed through her mind. He was absolutely right. Once her brother's debts had been paid, the Melrose family would have little left in the way of worldly goods, but that would not be a reason to hang their heads in shame. Quite the opposite, in fact. They could be proud of the way they were handling the crisis.

She smiled at Millie and Fred. 'Let's all choose a book and then go to the teashop. Shall we?'

Fred hesitated. 'We don't like to let you keep paying. You sure you can afford it?'

'Today I can.' She had enough money in her purse for this treat. It gave her great pleasure to see their excited faces as they scuttled off to find themselves a book each.

This didn't take long and they were all soon settled in the teashop. Millie and Fred's faces were glowing now and Gertrude felt her spirits lift. Everything was going to be all right. She just knew it.

'We didn't think you was coming, Miss.' Millie peered at Gertrude, her expression concerned. 'You all right? You look tired.'

'We have a family crisis and I haven't been sleeping well.' Much to her shame, tears filled her eyes.

Millie grabbed her hand, holding it tightly. 'Oh, I'm sorry. Have you lost someone?'

She nodded, and needing to talk, she told them about Edward. She didn't know why she felt so at ease in their company, but she did. She didn't make friends easily, because she found the chatter of girls her age boring and silly. These youngsters were not like that, and they listened with rapt attention as she poured out her hurt.

'That's bloody awful!' Fred declared when she'd finished. 'Excuse the language, Miss. It sounds like your brother got in with rigged games.'

'What do you mean?' She felt better now. Talking about it to people who weren't involved had helped a lot.

'Cheating. If that was so, then he wouldn't have stood a chance.' Fred rummaged in his pocket and brought out a pack of dog-eared playing cards. He began to manipulate them in a way that astonished her. He seemed to be able to make any card he wanted appear in his hands.

'How do you do that?' she gasped.

He smirked. 'I had an uncle who used to work as a magician in the music halls. He's dead now but he taught me lots of things with cards. No one would beat me if they was playing with me. But I wouldn't do that to anyone. I wouldn't cheat. We ain't got much, but we're honest. Dad says that's worth more than all the gold in the world. We got our pride.'

Gertrude couldn't believe what she was hearing. These youngsters had so little, but they took pride in being honest and trustworthy. Dear Lord, she thought, there were many from wealthy families who could learn from them. But the boy had made her think. Had her brother been cheated out of the money? How she wished there was a way to find out.

'Hope I ain't upset you, Miss. I could be wrong, but it sounds as if he played with the wrong blokes. No one loses all the time, and if they'd been decent they wouldn't have kept taking his money.'

'You haven't upset me. You've given me a lot to think about. Now –' she changed the subject – 'I asked you to bring me a sample of your work. Did you remember?'

The girl slid a sheet of paper out of her pocket and, smiling shyly, pushed it across the table.

'This is beautiful!' Gertrude exclaimed as she studied the writing. 'Where did you learn to do this?'

'I had a nice teacher at school and he was ever so good. His writing was better than I can do. He had proper pens and he let me use them.'

'This is excellent, Millie.' She smiled as the girl beamed proudly at the praise. 'Did you bring something, Fred?'

He nodded and put a small wooden box on the table. He gave it a polish with his sleeve before handing it over. 'It ain't the best wood, but I go and search along the river banks for bits washed up. Sometimes I'm lucky and find a really nice piece, but I use everything I can get. It's a cigarette box.'

She couldn't believe her eyes. It had been well put

together. The lid fitted perfectly and he'd even carved the head of a dog on the top. Because of her father's business she knew a bit about wood. From a young child she had listened to him talking about the furniture he made and had often gone with him to watch the men working. 'This is really well made, Fred. Even my father would not be ashamed of this.'

They were now beaming at her, obviously thrilled with the compliments.

'You are both very talented. May I borrow these? I'd like to show my father. I'll bring them back next week. I'll give you my address so you can collect them sooner if you want them.'

'Oh, that's all right, Miss. We trust you, don't we Fred?'

''Course we do. You keep them as long as you like. Your dad interested in wood?' Fred asked.

'Yes, he has his own business making quality furniture.'

The boy's mouth dropped open. 'Melrose! Your dad got that place in Putney?'

'That's right. Do you know it?'

He stared at her in amazement, leaning on the table eagerly. 'Everyone knows Melrose furniture. It's the best you can get. I go there sometimes just to watch them working. When the weather's good they leave the main door open and I can see in. Cor! Fancy that.'

'Have you tried to get a job there?' she asked.

He shook his head sadly. 'They wouldn't take on the likes of me. But the foreman's a good bloke. He gives me a cup of tea sometimes. Haven't seen the boss though – your dad I mean.'

It saddened her that they should feel no one would want them because they were from the slums. Why should it be a handicap? They were intelligent youngsters. Taking a small notebook and pencil from her bag, she gave it to Millie. 'Would you write down your full names and addresses for me, please?'

They did so without hesitation and Fred gave the book back after checking that Millie had done it neatly. 'We live next door to each other and we've been friends all our lives. Millie ain't got no dad so we look out for her and her mum. My dad works at the docks and both our mums take in washing when they can get the work. None of the work is regular like and some weeks there ain't much at all.'

Millie nodded, her little face serious. 'Me and Fred hate it because we can't find work. A bit of extra money would help. I could go into service, but I can't leave Mum. I'm all she's got.'

'Don't give up hope,' Gertrude told them, but the words sounded hollow to her ears.

'We won't do that.' Fred tapped the box in front of him. 'I make some of these when I can get the wood and take 'em down the market. I sell one or two now and again. It ain't much, but it all helps.'

'I'm sure it does.' She glanced at the clock on the wall. 'I must be going, but I'll try to meet you the same time next week. And wait in the shop this time,' she told them sternly.

'All right.' The girl's expression sobered. 'Thanks for the food and books again. We hopes it all works out well for you.'

'Thank you, Millie.' She smiled at Fred. 'Everyone needs a dream, that's what you said, isn't it?'

'That's right, Miss. It keeps up your spirits.'

'I'll remember that.' She turned and waved as she walked up the street. Now she must see David before returning home.

Like the Melrose family, the Gardeners were in business. David's father had an office near the London Docks. She didn't understand what they did, but David had explained how they bought and sold anything, often working for someone wanting to purchase a cargo. They made a decent living, but were not wealthy. David had been around ships all his life, and was extremely knowledgeable about all aspects of shipping.

The wind was a biting northerly as she reached his house. She knew he often came home for his midday meal, and she hoped he was here today.

She was in luck and he took her into the sitting room, where there was a welcome fire.

'You look frozen,' he remarked as he took her coat. 'Are you staying for lunch?'

'No, thank you. This is just a brief visit. We were wondering if you have any news of Edward.'

'Not yet. I've checked with everyone he might have gone to, but he hasn't been seen.'

'Where could he be?' She stared at the fire, watching the flames dancing, and felt sick with worry. 'Do you think he's left London?'

'It's a possibility, I suppose. I would have expected him to stay close to the familiar, but if he has left London then he will be hard to find. I'll keep looking.' He gave her an understanding smile, changing the subject. 'I see from the package you're clutching that you've been to the bookshop again.'

She nodded, and told him about Millie and Fred, showing him their work.

'Hmm, the girl has a neat hand. What kind of an education has she had?'

'I don't know, but she's intelligent. Fred is an interesting boy. He can make a pack of cards do his bidding and said that Edward might have been cheated.' Gertrude gazed anxiously at her friend. 'Do you think he could be right?'

'The thought has already occurred to me. He lost a terrible amount of money, and no one could be that unlucky. Most people win from time to time.'

'I wish we could prove the men he played with were cheats.' She sighed. 'But there's little chance of that.'

'The Hayworth brothers are powerful men. Edward always played with them and they appear to be the leaders of the group. It would be useless accusing them of being cheats without firm evidence.'

'And that we don't have.' Her mood plummeted. It all seemed so hopeless.

Chapter Seven

David watched Gertrude walking up the road and his heart ached for her and her family. She was desperately worried. He hadn't said anything to raise her hopes but as he'd listened to her talking about Fred, he'd had an idea. He was going to need the help of someone with influence if he was going to put the idea into action, and Alexander Glendale would be the ideal person. With his influence, no doors were closed to him. If David sought his help then he would have to be told the whole story, but it was already common knowledge about Edward's enormous debts. Gertie and her family had not tried to hide the disaster, so he wouldn't be breaking any confidences. He was aware that Glendale had been taking an interest in her, and if he was reading the signs correctly, it was a serious interest.

He gazed out at the bustling activity of the Port of

London. Glendale had always treated him in a friendly way, and he liked the man. They had even been able to sell a cargo for him when he hadn't had the time to deal with it himself.

Yes! He'd go and see him. The man was always straight, and if he didn't want to help he wouldn't hesitate to say so. If he went now it might be possible to catch him while he was at lunch.

With his mind made up, David closed the office and hailed a cab, anxious to get to Park Lane as quickly as possible.

The butler answered the door and showed him to a waiting room. 'I'll see if he is free, sir.'

'Thank you.' While waiting he studied the paintings on the wall, pleasantly surprised. They were all beautiful landscapes. Not one dark, dreary picture among them.

The door opened and he spun round to face the impressive man who had just entered. He topped David's six feet by at least three inches. His green eyes held warmth as he greeted his visitor.

'Hello, David. How's your father?'

'He's well, Mr Glendale. I apologise for calling on you like this, but if you could spare me a moment, I have something of importance I would like to discuss with you.'

'No need for such formality. Call me Alex, if you please. Come into the sitting room, where we can be more comfortable.'

This was a promising start, and he stifled a sigh of relief. Glendale had a reputation for being distant and brusque at times, but David had only ever found him agreeable.

They had met many times, but he was always conscious that Alexander Glendale was from an influential family. David's father was highly respected, but they didn't have the wealth and prestige of the Glendale family.

'What would you like to drink?' Alex was standing by a table with an array of decanters.

'Whisky, please.'

After pouring them both a whisky, Alex sat down.

David didn't waste any time. 'Thank you for seeing me. I need your help, Alex.' It sounded wrong addressing him by his Christian name, but he'd been told to do so.

'Go on.'

He watched Alex's expression change as he went into detail about the trouble the Melrose family were in. By the time he had finished, Alex was on his feet, fury evident on his strong features.

'This is intolerable!' he exploded. 'I'd heard Edward was in debt and his father was going to pay it for him, but I had no idea they were about to lose their home. This can't be allowed. What can we do?'

'Well, I have a plan.'

Alex sat down and leant forward. 'Tell me.'

Half an hour later there was silence as the plan was considered. Then Alex nodded. 'Bring the boy to me, and don't mention my involvement to anyone, especially Gertrude. The last thing we want is for her to interfere.'

He laughed at the wry expression on Alex's face. 'Not a word, I promise. I see you're under no illusions about her character.'

'None at all.'

He was struck by the realisation that this strong man and Gertrude would suit each other very well. He doubted it would be a tranquil union, but it would never be dull. 'I don't understand why she's so hostile towards you.'

'Perhaps she fears I would curb her independent nature.'

'And would you?' David couldn't help asking.

'I've never broken a spirited horse, and I wouldn't do the same to a human being. Now, let us return to the problem in hand. I would love to see those men shamed, whether they are cheating or not. Their conduct towards Sutton Melrose is criminal. You approach the boy, and in the meantime I'll see if there is a way to stop them losing their home. Gertrude may not like me, but I have a lot of respect for her parents.'

'It would be a relief to me if you could, but they won't take money from anyone. They consider this their problem and they must deal with it.'

'I am aware of that. I would not insult them in that way. No, I will have to think of something they would accept.'

David stood up. 'I'll go to the bookshop tomorrow and find the boy. When would it be convenient to bring him here?'

'I'll be at home after two o'clock.' Alex held out his hand. 'Thank you for coming to me. We'll see if we can sort out this mess between us.'

David felt as if a great weight had been lifted from him as he walked away from the house. Alex was a good man to have fighting for you.

* * *

How to approach Sutton Melrose with a proposal he would be able to accept had kept Alex awake most of the night. The Melrose family had their pride and would turn him down immediately at any hint of charity. The situation was delicate, but he had to see they didn't lose their home. The only way he could do that was to make this a strictly business deal. Since his own family tragedy, he had had a greater understanding of the suffering of others. He was in a position to help, and he was damned well going to.

He grimaced as he walked towards the front door. Gertrude was going to dislike him even more after this, but he had never stood a chance of winning her, so he would ignore her scorn. Gambling was a regular activity in the army and what the men did with their money was up to them, but he'd never tolerated cheating, and he wouldn't now!

Fortunately, Sutton Melrose was alone and Alex was immediately shown into the library. He was shocked by the man's appearance. Some of the bruises were still visible. He had aged ten years and Alex wanted to lift some of the burden if he could. And that wasn't just because of the feelings he had for the daughter; he liked and respected her parents. The fact that their son was putting them through this made him angry.

After the usual greetings were made, Alex wasted no time in setting out his proposal, making sure it was presented as a business venture on his part. He knew this was the only way Melrose would agree to the transaction.

An hour later he was with his bankers, making arrangements for the money to be transferred that very day.

Satisfied with his morning's work, he returned home and waited to see if David would bring the boy to see him. It would be interesting to see if the youngster was as good as Gertrude believed.

On the stroke of three, David ushered two scruffy youngsters into the library. The boy had locked his gaze on Alex, his eyes wary. The girl was turning round and round as she took in every detail of the room.

'Millie insisted on coming as well,' David explained.

She stopped at the sound of David's voice and studied the tall man for the first time. 'You don't think I'd let Fred come here on his own, do you? You might be posh, but that don't mean you ain't up to no good. Mr Gardener said he was Miss's friend so we trusted him, but we don't know nothing about you.'

'What you want me for?' Fred spoke, still suspicious.

'Miss Melrose told Mr Gardener that you're clever with cards. I'd like you to show me.' Alex pulled a cord and when the butler appeared, said, 'Bring refreshments for my guests, please, Hunt.'

'Yes, sir.' His expression remained composed, showing no disapproval about the strangeness of his master's guests.

'Right.' Alex placed two chairs at a small table, motioning Fred to sit opposite him. 'Sit in the chair next to Mr Gardener,' he ordered Millie.

After giving the pale gold satin chair a careful examination, she sat on the floor.

'What are you doing down there?'

'I can't sit in that! I'll make it all dirty and then you'll tell me off.'

David was shaking with silent laughter and Alex was only managing to keep a straight face with difficulty. Without saying a word, he stood up, lifted the girl off the floor and dumped her in the chair, then sat down again.

She bristled, offended. 'Well, don't swear at me if I mess up your posh chair!'

'I won't. I don't care if you're covered in mud, you will sit properly when you're in my house.'

She snorted, not a bit frightened of this important man. 'I don't suppose you have to bother about cleaning.'

'That is done for me. Now, will you be quiet for a while?'

'Suppose.' She folded her arms and glared at David. 'Is he a friend of Miss Melrose?'

'Not exactly.'

'Thought not. She's got more sense than to let herself be bossed about by him!'

'Millie.' Alex spoke quietly, but there was no mistaking the authority in his tone.

She clamped her lips together for a moment, wriggled in the chair, and then said, 'I don't like you very much.'

'You are not alone,' Alex remarked dryly. He turned his attention back to Fred, who had been watching the exchange with amusement. Placing a new pack of cards on the table, he pushed them towards the boy. 'Let's see what you can do.'

Fred ignored the new cards and pulled his own, dogged-eared ones from his pocket. 'What you want me to do?'

'We'll play Brag. Deal me a winning hand.'

68

For the next fifteen minutes, Alex watched Fred carefully, as he was dealt one winning hand after another. The boy seemed to be able to make the cards do whatever he wanted, and it was impossible to see how he did it.

A maid arrived with a trolley laden with sandwiches, cakes, tea and fresh fruit juice. After bobbing a curtsy to her master, she smiled at Fred and Millie, who were staring at the food in wonder. 'Shall I serve, sir?'

'No thank you, Daisy. We'll help ourselves.'

As soon as she'd left, Alex handed Fred the new pack of cards. 'Before we eat, show me again with these.'

'Mine ain't marked, but if that's what you want.' He smirked, broke the seal on the pack, removed the cards from the box, shuffled and dealt. The result was the same.

Sitting back, Alex looked across the room at David. 'He's good.'

'What's all this about?' Fred asked. 'Why you interested in card tricks?'

'I'm going to ask you to help me. But let's eat first. Millie, can you pour the tea?'

'Course I can.' She was off the chair in a flash, eager to get at the food. She waved her hands at the men. 'Me hands is clean. I washed them before we come here.'

As the girl busied herself pouring the tea, with her tongue sticking out slightly in concentration, Alex watched her every move. If he had seen these children in the street he wouldn't have given them a second look. He was ashamed of himself. They were desperately poor, but clearly bright. He wondered what they, and many like them, might achieve with a good education. He wished he could do something for them. His desire to help people in need was growing in him. It gave a feeling of purpose and structure to his life, something that had been missing since he left the army.

He smiled and nodded his thanks when Millie handed him a cup of tea. There was hardly any milk in it, but he guessed that would be used sparingly in her home.

'That all right?' she asked.

'Perfect, thank you, Millie.'

She beamed, warming to him at last. 'You want something to eat? There's lots.'

'I'll have a sandwich, please.'

Turning back to the trolley she began to count the sandwiches.

'What are you doing?' David asked.

'There's four of us so they've got to be shared properly. Got to be fair.'

Alex's jaw clenched as he watched her earnest little face. He'd always had a life of plenty, and this scene humbled him.

David put the plates in her hands. 'You don't have to worry about that. If we eat everything the maid will bring more. Hand the plates round.'

'Empty?'

'Yes, then you offer the large platter of sandwiches and we all take what we want.' When she rushed towards Fred, he stopped her. 'You serve Mr Glendale first.'

Fred was ginning, more relaxed now. 'That's 'cos he's top of the heap,' he told Millie.

'That right?'

Alex couldn't stop himself from chuckling. 'Not quite top of the heap. Now Millie, if there were ladies here, they would be served first, and then the men.'

With the point cleared up to her satisfaction, the girl happily trotted around seeing that everyone had lots to eat, including herself. It looked as if a plague of locusts had hit the table by the time they'd finished.

Eyeing the empty plates, Alex asked, 'Would you like anything else?'

'Couldn't eat another crumb,' Fred declared, patting his stomach.

Millie nodded agreement, giving Alex an impish smile. 'When Miss takes us to the teashop she gets them to give us some food to take home. She's ever so kind.'

Without saying a word, he rang the bell for the trolley to be removed. While the maid was doing this, he said, 'Daisy, ask cook to prepare a basket of food for both Mille and Fred.'

'At once, sir.'

After the maid left the room, Fred gave Alex a determined look. 'You being kind to us don't mean I'm gonna do what you want. I don't get involved in nothing criminal. I promised my dad. He said just because we're poor don't mean we have to sink into the gutter.'

'And he's quite right. I'm not trying to bribe you, Fred. Listen to what I have to say and then make up your own mind.'

'Fair enough.'

Alex sat back, his respect for these youngsters growing by the minute. 'The men Mr Melrose gambled with are members of my club and I would like to find out if he was cheated. If you were able to watch them, could you tell if they were manipulating the cards?'

'That all you want me to do? Just watch?'

Alex nodded.

'Hmm. They'd have to be very good for me not to see . . .' He paused. 'But I'd have to be near them for some time.'

'That can be arranged. The gamblers eat and drink a lot and I can get you in to clear the glasses and plates. I'll be there with you all the time. Will you help us, Fred?'

He almost held his breath while Fred looked at Millie, silent messages passing between them.

Eventually, Fred turned back to him. 'Will you help Miss and her family if we find out her brother was cheated?'

'You have my word on that.'

'Hmm, you don't look like a man who'd break his promise.'

'I'm not.'

'All right, I'll do it. But how are you gonna get me into your club? It must be posh. You being rich and all that.'

'You can leave that to me.' He wasn't sure how this was going to turn out, but at least they would be doing something for the Melrose family.

'Cor!' Millie was beaming. 'Wait till we tell Miss.'

'She mustn't know about this,' David said quickly. 'Promise me you won't say a word.'

'Why?' Fred was puzzled.

'Miss Melrose wouldn't be pleased to know I was helping her,' Alex explained, deciding to be completely honest with the youngsters.

'Why?' Millie asked this time.

'Because she doesn't like me.'

'You been nasty to her?' Millie eyed Alex with suspicion.

'No, I've always treated her kindly. I have great affection for her and her family.'

'Why don't she like you then?'

David smothered a laugh. These youngsters were not going to let this subject drop.

'Do you like everyone you meet?'

'No, 'course not.' Millie was now standing close to Alex, frowning. 'Most girls would fall over themselves to get at you. You being so posh and all that.'

Out of the corner of his eye, Alex could see David almost crying with silent laughter, and he was having the same difficulty, but managed to keep his composure. 'Those things do not impress Miss Melrose.'

''Spect not.' Millie glanced at Fred. 'She's not a snob, is she?'

Her friend nodded vigorously in agreement.

'Indeed not.' He thought it was about time he took control again. 'I'll contact you when the arrangements have been made, Fred. Will you give me your address?'

This was quickly written down, and armed with baskets of food, they were sent home in Alex's carriage, much to the youngsters' glee.

When they were alone again, Alex and David settled down with a large whisky each.

Alex raised his glass. 'Here's to success.'

'I'll drink to that.'

Chapter Eight

'Come into the library.' Sutton urged his wife and daughter into the room. 'I have something to tell you.'

Gertrude studied her father's face and was relieved to see him looking more relaxed. This was a terrible time for all of them, but her dear father was the one desperately trying to settle the matter, and the strain showed.

When they were seated he glanced at each of them, a brief smile touching his lips. 'You'll be pleased to know that the debt has been settled.'

'Oh, that's wonderful!' Florence sighed with relief. 'But how did you manage it, my dear? We haven't sold the house yet.'

'Yes, we have. I had a visit from Alexander Glendale this morning.'

Gertrude tensed, but she said nothing – with difficulty.

Her father continued. 'He'd heard of our urgent

need and made an extremely generous offer for this house. It was enough to clear the rest of the debt. I accepted. The money arrived from his bankers two hours ago and I've paid those men. We'll have no more trouble from them.'

'That is good news, darling.' Florence managed a smile, but couldn't stop her voice shaking. It had happened. The home she loved was no longer theirs. 'When does he want us to leave? I must get in touch with Hanna.'

Gertrude knew her mother would be heartbroken to leave this house. They all would be. And it was awful to hear that Mr Glendale had bought it.

'We don't have to leave.'

'What?' Her head came up and she gripped her mother's hand as it began to tremble.

'Explain, please.' Florence whispered.

'He has bought the house as an investment—'

Gertrude snorted.

'I know you don't like him, Gertie, but listen, and then I would expect you to find gratitude in your heart for his kindness. And make no mistake, this is an act of unselfishness. He didn't fool me that this was purely a business venture. He came to help us and presented it in a way he felt I could accept with dignity.'

She lowered her eyes at her father's rebuke. 'I'm sorry, Father.'

He nodded and continued. 'He explained that he had no plans for the property and so we could continue to live here. The rent he has set is ridiculously low. This I also accepted, because it will mean we can stay here.'

'That is very kind of him.' Florence couldn't hide her relief. 'I am so pleased we won't have to leave.'

Sutton smiled at his wife. 'You have been courageous, my dear, and I'm grateful for your support. There is one more piece of good news. Alexander said that we may purchase the house back at the price he paid for it when we are in a position to do so.'

'That's wonderful!' Florence exclaimed.

'Don't get too excited,' he warned gently. 'It will take time, for we have run ourselves dry. But we still have the business, and with economies and hard work we shall recover.'

She was pleased they didn't have to leave the home her parents had lovingly built up together, but Gertrude was suspicious about Mr Glendale's motives. Why on earth would he want to buy their house when he had so much property already? And from all accounts, he was also building up a thriving business in shipping. She was worried. Seeing the relief on her mother's face, she chose her words carefully. 'I don't understand why he has done this. Did he ask for something in return?'

Her father sat back and studied his daughter intently. 'No, he did not ask for your hand in marriage.'

'I didn't mean that,' she said hastily. But truthfully, it had been the first thing to come into her head.

'Yes, you did. He's made no secret of his affection for you, and I believe this is why he's helping us in this way. I can see no other reason for it. But he's not a fool, far from it. He knows you dislike him, and is too much of a gentleman to force his attentions on you. We cannot fathom why you feel such animosity towards him – and I suspect neither can you.'

She squirmed in her seat. Her father knew her too well, and what he said was true; she had no idea why she'd wanted to run the other way as soon as she'd seen Mr Glendale for the first time. It was all quite illogical. 'He makes me uneasy when he's near. Such a strong personality swamps me. I'm sorry, I know I'm being unreasonable, but I can't seem to warm to him.'

Florence stood up. 'I shall write a letter tonight, and you will do the same, Gertrude. We must also let Hanna know. I expect she'll be relieved to know we won't be moving in and disrupting her life.'

'Of course I'll write.' Her mother had made it an order, not a request. But she knew it was going to be a difficult letter to word. He might not be asking for anything at the moment, but what would happen in the future? They would be at his mercy, and that didn't sit easily with her. She knew enough about her father's business to be sure it would take a long time before he was able to buy back the house. Maybe years. Her parents liked and respected Glendale, but she had always found him to be a cold man.

Her mother left the room to tell Cook they were now ready to eat, but Gertrude stayed where she was, lost in troubled thought.

'Don't look so downcast, my dear.' Her father rested his hand on her shoulder. 'We have the worst behind us now.'

'I know, but I'm uneasy about this arrangement.'

'Don't be. If things should go wrong, then we can move in with Hanna. It would have broken your mother's heart to leave this house. I have taken Alexander at his word for her sake. He has the reputation of being a man who is honest in his dealings.'

She nodded. 'I don't doubt that, but he seems to lack warmth.'

He squeezed his daughter's shoulder. 'I agree he guards his emotions, but let's accept this piece of good fortune and take each day as it comes. The debt has been paid, and we can stay here, even if it no longer belongs to us.' Sadness filled his eyes. 'I've robbed Florence of her son. I didn't want to take her home from her as well, and I grabbed at this reprieve, even if it turns out to be short.'

She could feel the mental strain he was under and reached out to comfort him. 'Father, you had no choice. Not only had Edward left awful debts, but you had been attacked and your family threatened. Mother understands you only did what you felt you had to.'

When he spoke, his voice was husky with grief. 'I know, but it doesn't make my decisions any the less painful. He's ruined us, and I couldn't risk any harm coming to you and your mother. Material possessions mean nothing when weighed against both of you. Your lives are precious to me.'

'Do you really believe those men would have carried out their threat?' she asked quietly.

He shrugged, and then sighed deeply. 'I could not take that chance. Please don't mention this to your mother, but

I want you to be aware that we may not be able to regain the comfortable position we once held.'

She gazed into his troubled face. He had always spoken to her frankly, and he was doing that now, alerting her to the seriousness of their position. 'You mean it's unlikely we'll be able to buy this house back?'

'The word I would use is impossible. Oh, I could eventually save enough if the business grows, but times are hard and it will take many years. Will Alexander wait that long?' He grimaced. 'I doubt that very much. He's a good businessman and he will not want to have an investment standing idle for any length of time. I knew that when I made the agreement, but the debt had to be paid, and he was giving me a way to do that. I had to take his offer, as there was no choice. You understand, don't you?'

Gertrude felt sick when she nodded. Her father had been putting on a brave face for his wife's sake. She was grieving for the loss of her son, and she had been given some small comfort to know they could remain living in the house she loved. The pain she felt for her parents was physical, making her clench her teeth. And for the first time in her life she hated her brother for doing this to them. How could Edward have been so selfish?

'If there's anything I can do, you must let me know,' she said.

'There is something. Will you come and work with me, Gertie? I'm going to need all the help I can get at the workshop. The business is our only asset now and we must work hard to expand it if we can. It's not as profitable as it should be.'

'Of course,' she agreed instantly, then glanced up and smiled. 'I'm not much good at sawing wood.'

He laughed for the first time. 'I believe you'd be good at anything you tackled, but I'll need you to look after the paperwork for me. I'll expect your best handwriting.'

She smiled at his attempt to make a joke.

'I'm going to need you, and so is your mother.' He lifted her chin so he could look into her eyes, serious again. 'There's hard work in front of us, Gertie.'

'I'm not afraid of that. We'll get through this, whatever happens,' she declared confidently. 'Something will turn up, you'll see.'

'Ever the optimist.'

'Of course. Ah, there's the dinner gong. Now we must smile.' They walked arm in arm to join Florence, but the brightness of her expression belied the heaviness inside her. She prayed that Mr Glendale could indeed be trusted not to turn them out for a year or two. They all needed time to come to terms with the mess they were in. She doubted if her mother could have dealt with the loss of her son and the house all at once. How she hated to be at the mercy of anyone. But it was no good riling against it. Their situation was grave, and she would do anything she could to help.

The most important thing at the moment was to find Edward and know he was safe. Then perhaps it would be easier to come to terms with the rest.

The next morning, Alex was up early as there was a busy day ahead of him. His first call this morning would be to his club. He usually shied away from using his position, but he was going to call in a favour to get Fred into the gaming room. Then he would see David before going to the boy's parents. There was no way he would involve the youngster in this if they objected.

With the day planned, he helped himself from the various breakfast dishes. As usual, he was the only one there. Two years ago his mother, father and sister had died within a year of each other. His sister died of a fever, then his father of a massive heart attack, and his mother of a broken heart. She just seemed to lose the will to live.

The food in front of him was forgotten as the memories flooded in. He had been set for a military career, but he'd had to resign his commission and return home to take care of the family estates.

The grief that had swamped him on his return would never be forgotten. This large house had always been full of lively people, and the emptiness had nearly destroyed him. But he was a fighter and could not allow that to happen. He knew people considered him cold and unfeeling, but that facade had been necessary. It was the only way he'd been able to survive the loneliness and grief.

Pushing away the now cold food, he glanced down the table and pictured Gertrude sitting there. But that wasn't going to happen, and it was time he dismissed the desire. She didn't like him and he wouldn't waste time trying to change her mind. He didn't believe he was a vain man, but there were several young women who would marry him for his money. But he had grave doubts that he could ever commit himself to a woman who only wanted wealth and position. His parents had loved each other deeply, and he wanted the same for himself. Foolish!

The butler arrived holding a silver tray. 'The post has arrived, sir.'

'Thank you.' He took the letters, pleased to have his sombre thoughts interrupted.

The first letter was from Florence Melrose, thanking him for allowing them to remain in the house. It was beautifully written and he was pleased his offer had been accepted with such dignity. The next note lacked sincerity and he guessed it had been written out of duty. Gertrude had managed only a couple of sentences, and her gratitude was grudging. Giving a snort of disgust, he tossed the note down and muttered, 'My God, Gertrude, what have I ever done to you? You didn't mean one word of that! Your stiff note shows clearly that you resent the fact it was me who came to your aid. Well, I'm going to do a hell of a lot more. And when I've sorted out the mess your brother has left you in, I'm going to dismiss you from my thoughts and find myself a willing, docile wife!'

After reading the rest of the letters, he left the house and headed for the club. This must be settled before he saw Fred's parents. He had no intention of telling the club why he wanted the boy in the gaming room. It would be enough to indicate that he was interested in helping the boy and wanted to see if he was a good worker.

* * *

Two hours later, Alex made his way to David's office. It was situated close to the Port of London where all the shipping action took place.

'Everything's set for tonight,' Alex told David as soon as he walked in. 'Now I need permission from Fred's parents.'

'Of course.' David was already grabbing his coat. 'I'll go now.'

'We'll both go. I have my carriage waiting outside.'

That stopped David in mid-stride. 'The two of us turning up could cause quite a stir.'

'I doubt it.' Alex's eyes shone with amusement. 'If the parents are anything like their children I don't suppose they'll even raise an eyebrow.'

Both men laughed, and for the first time that morning Alex's mood lifted.

They left the carriage at the end of Tanner Street and walked to where Fred lived, thinking this might attract less interest. They were wrong. A large group of scruffy children attached themselves to Alex and David. A small boy of around four danced along in an effort to keep up with Alex's long stride, never taking his eyes off the fine gentleman.

'What you doing here?' the boy asked breathlessly.

Alex slackened his pace and smiled down at the child. 'We've come to see Fred and Millie.'

Emboldened by this show of friendliness, a slightly older boy pushed the other one roughly out of the way. 'What you want with them?'

'That's my business, young man.' Alex stopped and

looked around for the child who had first spoken to him. He was standing at the back of the group and scowling at the other boy. He looked defiant, but his bottom lip was trembling. Alex beckoned him forward, holding out his hand. 'Come and show me where Fred lives.'

The boy rushed forward and took hold of the proffered hand, his little face wreathed in smiles now.

'What's your name?'

'Johnny, sir.'

'And where do you live, Johnny?'

'Next door to Millie. We're at the end of the street.'

Alex began walking again, slowly this time so all the youngsters could keep up with them. He took in every detail of the squalid houses and the assortment of ragged clothes the children were wearing in an effort to keep out the cold. He glanced at David, who was carrying a little girl who'd had trouble walking. The two men were now grim-faced.

'This isn't right, David. What chance do these poor little devils have in life?'

'Very little.' He settled the girl more securely in his arms. 'This one needs medical treatment or she's never going to be able to walk properly. She can't talk very well either, but I think she said her name's May.'

Reaching out, Alex turned May's face towards him. 'Where do you live, May?'

She pointed to Johnny. 'Near.'

'How old are you?'

She screwed her face up in concentration and Johnny tugged at Alex's hand. 'She's three, but she ain't that old in her head. And there's summat wrong with her legs. Her mum and dad can't afford no doctors though.'

'After we've seen Fred, I want you to take me to her house. Will you do that?'

Johnny nodded, gazing up in admiration. 'You a doctor?'

'No, but I know a very good one.'

'You look rich. Never seen clothes like you're wearing. I can see my face in your shoes.' Johnny studied David. 'And you look right posh too.'

'Thank you, Johnny.' David winked at Alex. 'But I'm not as posh as him.'

The boy could hardly contain his excitement as he shouted to the rest of the children. 'Here, I'm holding the hand of a lord!'

'I haven't got a title, Johnny.'

'You must have, 'cos you're ever so posh. You don't have to hide it from us!'

Alex laughed as one of the older girls ran in front of him and gave a tottering curtsy. 'How do I get out of this, David?'

'I wouldn't try. It's giving this crowd a lot of pleasure. They'll be talking about this for ages. But you do have a title, Alex, your rank as Major. Most officers keep that title for life.'

'I'm not in the army now and wouldn't dream of calling myself Major Glendale.' Alex grimaced at the very thought.

'Hey, Lord!' Johnny tugged on Alex again. 'I try and look after May. Can you help her? She's a nice little thing and she ain't daft really.'

'I'll talk to her family.'

Johnny beamed. 'Fred told us about you. He said you was all right. He said you'd given him and Millie lots of grub. We all had a bit.'

'Ah, here comes the whirlwind,' David said as Millie hurtled towards them.

Skidding to a halt, she stopped in front of them, laughing. 'You got quite a crowd there.'

'Hello, Millie. We do seem to have gathered a large following.' Alex smiled, surprised at how pleased he was to see the precocious girl again. 'Is Fred at home?'

'No, he's down at the market trying to sell some of his boxes. He'll be back soon though. Can you wait? Mum'll give you a cup of tea.'

For the next hour David stayed in the background and watched Alex deal with the children and their families. He did it with ease, and David was astonished to see this side of the usually stern man. Oh, he laughed and joked, but there was always something in his eyes that made people cautious around him. Not once did he appear ill at ease in the dingy surroundings.

Millie's mother had insisted on serving tea in the front room. The furniture was old and torn, but it was clean and there was a vase of wild flowers on the window sill. Johnny brought May's parents over and remained himself, seeming reluctant to leave the tall man who had befriended him. May sat happily on David's lap all the time, never speaking, but her eyes darted around, taking in everything. Millie ushered in Fred's mother, and everyone waited expectantly to hear why these important men had come.

Alex explained what he needed from Fred, and after extracting a promise that no harm would come to him and he would be well looked after, the mother agreed. Then Alex told May's parents he would like to send a doctor to have a look at their daughter. When he assured them they wouldn't have to pay for the service, they accepted eagerly.

With everything settled, the two men took their leave, and Johnny insisted on accompanying them back to the carriage. He stood well back from the horse, not sure about being so close to the big animal. 'Will you come again?' he asked, looking crestfallen as they prepared to leave.

Alex stooped down in front of the boy. 'I promise I will. And I want you to do something for me.'

'Anything!'

'May needs fresh fruit. You all do.' He gave Johnny some coins. 'I want you to buy some with that and share it out.'

The boy nodded. 'I'll get a big bag of apples and oranges so we can all have a piece each.'

'Good lad.'

As they drove away, David couldn't keep his eyes off his companion. This had been a very revealing visit.

'Say what you're thinking,' Alex told him, amusement in his eyes.

With a short laugh, David said, 'I'm beginning to realise that under that stern exterior is a man with a soft heart.'

'It wouldn't do for a story like that to get around,' Alex said, giving a wry smile. 'And you're quite wrong.'

'I don't think so.' His respect for Alex had been growing by the hour. He couldn't help wondering how many other charitable deeds he did on the quiet. 'But I'll keep my opinion to myself.'

'Have dinner with me this evening. We'll dine at my house, where we can talk in private. We have much to discuss.'

Chapter Nine

'Has David been able to find out where Edward's gone?' Florence's face was lined with worry as she watched her daughter fastening her shoes.

Gertrude looked up. The concern about leaving the house had been removed for the time being, and her mother's whole attention had turned towards finding her son. She spoke gently. 'He hasn't said anything, but he's promised he'll do all he can.'

Her mother nodded. 'He's always been a good friend to both of you. Will you see him today and ask?'

'I'll go in my break time.' She stood up and surveyed herself in the long mirror. The dark grey dress was modest and neat. 'Will I do? I've never worked before.'

'You look charming as always, but I don't like the thought of you working at the factory.'

'It's necessary, Mother.' Her smile was tinged with

sadness. 'You wouldn't be so concerned if I were a boy, would you?'

'Of course not. Edward should be doing this. It's his place. But he never showed the slightest interest in the business. All he did was gamble away everything your father has worked for.' Her mother gave a ragged sigh. 'But he's my son, and I need to know he's all right. I'm half out of my mind with worry. I can't sleep.'

Stepping forward, Gertrude clasped her mother's fluttering hands. 'Shush, you mustn't upset yourself like this.'

Florence gazed at her daughter with pleading eyes. 'Where has he gone? If I could know he's safe, then I'll be all right.'

'He'll be able to take care of himself, you'll see. Now, what are you going to do today?' she asked, quickly changing the subject.

'Hanna's coming and she'll keep me busy.'

'Good.' Gertrude pulled a face. 'I must go. If I'm late on my first day I'll be told off.'

'Your father would never do that. From the moment you were born he's adored you. He'll be so proud to have you working beside him.'

'And I shall be proud to do it. Enjoy your day with Aunt Hanna!'

As Gertrude left the house, the smile on her face disappeared. If her mother continued to fret over Edward, she would make herself ill. She would do whatever had to be done to find her wayward brother. 'Damn you, Edward!' she muttered angrily. 'Where the devil are you?'

When she arrived at the factory, her father introduced her to the rest of the workers, many of them had been there for years. They were all aware of the gravity of the situation, for Sutton had been open and honest with them, and there was an air of determination about the workshop. Orders were being sought from anywhere. Their furniture had always been of the highest quality, selling to the more affluent, but now they were taking on more modest assignments. In fact, no job, however small, was being turned away.

Gertrude had a sharp mind, always willing to learn new things, and she blessed that ability now. Her father started her on the more simple tasks, going through each step patiently, until she became familiar with the system. She loved working with him and was eager to show she was capable of being an asset. She couldn't understand why her brother had continually refused to have anything to do with the business. It was quite stimulating.

After only an hour, Sutton smiled at his daughter and stood up. 'I can see the office is in good hands. I'll leave you to it. Just call if you come across anything you don't understand.'

'Yes, Father.' She felt so proud.

'And don't forget to take an hour for lunch at one o'clock.'

'I won't, and don't you forget either.'

He nodded and left the office.

The morning flew by. There was no sign of her father at one o'clock, so Gertrude decided to take the chance to see David. He nearly always went home for a meal around this time. Perhaps she would be invited to dine with him. She hoped so, because she was ravenous.

He was eating when she arrived. 'Sorry to disturb you, but I've only got an hour.'

'Why's that?' he asked, standing up to greet her.

'It's my lunch break.' She eyed the food on the table and willed her stomach to stay quiet.

He frowned and pulled up a chair. 'Sit down, Gertie. What are you up to?'

'I'm working for Father.' When she saw the look of disbelief on his face, she explained. 'We have no choice. It will take a very long time for us to recover, though please don't tell Mother. She's worried enough about Edward, and that's why I'm here. Have you been able to find him?'

'No, I'm sorry,' he said gently. 'I've enquired in all the places he used to frequent, but no one's seen him. I've also checked with many of the ship owners to see if he signed on as crew for them, but if he did he didn't use his own name.'

She was shocked. 'He wouldn't do that, would he? Go to sea, I mean.'

'It was a possibility I had to check.'

She sighed in disappointment as she toyed with the salt pot on the table. Her mother wasn't going to take this news well.

'Would you like something to eat?' he asked.

'Yes, please.' She waited while the maid served her. 'What am I going to do? I've promised I'll find him. Mother needs to know he's all right, and so do I.'

'I've done all I can, but there is one man who could probably help.'

She looked up eagerly. 'Who?'

'Alexander Glendale.'

Her knife and fork clattered on to the plate, her eyes filling with disbelief. 'I can't go to him! He's our landlord, for heaven's sake! And what the devil can he do that you can't? You know Edward, he doesn't.'

'Gertie!' David stopped her as she took a breath to continue her tirade. 'I don't know what's the matter with you. One mention of Alex and you start to spit like a frightened cat. He's a good man.'

She gave an inelegant snort.

'Has it occurred to you,' he continued, 'that he bought your house to help you? That he did it out of respect and compassion for your plight?'

The expression on her face said she thought her friend had lost his mind. Compassion? He was too cold to have such feelings!

Watching her intently, David said, 'I do believe you're frightened of him.'

'I am not!'

'All right, let's talk this through, then you can prove it and go to see him.' David took a deep breath. 'Now, as I've told you, I've searched everywhere I can think of, but there's no sign of Edward. He's out there somewhere, on his own and without money. For the first time in his life he's got to provide for himself. His immediate need would be to get food and a roof over his head. Think carefully. What does Edward like to do – except gamble, of course?'

She chewed her lip. It frightened her to think what her brother might be going through. He had been disowned by his family and was probably too ashamed to go to friends for help. 'He hasn't any skills . . . Apart from socialising, he's only ever shown an interest in horses.'

'Exactly.' Pushing away his empty plate, David sat forward.

'Would he have left London and gone to work at a stud, or something like that?'

'Well, if he has, it would be one we don't know, because I think he doesn't want to be found. This is where Alex might be able to help. He has estates in the country, and his reach is wide. He was an officer in the cavalry before he had to resign his commission and return home. He knows a lot about horses, and even owns his own stud in Kent to supply the army.' He let her think about this for a moment. 'The Glendales have always been a highly respected family, and one of enormous wealth. His influence is wide ranging, and I believe he's our best hope, so put aside your dislike and ask him for help.'

'Couldn't you ask him?' she asked hesitantly.

'No, this is something you must do.' He paused. 'I never considered you to be a coward.'

That hurt! And he was right; she was being unreasonable – again! 'I'll think about it.'

Unable to sleep that night, Gertrude sat up and hugged her knees. David's accusation that she was acting like a coward had unsettled her. Was she? He was a good friend and had always spoken frankly to her. He didn't say things he didn't mean.

Resting her head on her knees, she tried to take an

honest look at her feelings. She didn't like Alexander Glendale; hadn't liked him from the moment she'd set eyes on him. But why? He was a pleasant-looking man; some said handsome, but she wouldn't go that far. What had struck her most was his size. He stood a head above most people, and was even taller than David, who was six feet. When he'd turned his gaze on her she'd felt as if something had hit her. The green of his eyes was startling against his black hair. There was an aura of strength emanating from him and he must have been a commanding figure in his uniform. When he walked into a room he seemed to fill the place; all eyes turned towards him. Not a man to be comfortable around, and that was the mystery, because he'd never done anything to earn her animosity.

Her sigh was ragged. Putting that aside, she hesitated to go to him for two reasons. One – she considered him to be a cold, unfeeling man, and couldn't believe he would even be interested enough to help. Two – she really didn't see what he could do. As far as she knew, he had never spoken more than two words to Edward. Oh, David had made some good points in his favour, but she still felt it would be a waste of time. She was desperate though, not knowing which way to turn. She had to do something – anything!

Sitting in the same position, she mulled everything over. Perhaps David was right? Perhaps Glendale did frighten her a little. She didn't think she had seen him smile – not really smile. But none of that was important. Her brother must be found, and every avenue, however unlikely, had to be considered.

Sliding back into the bed, she pulled the covers up to

her chin. He was a man of influence and might have more chance of tracing her brother. But she didn't relish the thought of approaching him.

With a growl of frustration, she thumped her pillows into shape. What choice did she have? When she'd told her mother there wasn't any news, the distress in her eyes had torn Gertrude apart. She had to do something! And her personal feelings didn't come into this. What was the worst he could do? Allow her to beg, and then refuse?

Her mouth set in a tight line. Well, she was strong enough to take rejection. At least she would know she'd done everything she could. And it would be interesting to see if the man had a heart.

She would visit him tomorrow in her lunch break.

Chapter Ten

'Everything's set, David. My housekeeper has some decent clothes for Fred, and if they don't fit she will soon make the alterations. The boy will be here by six o'clock, so we'll dine here and then go to the club.' Alex's mouth turned up at the corners. 'Oh, and Millie's insisting on coming as well.'

'Good heavens!' He shook his head. 'What are we going to do with her?'

'I'll put her in the kitchen. With all that food around her she won't move.'

'Good idea. I suppose she's coming to look after Fred?'

'So she says, but truthfully, I don't think she wants to be left out. Will you join me for lunch?'

'Thank you, I'd like to.'

At that moment the butler entered. 'There's a Miss Melrose to see you, sir.'

'Oops!' David stood up. 'That's my fault. I told her to come and see you, but I didn't believe she'd do it.'

'She doesn't know about our plan, does she?'

'No, she wants to ask a favour of you. I'd better not be here. She'll be suspicious if she sees me.'

Alex's eyes glinted with amusement at David's discomfort. 'Wait in the dining room.'

David shot through the door, closing it firmly behind him.

'You may show Miss Melrose in.' Alex stood by the window, his back to the door. This was intriguing. The first time he'd seen her he had been attracted to her lively nature and intelligence, and decided in that instant he wanted her as his wife. Before approaching her, he'd spoken with her father who had insisted that his daughter must make her own choice, but Sutton had given his approval. He'd thought it would be a reasonably smooth courtship from then on. How wrong he'd been! No matter how hard he tried to engage her interest, she shied away from him. He wasn't a man to waste his time on a hopeless cause, but still he clung to the wish to make Gertrude his wife.

The door opened. 'Miss Melrose, sir.'

He waited for the butler to leave before turning. She looked tired and ill at ease, but her head was high and her gaze steady. He liked that. Damn it! He liked everything about her.

'I apologise for calling on you unannounced,' she said, as soon as he was facing her. 'But I would be grateful if I could have five minutes of your time, Mr Glendale.'

A stiff, well-rehearsed opening. Dipping his head in

agreement, he indicated a chair. 'Please sit down.'

'I'll stand, as this won't take long.'

He wasn't going to have that! 'You are not standing before a headmaster awaiting a rebuke, Miss Melrose. Sit down, please.'

It wasn't a request, it was an order, and he watched emotions flashing through her violet eyes. She wanted to refuse, but after a brief hesitation she settled in the chair. He sat behind his desk and waited.

After drawing in a deep breath, she began. 'You are aware that my family have turned Edward out, and I am concerned about my mother's health. My father had every right to send Edward away, but my mother and I would be relieved to know where he is. I've had the help of a friend, but we've been unable to find any trace of him.'

When he didn't speak, she continued. 'At his suggestion I've come to ask if you could help. I don't know what else to do.'

She looked wretched for a moment, and then recovered her composure. 'But I'm wasting your time. I shouldn't have come.'

'Has your brother ever mentioned something he would like to do, or somewhere special he wanted to go?'

She was halfway out of her chair when he spoke, and sat down again at once. 'I can't recall him ever being interested in anything particular. He liked riding and was an excellent horseman.'

'Nothing else? Did he want to travel?'

'He never mentioned it, but he didn't tell me everything. He would have spoken more freely to David Gardener.'

'I'll ask him.'

Her gaze locked on to his in surprise. 'You'll help?'

He nodded. 'I'll do what I can, but I make no promises.'

'I wouldn't expect you to.' She stood up, clearly relieved. 'Just knowing you'll try to find Edward is enough. Thank you.'

Alex was also on his feet. 'Don't raise your hopes too much. Your brother could be anywhere by now. I'll contact you if I have any news.'

'Could you do that discreetly? Father doesn't know we're looking for Edward, but Mother needs to know he's all right.'

'I understand.'

Dredging up a faint smile, she left the room.

He stood by the window and watched her walk up the road. She was an independent girl, used to making her own decisions, so it had been hard for her to come pleading for help. But it was terribly important to her and her mother's peace of mind that her brother was found.

His mouth set in a grim line as he turned away. He had never seen her looking so dispirited. He'd been attracted to her natural sparkle and bright intelligence. Now that brightness had faded, and he hoped it hadn't been extinguished. If he ever got his hands on Edward Melrose he would be tempted to shake him until his teeth rattled. How could the thoughtless boy have put his family in this degrading position? He admired the way they were dealing with the shame. There had been no attempt to hide their son's gambling or huge debts. The Melrose family had drawn closer together, making no secret of the difficulties they were now facing. Such courage and dignity . . .

'Will you help?'

At the sound of David's voice, Alex turned and walked back to his desk. 'I don't know how I can succeed when you've failed, but I'll do what I can. Tell me all you know about Melrose over lunch.'

By the time Gertrude arrived back at her father's factory, she had regained her composure. She thought she'd managed the unpleasant task quite well, but was ashamed she hadn't been a little more gracious. Her emotions were in turmoil, and standing in front of him had unnerved her. She didn't know how she'd got through the meeting. His steely gaze never left her face, and she'd been sure he was going to refuse. But he had agreed to see what he could do, and she couldn't ask more than that. After all, this wasn't his problem, and he didn't need to get involved. But her relief had been immense. David thought highly of Alexander Glendale, and she trusted her friend's judgement.

Once back in the office, she remembered Fred's wooden box. She had brought it with her and it was sitting on her desk. She smiled at the thought of the two likeable youngsters. The memory of their joy in the teashop was like balm to her distressed mind. She'd go to the bookshop on her day off and hope they were there. They mustn't think she had abandoned them and was going to keep their possessions.

'Did you have a good lunch?' her father asked, sitting in the chair next to her.

'Yes, thank you,' she lied. There hadn't been time to eat, and Mr Glendale certainly wouldn't have invited her to eat with him. He hadn't even seemed pleased to see her. So much for his supposed interest in her. But what else did she expect? He'd probably got fed up with her disinterest, and abandoned that idea by now.

'What's this?' Her father reached out for the box.

'I've been meaning to show it to you, but so much has been going on. The young boy I told you about made it.'

'Hmm.' Her father examined it closely. 'It's crude but well-constructed. The joints are excellent, and the carving on the top shows real promise. Has the youngster got a job?'

'No, and he needs one.'

Sutton stood up, still holding the box. 'Bring the boy to me, and I'll see what I can do for him. I'm not promising anything,' he said when he saw the pleasure on his daughter's face. 'We're not in a good position at the moment, but I might be able to take him on as an apprentice. I'll have to talk to him first, though.'

She knew her father and was pleased with his response. If he were really interested in Fred's work he would help him. 'I'll see him on my day off on Thursday.'

'No, go tomorrow morning and bring him here.'

'All right.' She watched him leave and could hardly contain her excitement. It was turning out to be a good day after all.

Aunt Hanna joined them for dinner and her lively company kept the conversation flowing. She was like a fresh breeze lifting their thoughts and making them smile. Gertrude knew that Hanna's life had been far from easy. She had been married at the age of seventeen to a much older man chosen by her parents. He'd been an odious man and treated the gentle girl harshly. When she had failed to give him the children he demanded he'd cast her aside and taken a mistress, flaunting her in public. But his wife was made of stern stuff and she had weathered the storm, somehow managing to hold on to her dignity. He'd died when Hanna was only twenty-nine, leaving her the small house in London and very little money, most of his fortune going to the other woman.

Gertrude held her aunt in high affection. She was always cheerful and optimistic, never once showing the slightest sign of being bitter about the way she had been treated. She always declared that she had come out of the experience a much stronger person. When she told them that all would be well in the end, they agreed that she was probably right. But Gertrude knew the future was uncertain and their lives would never be the same again. Her father would work himself to exhaustion in an effort to pull them out of the financial mess Edward had left them in. And although her mother did not appear to have noticed, she *had* lost her home. The chances of buying it back were remote.

How Gertrude longed to be able to remove their burdens . . .

'Excuse me.' Sutton stood up. 'I'll take my coffee in the study.'

'Don't work too late,' Florence scolded her husband gently. As soon as he'd left the room she turned to her daughter. 'Did you see David? Is there any news?'

'I'm afraid not. He suggested I ask Mr Glendale for help, and I saw him today. He said he'd do what he could, but I wouldn't hope too much,' she warned. 'I can't see what he can do, but David seems to think a lot of him, and I didn't know what else to do.'

'That was good of him to agree,' Hanna said, nodding in approval. 'You did the right thing.'

Gertrude pulled a face. 'He didn't seem too pleased to see me.'

'Nonsense!' Florence exclaimed. 'He told your father he thinks a great deal of you.'

'That was months ago, and I've hardly spoken to him since.'

'Because you scuttle away whenever you see him.' Hanna looked accusingly at her niece.

'I do not *scuttle* away.' She was indignant. 'I avoid him, that's all.'

'Of course you do, and if he wasn't delighted to see you then he's given up on you. He doesn't need to waste his time on an unwilling girl. There are plenty more who would welcome his attention. He has a wide choice, for even titled families would be pleased to have him as a son-in-law. He needs a wife and children of his own, so I expect he's found someone else by now.'

'I hope he has,' Gertrude said defiantly.

'Will you two stop arguing?' Florence stopped them.

'Sorry.' Hanna glanced at her niece and winked. 'If I was twenty years younger I would be running towards him, not away.'

They laughed as her aunt patted her hair into place.

'Do stop that, Hanna,' Florence chided. 'You could have remarried a long time ago, but you would have none of it. Gertrude, do you really believe he will try to find Edward?'

'He said he'd try. That's all I can tell you.' Her mother was clutching at this straw, and she didn't want to raise her hopes too much. 'We must be patient.'

'I'm told that Alex never breaks his word.' Hanna smiled encouragingly at Florence. 'Don't give up hope.'

Florence nodded. 'He's a resourceful man and I'm sure he'll help all he can. Look how he stepped in to see we had enough money to pay off the debt and still remain in our home.'

Yes, just look! Gertrude didn't speak the words or allow her misgivings to show. Her mother was drawing some comfort from his involvement and that's all that mattered.

For the moment.

Chapter Eleven

'Let's have a look at you.' Alex turned Fred around and examined him from every angle. 'You've done a good job with him, Mrs Jenkins.'

The housekeeper straightened Fred's tie. 'Thank you, sir. I had to alter the clothes rather a lot. The boy's far too thin, but he does look presentable now.'

'Indeed.' Alex glanced across at Millie, who was grinning at her friend. 'Can you find something for Millie? She insists on coming with us and I shall have to leave her in the club kitchen with Cook for a while.'

'Hmm.' Mrs Jenkins whipped a tape measure over the startled girl. 'Young Daisy's about her size. I'll see if she's got something suitable.'

'Good. Tell Daisy I'll buy her two new frocks to replace the one she gives to Millie.'

'One will do!' the housekeeper said in a disapproving

voice. 'The girl wouldn't expect more than that.'

'I said two.'

The housekeeper sighed. 'Very well, two it shall be, but you are far too generous.' Then she left the room.

''Ere.' Millie sidled up to Alex. 'Do you let her talk to you like that? You're the big man around here, ain't you?'

He laughed quietly. 'Mrs Jenkins has been with the family for a long time. She practically brought me up, and does take liberties some times.'

'And you don't mind? I mean I've watched all the others treat you like you're the boss. You gives an order and they jump, fast.'

''Course they do,' Fred told his friend. 'He was an officer in the army and expects to be obeyed smartly.'

'How do you know?'

The boy smirked. 'There's a picture of him in the other room. Mrs Jenkins told me you was a cavalry officer while she was making the clothes fit me.'

Millie was through the door like a shot and they could hear her running around the room. Then she returned clutching a silver photo frame. She hurried over to David. 'Look at this! That horse is huge, and don't Sir look fine in his uniform.'

'Splendid,' David agreed.

She spun round and trotted up to Alex, pulling on his sleeve. 'Sit down, you're too tall.'

When he did as ordered the girl leant on him so he could see the photograph. She began to point to parts of his uniform, asking, 'What's this called? And what's that for?'

Fred shook his head and grinned at David. 'She's got to know everything. Questions, questions, all the time. Drives her family mad. Been like it from the minute she could talk. Still, he doesn't seem to mind, does he?'

Before David could answer, the housekeeper swept into the room again. Seeing Millie holding the silver frame, she said sharply, 'Put that back where you found it, girl!'

Millie rounded on her, indignant. 'I'm asking him to tell me about his horse and the uniform. And I ain't gonna keep the picture. I'm not a thief!'

'Of course you're not.' Alex stood up. 'Did you find something for Millie to wear?'

'Daisy's given me her best frock.' The housekeeper studied Millie's hurt expression and gave a brief smile. 'I didn't mean to imply you would steal the picture, young lady. I was pointing out that you shouldn't pick up things when you're in someone else's house.'

'Oh.' Millie looked up at Alex. 'Sorry, I didn't know. You should've told me. We wouldn't do nothing wrong to you, would we, Fred?'

''Course we wouldn't. And he knows that, don't you, sir?'

'I certainly do. You are both very well-behaved and I trust you completely in my home.'

Millie nodded, relieved. 'Miss takes us to a posh teashop and she ain't ashamed of us.'

'They was shocked the first time we went there. Bet they wouldn't mind if I went in looking like this though.' Fred smirked and looked down at his smart suit.

'They wouldn't know who you was,' his friend laughed.

Alex turned her towards his housekeeper. 'Go with Mrs Jenkins and see if the frock fits you.'

She gave the picture a tender look, running her fingers gently over the embossed frame. 'Ain't this lovely? I'll put the picture back first. I know where it was.'

'Thank you, Millie.' He watched her walk out of the room with the housekeeper, his expression thoughtful. He rang for the butler who appeared immediately. 'Ask Daisy to come and see me.'

As the butler left, the door to the other room opened and the housekeeper came in. 'It's a perfect fit. Come on Millie, show everyone how pretty you look.'

Her face appeared round the door, looking very uncertain about letting them see her.

Fred burst out laughing. 'Don't be daft. Millie, you ain't never been shy in your life.'

Giving a defiant toss of her head, she stepped into the room. 'Don't laugh then! It touches the ground. I'll fall over in the blinking thing.'

'That's how it's supposed to be.' David fought to keep a straight face. 'You look lovely, Millie.'

'Think so?'

''Course you do,' Fred told her. 'You look real grown-up.'

'Hmm.' She still looked uncertain as she ran her hands over the material. 'Suppose it's a pretty blue.'

'It's splendid,' Alex said, just as the door opened and the young maid appeared.

She bobbed in front of him. 'You sent for me, sir?'

'Yes, Daisy. Thank you for giving Millie your frock. You may choose any material and the dressmaker will make you two to replace it. Now, I know you've finished for the day, but I want you to come with us this evening to keep Millie company. I'll see you are recompensed for your time. We shall be leaving in half an hour.'

'I'll be ready, sir.' As Daisy passed Millie, she whispered, 'The frock suits you.'

The club was quiet when they arrived. It would be another hour before the evening really began. After installing Millie and Daisy in the kitchen with strict instructions that they were not to move from there, Alex, David and Fred went to the gaming room.

David watched Alex in operation. The army officer was evident. He had planned the evening with military precision.

After setting two tables with glasses and plates, he gave Fred a tray. 'Clear the tables,' he ordered the boy. 'Remember, men will be sitting there so don't jostle them. Remove only the glasses you can easily reach. Don't speak or make a noise. They will not be pleased if you break their concentration.'

The boy nodded and set about the task. When his tray was full, he asked, 'How was that?'

'Very smooth,' Alex told him. 'Once you have enough glasses, you take them to the kitchen to be washed.'

'Right.'

'All the time you're working I want you to keep an eye on the players. I'm not going to point out the men we believe are cheating. We mustn't let them know they are being watched.'

'They won't even know I'm here. Where will you be?'

'At the table in the corner.' Alex pulled out a chair. 'Fancy a game of cards, David?'

'But you don't gamble. Everyone knows that.'

'Perhaps I'm so bored away from the army I need a little excitement.' He unbuttoned his jacket and sat down.

'I suppose some might believe that, but what if others want to join us?'

'Let them. Neither of us are known gamblers and we need to blend in.' Alex turned his attention back to Fred. 'You will work for two hours and then the usual boy will take over. If at any time you feel you can't manage, or need to talk to me, place an empty glass on our table. I'll meet you outside. Is that clear?'

'Yes, sir, I knows what to do. You can rely on me.'

'Good lad.'

The door opened and the room began to fill. David was relieved to see that they all had full tables and there wasn't any danger of them being invited to join the others. Though from the curious glances many cast at Alex, it was obvious some would have liked to snare him, as he was reputed to be one of the richest men in the country.

Alex placed money on the table to make it look as if they were really playing, and thankfully, no one else asked to join them. He had an air of boredom about him, making David realise he was a consummate actor, and far more skilled at brag than would have been believed. If any of the others had drawn him into their games, they would have been in for a shock.

He fought to hide his amusement. 'I had the impression

you didn't know anything about playing cards?'

'I never said I couldn't play, I just don't agree with gambling.' Alex gave a wry smile. 'You learn a lot of things in the army, but I'm not skilled enough to spot cheats.'

'Nor me. And you're letting me win all the time,' David remarked dryly as he dealt another hand.

The boy moved quietly and no one was giving him a second glance. He didn't come near them and David began to worry this evening was doomed to failure.

It was almost at the end of the two hours before he came over to their table. Having his back to the room he gave Alex a sly wink as he leant over to pick up a glass. 'Got 'em, sir!' he whispered, then left carrying a full tray.

As soon as Fred had disappeared, Alex threw down his cards, and said in an audible voice, 'You win again. I don't think gambling is for me.'

'Try another hand.' David joined in the subterfuge. 'Your luck might change.'

'I doubt it.' Alex stood up. 'Let's get something to eat.'

David collected the money from the table. 'Good idea, I'm ravenous.'

Once outside, David tried to give Alex the money, but he waved it away.

'But it's all yours.'

'Give it to the youngsters. And include Daisy. She's given up her time off to be here. They all deserve it.'

'All right,' he agreed, although he knew Alex had already slipped them some money, along with the new clothes. But he was right, they did deserve it.

Fred was tucking into a large piece of fruit pie when

they walked into the kitchen. 'This is good,' he grinned.

Millie was watching her friend with a glint of pride in her eyes. 'All that running around's made him hungry.'

Scooping up the last morsel, Fred swallowed, and then turned his full attention to Alex. 'They're good. It took me a while before I spotted them. Those poor devils playing with them didn't stand a chance.'

'Who was it?' David could hardly contain his excitement.

'Second table on the right as you come in the door. Was they the ones you're interested in?'

'Yes. Well done, Fred. Explain what they were doing.'

'Well, there was three of them working together.'

'Three?' Alex and David spoke together.

'I'm sure of it. The one with his back to the door was good at handling the cards. Not as good as me, though.' He smirked. 'The one on his left was working with him.'

'They're brothers,' David told the boy.

'Not surprised, but their ace was the man at the table opposite them. He could see what cards their victims were holding.' Fred guzzled a glass of milk one of the kitchen staff had put in front of him. One look at these kids and everyone wanted to feed them. 'They had a system of signals. I nearly missed him. I wasn't sure at first, so I blocked his view once and he pushed me out of the way. They were letting the victims win now and again, but only when there wasn't much on the table. There was quite a lot that time so I knew then what they was doing.'

'Describe this other man.' Alex's eyes were narrowed.

'Dark hair.' Fred frowned. 'Not like yours. Reddish dark.'

'My God!' Alex exclaimed. 'Are you sure, Fred?'

'No doubt about it. Why, do you know him?'

Alex nodded, fury glinting in his eyes. 'His name's Shawbridge.'

'Michael Shawbridge,' David said in awe. 'Wasn't he going to marry your sister?'

'Oh, you don't want to let him do that,' Fred said in alarm. 'He's up to no good with those others.'

'My sister's dead. I was sad for them that the wedding never went ahead and they'd had a short time of happiness together, but now I've found out about this, I'm glad it didn't.'

Fred looked upset. 'I'm sorry your sister died.'

Alex tapped Fred on the shoulder in a friendly gesture. 'So am I, Fred.'

Millie rushed over to him, concern on her face. 'Ain't you got no other brothers and sisters?'

'Unfortunately, I haven't.'

'We got lots.' The boy pulled a comical face, lightening the atmosphere. 'You can have some of those, if you like.'

'That's very generous of you.' Alex chuckled.

The way the conversation had been going worried David, but once again, Alex had shown himself able to cope with any situation. He wished Gertrude hadn't taken such a dislike to Alex. He had a strong feeling the man was lonely, and they would have been admirably suited.

'It's awkward you knowing one of them so well,' Fred remarked, 'but what are you going to do about these men? They ought to be stopped.'

'Can you get the money back they took off Miss's brother?'

'I doubt that, Millie. It would be hard to prove he had been cheated, but I'll find a way to put a stop to them.'

'You just tell me if I can help,' Fred said angrily. 'They've harmed Miss and her family. She's been good to us and don't deserve to be hurt like this. It ain't right.'

'No, it isn't. Your part in this is now finished, and I thank you very much. David, will you see our young friends and Daisy get home safely? Take the carriage. I'll get a cab when I'm ready to leave.'

'What about the clothes?' Millie asked.

'You may keep them.'

'You sure? We've had lots to eat.'

'I'm sure.' Alex smiled warmly at them. 'I do believe you've enjoyed yourselves.'

Fred grinned. 'It was exciting, and thanks for the clothes and everything. We'd like to know what happens.'

'I'll make sure you hear the whole story.'

'Don't leave nothing out,' Millie told him. 'We don't like people who does things like this to Miss. She's our friend.'

'Take them all home now,' Alex said, turning to David.

'Of course.' Then he said quietly, 'These are ruthless men so be careful, Alex.'

'Always.'

The last thing he wanted to do was leave Alex alone, but the children had to be taken out of harm's way. No one must ever know they had been involved.

Once in the coach, he shared the coins between the three

of them. Daisy hesitated. 'But I get paid, sir. I shouldn't take this.'

'I've been told to share out the money and that's what I'm doing. It's all right for you to take it, Daisy.'

'Thank you, sir.'

'Gosh.' Fred was examining the money in his hand. 'This is too much.'

'It isn't nearly enough for what you've done tonight. We're very grateful.'

Millie was still counting the coins. 'Mum don't earn this much in a month. I'll give it to her.'

'Keep a little for yourselves. You've all deserved that money this evening.'

'We could buy ourselves a book each,' Fred told his friend. He gave David a worried look. 'What we gonna say to Miss when we see her? It don't seem right to keep secrets from her.'

This was worrying him as well. 'We must respect Mr Glendale's wishes and keep his name out of it for the time being. I'll have to tell Gertie's family though, but I'll say the man helping me doesn't want to be named for reasons of safety. They won't question it after the attack on Mr Melrose.'

'Hmm.' Millie chewed her bottom lip. 'We'll say the same thing then. We don't want him to get bashed up, do we?'

Everyone agreed, and David tried to relax for the rest of the journey. But he couldn't help wondering what Alex was up to at the club.

Chapter Twelve

There was no sign of Fred and Millie at the bookshop the next morning. Gertrude knew they could be anywhere and tracking them down might take all morning, and she couldn't spend too much time away from work. Her father was struggling to increase the business in order to pull them out of the mess Edward had left, and he needed her. After waiting around for half an hour she left a message with Mr Partridge and hurried back.

During the day she kept expecting Fred to come, but he never did.

When they arrived home in the evening, David was in the sitting room with Florence. He looked tired and worried when he greeted them.

'What's happened?' Gertrude asked, with concern.

'I have something to tell you, but –' he glanced directly at Sutton '– before I say anything, I need your promise you won't take any action of your own. The situation is being dealt with.'

Sutton indicated that David should sit down. 'You'd better tell us what this is about.'

'Your word first, please.' He was uncomfortable about insisting, but it was necessary.

'You have it.'

'And you, Gertie,' David insisted. 'No member of the Melrose family must appear to be involved in any way. It could be highly dangerous, and I know you too well.'

'I'll keep out of it,' she promised, very worried by now. 'For goodness' sake, tell us what's happened.'

He then gave a brief outline of the events of the previous evening, omitting where this had taken place, and Alex's involvement.

Gertie jumped to her feet, furious. 'You had no right to ask Fred to do this! What were you thinking of?'

'No one knows, and he wouldn't be recognised. I saw him safely home as soon as he'd identified the cheats. We had his parents' permission, and Fred was eager to help.' David spoke firmly. 'Eager to help you, Gertie.'

'We? Who else is involved?' her father demanded.

'I can't tell you. It's his wish to remain anonymous.'

'That isn't acceptable!' Sutton was also on his feet, a deep frown furrowing his brow. 'The fact that Edward might have been cheated only makes him appear more foolish—'

Florence gave a quiet sob of distress. 'Oh, my poor, misguided boy.'

'I'm sorry, my dear.' He took hold of his wife's hand

as he spoke to David. 'What does this man intend to do about these scoundrels?'

'I don't know. He's also keeping me out of it. Fred is the only one with skill enough to spot them cheating and . . . my friend will not allow him to speak out against them.'

'I should think not!' Gertie was still seething. 'If I ever find out who this person is, I'll tell him what I think of him. How dare he take a young boy into a gambling den.'

'He was, and is, quite safe.' David could understand her concern for the youngster. 'We've made sure of that. The fewer people who know the details, the safer everyone will be.'

'Is there any chance of getting our money back?' Florence spoke in a hushed voice, terribly distressed by these revelations.

'Not without charging them, and we can't do that without Fred's testimony.'

Sutton nodded in agreement. 'The boy can't be exposed to such danger. It's a dilemma, but something must be done or they will continue to cheat others.'

'All I can tell you is that they are going to be stopped.'

Gertrude had calmed down, and anger had been replaced with worry. 'I don't like the sound of this. These men are vicious, as father well knows. Please be careful, and your friend, as well.'

'I'll take care.' He smiled at last. 'And my friend is more than capable of looking after himself. Don't go asking Fred and Millie who he is because they're also sworn to secrecy.'

Blast! That's just what she had intended to do.

'Don't make them break their word,' he insisted.

She sighed inwardly. 'All right. But I don't see why this friend of yours, whoever he is, has to be so secretive about his identity to us.'

'It has to be this way, so don't pry, Gertie. I'm not accusing you of being a gossip, because I know you're not, but it's better if you don't know too many details.'

'David's right,' her father agreed. 'We must be grateful someone is prepared to unmask these men. It needs to be done, and it's vital this man works in secret, for everyone's sake.'

'I'm glad you understand.' David was relieved. 'Now, if you will excuse me . . .'

'Of course.' Sutton shook his hand. 'You'll keep us informed?'

After he had promised he would, Gertrude saw him to the door. 'Do you know if Mr Glendale has done anything about finding Edward?' she whispered.

'I really don't know, but he's hardly had time. And I honestly don't know where he should start the search.'

She gave him an exasperated look. 'Then why did you urge me to seek his help? I could have saved myself, and him, the embarrassment. I felt he was too polite to refuse.'

'He wouldn't have been embarrassed. Alex thinks highly of you and your parents, and he might have fresh ideas. I didn't know what else we could do. Goodness knows I've tried hard enough, but Edward seems to have disappeared. He has questioned me in detail about Edward's habits.

He's set his mind to it, but you must be patient. He's a busy man.'

'Oh, don't say that.' She chewed her bottom lip in worry. 'It makes me feel even worse about asking him. He doesn't have to do this, and if he's so busy, how is he going to find the time?'

'He'll find it. You've got to learn to trust him. We need all the help we can get. And if it weren't for him, you would be living with your Aunt Hanna, crammed into her small house, or still struggling to pay the debt. I know how independent you are, but a little trust and gratitude would not go amiss.'

His rebuke hit its target and she lowered her eyes in shame. What was the matter with her? 'I'm sorry, and you're quite right. I've always been far too independent.'

He chuckled then. 'I'll say you have. Even when you were a toddler, if we tried to help with something, you would push us away, saying, I can do it! I can do it! Relying on others doesn't come easy for you.'

'I know I'm unreasonable at times, and I can't understand why Mr Glendale once found me attractive enough to approach Father.'

David was still smiling, remembering the feisty, independent little girl, who hadn't mellowed much now she was grown. But he still adored her, and so did everyone else who met her. 'I don't think you have to worry about that now. You've left him in no doubt about your feelings for him. I've heard a rumour that he's showing interest in someone else.'

'Oh . . . Who?'

He bent and kissed her cheek. That had given her something to think about! 'I haven't the faintest idea. Goodnight, Gertie.'

Sleep eluded Gertrude that night, though she was desperately tired. It would be bad enough if her brother had lost all that money in honest games, but to know he had probably been cheated made him look even more foolish. Her mother had said very little, but she'd clearly been devastated. No matter what he'd done, he was still her son, and nothing would stop her loving him.

She punched her pillows in an effort to get comfortable, but it was a waste of time. Her mind was a jumble of worry, anger and something else she couldn't quite grasp.

David had been uneasy about delivering his news and she understood that. Who was this friend of his? If he wouldn't tell them who it was, it must be someone they knew. But using Fred like that was wrong! If she ever found out who he was, he would receive the sharp end of her tongue for involving the young boy in this crazy scheme. But she couldn't deny these men needed to be exposed as cheats, for goodness knows how many others were suffering because of them.

Damn! She sat up, bent her knees and rested her head on them. Her stomach was rebelling. She hated feeling so helpless. Her parents had aged in a short time, and it was terrible to watch them suffering so much. If only there was a way to make them happy again. It would help her mother to know her beloved son was surviving out there on his own. All David's efforts to find him had failed, and as much as she hated to admit it, Mr Glendale was their only hope now.

Her sigh was ragged as she settled down again. Sleep. She must sleep. It was impossible to think clearly when she was so tired.

Drifting between consciousness and sleep, ideas on how she could ease her parents' burden drifted through her mind. But there seemed no way out of the mess they were in. All she could do was take each day as it came, and do the best she could.

It had been painful parting with his grandfather's pocket watch. All the time he had been losing at cards he'd held on to it, determined not to part with this item he loved. But there was nothing else left to sell. Even his decent clothes had been pawned as he'd moved from one cheap lodging house to another, always on the move to avoid being found or recognised. His shame was crushing and the only thing on his mind was to somehow redeem himself. And until that day he wanted to remain in the shadows, hidden from sight. Lacking any practical skill, he had tried to get labouring work at the docks. But there were too many hungry men fighting for work. He'd tried to get work as a ditch digger, but even there he had failed. His accent and unblemished hands showed him as a man not used to hard work. He deeply regretted his idle life. If he'd worked with his father, as he should have done, then he might be more fitted for surviving in this harsh environment. But he hadn't, and it was no good wishing. He was a fool. His family had given him every opportunity in life, and he'd thrown it back in their faces. He didn't know how they were coping with the aftermath of his stupidity, and he was frightened to find out. It was going to be terrible for them because his losses had been enormous, and if he knew the details of their suffering it would destroy him.

He counted out the money and put aside enough for the rent. At least he could pay the landlady when he left in the morning and wouldn't have to creep away in the night.

After he had accepted that he wasn't going to be able to find work of any kind, there had been only one avenue left open to him. It was going to be hard, but he was determined to prove to his family – and himself – that he could amount to something. This was now a burning desire, and might be an unattainable dream, but no matter what the future held, he wouldn't let the dream fade. It would probably take him the rest of his life, but he would pay back every penny he had lost. And if he didn't survive, at least they would know he had tried and given his all.

His meagre belongings were packed. Tomorrow he started a new life, and he was dreading it.

Chapter Thirteen

It was impossible for Gertrude to concentrate on her work. She hated not knowing what was going on, and was sick with worry. David had said they must not be involved because of the danger, and he never exaggerated. She had tossed and turned last night trying to place the other man involved. David had a wide circle of friends and acquaintances, and it could be any of them. The fact that they had involved Fred was even more worrying, and they shouldn't have done that! She'd become very fond of the youngsters, and felt protective towards them.

Taking a deep breath to calm the agitation, she forced herself to get on with the paperwork in front of her. Had Fred been to the bookshop yet? If he didn't come today then she'd have to go and find him. She wished he'd come. But it was no good fretting like this when she had work to do.

It was nearly twelve o'clock when she saw the youngsters peering in the door. With an exclamation of relief, she leapt to her feet, rushing to meet them.

'Thank goodness you're here!' She urged them inside. 'Are you all right?'

'Yes, Miss.' Millie grinned. 'We got your message just now and Fred couldn't wait to get here.'

The boy wasn't taking any notice of them; he was too busy running his hands over a finished table. 'Cor!' was all he said, dropping to his knees to examine the legs.

Gertrude smiled for the first time that day and peered under the table at him. 'I showed my father your box, and he wants to see you.'

'What?' He came up so quickly his head caught the corner of the table.

'Do you like that, young man?'

Fred nearly lost his balance as he spun round to face the man who had spoken. 'Yes, sir. Lovely bit of wood, sir. Oak at its best. Them joins is perfect, sir. And the polish . . .' He sighed in ecstasy.

'We pride ourselves on good workmanship.' Sutton was looking highly amused at Fred's reaction. 'Would you like to have a look at the work going on here?'

'Oh, yes please, sir!' Fred was quite breathless with the excitement of it all.

'This is my father,' Gertrude said, when she could get a word in.

'And you must be Millie and Fred. My daughter has told me about you. Gertrude, will you give Millie some tea while I have a talk with Fred?'

'Of course.' She led the young girl to the back of the workshop where they had a small kitchen.

'I was very worried when David told me Fred had been asked to see if some men were cheating at cards.' Gertrude handed Millie a plate of biscuits. 'That was a dangerous thing to do.'

'We was quite safe.' The girl was already munching on one biscuit and holding another in her hand.

'We?' Gertrude spun round, leaving the water to boil. 'Were you there as well?'

''Course. I wouldn't let Fred go on his own. I didn't see none of the men though. I was in the kitchen with the cook and D . . . Er, the other man made one of his servants stay with me.'

This just got worse! David had kept quiet about this, and she was furious. 'A gambling den is no place for youngsters of your age.'

Millie laughed. 'It weren't no gambling den, Miss. It was proper posh. And as soon as Fred had spotted the cheats, Mr Gardener took us straight home.'

Now she was even more puzzled. 'What was this other man going to do when you left?'

'Dunno. He just said he had things to do and he wanted us out of the way.' Millie studied Gertrude's worried expression. 'Don't you fret none, Miss. This man's tough. He can look after himself.'

'Strong, is he?' she asked innocently.

Millie soon realised what Gertrude was doing. 'Can't tell you no more. We promised, and I already said too much. That water's gonna boil away,' she pointed out.

'Oh, damn!' Gertrude muttered as she grabbed the kettle. While waiting for the tea to draw, she said, 'I promised I wouldn't ask you any questions, but I do hate not knowing what's going on.'

"Spect you do.' Millie nodded in sympathy. 'But your friend and this other man are working in secret to keep all of us safe. They came and saw our mums before we did this. They left their carriage and walked down our street, causing quite a stir, I can tell you. They sat in our house and drank tea, as easy as you like. My mum was in quite a state and had a job to pour the tea.' She giggled. 'But they talked away just as if they was in a palace. Didn't know posh gents could be so nice.'

Gertrude was bursting to hear more.

'Millie!' Fred's voice put a stop to their conversation. 'What you been saying? Remember our promise.'

'I haven't said his name!' She looked hurt at her friend's rebuke. 'I won't say nothing to put him in danger. He's a good bloke.'

Fred grinned, relieved Millie hadn't let anything vital slip. 'And Johnny keeps running up the road to see if he's coming again.' He glanced at Gertrude apologetically. 'Sorry we can't tell you everything, but we always keeps our promises.'

'And so you should.' Sutton walked in. 'My daughter has an insatiable curiosity.'

'Insat . . .' Millie frowned. 'That's a new word to me. What's it mean?'

'Impossible to satisfy,' Gertrude explained, pulling a

face. 'But this concerns us, Father. I can't see the need for all this secrecy.'

'Because this man, whoever he is, is not only trying to shield us from any unpleasantness, but also to keep Millie and Fred safe.'

'You'll know when he's dealt with these men,' Fred told her.

'And you believe he will expose them?'

'No doubt about it. If he sets about something, then he'll do it. He's that kind of man.'

He sounded so sure and the secrecy was frustrating. David knew plenty of men in the shipping business. It must be one of them he'd gone to for help, probably one of the ship owners. 'In that case, I'll have to wait patiently.'

'We all will.' Sutton turned his attention back to Fred. 'Tell Millie your news.'

'Oh.' Fred started to hop from foot to foot in excitement, fairly bursting with pride. 'I'm gonna work here! Mr Melrose's gonna teach me everything about working with wood. I'm to be his apprentice!'

Millie erupted with a shout of glee. 'Thank you, sir! All Fred needs is a chance. Thank you, thank you. When do you start, Fred?'

'Tomorrow!'

'Let's get back and tell your mum and dad. They'll be so proud of you working for one of the best in the business.'

Sutton was smiling at their pleasure. 'Off you go. I'll see you at eight in the morning, young man.'

'I'll be here, sir!' He grabbed Millie's hand and they rushed out of the workshop.

Gertrude watched them disappear and squeezed her father's hand. 'That was kind of you. Can you afford to take him on at the moment?'

'We'll manage.' He smiled at his daughter. 'I wish we could do something for the girl as well.'

'So do I. She was overjoyed for Fred though. I'll have a word with David and see if he can help find her a job. Her handwriting is excellent.'

'Good idea. They're bright youngsters and deserve a helping hand.'

The desire to confront the gamblers the night before had been tempting, but Alex had not considered it a wise thing to do. He didn't want to draw attention to Fred, so this would have to be done stealthily by sowing seeds of suspicion. By the time word reached the Hayworth brothers it would have gone through many people, making it difficult for them to find out where the accusation had originally come from.

First he would make a call on Michael Shawbridge. He wasn't sure if the damned fool deserved to be alerted to the danger, but his sister had loved him, and Alex felt he owed him the chance to get away from the brothers before their cheating became public knowledge. He would invite him to dine with him at the club, and as he did this from time to time it wouldn't be thought unusual. After his sister had died he'd made a point of keeping in touch with Michael. After all, he had nearly become a part of the Glendale family.

Fastening his pocket watch in place, he gave a sad sigh.

Who would have believed such tragedy would befall them. He was now the only Glendale left . . .

Would the pain never leave him?

Giving a disgusted grimace, he turned away from the mirror. Self-pity was a trait he despised. It was time he stopped yearning for a girl he couldn't have and set about building the family again.

His long, determined stride took him out to the waiting carriage. That was a problem he would address soon, but for the moment he had several other urgent matters to deal with.

Michael accepted the invitation with pleasure and they went straight to the club. During the meal, Michael soon mentioned his surprise at seeing Alex in the gaming room the night before. 'I didn't know you liked to gamble,' he said, smiling with amusement.

'I don't. I had a deal to make with Gardener Shipping and we were just passing the time before dining.'

'How many ships have you got now, Alex?'

'Two, but I'm thinking of buying another one.'

'It's a lucrative business then?'

'Not at first,' he told him, 'but it's beginning to show a profit. I enjoy the cut and thrust of buying and selling cargoes.'

'You may deny that you're a gambler,' Michael laughed, 'but I'm not so sure that's true. You ought to join us tonight. There's room at the Hayworths' table.'

Shaking his head, Alex leant back, making sure the other diners could hear what he said. 'I'm not a fool, Michael. They appear to be too lucky – if luck comes into it.'

'What do you mean?'

'Surely you've heard the rumours?' Alex refilled their wine glasses.

'No.' Michael glanced around quickly to see if any other diners were listening. He leant forward and spoke quietly. 'What rumours?'

'I've heard it mentioned that they appear to be very clever with cards.' He didn't bother to lower his voice. 'There might be nothing in it – you know what London is like when it comes to gossip – but if I were you I'd keep well away from them just in case accusations begin to fly.'

'I don't play at their table.' Michael looked agitated.

'Ah, that's right, you were on the next table.' Alex smiled and called the waiter over to order brandy for them.

'Er . . . who told you about this?'

Alex frowned as if trying to remember. 'I was at a function last week given by Lord and Lady Shearing, and it seems some young men have got themselves into debt after playing with the Hayworths. It appears to have raised doubts as to the honesty of the games.'

All colour drained from Michael's face. 'Really? Rumours like that could ruin a man's reputation. Is there any proof of this?'

'I couldn't say. I'm only repeating what I heard. I wouldn't have said anything, for London is rife with tittle-tattle, and I usually take little notice, but I believe you are acquainted with them and should know what is being said.' He swirled the brandy around in the glass. From the look on Michael's face, he knew he had made his point and he hoped the damned fool would now distance

132

himself from the Hayworth boys. He had done his duty by Michael and his sister, now it was up to the man to use some sense. He was aware many around them had been listening attentively; now all he could do was wait for the news to spread. And it would, like a raging fire.

Alex flicked open his watch. 'Thank you for joining me, but I'm afraid I have another appointment. We must do this again soon.'

'It has been most enjoyable.' Michael had regained a little of his composure and stood, smiling. 'Do you ever stop working?'

'I like to keep busy.' He shook hands with Michael and walked out of the dining room, stopping to speak briefly to several men on the way.

There was a grim smile on his face as he climbed into his carriage.

Now let the rumours begin to fly!

Chapter Fourteen

After another busy day, Gertrude arrived home alone. Her father was working himself too hard, and all her pleas had been unable to make him stop and come home for dinner. He had always been a quiet man, relaxed, never showing signs of irritation, but now he spoke sharply far too often. The change in him concerned her.

Removing her coat and hanging it in the hall, she was about to open the drawing room door when she heard a sound. Did her mother have visitors? She certainly hoped not because it would be difficult to be sociable tonight. Taking a deep breath, she turned the handle and walked in.

Her mother was the only one in the room. She was standing by the fireplace, sobbing. It was a heart-rending sight.

'Mother!' Gertrude rushed to her side.

Florence spun round, making an effort to pull herself together, but the tears were unstoppable.

'Has something happened? Have you had news of Edward? What's happened to upset you so? Sit down and tell me why you're crying like this.'

'I'm sorry you had to see me in such a distressed state, my dear, but I was overwhelmed with sadness.' Florence wiped her eyes, then clasped her hands together tightly. 'Please don't tell your father. He has enough to worry about.'

'I promise. Is there anything I can do?'

Shaking her head, her mother settled back in the chair. 'I'm out of my mind with worry about Edward, imagining all the terrible things that could have happened to him. Your father shouldn't have turned him out with nothing. How is he going to manage? He's never had to fend for himself.' She began to shake. 'And there's this house. I'm here all day and it isn't the same. Everything I touch belongs to someone else. All the items we've lovingly collected over the years are no longer ours . . .'

'What do you mean?' Her mother must be confused. 'The contents are still ours, surely? Father only sold the house.'

'No.' Florence looked at her daughter, anguish in her eyes. 'The house and entire contents were sold together. All we own are our personal belongings.'

She was stunned and furious at the same time. Why hadn't she been told? They didn't even own the chairs they sat on, or the beds they slept in! 'This can't be? The sale of the house alone would have cleared Edward's debt.

135

We'd already raised some of the money. You must have misunderstood, Mother.'

'There was interest added because of the delay in settling the full amount.'

'This is disgraceful! We should have refused to pay and gone to the police.'

'Your father wouldn't take the risk. They'd made it clear your life was in danger if Sutton didn't do as they said. The beating he'd received convinced him they would carry out their threat. He would protect us with his life, Gertrude, you know that.'

'He should have told me it was that bad. He should have told me.'

'I only heard the full story last night and that's why I'm so upset. We'll never be able to buy back the house and the contents. And I don't know if Edward is dead or alive.'

The despair in her mother's voice was distressing and Gertrude tried to think of something comforting to say, but all she could come up with was, 'Father will do everything he can.'

'And kill himself trying.' Florence's mouth set in a grim line. 'I've lost my son; I don't want to lose my husband as well. We've got to stop him working so hard. But how?'

'We could move in with Aunt Hanna. Then he won't have to worry about the house.'

'I've already thought of that, but I know your father. If he believes I'm upset and cannot live in the house because it no longer belongs to us, then he'll work even harder to make sure we can buy it back. He knows how much I've always loved our home.' She gave a helpless shrug. 'That wouldn't work.'

'You're quite right,' Gertrude had to agree. 'We'll have to think of something else.' Relieved to see her mother more composed, she said, 'I'd better go and change for dinner.'

'Sutton won't be joining us, of course.'

'No. Sorry, Mother. I did my best but he wouldn't listen to me.'

Once upstairs and alone, she began to go over everything her mother had told her, frantically searching for a glimmer of hope. The future was uncertain. It might help if Edward could be found. What was Mr Glendale doing? He'd promised to try and trace her brother, but there had been no word from him. She knew she was being unreasonable again. After all, there had hardly been time, but this was urgent! Didn't he realise that?

Oh, stop blaming him for your problems, she chided herself, knowing she had a bad habit of jumping to the wrong conclusion. *Be honest, it wouldn't have been surprising if he'd refused after the way you've treated him.*

The next morning Alex studied the papers on his desk, running his hand through his hair as he decided what to do first. His commitments were piling up and everything was urgent. If there were to be any chance of coping, he would have to deal with this like a military campaign.

A cup of tea appeared by his hand and he looked up at his butler's disapproving expression. 'Damn it, Hunt, how did you learn to move so silently?'

'Years of practise, sir.'

Alex gave a snort of amusement. 'I could have done with you in my regiment.'

'Thankfully I'm too old for that. Breakfast is ready for you. Cook will be offended if you don't eat.'

After gulping down the tea, Alex stood up. 'I'd better not do that!'

'Indeed not,' the butler said dryly.

'There's something you can do for me. I need a reliable man to make some enquiries for me. Could you find me someone like that?'

Hunt furrowed his brow for a moment, and then nodded. 'I believe I know the very person.'

'I thought you might.' Anxious to get on with the day, he headed for the dining room. 'Have him here this evening. I'll be out most of the day.'

After doing justice to the excellent food, he went straight to the Gardener's offices, holding a folder bursting with papers.

'Ah, I'm glad you're here, David,' he said as he swept in. 'I need your help.'

David leapt to his feet. 'What can I do for you?'

'I've got too much for one man to deal with.' He sat down and placed the folder in front of David. 'One of my ships, the *Falcon*, is due in any day now with a cargo of tea, and anything else the captain picked up on the voyage. I'd appreciate it if you would deal with it for me. The usual fee, of course.'

'I'll handle that for you.' David began to sort through the papers. 'I don't need all this.'

'I'm hoping you do.'

David looked up sharply. 'But the *Sea Imp*'s papers are also here, and your negotiations to buy *Gipsy Wanderer*!'

'I'd like you to act as my agent. Buy and sell cargoes as you think fit, and I've given you the price I'm prepared to pay for *Gipsy*.'

It took a few moments for this to sink in. He was being offered the chance of a lifetime! David took a deep breath, hiding his excitement well. 'I'd be honoured to represent you.'

'That's a relief!' Alex was already on his feet. 'Have the papers drawn up and bring them over this evening. Seven. And you'll dine with me?'

'Thank you.'

Alex strode towards the door, and then he stopped and looked back. 'I'm taking my doctor to see little May now. I sent word to say we're coming. Could you find the time to join us? It will only take about an hour. The little girl might be frightened of the doctor and she took a liking to you. Your friendly face could help.'

'I'd love to come, sir. I'll still have time to complete the necessary papers.'

'Good, May will be pleased to see you again. Oh, and the name is still Alex. You seem to have forgotten that.'

'So I have. It's even harder to address you by your Christian name now I'm in your employ.'

'You'll get used to it. Now, let's collect the doctor and see if anything can be done for that little girl.'

As soon as May saw David, she held out her arms, begging to be picked up. Johnny skidded into the house along with six other children. There wasn't room to move in the tiny house and May's parents became agitated, trying to push them all out the door again.

'You stay here, David,' Alex instructed, 'while I deal with this crowd.'

'C . . . Come into the front room,' May's mother said, clearly in awe of the imposing doctor. She was clasping and unclasping her hands as she gazed at David holding her daughter in his arms. Then she turned to Alex. 'Please, sir,' she whispered. 'We ain't got the money to pay for such a posh doctor.'

'You won't have to.' He smiled warmly, trying to put the woman at her ease. 'Doctor Stevens is my own physician and is doing this at my request. He's a skilled surgeon, and if anything can be done for your daughter he'll tell us.'

May's father hadn't said a word so far, but now he stepped up to Alex, a hint of tears in his eyes. 'Thank you, sir.'

With a slight inclination of his head in acknowledgement, Alex said, 'You join your wife, while I deal with these youngsters.'

The children were still crowding the doorway and Alex ordered, in his best military tone, 'Outside everyone!'

Johnny stuck close to his side until they were in the street. Then he began to rummage in his pockets until he found a tatty piece of paper. Catching hold of Alex's arm he held it out to him. 'My dad said I got to give you this to show what I spent. There's a penny change.'

Alex was astonished. It was a record of every piece of fruit Johnny had purchased with the money he'd been given.

The boy was shifting from foot to foot as Alex studied the account. 'My dad made me show him everything I bought and he wrote it down. Er . . .' Johnny eyed the grubby piece of paper and chewed his lip. 'Dad said I was to keep it clean. Hope you can still read it. We all had an apple and orange each, and I gave May two oranges and two pears. She likes those. We all thought they was smashing. Didn't we?' he asked the assembled children.

There was a chorus of agreement and Johnny was looking a bit sheepish now. 'Um . . . I know you said I was to buy fruit – and I did – but you give me a lot of money so I got a bag of gobstoppers and shared them out as well . . . Er . . . I saved one for you.'

'Why thank you, Johnny.' Alex accepted the bag, looking suitably impressed with the gift. 'I'll enjoy that tonight when I'm relaxing after dinner.'

The boy was now beaming with relief. 'Here's your change, Lord.'

'You keep it and buy a few more sweets, and –' Alex took a few coins out of his pocket – 'more fruit. It's most important you all have enough fresh fruit.'

The children were crowding round to see how much money Johnny was holding. 'Cor,' one said. 'Can we have a banana this time? I ain't never had one of those before.'

Tucking the money safely away, Johnny said, 'You can all come with me and choose what you want. That's fair, ain't it, Lord?'

'Very fair, Johnny. And I'm not a lord.'

''Course you are.' Johnny wasn't going to have it any other way.

Alex gave up. 'I would like to meet your father. Is he at home?'

'Not today. He works at the docks when there's ships in.'

'What about your mother? Can I meet her?'

'That's me, sir.' A woman stepped out of the crowd now gathered in the street. 'Agnes Bell, sir.'

'I'm pleased to meet you, Mrs Bell. You have a fine son. Would you please thank your husband for keeping such an accurate record of the money spent.'

'I will that, sir.' She smiled proudly at her son. 'He's a good boy, and a big help to me. Always ready and willing, he is.'

'Ow Mum!' Johnny wriggled in embarrassment. 'Lord don't want to know things like that.'

At that moment Millie arrived, out of breath.

'Where's Fred?' It was unusual to see her on her own.

'He's got a job! Miss's dad's given him work at the furniture place. Fred's so excited. He's started today. Miss is working there as well, but we didn't say nothing about you. She asked though, but we kept quiet.' Millie took a deep breath. 'I miss him. I've been trying to get a job as well, but no luck yet.'

'I might be able to help.' David walked out of the house. 'I've just taken on more work and could do with extra staff. I know you have a neat hand, so would you like to try working for me? I'll need you to run errands and generally be my helper. Do you think you could do that?'

Her eyes opened wide and she jumped up and down.

'Oh yes, sir! Please, sir! I'll work hard.'

He handed her a card. 'That's where I work. Be there by nine o'clock tomorrow morning and we'll see what we can arrange.'

'I'll be on time.' She gazed at the two men, tears of gratitude welling up. 'It sure was a lucky day when we met Miss. Because of her, we met you. You been able to do anything about those men?'

'I'm working on it.' Alex gave her a sly wink. 'There appears to be a nasty rumour going around that they're not to be trusted.'

'Wonder how that started?' She giggled.

'I wonder.' His expression was one of innocence.

'Oh, you're a card! I think I like you ever so much. I didn't at first, 'cos you seemed too bossy, but you ain't really.'

'Thank you, Millie. I like you too.' Alex turned his attention to the doctor, as he joined them. They stepped away from everyone so they could talk in private. 'What's the verdict?' he asked quietly, praying he hadn't raised the parents' hopes for nothing.

'It was a difficult birth and the child was injured. There wasn't proper medical care at the time, but I believe it can be put right. It will probably need an operation and the treatment will be expensive.'

'Do whatever is necessary and send all the bills to me. Let's talk to the parents.'

Fifteen minutes later, after saying goodbye, the three men were back in the carriage.

After dropping off the doctor, Alex insisted on taking

David back to his office. 'You'll join me this evening at home. We have a lot to discuss, but right now I have more rumours to spread.'

Just before David arrived that evening, Alex's butler brought in a man who could make enquiries and, hopefully, discover the whereabouts of Edward Melrose. He appeared capable and was engaged.

Relaxing with a large whisky, Alex ran over the day in his mind, well satisfied. The doctor was now in charge of little May's treatment, David had been engaged as his agent, relieving him of a lot of work, and he had made a start in tracing Edward. He hoped the man – Grant – was as efficient as his butler believed. And he didn't think it would be long before the card cheats began to be shunned by society. It had been a productive day.

Chapter Fifteen

The office routine was becoming easier for Gertrude. Working for her father was a blessing, leaving her little time to dwell on their precarious situation. Last night her father had promised he would shorten his working day, but she knew it was going to be difficult to make him keep to the promise. The business had to expand if they were to have any chance of recovering from the mess Edward had left them in.

She had arrived early this morning, determined to get through as much paperwork as possible. The more she could take on, the less there would be for her father to deal with in the evenings. They had let a couple of their staff go in an effort to lower their running costs, but she couldn't help wondering if it had been a false economy.

Shuffling through the pile of work on her desk, she was

startled when Fred burst into the office, his face alight. 'Millie's got a job as well!'

'That's wonderful!' She caught his mood and smiled happily. 'Where?'

'She's gonna work for Mr Gardener and starts today!' Fred could hardly contain himself. 'Oh, Miss, ain't it smashing?'

'Do you mean she's working for David, or his father?' She wasn't sure she'd heard correctly, as Fred was gabbling in excitement.

'Your friend. He was gone by the time I got home, but Millie was waiting for me at the top of the street.'

'Well, that is good news.' She pursed her lips. 'Are you saying that David called at Millie's house to offer her a job?'

'Not just for that. He was there with –' he ground to a halt, shuffling his feet anxiously – 'with the other man. The one we can't tell you about.'

'I see. And is it all right for you to tell me what they were doing there?'

He pursed his lips. ''Spect so. We only been told not to say his name.'

'Then you won't be breaking any promises, will you?' She waited expectantly.

The doubtful expression left Fred's face. 'This other man's helping one of our neighbours, and Mr Gardener comes too 'cos they're friends.' Fred smirked. 'They came walking down our street again, easy as you like, but this time they had another man with them. Caused quite a stir. Millie's mum made tea and they sat chatting like it

146

was normal for them to be in the slums. Didn't turn their noses up, nor nothing. We like them for that, and the kids can't wait for them to come back. One little girl sat on Mr Gardener's lap all the time. Real happy she was, and Johnny won't leave this other man's side. I'm so happy Millie's gonna work for Mr Gardener. Real nice gent, he is. And so's the other one.'

'I know David is a kind man, but I'll have to take your word about the other one.' Now there was a third man, as well. What on earth were three of them doing down Fred's street?

Fred eyed her intently. 'Mr Gardener's friend is special like – he cares about other people even if he don't know them.'

'I look forward to meeting him when this is all over.'

Fred nodded. 'Got to go. Time to start work.'

He hurried away with a spring in his step and she was so pleased. Having a job was very important to them. At lunchtime she would call on David and thank him. Thinking of her friend, she gave a sigh. It would please both families if they fell in love, but they couldn't think of themselves as anything but brother and sister.

The hammering and sawing of the workshop faded into the background as she concentrated on the work in front of her. It took a while before she became aware of a commotion. Looking out of the office window, she was surprised to see their maid talking to her father. Annie was waving her arms in agitation, and then she turned and ran out of the workshop. Which was surprising because she was no longer young. They'd let the other staff go, but

Annie wouldn't leave, saying that this was her home, and as long as she had something to eat, she didn't care if she had any wages. They were managing to pay her, of course.

One look at her father's face and Gertrude knew something dreadful had happened. She met him as he strode towards her.

'We must go home at once. Your mother has collapsed. The doctor's been sent for. Fred,' he called. 'Run outside and see if you can find us a cab.'

The boy tore off as fast as his legs would carry him.

'Did Annie know what's wrong?' Gertrude asked, her heart thudding uncomfortably. She had to run to keep up with her father.

He shook his head. 'This has all been too much for her, and I blame myself. I should never have sent Edward away.'

They scrambled into the cab Fred had managed to get them and she was shaking with anxiety. 'It isn't your fault, Father. You mustn't blame yourself. It might not be too bad. Mother could just have fainted and Annie panicked.'

'I pray to God you're right,' he said, grim-faced.

That hope was dashed as soon as they hurried into the bedroom. Florence had lost all colour, her eyes were closed and she was breathing raggedly. The doctor was already there and he motioned them to stand still and be quiet while he carried out his examination.

Sutton ignored him and rushed to his wife's side. 'Oh my dear,' he whispered huskily. 'We're here. We're here.'

'She's unconscious.' Doctor Andrews laid his hand on

Sutton's shoulder. 'Come outside and I'll explain what's happened.'

They followed the doctor out of the room. Gertrude was numb with grief. Her sweet mother was very sick.

'I want the truth,' Sutton demanded.

'Your wife has had a seizure and is unconscious. She should be in hospital, Mr Melrose, but moving her would do more harm. I've sent for nurses to care for her.' He gave them both a sympathetic look. 'I have seen some people recover, but I must warn you it will take a long time. Your wife is very ill.'

A young woman came up the stairs and the doctor nodded. 'Nurse Steadman, this is Mr Melrose and his daughter. Come with me and I'll explain the situation. Another nurse will be arriving to take over the night duties.'

'Yes, doctor.' She nodded acknowledgement to them.

'You will give us ten minutes and then you may both come in.' Sutton's head was bowed in anguish as they waited, and she clasped his hands; they were icy cold with shock. 'Mother will come through this.' She tried to inject confidence into her voice. 'We'll nurse her back to health, no matter how long it takes.'

When her father didn't speak she knew there was another pressing worry on both of their minds. Prolonged medical treatment was going to be expensive. 'I still have a few pieces of jewellery. I'll sell those.'

He nodded and squeezed her hand. 'Your mother comes first. I'll see if I can sell the business.'

'No!' She wasn't going to let him do that if it could

possibly be avoided. They had given up everything else in order to keep the business in the family. 'Don't do anything yet, please. We'll manage. Mother may make a quicker recovery than the doctor believes.'

His mouth set in a grim line as he nodded. 'All right, but your mother will have the best care available no matter what the cost. It's the only thing I care about now.'

'I agree. Whatever has to be done will be done, but let's see how things go before we make any decisions.'

'Oh Gertie, if only your brother had been born with a fraction of your good sense we wouldn't be in this mess now. Your mother's collapse is due to all the stress and worry.'

The bedroom door opened and the doctor came out. 'You may go in now. I'll be back in the morning to see how Mrs Melrose has weathered the night.'

Sutton rushed to his wife's side, pulled a chair up next to the bed, sat down and took hold of her limp hand. He remained silent, eyes fixed on his wife's face.

'Don't let him stay there all night,' the doctor told her. 'I don't expect any change for a while.'

The way he said it made her glance at him sharply. 'Do you have any idea when that might be? The truth, please.'

'It might be a few hours, days, or even weeks. I'm sorry, Miss Melrose, but all we can do is wait.'

And that was what they did. They waited through the night, next day and another night. There was no change. Hanna had arrived the previous evening, much to Gertrude's relief, and they managed to make her father get some sleep.

At breakfast she urged, 'Go into work today, Father. There's nothing you can do here. Aunt Hanna and I will stay with mother and help the nurses.'

'I can't leave her.'

'She doesn't know you're here,' Hanna told him firmly. 'I'll send for you at the first sign of a change in her condition.'

He stared out of the window, deep in thought. 'It's started to snow. Your mother loves to see the garden covered in a white blanket.'

'She'll see it.' Gertrude didn't know how she was managing to speak. Not only was she worried about her desperately sick mother, but she was also concerned for her father. It had seemed as if things couldn't get any worse for them – but they had! They were living the worst kind of nightmare.

'Yes, of course she will.' Sutton turned away from the window and straightened up. 'You are to send for me at once.'

'Immediately,' Gertrude assured him, watching his inner struggle and praying he would go back to work. The business needed him, and he needed a break from the sick room, or he would also become ill.

When he still stood where he was, undecided, she said firmly, 'Mother and I need you fit and strong. What will happen to us if you collapse as well?'

'I don't want to leave her, but you're quite right.' He ran a hand over his eyes. 'Seeing her like that is killing me. I feel so bloody helpless. I swear if Edward turned up now I would strangle him.'

Gertrude stifled a sigh of relief. Her father had been like a man in a dream, not speaking or showing emotion. Now his eyes were blazing. He was awake, angry and ready to fight. That was much better. 'So you'll go to work?' she asked gently.

'Do as Gertie suggests, Sutton.' Hanna poured herself a cup of tea. 'You're getting in everyone's way. At least at the workshop you'll be doing something useful.'

He glared at his sister. 'How the hell can I concentrate on business?'

'Because you've got to.' Her expression softened as she studied her brother. 'I know it's hard, but Gertie's right, we need you. I'll help all I can financially, but my funds are all too limited, as you know.'

'Oh hell!' Sutton looked stricken. 'I'm sorry Hanna, but you mustn't beggar yourself because of us. Gertrude, I'm going to leave this responsibility to you. Let me know when we urgently need more money and I'll see if I can get a loan against the business.'

She nodded, determined that she would do anything to stop him placing the business in jeopardy. 'I have a few pieces of jewellery to sell. The money from those should help a little.'

'Sell your mother's as well. I'm sure she won't mind. That should meet the immediate medical costs.'

'I'll do that today.' She hesitated. 'I could ask David—'

'We will not borrow money from our friends, Gertie! This is a family matter and we'll deal with it ourselves.'

'Of course we will.' Hanna handed her brother his hat and coat. 'Now go.'

As soon as they were on their own, Hanna turned to Gertrude. 'I'll stay with Florence while you go and do what you have to. Never mind what your father says, get money from anyone. I spoke to the doctor last night and he believes Florence is going to need nursing for quite a long time – night and day. From today we are going to have a team of four nurses working shifts. She must not be left alone for a moment.'

The room began to swim. 'Four nurses?'

'Don't you go all weak on me!' her aunt reprimanded firmly.

'Sorry.' She took a deep breath. 'What are we going to do, Aunt?'

'The best we can, my dear.'

Chapter Sixteen

The amount the jeweller had offered for her precious pieces had been insulting. Gertrude was furious as she stormed up the road. Because she was a young woman on her own he'd thought he could cheat her. Well, she wasn't going to allow that. One member of the Melrose family had let himself be conned by cheats, and she wasn't going to be the second!

Without hesitation she called a cab and was on her way to see David. This wasn't unusual because she had always turned to him when she needed help.

'Hello, Miss.' Millie jumped to her feet as soon as Gertrude walked into the office, her face wreathed in smiles.

Her anger faded when she saw Millie's happy face. 'How are you getting on? Do you like working here?'

'It's smashing. Fred's happy too. We was all sorry to hear about your mum. How is she?'

'Not at all well. Is David in?' she asked, changing the subject as her voice trembled.

'He's just popped out.' Millie pulled up a chair for Gertrude. 'But he won't be long. Would you like a cup of tea?'

Before she could answer the door opened and David walked in.

'Gertie! How's your mother?'

She just shook her head, eyes misty, and he crouched down in front of her. 'Is there anything I can do?'

Taking a tight hold on her fragile emotions she nodded. 'I've come to ask you to do something for me.'

'Let's go into my office at the back and you can tell me all about it.' He held the door open for her, and said, 'Millie, watch the office for me. I don't want to see anyone for a while.'

'Yes, Mr Gardener.'

Once they were alone she poured out her worries, fears and anger. 'Would you sell some jewellery for me? You'll have more chance of getting a fair price.'

'Is this necessary?' he asked gently.

'Yes, and it's only the start. According to the doctor, mother's recovery could take a long time.' Much to her shame, a tear trickled down her face and she swiped it away. 'It's terrible, David. She doesn't move or even open her eyes. The nurses know how to feed her liquids and we need them. There's a nurse with mother the whole time, and the doctor's in and out all the time . . .'

'I understand.' He picked up the packet of jewellery she'd placed on his desk. 'I'll sell these for you, and make sure you get enough to tide you over for a while. I'll be able to add a little to it as well.'

'Father said I mustn't ask you for money.'

'You haven't asked, I'm offering.'

'Thank you.' Her voice was thick with emotion. 'I'll do my best to pay you back.'

'No, you won't!'

He sounded angry, and she'd never seen him lose his temper before. 'Have I upset you?' she asked. 'I'm sorry to be so weak. I should be able to deal with this on my own, but I'm swamped. So much has happened in a short time and I'm finding it difficult to handle.'

'I'm mad, Gertie, but not at you. It hurts to see the family I love in this dreadful situation, and all because of one selfish bastard! And don't you dare apologise for showing your emotions. Many would be helpless faced with such a disaster, but you're a fighter, and you'll keep doing that until you walk out the other side of this nightmare. I'm proud of you.'

His confidence strengthened her and she touched his hand gratefully. 'If we could find that selfish brother of mine it might help mother's recovery.'

'Maybe. I've got some business to do with Alex, so would you like me to ask if he's made any progress?'

'Oh, thank you.' She hesitated, swallowed what little pride she had left, and said, 'Fred told me the man involved in finding the card cheats is helping a little girl who lives in his street . . .'

David's eyes narrowed.

'You needn't worry, he hasn't told me his name. But

I was wondering . . .' She rose to her feet, furious with herself. 'Hell and damnation! I won't do this. I won't beg. We'll manage. We still have some of mother's jewels, and she'll get better quickly. I know she will. And we'll rebuild our lives. It doesn't matter how long it takes. We can do this. I'm frightened, but I won't beg. I won't!'

'Easy now.' He was leading her back to the chair.

She sat down and gazed at her friend with tortured eyes. 'Mother will recover, won't she, David? I dread to think what will happen to father if she doesn't.'

'Of course she will.' He stooped down in front of her and took hold of her hands. 'Just hold in there, Gertie. I know you've got the strength and courage.'

The smile she produced was wobbly. 'Will you keep reminding me of that?'

'Every day, I promise. And you must come to me whenever you feel the need to shout at someone.'

'You could regret that offer.'

'Never.' He shook his head. 'That's what friends are for.'

Millie joined David by the window as they watched Gertrude walk up the road. 'It hurts to see her suffering like this, don't it?'

'How much bad luck can one family have?' David growled in frustration.

'Hmm.' Millie looked up at him. 'But she's got you for a friend to help her through this. My mum says life's full of ups and downs. You have to work your way through the downs, and be happy in the ups.'

He couldn't help smiling at the girl's homespun logic. She was full of her mum's sayings, and there was a lot of sense in them. 'Your mother's a wise woman. Now, I must go out again, so will you be all right for a while? My father should be back any minute because he has an appointment in half an hour.'

Millie nodded. 'Mr Harrison's coming to see your dad. I've met him before and he likes a nice strong cup of tea.'

She grinned. 'I can manage.'

Knowing that was true, he put on his coat and left, heading for Alex's home. Millie was turning out to be a real asset. He'd certainly done the right thing in employing her. His father had been doubtful at first, but he now doted on the young girl, joking and laughing with her. She was sensible and not easily flustered, and more than that, she was thoroughly likeable. Everyone who came to the office adored her. She had brought laughter into the place.

His thoughts turned to business and he hoped Alex was in. The negotiations for the ship had stalled. The owners wouldn't accept their offer and were pushing for a higher price. He'd raised the bid slightly, but he had to know how far to go before he could proceed.

He was shown to the library where Alex was pouring over some accounts. He glanced up. 'Ah, David, how's it going?'

'Not well. They've raised the price by two hundred pounds, and quite frankly I consider the offer we've made to be a fair one. But they're still hesitating.'

'Hmm.' Alex sat back, deep in thought. 'Stick to our offer and if they demand more, walk away.'

'You could lose her,' he warned, knowing how much Alex had set his heart on adding this ship to his others. 'She's a fine ship.'

'I know, but trust me. We've made a generous offer, and if they think they are going to lose the sale they'll come after you. Their next price will be only a fraction higher than we've offered. Then accept.'

'Suppose they don't?'

'They will.'

David studied the man in front of him, constantly surprised. 'I thought you weren't a gambler.'

'There are times when you have to make a strategic retreat in order to get what you want. You tell them the deal's off and they won't even let you get out of the door.'

'I hope you're right.' He felt excitement and apprehension at the same time. He very much wanted to keep this job, and didn't want to mess it up.

'So do I.' Alex smiled wryly. 'But I have complete faith in you. I can't spare the time to do this myself. I've my other businesses to oversee, and more commitments than I can count at the moment. The doctor's starting May's treatment and I want to keep a close eye on that. Her parents are naturally worried. Then Edward Melrose has to be found. I've got a man working on it, but he's had no luck so far.'

'You know his mother's seriously ill?'

'So I've heard, but don't know the details. What exactly is wrong with her?'

'A seizure of some kind. She's unconscious, but if you

ask me her heart's broken. Edward was always her pride and joy.'

Alex's mouth tightened. 'The same thing happened to my mother.'

'Gertie came to see me this morning. She's desperate and I've never seen her like that before. She'd been trying to sell some jewellery and couldn't get a fair price. She's asked me to do it for her.'

'Sell her jewellery?'

'I'm afraid so. Her mother needs constant nursing, and that's costly. If the illness goes on for a long time, and that's the medical prediction, then they will have to dispose of her mother's pieces as well. It's devastating to see them suffering like this.'

'Have you got the items with you?'

'Yes, I'm going to sell them when I leave here. The money is needed quickly. Her father's threatening to sell the business to meet the medical expenses, but she's fighting to stop him doing that. It's all they have left.'

'She's right! Her family must keep the business.' Alex was now prowling the room, and then he stopped in front of David. 'Show me the jewellery.'

'I don't expect there's much of great value.' He emptied out the contents of the bag Gertrude had given him. 'She's never put much store in such embellishments.'

'An unusual young girl,' Alex remarked, as he bent to study the items on the table.

'She is, but she has her faults like all of us. Stubbornness is one of them. When she gets an idea in her head it's near impossible to reason with her.' He watched Alex examining the jewellery, and when he remained silent, David continued. 'Her intelligence and quick mind are things a lot of people find hard to deal with – especially men.'

'Then they are fools.' Alex held up a gold bracelet. 'I've seen her wearing this.'

'Ah yes, that was a present from her Aunt Hanna, and the only piece Gertie constantly wore.'

'Sentimental value?'

'Yes, but she won't let that influence her. Her family is more important than anything else.'

'That's a quality to be admired.' Alex sat back. 'Her father's right to take her into the business. Properly trained, she could turn out to be an asset to him.'

'I agree, and he should have done that as soon as it became obvious Edward wasn't interested.' David's eyes filled with sadness. 'He hesitated because he wanted his daughter to have a husband and family of her own. That's unlikely now.'

Alex looked up sharply. 'Why?'

'Well, look at the mess they're in. They've withdrawn from society because they can no longer entertain as they once did. Gertie's time is completely taken up with looking after her mother, and helping her father in any way she can. What chance does she have of a life of her own?'

'You think a lot of her,' Alex remarked, noting the worry lines etched on David's face.

He nodded. 'She's always been like a sister to me. Infuriating, funny and adorable. The Melrose house has been my second home since I was a youngster, and it's tearing me apart to see them suffering like this. If I could wipe it away I would, but the only thing I can do is be a friend she can lean on when things get too bad. And at the moment they're as bad as they can get.' He turned his gaze back to Alex. 'What do you think I can get for the jewellery?'

'How much do they need?'

'I've no idea, but if Florence's illness is a long one, as predicted, it will cost a great deal. All Gertie's asking is a fair price for the jewellery.'

'The only items of any value are the necklace and bracelet. I'll give you forty pounds for the lot.'

David held up his hands in protest. 'Even I know they aren't worth anything like that. Her father gave her the gold necklace, but it isn't that valuable. The only piece I can think of with any value is a diamond necklace her aunt gave her on her eighteenth birthday, but she's probably saving that for another time. I thank you for wanting to help, but she's no fool and will immediately be suspicious if I hand over that kind of money.'

'And she won't take charity, even if it comes from you?' Alex grimaced, already knowing the answer. 'All right, I estimate the most you will be offered is twelve pounds. I'll give you twenty.'

'The best offer made to her was five guineas, which was insulting. I'll put a little more to it and that should pay the immediate nursing costs. Thank you, Alex, you're a very generous man.'

'I'm a wealthy man who has no family of his own to care for. It gives me pleasure to help a few people in need.' His tone was dismissive. 'Now that's settled, go and buy me that ship, David.'

Chapter Seventeen

The negotiations went exactly as Alex had predicted and David was jubilant when he returned to the office.

'I can tell from your expression that you've made the deal,' his father said.

He waved the sale papers, laughing. 'The ship is Alex's. It's no wonder he's so successful. I would never have dared to take that chance, but he knew what he was doing. The owners panicked when they thought they were going to lose the sale. They knew they wouldn't get a better offer from anyone else.'

His father slapped him on the back, clearly delighted. 'Well done, son. Glendale will be pleased with the way you've handled this. You'd better go and tell him the good news.'

'Yes, I must see him at once. He's given me the authority to sign on his behalf, but I need his signature as well.'

He watched his son's animated expression. 'Glendale has put a lot of trust in you, and you enjoy the work, don't you?'

'I love it.' David's expression sobered. 'But running these ships is not going to leave me much time for our business. I'm uneasy about that.'

'I've already decided we need more staff, and have this very day employed a young man to join us. His name's Robert Spencer. He comes highly recommended and already has some experience in shipping.' His father smiled at Millie, who was listening with rapt attention. 'And we have Millie as well. She's a great help, so we'll manage, won't we Millie?'

The girl nodded eagerly. 'Yes, Mr Gardener. I love working here, and I learn quick.'

'You certainly do. I'm sure it won't be long before I can leave the office in your capable hands. You deal with everyone in a friendly way and they like that.'

She beamed at the praise, and David's father turned back to his son. 'You concentrate on working as Alexander Glendale's agent. This is a fine opportunity for you and you'll need to work hard to make a success of it. He's a shrewd businessman and you'll learn a lot from him. We'll turn the spare room at the back into an office for you.'

'Thank you.' David was overcome with gratitude. With him pulling out of the family business, his father was going to have to shoulder more of the work until the new man was trained. He was well aware of the sacrifice his father was making in letting him take on this work as agent.

'No need for thanks, I'd never hold you back. I'm

proud of you. It's going to be a challenging time for you, but nothing you can't handle. Have you found a crew for the new ship?'

He laughed. 'We've only owned it for an hour, but I'll start hiring tomorrow. The ship's in first class condition and can be put into service immediately. I've already put out the word. Alex has a good reputation so there shouldn't be any shortage of men willing to sail in one of his ships. Then there's a profitable cargo to find. And the Falcon's due in any day now . . . Oh, how I'd love to sail on one of the voyages. I could learn so much.'

'Perhaps one day you'll be able to, but one thing at a time. You'd better see Glendale first. He'll want to know how you've got on.'

David's smile held a touch of embarrassment. 'I'm getting carried away, but it's all so exciting.'

'Will you be home for dinner?' his father asked, as his son headed for the door.

'I doubt it. After I've seen Alex I have to visit Gertie.' He sighed deeply.

Millie caught David's arm. 'Tell Miss she's to let me know if there's anything me and Fred can do. I could sit with her mum to give her a break. I've been used to doing that when there's been sickness in our street.'

'I'll tell her, and I'm sure she'll be grateful for your offer. She does have nurses there all the time, though.'

'It helps to know people care,' she said wisely. 'When things get tough you can feel awful alone. Like Sir does.'

He gave her a startled look. 'What do you mean?'

'He ain't got no one to call his own. Stands to reason he

must get lonely sometimes. No matter how rich someone is, you gotta have family, or it don't mean nothing.'

'You're absolutely right. How did you become so wise?' he asked, smiling gently at her.

'Oh, I ain't wise,' she laughed. 'Mum says I was born knowing how people feel. I watch their eyes. You'd be surprised what they show. You ought to try it sometime.'

'I certainly will, and I'll tell Gertie about your offer.'

'Ta. We're right fond of her. She's got a good heart.' The girl cast him a knowing glance. 'Just like you and Sir. You both ought to be married with a load of kids.'

'Not yet.' He grinned. She was such an outspoken and appealing girl. 'There's too much to do.'

Alex was delighted with the deal, and they spent an hour discussing plans for the new ship. Then David made his way to see Gertie.

She was in the study, working on the business books, when he arrived. She had dark rings under her eyes and looked exhausted, but smiled warmly when she saw him.

'Where's your father?' he asked, not sure if he knew his daughter was selling her jewellery.

'He's sitting with Mother. Did you manage to sell the things I gave you?'

'I got twenty-two pounds for them.'

'But that was much more than I was offered. Who bought them?' She eyed him with suspicion. 'How much of that is your own money?'

'Only a little,' he admitted, feeling awkward, but he had to skirt around the truth. He'd wanted to put in more than he had, but Alex's offer was so generous he knew she'd be suspicious. 'I sold them to someone involved in shipping.'

'Not a dealer?'

'No, I got a better price this way.'

'You certainly did.' She took the money from him and held it in her hand. 'Thank you, David. This will be a big help, and I'm very grateful to you. But I wish you'd take back the money you've put in. Father will not be pleased if he finds out.'

'Now, don't argue about it,' he scolded, when she opened her mouth to speak again. 'You must let me help.'

'I wasn't going to argue.' She stood on tiptoe to kiss his cheek. 'As you said, that's what friends are for – and you're a true friend. One day I'll be able to repay you.'

He was relieved. Not only had she accepted the money, but she hadn't questioned him closely about the sale of the jewellery. He could see from her expression she was very relieved. 'Will that pay the medical bills for a while?'

'Oh, yes, it will last for a while.' She smiled hopefully. 'Can you stay and talk?'

'Of course.' He sat down, knowing she was desperate for some company, and took the drink she quickly poured for him.

'Tell me how Millie's getting on.'

He gave her the girl's message, going into detail about the conversation they'd had as he was leaving the office. 'It's incredible,' he laughed. 'There's so much wisdom in her. My father's delighted to have her in the office. She's so good with everyone who comes in.'

'That's wonderful! Fred's doing well and loving every minute of working for Father. He's eager to learn and the men, including my father, never tire of showing him new procedures. All they both needed was a chance, and I'm very pleased we've been able to give them that. Now, what else have you been doing?'

She seemed pleased to be catching up with the news, and he decided it was time to tell her something else. 'I've been given a new job, Gertie. It's a tremendous challenge and I'm very excited.'

'Really?' She sat forward eagerly. 'Tell me all about it.'

He watched her expressive face as he explained that he was Alex's agent with complete responsibility for his ships. 'I bought one for him today and got it for a really good price.' He grinned. 'What do you think of that?'

Her eyes opened wide, stunned. 'You bought a ship? On your own?'

He nodded, still smiling broadly as she shook her head in amazement. 'Don't you think I'm capable of doing the job?' he teased.

'You're more than capable, but what I can't understand is why Mr Glendale needs an agent.'

'He's got far too much to do at the moment, and added to his workload is the task of trying to find Edward. That won't be easy, as I well know.'

'Oh dear, I shouldn't have asked him, should I?'

'Yes, you should. He wants to help, Gertie.' He studied her intently. 'What you see on the outside is not the real man. He's a tough ex-cavalry officer and used to being in command, but if you dig beneath the surface there's a very different person. You made a snap decision when you first met him, allowing his strong personality to overpower you, and you've never taken the trouble to get to know him.'

'I know,' she sighed. 'It's a fault of mine, but I still can't change my opinion. And being unreasonable is another fault of mine.'

'True,' he readily agreed, making them both laugh.

'Still, I'm truly pleased for you. I know you'll excel in your job as his agent.'

'Thank you, Gertie. Your approval means a lot to me.'

'And I'm lucky to have you as my friend. If only Edward had realised your worth and listened to you, then we wouldn't be in this mess now. But it's no use fretting about what might have been. We have to deal with the situation we find ourselves in at this moment.' She tipped her head to one side and pursed her lips. 'Now you've become close to Mr Glendale, has he said how the search for Edward is going?'

'He hasn't said anything yet.' It hurt to see her eyes cloud with worry again. For a brief moment she had relaxed, but he knew just how hard the waiting was for her. 'He won't unless there's something positive to report. But you can be sure he's working on it.'

'Of course you're right, but I feel so helpless sitting here waiting for someone else to carry out the search. I'm sure it would help Mother's recovery if she could hear Edward's voice.'

'Is she still unconscious?' he asked, sad to see how much she was struggling to keep the tears at bay.

'Yes, but we talk to her all the time. The doctor said she might hear us . . .' She gulped back the emotion that was welling up. 'It's terrible. She has to get better! She has to!'

'Give it time, Gertie.' Faced with her anguish, he didn't know what else to say. She had always been a girl in complete control of herself, but this was trying her to the limit.

'Time.' She straightened up. 'Aunt Hanna says time heals, but if Mother dies I'll never speak to Edward again. I'll completely disown him, as Father has.'

'It won't come to that.'

'No, of course it won't. I'm being silly again, but I want him found so he can know what he's done to the family who loved him.'

Fury raced through him. 'If I get my hands on him I'll give him the thrashing he deserves!'

'I expect he knows, and that's why he's keeping out of the way.'

'He can't hide forever. Alex has an experienced man out scouring the country for him. He'll track him down.'

'Alex?' She glanced at him in surprise. 'You call him that to his face?'

'He told me to. We work together well and I like him. Sometimes, in unguarded moments, I can sense the sadness in him. I believe he's still grieving for his family, and I'm sure he misses army life. He never says so, of course.'

'I don't suppose he does.' Gertrude frowned. 'He doesn't show his feelings, and that's what I find so difficult about him. We've always been open about our feelings, expressing them with freedom.'

'That doesn't mean he hasn't got any.'

'Perhaps not.'

He'd been trying to make her change her mind about Alex, but no matter what he said, she wouldn't give way.

'Has this other friend of yours had any success in dealing with the card cheats?'

'What?' He was thrown off guard by her sudden change of subject.

'The gamblers. Has your mystery friend been able to expose them?'

'Oh, he's working on it, but he's got to be careful. No one must know what he's up to or it could lead back to any of us, and he's determined that won't happen.'

'I can see that.' Suddenly Gertrude's expression changed, her eyes opening wide. 'Why didn't I see it before?'

'See what?' The breath caught in his throat. He'd seen that look many times. She knew!

'This friend of yours is Mr Glendale, isn't it?'

'No. What makes you think that?'

'You always were a terrible liar, David. To gamble, Edward used to be invited to the best gentlemen's clubs. Of course it's him! How could I have been so slow? All the clues were there, and I just ignored them.'

He knew why she hadn't worked it out before this. She had been too worried about her family to put her sharp mind to solving the mystery of the nameless friend.

'Did he take Fred to his club?' When he still didn't answer, she exploded. 'Oh come on, your silence is enough to tell me I'm right. So talk!'

'We went to his club, yes.'

'Tell me about it,' she demanded. 'And don't leave anything out.' Cornered, and knowing there was no way to avoid it, he told her the whole story.

She nodded when he'd finished. 'Fred's a bright boy, but you were taking a terrible chance. What if those men had realised what he was doing?'

'Alex and I were there all the time. He'd promised Fred's parents he would look after their son, and he'd have taken on the lot of them to keep that promise.'

'You place a lot of faith in him.' Gertrude gazed thoughtfully into space for a moment, then turned back to him. 'It seems I am even more in Mr Glendale's debt. Fred said he was helping someone down his street.'

'Little May, she needs medical attention.' He smiled as he remembered the child he'd become very fond of. 'Alex took his own physician to examine her, and he believes something can be done for her. You should have seen May's parents. The hope in their eyes was heart-rending.'

'Why's he doing all this?'

'Because he can.'

'What sort of an answer is that?'

'The answer he gave me when I asked the same question.' David wasn't going to elaborate. Let her draw her own conclusions.

'The man's a mystery.' She was shaking her head in bewilderment. 'Do you know exactly what he's doing about those cheats?'

'No, he's keeping us all out of it.'

'Is he in any danger?'

'I would say it's the cheats who are in danger. He's a

strong man, physically and mentally, and a trained soldier. He can take care of himself.'

She nodded agreement. 'Does Father know any of this?'

'No, and I wouldn't worry him with it at the moment. He has enough on his mind.'

'I agree.'

'You mustn't repeat any of this,' he said as he stood up. 'Don't even talk about it to Fred and Millie. We don't want any attention focussed on them.'

'I understand.' She went with him to the front door. 'Thank you for the money. Let me know what happens, will you?'

'Promise.'

As soon as he was outside, David hailed a cab and directed him to Alex's house. He had to be told Gertie knew the whole story now.

Chapter Eighteen

The nurse was coming down the stairs as Gertrude closed the door. She was still stunned to know how much Mr Glendale was involved in her family's affairs. Why was he doing this after she had rejected him so rudely?

The nurse was smiling. 'Miss Melrose, your mother's awake and asking for you.'

Gertrude didn't stop to ask questions as she raced past the nurse to get to her mother. Every other thought was wiped from her mind.

'Gently, Miss.' The nurse caught her before she entered the room. 'Your mother is very weak. Talk to her quietly and naturally. Smile and let her know how pleased you are.'

Taking a deep, steadying breath, she nodded.

The nurse opened the door for her. 'I've sent for the doctor.'

As she stepped quietly into the room, Gertrude's eyes fastened on her mother. She was propped up on pillows, her face ashen, but joy of joys, her eyes were open. Her father was holding his wife's hand and talking quietly to her.

'Gertrude, come here,' Florence said the moment she saw her daughter. 'Need to talk to you.'

Her mother's words were slurred and hesitant, but Gertrude's relief was immense. Not only was her mother awake, but she knew who they were. Her mind did not appear to be impaired, as had been feared.

'Hello, Mother.' She smiled as she sat beside her father. 'We're so happy you're awake. You've had a long sleep.'

'Sorry.' Florence's eyes filled with tears. 'Silly old woman! Hurt you both.'

'You mustn't feel like that, my dear.' Sutton brushed the hair away from her face. 'We understand. It's been a terrible strain for you, and you couldn't help being ill.'

'Strain for you too.' There was anguish in Florence's eyes now.

'All that matters is you're back with us.' Gertrude leant forward. 'Now you must rest and get well again. You can leave everything to us, can't she, Father?'

'Completely.'

'Drink.'

Sutton held a glass to his wife's lips, and after taking several sips, she leant back and gave him a little push. 'Darling, I want to talk to our daughter.'

He stood up. 'I'll go and see if the doctor's arrived.'

When he'd left the room, Florence grasped her hand with surprising strength. 'Take care of him.'

'I will. Don't you worry about a thing.'

Closing her eyes, Florence fell silent as she struggled to find the words she needed. 'Worry,' she murmured, opening her eyes again. 'Worry about you.'

'There's no need. I'm quite all right.' She kept her smile in place.

Florence shook her head slightly. Her movements seemed to be restricted. 'No, not. If we die you have nothing – nothing!'

'You mustn't think like that!' she exclaimed, worried by her mother's distress. 'Neither of you are going to die.'

'Will . . . one day.'

'Please don't talk like this. You're tiring yourself, and all over something that isn't going to happen for a long, long time.'

'Must say . . .' She was having increasing difficulty finding the words, but determination shone in her eyes. 'You must have husband to care for you. Not worry then . . .' Florence slumped back, exhausted,

'I'll marry one day, Mother. Please don't worry about me.'

'Soon.'

The bedroom door opened and Sutton returned with the doctor and nurse. After giving her mother's hand a gentle squeeze, she left the room so the doctor could carry out his examination. As she waited outside she felt like crying. Her joy at seeing her mother awake had now turned to fear. Her mother was fretting about her, and if she carried on like that, another seizure was possible, and they'd been told it was unlikely she would survive another one. Somehow they had to stop her worrying.

Leaning back against the wall she clasped her shaking hands together. This was terrible. What was she going to do? How could she get married when she didn't even have a young man yet? And how was she going to meet someone now? They were no longer involved in the social round, and her time was completely taken up with looking after the household affairs, and helping her father with the business. And she wouldn't have it any other way. It was unthinkable she would leave them when they both needed her so much!

Closing her eyes, she tried to think of a way to ease her mother's mind. Perhaps she could ask David to pretend he wanted to marry her. An engagement might be all that was needed to stop her mother from worrying about her. Then when she was completely well again they could say they'd changed their minds.

It only took a few moments to see the flaws in that scheme, making her give an inelegant snort of disgust. They wouldn't fool her mother. She knew them too well. They had been friends from early childhood and had great affection for each other, but it would be like marrying her brother. David's mother had died when he'd been only four years old, and Florence had given the young boy the mother's love he so badly needed. He was a part of their family. No, her mother would not be fooled—

'Gertie.'

She started at the sound of her father's voice and opened her eyes. 'What does the doctor say? Is mother going to be all right?'

'It's too early yet, but he's pleased so far.' Her father studied her strained expression. 'What did she say to you, my dear?'

For a brief moment she considered keeping this from him, but it wouldn't be fair to do so. She'd never hidden anything from him, and this was something he should be aware of. 'Mother was worrying about me. She wants me to get married quickly. She says she'll stop fretting when she knows I have someone to take care of me.'

Sutton nodded, his face lined with fatigue. 'It would also ease my mind to know you were settled.'

'Oh, please don't think like that as well!' She was really alarmed. 'You and Mother mustn't start worrying about me. We're all going to get through this – together!'

'Of course we are. We've never had to worry about you, and we mustn't start now.'

'No, you mustn't! And we've got to convince mother of that as well. Everything's going to be all right. We've still got the business, and we'll eventually get back to where we were.'

Her father drew in a deep breath. 'There's something I haven't told you. Over the last year trade has dropped, and we're hardly making a profit at the moment.'

She felt as if the ground had just dropped from under her. All her hopes had been placed on the business. 'You should have told me. I'm the one who urged you to keep it. Would it have been better if you'd sold it and started up in a smaller way somewhere else?'

'I looked into that possibility, but it would be almost impossible to sell a low-profitable business at the moment.

We've got to turn it around first, and then we might be able to do something with it.'

'Does Mother know?' she asked, refusing to show just how distressed she was with this news.

'Yes. And I believe that's what caused her collapse.'

She nodded, understanding the situation now. 'That's what she meant when she said I could be left with nothing.'

'That's right, darling. Unless we can pull the business together it would just be a burden to you.'

'Then we'll make it profitable again!' She gazed up at her father, determination showing in her eyes. He had a defeated air about him, as if his wife's illness had taken all the fight out of him. Well, she had enough fight in her for the two of them! 'We will do it, Father!'

Before Sutton could say anything, the doctor came out of the bedroom. 'Your wife is fully conscious and mentally alert, Mr Melrose. I had feared there might be some confusion when she regained consciousness, but that is not the case.'

'Thank God!' Sutton heaved a sigh of relief.

'However, we must be cautious,' the doctor warned. 'Mrs Melrose's condition is still grave and this rally might only be temporary. The most important thing you can do is to keep her free from worry. I'll visit again tomorrow.'

The moment of elation had been short, but Gertrude refused to let the doctor's warning drag her down again. This was progress – and it would continue.

'He has just asked the impossible.' Sutton ran a hand over his face, looking haggard. 'How the devil are we going to stop her worrying? I've never been able to do that in all the years we've been married.'

'We must always be cheerful, and convince her all is going well.'

'I've handled everything so badly.' His mouth set in a grim line. 'This would never have happened if I hadn't sent Edward away. I should have made him stay and work until he dropped with exhaustion. That would have been punishment enough.'

'You've got to stop blaming yourself.' Her father looked as if he was at the end of his strength. 'After what Edward did you had no choice. Wishing you could change the past will do no good. Now is the only moment we can deal with, and we *must* remain hopeful. We have good news today, so let us be happy.'

'You're quite right, my dear.' He straightened up and smiled at his daughter. 'We must do all we can to see your mother makes a full recovery. And all she must see are our smiling faces.'

It was eleven o'clock before Gertrude went to bed. Her father was still with her mother, sitting quietly as she slept. The three of them had had tea together, and they'd told her mother amusing stories about Fred and Millie. When it had become a struggle for her to stay awake, they had stopped talking and let her drift off to sleep.

But sleep was something she was finding impossible to do. Her mother was still gravely ill, and her father was beginning to sink under the strain. The concern for her parents was bad enough, and the worry over what had happened to Edward wasn't helping. But the worst feeling of all was one of utter helplessness. It was as if events had a mind of their own and nothing they did helped. There seemed to be a new disaster around every corner.

She stared into the darkness, her mind a jumble of doubts and fears. It was going to be a long night.

Chapter Nineteen

The men around him were in high spirits, but Edward Melrose couldn't match their mood. This sudden turn of events had taken him by surprise, though it shouldn't have done. He was well aware of the situation in South Africa, and once again he had misjudged things. Why the hell didn't he think things through properly? It was becoming abundantly clear that he was lacking in common sense. His sister would never have made such a mess of her life, or that of her family. But what other choice did he have? It was the army or end up in a workhouse.

The memory of the night his father had disowned him and turned him out was a waking nightmare. He didn't hate his father for what he'd done. In fact, he admired him. It had taken courage, and Edward knew he'd deserved nothing less. He could still picture the anguish in his sister's eyes, and he hadn't had the courage to look at his mother.

He hadn't dared go to David to find out how they were coping. But that was probably for the best. He wasn't sure he could handle seeing them suffer because of him. He could never go back, his father had made that very clear, so perhaps leaving England wasn't such a bad thing to do. The shame would never leave him, and that was something he had to learn to live with – or die with. And where he was going there was a fair chance of the latter happening.

'Melrose!' The sergeant was standing by the hatchway and shouting at the top of his voice, scanning the crowded ship's hold for his prey.

'Here, sir!' Edward had soon learnt to respond at once. His pushed his way forward.

'Come with me.'

He followed, wondering what rough job he was going to be given now. The sergeant had soon noticed Edward was not the usual rough recruit, and it had become his mission to work every vestige of a gentleman out of him. He was sure he wouldn't be sailing out to fight the Boers so soon after joining if this man hadn't convinced the officers Edward was needed to care for the horses.

Sergeant Harris turned around and glared at him as they strode on to the deck. 'You needn't think your posh friends are going to save you, Melrose.'

'No, sergeant.' Edward wondered what on earth the man was talking about.

The instant he stepped on deck he knew, and his step faltered. Damn! What was he doing here? And how had he found him?

They stopped in front of Alexander Glendale and the

sergeant's surly manner disappeared. 'I can only allow you ten minutes, sir. The ship's preparing to get under way.'

'This won't take long. Thank you, sergeant.'

'Sir.' Harris came smartly to attention, turned on his heel and marched away.

Alex turned his cold green eyes on Edward. 'You really are a bloody fool, Melrose. Didn't it occur to you that you'd be sent to fight the Boers if you joined the army?'

The rebuke hurt because it was true. He bristled defensively. 'And what the hell was I supposed to do? I couldn't get a job anywhere! Why are you here?'

'Your sister asked me to find you. Your mother has been frantic to know if you're all right, and now she's had a seizure of some kind.'

Edward paled. 'How bad is she?'

'Very bad, I understand.' Alex removed a sheet of paper and a pen from his jacket, and then handed them to Edward. 'Write a quick note to your mother saying you're doing well, and she's not to worry. Don't mention anything about the army or where you're going. That will only add to her concern.'

He did as ordered, forcing his hand to stop shaking. This news was devastating. When he'd finished, he handed it back to Alex.

'Let's hope this helps.' He studied the man in front of him, not trying to hide his disgust. 'Do you know what you've done to your family?'

Edward wanted to shout and say he didn't want to hear. He should walk away, but his feet wouldn't move. This man would tell him no matter what he said. His mother was seriously ill because of him and he couldn't even go to her. He hadn't believed his shame and misery could get any worse, but it just had.

Hands clenched into tight fists, Edward endured a thorough examination by Glendale, and watched him give a slight shake of his head before saying, 'I think it better at this time that you don't know the full details. However, I want your promise that you'll keep in touch with me. Write whenever you can, and don't forget David Gardener. He's a loyal friend to you, and any news we receive will be given to your sister and mother. They will need constant reassurance that you are all right.'

Edward was well aware the imposing man in front of him had been an officer. It was all still there – the military stance and air of authority. And he suddenly realised that Glendale was a man of deep feelings – a man who cared about others. He could be trusted. He didn't have the faintest idea why he felt like that, but there was something about the man. 'I promise, and may I ask a favour?'

Alex inclined his head.

'Will you watch over my family for me?'

'I'm already doing that. Anything else?'

'Tell David I'll write as soon as I can.'

At that moment the ship erupted as orders were shouted and sailors began hauling on ropes.

The sergeant appeared. 'Sorry, sir, you'll have to leave. We're about to get under way. Back to your duties, Melrose.'

Edward was glad to get away. He didn't know what the future held for him, or if he would ever come back to these shores, but it gave him a small measure of comfort to know that Glendale and David were there for his family. He'd never been a particularly religious man, but his view of life had changed. He would pray for his mother's recovery, his father's well being and his sister's happiness. Though the hope that his father would some day forgive him was more than even the Almighty could bring about.

'Thank you for allowing Melrose to see me,' Alex said as the sergeant escorted him to the gangplank. 'How's he doing?'

'Not bad, sir. He's not been used to hard work, but he don't complain, even though I give him hell. Got the makings of a good soldier, if I'm not mistaken.'

Alex nodded. He knew this sergeant. He was tough when he needed to be, but would help any man through a difficult time if he thought he was worth the trouble.

'He's obviously been brought up as a gentleman, but never talks about himself.' The sergeant gave Alex a sly glance. 'Been in trouble, has he?'

'Needs to prove himself,' Alex said dismissively. 'Can't blame a man for that.'

'No, sir. Hard way to do it though by starting at the bottom like this.' Harris was clearly reluctant to let the matter drop. 'Bet you wish you were coming with us, sir.'

'I do miss the army,' he said, glancing around the deck and experiencing a pang of regret that he was no longer a part of this.

'And we miss you too, sir. You was a damned fine officer, and there aren't too many of them around.'

'Thank you.' He hid a smile, knowing Harris had said differently when he'd been a serving officer. 'Keep your eye on Melrose for me.'

'Friend of yours, is he, sir?'

'He comes from a family I have great respect for.'

'Right, sir. I'll see he don't get into trouble.'

'Good man.' Alex made his way off the ship, satisfied he might have eased Edward's relationship with Harris somewhat.

After leaving the ship, his first stop was at David's offices. As soon as he walked in, Millie leapt to her feet, smiling. 'Hello, sir, you want Mr Gardener?'

'Yes please, Millie.'

She shot through the door and could be heard calling, 'Mr Gardener, Sir's here to see you. Shall I make some tea?'

David appeared immediately. 'Come through, Alex. We will have a pot of tea, please, Millie.'

'Right away.' She sped away.

'Does she do anything at normal speed?' Alex asked, smiling in amusement.

'Haven't noticed it yet. She's more than willing, and I don't know what we'd do without her now. She can be left to tend the front office while we're both out. The clients love her. I can hear them laughing when they come in. Gives the place a good atmosphere.' David studied Alex for a while. 'You look worried.'

'We've got a problem. I've found Edward Melrose, but he's on a ship heading for South Africa.'

'What the hell's he doing going there?'

'He's joined the army.'

'Oh, damn!' David rubbed a hand over his eyes. 'The bloody fool! There's a war going on out there.'

'Exactly. I caught them just before they sailed and made him write a note to his mother saying he was all right.'

'But not that he's on his way to fight the Boers?'

'I didn't think it wise to mention that at the moment.' He handed David the note.

'They're going to wonder where we got this.' He gazed at it as if it would bite. 'What on earth are we going to tell them?'

They hadn't heard Millie come in until she put the tray of tea on David's desk. 'You could say it came here in the post.'

Both men looked at her in surprise, then David said, 'But Gertie would want to see the envelope, and know where it came from.'

Millie screwed up her face in concentration. 'I don't like keeping things from Miss, so you could perhaps tell her the truth. She could tell her mother the letter came here and I opened it and threw the envelope away. Didn't know it was important because I don't read anything.'

'Do you think Gertie should be told, Alex? And what about Sutton?'

'Hmm, I think they should both be told, and let them decide when Mrs Melrose is well enough to be told the truth.'

'Yes, that would seem the best thing to do,' he agreed, glancing at Millie. 'Thank you for the suggestion, but it wouldn't be right to blame you for something you haven't done.'

'That's all right, Mr Gardener. Mrs Melrose has to get better first. She can't take no more bad news. You'll be able to tell her the truth when she's feeling stronger. Now, you drink your tea before it gets cold.' She smiled broadly at Alex. 'Them biscuits are lovely.'

When she left the office, Alex shook his head. 'That girl has an abundance of good sense. Just imagine what she could have achieved with a proper education.'

David poured their tea and handed Alex a cup. 'Fred's the same. Thank goodness Gertie found them and we've been able to give them a chance in life. Any news of little May?'

'The doctor's operating soon, and he's hopeful, but only time will tell if she will walk properly again. I'm going to collect her and her mother when I leave here. We're going to the Melrose workshops to see if they can make her a special chair with wheels on. She's going to need something like that for a while.'

'Let's hope she makes a complete recovery, otherwise the poor little devil isn't going to have much of a life, is she?' David picked up the note again, looking doubtful. 'Gertie asked you to find Edward, and you've done that, so do you think you ought to be the one to tell her about this?'

'I'll do it if you wish.'

'Thanks. Let's pray Edward doesn't get himself killed out there.'

'Exactly! Now, while I'm here show me what cargoes you've managed to get for my new ship.'

Chapter Twenty

The sound of a child's laughter made Gertrude glance up sharply. Through the office window she could see a group of people around her father, including Fred, who was talking animatedly to a small girl being held by a tall man. Even from this distance he was easily recognisable, and she couldn't believe her eyes. What on earth was Alexander Glendale doing carrying a child? Fascinated, she couldn't take her eyes off the scene.

They were obviously discussing the merits of several small chairs, and her father was sketching on a pad. The little girl was put in one of them and all the men crouched down, deep in discussion. A poorly dressed woman was standing behind the chair and resting her hands on the little girl's shoulders.

After a while, Mr Glendale picked up the child again,

and left with the woman. Fred waved happily until they disappeared from sight.

She was bursting with curiosity and was pleased to see her father heading for the office. 'What was that all about?' she asked as soon as he came in.

'We've been asked to make a chair with wheels on for the little girl. She has difficulty walking and is being treated by Alexander's physician. He's going to operate on her soon, and then she won't be able to walk at all for a while.' Sutton was already busy making a detailed drawing.

She frowned. 'The service of an eminent physician will be expensive, surely.'

'Very, but without expert help she will always be disabled. I understand from the child's mother that Alexander is paying for the treatment and the chair.'

'That's more than generous of him,' was all she could think of to say.

'He's a generous man. Fred told me he's taking an interest in all the children in their street. He's very good with them, and visits regularly to check they are all right.'

'Well! That's a side of him I never knew existed.'

'You've never bothered to look closely, have you my dear?'

She shook her head. 'I'll need to revise my opinion of him. After I've had time to digest this.'

'I would say that's long overdue,' her father murmured, head bent over his work.

Accepting the rebuke, she stared into space, eyes closed as she focussed on the first time she had ever seen Alexander Glendale. He had walked into the room and every eye turned towards him. His strong character had overwhelmed her, and instinct told her this was not a man to get close to. He gave the impression of being completely unapproachable – a man of authority who would expect to be obeyed without question. When he'd declared his interest in her she'd been frightened. Her family were close, openly showing affection for each other, but there didn't seem to be anything gentle or loving about this imposing man. But she'd just seen him handle the little girl with tenderness, talking to her and smiling. That smile had transformed him. And the fact that he was taking an interest in children from the slums showed there must be a different man under his stern exterior. Had she been too hasty in her assessment of him – too harsh? Had she misjudged him so badly? She really thought she had!

'What are you doing here, my dear?'

Her father's voice broke her thoughts. 'Aunt Hanna's with mother, so I thought I'd collect some of the paperwork to deal with at home.'

'Would you send out the payment reminders as well?'

'Yes, of course.' She gathered up everything she needed. 'This will give me something to do. But I have an errand to run before I can start on it.'

'I know how busy you are, so do the work when you can.' He smiled affectionately at her. 'I don't know what I'd do without you.'

'Have you found him?' Hope flared in Gertrude when she saw who was waiting for her when she arrived home two hours later.

Alexander was studying her intently, a deep frown of concern furrowing his brow. 'Please sit down.'

She waved her hands impatiently, very aware of the tone of command in his voice. 'If you have news, please tell me.'

'I have seen your brother and he gave me this note for your mother.'

She took it from him, turning it over and over in her hands. 'Mother needs to see him. Where is he? Did you tell him how ill she is?'

'I told him. Sit down.' Alexander stepped forward, making her sink into the chair behind her. She was close to collapse. 'Read the note.'

With trembling hands she rested the paper on the arm of the chair before it was steady enough to read. The note was disappointingly short. 'All this says is that he's all right. What good is that? Tell me where he is and I'll drag him here if I have to.'

'That isn't possible, I'm sorry to say. He's joined the army and is on a ship bound for South Africa.'

Every trace of colour drained from her face, and she whispered, 'Oh no!'

Stooping down in front of her, he handed her a pristine handkerchief so she could wipe the moisture from her eyes. 'The ship was ready to sail when I arrived. I only managed to see your brother because I knew the sergeant. That short note was all we had time for.'

She took the handkerchief and dabbed her eyes, then twisted the fine cotton into a ball as she fought for composure. This was devastating news. It embarrassed her to appear so distressed in front of him, but she was so very tired of trying to be brave. She wasn't brave at all. What was she going to do now?

'May I offer some advice?' he suggested, as he stood up again.

'Yes, please.'

'Give your mother the note, but tell her you still don't know where he is.'

She nodded. 'I'll have to lie because I certainly can't tell her he's on his way to fight the Boers. That will make her frantic with worry.' She gazed up at him. 'What shall I tell father? He ought to know.'

'I agree. Would you like me to talk to him?'

'Oh, would you?' Her voice trembled.

'I'll go to the workshop when I leave here.'

'Thank you.' She stood up, holding on to the back of the chair for support. 'Forgive me, I haven't offered you any refreshments.'

'There's no need.' He moved towards her. 'You're exhausted. You must rest.'

Something inside her snapped. 'Rest? How can I rest? Father is working and worrying himself into an early grave. The business I believed to be sound is struggling to make a profit. My fool of a brother could get himself killed in a war, and my mother is dangerously ill. She's regained consciousness, but her recovery is being hampered by worry. Not only is she fretting about Edward, but she's afraid I'm going to be left with nothing. I don't care! I just want her to get well, and for her and father to be happy again. Nothing else—'

Alexander's frown deepened, then he took hold of her arms and made her sit down again. With two strides he'd reached the drinks table and poured a brandy. Handing it to her, he said, in a tone of voice only a fool would disobey, 'Drink this.'

The strong liquid made her cough and she couldn't take more than a sip. Her show of weakness made her ashamed. 'I'm sorry. I'm embarrassing you.'

'Stop apologising, Gertrude!'

That made her bristle with indignation. She wouldn't be spoken to in that tone of voice! She might be down, but she still had some fight in her. Forcing her legs to remain steady, she stood to face him. 'I was trying to be polite. And just because you own us doesn't mean you can order me around. Thank you for bringing me news of my brother, and the offer to tell my father, but on reflection I believe it will be better if I break the news to him.'

'Don't be stubborn. You're clearly in no fit state to shoulder this burden alone.'

'I am perfectly capable! The news about Edward has been upsetting, and for a moment I was confused. But I'm all right now. I'll do whatever has to be done for my family. Somehow I'll stop mother worrying about us.'

He hesitated for a moment, then said, 'There's one way you can ease your parents' difficulties and concerns.'

'Oh?' Despite her anger, she was ready to listen.

'Marry me and I'll give you the house as a wedding gift. I—'

'How dare you!' she exploded. He was trying to buy her. That hurt so much she clutched her sides, feeling physical pain. She'd begun to think about him in a more kindly way, and then he does this to her. It was cruel. Her first assessment of him had obviously been the correct one.

'Let me finish.'

'I am not for sale, Mr Glendale.' She lifted her head in defiance. 'And the fact you think I am is insulting!'

He didn't have a chance to reply because the door opened and Hanna swept in. 'Stop shouting, Gertie. What's going on here?'

'Mr Glendale is leaving, Aunt.' Then she turned on her heel and stormed out of the room.

Fifteen minutes later there was a firm tap on her bedroom door. She knew who it was. 'Come in.'

Her aunt sat next to her on the bed. 'He wants to apologise for upsetting you.'

'No!'

'Don't be so damned stubborn, Gertie. I don't know what went on between you down there, but he's gone to a lot of trouble to trace Edward, at your request. At least have the decency to thank him for that, and listen to his apology.'

'I've already thanked him.' She stared at the note still clutched in her hand. 'He told you Edward's joined the army then?'

'Yes, the bloody fool. Why the blazes didn't he come to me? But we'll discuss this later. Put aside your wounded pride and listen to Alex's apology.'

'He hurt me.'

'He knows that, and believe me, that's the last thing he would want to do.'

'You always talk about him as if you know him well.'

'My husband was acquainted with the Glendales. I've known Alex since he was ten years old.'

She gave her aunt a startled look. 'I didn't know that.'

'There's a great deal you don't know about me. I never talk about those years. They are best forgotten, but I will tell you a little about Alex. His great grandfather came from Scotland. He was a shrewd man and soon began to build up the family fortune. Each male has carried on the business. When Alex's father, and then his mother and sister died so tragically, he was left with no choice but to resign his commission in the army and return home. He has inherited the sharp business mind, and although I know it was the last thing he wanted to do, he left the life he loved and came back to deal with the family affairs. He's a strong man, which is a blessing or he would not have survived such devastating losses, but that doesn't mean he is without feelings. He's still trying to pull his shattered life together. He understands only too well what our family is going through, and that is why he has spent time helping us.' Hanna stood up. 'You're an intelligent girl, but you should have grown out of this habit of making hasty judgements about people and situations, and I'm going to be very cross if you don't start acting your age. You're a woman now, Gertie, not some silly child who throws tantrums every time someone upsets her.'

She flinched at the merited rebuke, and nodded.

'Good.' Hanna opened the door. 'Show him how gracious you can be.'

Chapter Twenty-One

At least Gertrude had allowed him to apologise, but he hadn't been prepared to do more than that. He'd upset her, and for that he was very sorry, but she had reacted so quickly to his suggestion that he hadn't had time to tell her why he was making the proposal. When she'd said she would do whatever she had to for her family, he had spoken without thinking. He swore under his breath. As if she wasn't suffering enough, he'd caused her more distress. He would never forget the pain in her eyes as she'd accused him of trying to buy her, and to be truthful, that's exactly how it had sounded. But if she'd only continued to listen he'd have been about to tell her how he felt. He should have done that first, of course, but he hadn't. The trouble with him was he was used to giving orders, and he had appeared abrupt in his handling of a sensitive girl. Much too late to recognise that now; the damage had been done.

Still muttering curses, Alex walked. He didn't know where, or care, oblivious to the cold drizzle. Hadn't he told himself repeatedly that Gertrude was not for him? Had he listened? No, he damned well hadn't. The dream of winning her had persisted. Well, he'd better conquer that desire. Now!

'You're getting wet, sir.'

He started, unaware his carriage was following him slowly. He hadn't even heard the clip of the horse's hooves on the road. Without saying a word he climbed in, settled in the plush seats and closed his eyes. When the horse began to canter, he sat up and opened his eyes again.

What was done couldn't be changed, though he would give anything to be able to take back those hasty words. He'd ruined whatever slim chance he might have had with her, but that would not change his desire to help them. The loss of his own family had made him more aware of the suffering of others. He couldn't change the world, but he could help a few people along the way.

His own life needed to be put into order as well, and he'd spent enough time on something that could never be. He'd done all he could for the Melrose family at the moment, and now it was time to retreat.

'Where to, sir?' the driver called.

'Home.' Home, he thought bitterly. Once it had been, but now it was just a huge, empty shell. He would make sure May was all right and then go to his Hampshire estate. The peace there would help him sort things out in his mind. It was time to lay some ghosts. He should have done it months ago.

The carriage stopped and he got out. 'I won't need you again today, Dickson.'

His butler was waiting at the door, shaking his head in disapproval as he removed his master's wet coat. 'Mr Shawbridge is waiting to see you, sir. Shall I tell him you are unavailable?'

The last thing he wanted at the moment was a visitor, but he'd better see Michael. 'No, I'll see him. Where have you put him?'

'In the library, sir.'

Alex entered the room and walked straight to the drinks table, as Michael leapt to his feet. After pouring two large brandies, Alex sat down. 'Please sit down. What can I do for you, Michael?'

Before speaking, his visitor took a large gulp of the brandy. 'I thought you'd like to hear the news. The Hayworth brothers have been expelled from the club for cheating. There's one hell of a row going on.'

Michael was clearly ill at ease and he hoped the damned fool hadn't also been caught. 'And have they also connected you with them?'

'No!' he declared in alarm. 'You know, don't you?'

Alex nodded.

'Oh God! Now I understand your warning to me, and I thank you. I've been an idiot, but I'll never get involved in anything like that again.'

'You'd be wise to choose your friends more carefully.'

'I never took any of the money.' Michael gulped down the last of his drink. 'It just seemed like a bit of fun, but that's no excuse, is it?'

'No, it isn't. People have been hurt, and that is unacceptable.' Alex refilled the glasses, well pleased with the news, but still concerned for Michael. He was sure the young man didn't mean to do anything dishonest, but he was so easily led, and the brothers were very persuasive. 'Will they implicate you?'

'Unlikely. Their reputations are ruined, and no one will believe anything they say again. They left for France this afternoon, and it will be a long time before they can return. The people they cheated are clamouring for their money back. They won't get it, though.'

'Not a chance.'

'Er . . .' Michael turned his glass round and round in his hands. 'I'm moving to Suffolk, Alex. I've met a girl, Frances Handley, and we're to have a Christmas wedding.'

It was the kind of news that helped to lift some of the gloom from him, and he smiled, genuinely pleased. 'Congratulations, I've met the family and she'll make you a fine wife.'

The worry cleared from Michael's face. 'I know she will. Thank you. I wasn't sure how you'd take it.'

'My sister has been dead for nearly two years, and you cannot live in the past. I'm delighted for you. I shall expect an invitation to the wedding.'

'You're already on the list.' Michael smiled and sat back, relaxed at last.

They talked for another hour and then Alex was left to dine alone. It was satisfying to know the brothers had been exposed with no hint of Fred's involvement. There was no chance of the Melrose family getting any of their money back, but it was a victory nonetheless. There was a measure of justice in their banishment from this country.

He gazed into the fire, watching the multicoloured flames dancing, and he took a deep breath, relaxing in the warmth and quiet. He'd told Michael he couldn't live in the past. It was time he took his own advice and moved on with his life.

Pacing restlessly, Gertrude looked out of the window for the fourth time.

'Do sit down, Gertie!' Hanna scolded. 'I swear you're making me quite dizzy.'

She did as ordered, fingering the note in her hand. 'I wish Father would come home. I won't tell Mother we've heard from Edward until I've spoken to him.'

'And you're quite right not to. But you should have told him your mother asked you to trace Edward.'

'I know I shouldn't have kept that from him, but he's never shown any interest in finding him. Now I hope he'll be relieved that we can put Mother's mind at ease. But I need to ask him how much he thinks we should tell her.'

'Very little, I'd say.' Hanna tipped her head to one side, listening. 'Ah, here he comes now.'

'How is she?' he asked, as soon as he walked into the room.

'Sleeping at the moment.' Hanna handed her brother a glass of whisky. 'Sit down. Gertie has something to tell you.'

It took her no more than ten minutes to explain about the search for Edward. When her father made no comment, she held out the note. 'I apologise for not being honest with you, but Mother didn't want you to know how bad she felt. Please read the note.'

He made no attempt to take it from her. 'What does he say?'

'Only that he's all right and Mother is not to worry about him. She desperately needs to know Edward is safe, but how much do we tell her?'

'You're the only one who can make that decision, Sutton,' Hanna told him.

He drained his glass and put it on the small table beside his chair. 'Give her the note and say it was delivered here by hand, but no one saw the messenger. She must *not* be told the blasted idiot has joined the army.'

He stood up, clearly angry. 'Is that understood?'

'Yes, Father.' Gertrude watched him stride out of the room. 'He's furious with me. That's the first time I've ever been anything but open and honest with him.'

'It isn't that. He's blaming himself for Florence's illness, and he's distressed Edward is going to be in such danger.'

'But he doesn't care what Edward does.'

Her aunt gave her a sad glance. 'He cares, my dear. He sent Edward away because he knew his son would sink further into trouble unless he was brought to his senses. The way he did it may seem brutal, but it had to be done, and I believe it was the right thing. Edward is now in the army and the discipline will make or break him. I'd bet on it being the making of him.'

'I never thought of it like that. I believed Father sent him away because he hated him for what he'd done to us.'

'No, my dear. Sutton has constantly urged Edward to come into the business and live a useful, productive life, but the boy kept making excuses, saying he would consider it in a few months. But he never intended working. He was out of control.'

'Poor Father, what a terrible burden for him to carry.'

'It is, but he'll survive with our help. Don't be deceived by his gentleness, he's a strong man. Now, why don't you go and see your mother?'

Gertrude rushed over to her aunt and gave her an affectionate hug. 'You're so wise and sensible. I don't know what we'd do without you in this crisis.'

'You'd manage. You're just like your father, though you don't realise it yet. Now, off you go.' Hanna waved her away.

Her aunt always managed to put things in their proper perspective, Gertrude thought as she made her way up to her mother's room. And if she had inherited even a small amount of her father's character, then she was blessed indeed. The problem was she didn't feel strong; she was floundering, close to panic some of the time. It was only the love she felt for her brother and parents that stopped her crumbling. The only person she ever let her guard down with was David.

Quietly opening her mother's door, she peered in. 'Is she awake, nurse?' she whispered.

'Come in, Miss. Your mother's had a wash and change of nightclothes, and she's more comfortable now.' The nurse straightened the bedclothes. 'Stay for a while, but don't tire her.'

'I won't.' She walked towards the bed, a bright smile on her face. 'I have good news, Mother.'

'Edward?'

She nodded, sat on a chair by the bed and held out the note. 'He's written to you.'

'Read it to me.'

As she read her brother's brief words, she saw the tears gather in her mother's eyes.

'Oh, thank God! He's all right! Where is he? I want to see him. Need to see him.'

'Edward doesn't say where he is.' She was trying not to say more than was necessary. 'But he's fine, and I expect he'll write again.'

Her mother took the note from her, kissed it, and then clutched it to her heart. With a sigh of relief she closed her eyes.

Believing she'd fallen asleep, Gertrude began to stand up, sad for her mother's suffering, and knowing it wasn't going to be possible for her to see her son for a very long time.

'Got to find our daughter a husband,' her mother murmured. 'Got to have someone to take care of her.'

Gertrude sat down again, dismayed to realise her mother was still worrying about her.

The nurse touched her shoulder. 'She's talking in her sleep, that's all. Knowing her son's all right will help her rest easier.'

'That's what I'd hoped, but she's also worrying about me.'

'Only natural.' The nurse smiled understandingly. 'A mother is always concerned about her children, and

I'm afraid worry is also a result of the illness. She feels helpless, you see.'

Afraid she was going to break down, Gertrude left quickly and made for her own room. It was vital her mother didn't worry, especially about her. What was she going to do? She couldn't conjure up a husband!

The tension inside her was unbearable and there was no relief from tears. Her eyes were dry. She knew the answer to the problem had been there when Mr Glendale had suggested they marry. And what had she done? Insulted him and stormed away.

Fool! Damned fool! It would have been a loveless marriage, but there were still many marriages of convenience. He needed a wife; needed a family of his own again. It might not have been so bad; he was a good man. Everyone said so. But she found him so disturbing . . .

Sitting on the edge of the bed, she rested her head in her hands. He'd never speak to her again. When she had gone back downstairs he'd told her she had stormed out before he'd had a chance to explain the reason for his offer. He obviously hadn't been prepared to tell her then, and how could she blame him? After being snubbed so rudely it was understandable that he'd keep his reasons to himself.

She should have listened to what he had to say. But it was easy to be wise after the event, and it was a bad habit of hers to react too quickly without hearing the whole story. She would have to make sure she learnt from this.

Chapter Twenty-Two

'Two young people to see you, sir.'

Biting back a curse, Alex glared at his butler. The last thing he wanted tonight was visitors.

'Millie and Fred, sir.' Seeing the scowl on his master's face, he asked, 'Shall I tell them you're not at home?'

'No, of course not.' Perhaps it was for the best. The lively youngsters would certainly keep him from brooding. 'Send them in.'

'And shall I ask Cook for refreshments?'

The butler's dry tone of voice made him smile, lifting the unhappiness he was feeling. They only had to appear and Cook wanted to feed them. 'Better make it a large selection.'

'Of course, sir.'

As soon as Hunt left the room, Fred and Millie tumbled in, beaming with excitement.

'We've seen May, and the doc says the operation went well and there's a good chance she'll be able to walk properly.' Millie couldn't stop smiling.

Alex was surprised. 'I didn't think the operation was for a few days yet. I had intended to be there.'

'The doc did it today,' Fred told him. 'He said it wasn't as bad as he'd first thought, so he did it straight away. She didn't have time to think about it so she wasn't too frightened. And the chair you ordered will be ready in a couple of days. Mr Melrose is hurrying it along.'

'That is good news.' He was delighted. 'Sit down and tell me how she is.'

'A bit dopey, you know, but she smiled when we told her she was gonna walk like everyone else soon. We can't get Johnny away from her side. Loves that little girl, he does. They don't usually let children in the wards, but they said he could stay with her for a while.' Millie sat on the satin chair without giving it a second glance this time.

'And her mum cried,' Fred said. 'Her dad was close to tears as well when the doc spoke to him. Real happy they was with what he told them.'

Millie nodded. 'They said there's no way in this world they could ever thank you enough.'

'Knowing she's going to be able to walk properly again is thanks enough.' Alex smiled. 'Are you hungry?'

'We're always hungry,' the girl laughed. 'You know that.'

'So I do.' The door opened and the maid wheeled in a trolley laden with food.

Daisy smiled with pleasure when she saw Millie was wearing the frock she'd given her.

'Did you get your new frocks from him?' Millie looked pointedly at Alex.

'Yes, two as promised.'

'Good.' She gave a satisfied nod.

'Thank you, Daisy.' Alex struggled to keep a grin at bay. 'We'll serve ourselves.'

'Very well, sir.' The maid smiled again at the two youngsters as she left.

'Oh, I nearly forgot.' Fred fished in his pocket and handed Alex a sheet of paper. 'Johnny said you was to have this. It shows what was spent. And when are you coming to see him again?'

'Tell him I'll be along some time tomorrow.'

'Right. He was at the hospital with May's mum and dad. Gets worried about her, he does, and took her a bag of fruit. It's all down on the paper, he said to tell you.'

The butler slipped in quietly. 'Mr Gardener to see you, sir.'

'Show him in, Hunt.' Alex noted the rapidly depleting trolley. 'And ask Cook for more tea and food.'

'Yes, sir.' Hunt's mouth twitched. 'Cook asked if the young people would like a basket of food – each – to take home? With your permission, of course, sir.'

'I'm sure they would.' Alex looked at the youngsters, who were nodding vigorously. 'Thank Cook for us, Hunt.'

'Of course, sir.'

'Oh, and have the carriage made ready to take Fred and Millie home.'

'You don't need to do that. We can go on the bus, can't we, Millie? We got enough for our fare now we're working.'

'No, it's bitterly cold. You keep your money for something else.'

'Thanks.' Millie helped herself to the last sandwich. 'We give most of what we earn to our mums, but we're saving up, as well.'

'Hello, Mr Gardener,' Fred said as David walked into the room. 'We've been to see May. She's gonna be all right.'

David looked surprised as he shook hands with Alex.

'They operated today,' Alex explained. 'The doctor made a quick decision to do it right away. It went well evidently, and he's hopeful for the little girl.'

'That is good news!'

Daisy returned, carrying two baskets of food. She put them down near Fred and Millie. 'Fresh tea is on its way, sir.'

The butler was right behind her. 'The carriage is ready, sir.'

Alex stood up. 'Thank you for coming to let me know about May.'

'The doc asked us to let you know. He couldn't come himself 'cos he's ever so busy.' Fred nudged Millie. 'Time we went. Sir and Mr Gardener got business to do.'

'Thanks for the grub.' Millie eyed the basket. 'It's good of you, but you don't have to give us so much now we've got jobs.'

'Cook would be very upset if you didn't want her food. It gives her pleasure to know you enjoy her cooking.'

'Ah . . . well, we wouldn't want to upset her. Would we, Fred?'

'No fear. Best food we've ever tasted, and we share it out.' Fred turned to David, his expression worried. 'You seen Miss? Is she all right? How's her mum?'

'Her mother's still very ill. This is an unhappy time for her and her father.'

''T'aint right!' Millie declared. 'She ain't done nothing to deserve this. That brother of hers ought to be ashamed of himself. You tell her to send for us if there's anything we can do. She's so kind. You looking out for her, Mr Gardener?'

'We both are.' David nodded in Alex's direction.

'That's good.' Fred scowled. 'She needs friends at a time like this. We'll do anything for her. She's only got to say. Ain't that right, Millie?'

The girl nodded. 'That's right. 'Cos we're her friends too.'

Hunt appeared in the doorway. 'The horse is getting cold, sir.'

After saying a hasty goodbye, they watched the youngsters climb into the carriage and disappear up the road.

'I'll go and see May tomorrow.' David took a cup of tea from Alex and sat down. 'Where is she?'

'Whitechapel.' Alex let out a deep sigh.

'You all right?' David asked, concerned by Alex's drawn and tired appearance.

'I made a mess of my meeting with your friend. She took offence at something I suggested, and that was the last thing I wanted to do.'

David knew he was talking about Gertie. It was all too obvious. 'Wasn't she relieved to know her brother was all right?'

'She was pleased to have the note to show her mother.' Alex stood up, resting his hand on the mantelpiece and staring into the dancing flames. 'She looks near the end of her strength, and when I suggested a way to ease their problems, she asked her aunt to throw me out.'

'Oh, Gertie!' David muttered under his breath. 'She's too proud, and reacts badly to any hint of charity.'

Alex's laugh was devoid of humour. 'The price was too high for her.'

When Alex said no more, David didn't probe further. What this was all about was between the two of them. 'And did Hanna throw you out?'

'No, she made her niece face me so I could apologise.'

'You had to apologise for offering to help?' David could picture the scene. A furious Gertie, and Hanna laying down the law. No man would stand a chance between the two of them, and they would test anyone's patience.

Sitting down again, Alex grimaced. 'The situation was ridiculous. You may laugh. I know you're finding it difficult to keep a straight face.'

That was all David needed, and he began to shake with laughter. 'I'm sorry, but I know those two, and if the pair of them set about me, I'd run like hell! I've known Gertie nearly all my life and love her dearly, but she is difficult to handle at times. I could never understand her stubborn streak because she has such a caring nature, and would help anyone in trouble.'

Alex nodded, amused now. 'She didn't even let me finish what I was saying.'

'She often admits to being unreasonable at times, and once she's formed a firm opinion it's hard to make her change her mind.' He was serious again. 'Don't be too hard with your judgement of her. She's half out of her mind with worry for her family, and I expect that's why she reacted so badly.'

'I dare say you're right. She's in dire trouble and has her pride. I can't blame her for that, but I now feel I've done as much as I can for her. As you are aware, I did at one time harbour a hope that we would become better acquainted. Regardless of her faults – and we all have those – I liked her the moment I set eyes on her. She has a pleasing personality and a lively intelligence, and I felt she would make an ideal wife for me.' Alex frowned. 'I would soon become bored with a docile wife.'

'She might yet come to care for you,' David suggested, trying to give comfort.

'Not after today. I've been defeated and I'm battle weary. I have a lovely house in the heart of Hampshire and I'm thinking of going there for a while.' He sighed deeply, rubbing his forehead. 'It's full of memories and that's why I haven't visited it since I returned home. It's time I laid a few ghosts and got on with my life.'

Chapter Twenty-Three

'What on earth did you do to Alex?' David asked Gertrude when she came into his office the next day. 'I've never seen him so depressed.'

She looked uncomfortable. 'He insulted me.'

'Come on, I don't believe that. He's a gentleman through and through.'

'I don't want to talk about it. He apologised, and that's an end to it.'

David sighed deeply. 'Whatever happened is between you and Alex, but you've now lost the best support you could have. He's done a lot for you, and I wouldn't be surprised if you've seen the last of him.'

'Don't you think I know that?' Her bottom lip trembled. 'I'm sure he didn't mean it the way it came out, but I won't be bought. I feel beaten down enough without being offered money to . . .' She shook her head vigorously. 'Never mind.'

'He didn't make an improper offer, did he?' David's eyes narrowed as he studied her.

'No, of course not!'

'Then what are you talking about? His help so far has been given freely, without thought of reward. Tell me, Gertie. You've never kept things from me before.'

'He offered to give me our house as a wedding present if I married him. I know he wants a wife. I understand his need, but he's the most eligible man in London, so why on earth did he make an offer like that? He could have any girl he wants.'

'Except you,' David said sadly. 'He told me you didn't let him finish what he was saying.'

'What was I supposed to do? Stand there and let him humiliate me?'

'If you'd had the decency to hear him out I'm sure you would have found that "buying" you was not his intention. I've come to know him well lately, and if I've read the signs right, Alex is in love with you.'

'Don't be ridiculous! He might have shown an interest when he first returned home, but that was ages ago, and now he knows me better I'm sure he's changed his mind. He needs a docile, obedient wife, not someone who is argumentative and has a mind of her own.'

'How do you know that's what he wants?'

'That's what every man wants, isn't it?'

'Oh, Gertie.' David was shaking his head in dismay. 'You don't know the first thing about men, do you? Think about it. Why would he have bought your house and then let you remain living there? Why would he expose the

216

men who cheated your brother? And why would he take the time and trouble to trace Edward? He's been home for more than a year, leaving the army he loved in order to take over the family responsibilities. He needs to have a family around him again. He could have had his pick the moment he came back, but he's wasted his time on someone who's made it clear she despises him.'

'I don't despise him!' she declared defensively.

He put his hand under her chin to make her look up at him. 'I think his feelings for you are more than liking. Turn him down if you must, but at least do it graciously. You're a bloody fool, Gertie.'

She stepped back, trembling, and grabbed hold of the desk to steady herself. He'd never spoken to her like that before, and it hurt. With hesitant steps, she walked towards the door.

'Where are you going?'

'To find a jeweller.' Her voice was faint.

'I said I'd sell anything for you. Give it to me.'

She shook her head. 'You've done enough. Everyone's done enough. It's time I stopped relying on others and started taking control of myself.'

'Don't be stupid. Give me the jewellery.'

Suddenly she spun round, eyes blazing. 'Stop calling me names, David! I'm lost! Don't you realise that? My life until now has been comfortable, secure, and surrounded by people who love me. No demands were made on me. As long as I was happy, my parents were content. Now that's all gone and I'm floundering like a fish out of water. My parents are suffering and I'm helpless, unable to ease their pain. I'm sorry to have failed you and Mr Glendale. I'm trying to do what's right, but I can't think straight. Nothing in my life has prepared me to cope with this terrible crisis, and I'm letting everyone down—'

He watched in horror as silent tears ran down her cheeks. The lovely, happy girl he'd known for so long had disappeared before his eyes. Standing in front of him now was a confused and heartbroken woman. She had been coping well, or so he'd thought, managing to keep a smile on her face, but her mother's illness was clearly tearing her apart. Her foundations in life had been torn from under her.

'Oh, don't do that!' He stepped forward and held her in his arms. 'I'm so sorry. I shouldn't have said those harsh things to you.'

'I deserved them,' she murmured, burying her head in his shoulder. 'You're quite right. I'm impossible.'

'We've always known that, haven't we?' he teased gently.

She made a sound something like a laugh and a sob combined. Then she looked up, pleading in her eyes. 'Be patient with me, please. Don't turn against me. I couldn't stand that.'

'I'll always be here for you. We're all under strain and must try to understand each other.'

Nodding, she stepped back, wiped her eyes and took a deep breath. 'I always considered myself to be a strong person, but I now know that isn't so.'

'You listen to me. Don't believe that about yourself because it isn't true. You're trying to cope with a living nightmare. I haven't seen your mother, but it must be terrible watching her day after day, not knowing if she's ever going to recover. Many would sink under the strain.'

'I know I mustn't, and that frightens me. Father needs me as well.' She straightened up. 'I'll apologise to Mr Glendale if he'll see me. Do you think he will?'

'I don't know. And he told me he was going to the country for a while.'

'Oh, when?'

'He didn't say, but soon, I expect.' He was relieved to see some colour coming back to her face.

'Then I mustn't waste any time.'

'Are you going to give me the jewellery?' he asked gently as she made for the door.

'No, you've got enough to do. I'll deal with it myself.' Her smile gave a glimpse of the girl she really was. 'And I won't let them cheat me!'

'That's my girl.' He didn't argue, seeing it was important to her. Her confidence had been shaken, and she needed to regain her sense of self-worth.

The office door opened a crack and Millie's worried face appeared. 'I've made a strong cuppa, Miss. Have one before you go. My mum says it puts a spring back in your step when you're feeling down.'

'And she's quite right.' He took hold of Gertie's arm and led her to a chair. 'You join us as well, Millie. And have we got any of those shortcake biscuits left?'

A rustling sound came from the outer office, then the door opened wide and Millie came in carrying a tray laden with tea and the requested biscuits. There was also a small parcel tucked under her arm.

'Thanks, Millie.' Gertrude managed a tight smile. 'Just what I need.'

After placing the tray on the desk, Millie handed Gertrude the parcel. 'Me and Fred got you this as a little thank you for all you've done for us. Hope you like it.'

'Oh, you shouldn't be spending your money on me.'

'We thought it would cheer you up. And it didn't cost much.' She smirked. 'We beat old Partridge down.'

'That's very kind of you.' She removed the paper wrapping and studied the book in her hands, swallowing hard to keep the tears of gratitude at bay. The fact that Fred and Millie had thought of her in this way was balm to her troubled mind.

'How lovely!' she exclaimed. 'Look, David, a book of poems by all the famous poets.'

'Ah, you'll enjoy that.' He leant across to get a better look.

'I will.' She stood up and kissed Millie on the cheek, much to the young girl's surprise and pleasure. 'Thank you. I'll treasure this.'

Millie beamed. 'We wrote in the front.'

When she opened the book at the front, there in the girl's beautiful writing were the words, 'Hold on to your dreams.'

'Fred told me what to put. He said it was important 'cos in the bad times we must always have something to hold on to – some hope for the future. Might sound daft to you, but that's how we think.'

'It isn't daft, Millie. And I promise to do my best to remember. If I start to forget, all I'll need to do is read this lovely book. I'll pop into the workshop on my way home and thank Fred as well.'

'That'll please him.' She set about pouring the tea. 'I don't know nothing about poetry, but Mr Partridge in the shop said it was good and you'd like it.'

'He knows my taste in literature.' She gave a wistful smile. 'I do miss my visits to the shop. I used to spend ages rummaging through the shelves to see what I could find.'

'You'll be able to do that again.' Millie handed around the biscuits. 'Won't she, Mr Gardener?'

'Of course.' He sat back, happy to let the young girl chat away, relieved to see Gertie's composure returning.

'Things change and we can't do nothing about it, but things have a way of working out. When we look back on the bad times we can often see something good come out of it. We have to look real hard at times, but Mum says there's always a spark of good there.'

Amusement spread across David's face. 'You're a philosopher, Millie. How did you become so wise?'

'You're teasing me again, Mr Gardener. I ain't wise. I've just taken lots of knocks in life, and you have to learn not to let things get you down. Many times I've felt like grizzling, but Mum and Fred are the wise ones and they soon puts me right.' She sat down and leant forward. 'We sits down with a cuppa and we think of all the things we would like to do. Many of those dreams won't come true, but that don't matter. It gives us something to hope for.'

'Fred told me your big dream was to get out of the slums and live in the country.' Gertrude was fascinated.

Millie couldn't be more than sixteen, but she was mature beyond her years.

'Oh, that one isn't just a dream, it's something we're gonna make come true. Even if it takes us till we're old and grey. We're gonna get out of the filth and poverty, and take our families with us.' She nodded her head, her mouth set in a determined line.

The feeling of inadequacy and fear that she would not be able to cope much longer had eased since she had talked to David and Millie. David had been quite right to point out her failings. That had made her take a good look at herself, and she didn't like what she'd seen. Her conduct towards Alexander Glendale had been down-right rude from the moment she'd met him. *She* was the one who needed to apologise, and she would do that now. Then she'd call in and thank Fred for his thoughtful gift.

There was fresh purpose in her step, and she blessed her friends for waking her out of the gloomy frame of mind she'd allowed herself to slip into. What good was she going to be to her parents if she continued in that way?

The first jewellers she came to was a smart shop, and she marched in, determined not to be intimidated this time.

Fifteen minutes later she walked out well-satisfied. Not only had he given her what she considered a fair price for her mother's necklace and small ruby and pearl brooch, but she still had some pieces left for another day. She now had enough to pay the nurses for the next two weeks, but there was also a little she could use on fares. There was a lot she needed to do today, so it would help to travel by cab, as it would save time. She didn't like to be away from her mother for any length of time, in case she called for her.

It wasn't long before she was climbing the steps at Mr Glendale's home.

'I'm sorry, Miss Melrose, but Mr Glendale isn't at home, and I don't know when to expect him. Perhaps you'd like to leave a message?'

'No, thank you. I'd rather see him in person.' This was disappointing because once she'd made up her mind to do something then she liked to get on with it. And her apology could not be put in a short note. 'Do you know if it would be convenient for me to call sometime tomorrow?'

'He will be away for a while,' the butler told her.

'Away?' She was too late! He'd gone already.

'Yes, Miss Melrose. Would you like me to let him know you called?'

She shook her head. 'That won't be necessary. I'll see him when he returns.'

And I hope I don't lose my nerve while I'm waiting, she thought as she walked away.

Chapter Twenty-Four

The house had a neglected, unlived-in air about it. The staff had done their best to make it ready for him, but he'd given them little warning of his arrival. He should have come sooner, but he hadn't been ready to face it. The house had been a happy family home and was full of memories, but this had to be done. It was no good delaying it any longer.

It was February now, but spring was still a long way off. With his collar pulled up and hands in his pockets he wandered through the garden, head bent against the biting wind, and the memories flooded in. Stopping, he gazed up at the large tree he'd climbed at the age of nine and got stuck. His father had had to climb up and coax him down. His little sister had taunted him until he'd climbed it again the next day to prove he could get up and down by himself. It was an act of bravado but he'd always been very determined, even at that young age. Nothing dented his confidence and failure was not a word in his vocabulary. If he failed at something he would keep on until he mastered it.

He gazed at the bare branches. Where was that boy now? Where was the confidence and determination? Had it died with his family?

'No!' he said out loud, clenching his hands into fists. The tragedy that had befallen his family had torn his life apart, but he was still the same person, and would damned well prove it!

Stripping off his coat, he hung it on a low branch, spat on his hands and began to haul himself up. He didn't stop until he reached the very top branches, then he gazed across to the house. How he loved this place. There were only happy memories here and he couldn't understand why he had been so reluctant to come. He'd been blessed with a loving family, and he would have one again. Gertrude wouldn't have him; that was a disappointment, and had done nothing for his confidence, but he'd find someone else. If he chose carefully, he should be able to make a happy marriage. Perhaps not with the passion he felt for that other spirited young lady, but there would be someone else for him. Deep down he knew he was trying to talk himself into accepting second best, and he wasn't sure he could live with that. He gazed across the tops of the bare trees, picturing what they would be like in the spring, in full bloom. He smiled as he drank in the tranquil scene, feeling it soothe his thoughts.

'Sir, are you all right?'

The sound of his butler's anxious voice reached him and he peered down. 'Hello, Hunt, when did you arrive?'

'Just this moment, sir. I thought I'd better see that everything was to your liking here.'

'Ah, checking up on the staff, are you?'

'It's my job, sir.' Hunt sounded offended. 'There was little time to prepare.'

'I know, but you needn't have worried. I've slept in many uncomfortable places whilst in the army – even ditches from time to time.'

'Quite so, sir,' Hunt remarked dryly. 'Are you planning to make your bed in that tree?'

Alex tipped his head back and laughed – really laughed – for the first time, easing some of the grief and pain he'd felt since his return home. The relief was palpable and made him take a deep breath. The past was gone and not one moment could be changed. The family disaster had happened, and that would always be a source of great sadness to him, but the good memories would always be with him. No one could take those from him.

'Are you coming down, sir? Cook will not be pleased if dinner is spoilt. She's made your favourite steak and kidney pie.'

'Has she?' It was only then that Alex realised just how hungry he was. He began to climb down, his long legs making easy work of the descent.

Jumping the last few feet, he landed lightly and grinned

226

at his butler. 'Just wanted to see if I could still do it.'

The corners of Hunt's mouth twitched, but he said nothing as he held out the coat for his master.

'I'm glad I came,' he said, shrugging into the coat.

'Yes, sir, it was the right thing to do, and the staff are delighted to have you home.'

Home – yes, this place had always been regarded as their home. 'I should have come sooner.'

'You're here now.' Hunt opened the front door. 'Perhaps you'll stay for a while?'

'Yes, I think I will.'

The butler gave a satisfied nod. 'It was good to hear you laugh again, sir.'

'It felt good.'

A week later, David received a letter from Alex asking him to come for a few days, so they could discuss expanding the shipping line. He was also asked to bring May, her parents, Johnny, and Millie and Fred if they could be spared from their jobs for a short time.

When David told Millie, she exclaimed, 'Crumbs, where's he gonna put us all? How big's his house?'

'I've no idea. My father said you could take four days as a holiday. Would you like to come?'

'Oh yes. Do you think Mr Melrose will let Fred off work?'

'I'll go and see him right away. Little May's out of hospital now, so will you go and see her parents? Tell them Mr Glendale's arranged transport.'

'What, now?'

'Yes, Millie.' David's father came into the office, smiling. 'You'll enjoy the country, even if it is still winter.'

'Thanks, Mr Gardener.' Millie was scrambling into her hat and coat, her face glowing with excitement. 'I ain't never had a holiday before.'

'Only four days. See she's back on time, David. I can't do without her for longer than that.'

It took David the rest of the day to make the arrangements for their journey. Sutton had readily agreed to Fred taking a few days off. May's father couldn't come because he would be working at the docks. Work was so hard to come by it was never turned down, not even one day. Johnny did a cartwheel when he heard about the trip.

There hadn't been time for David to see Gertie to tell her he would be away for a few days, and he hoped she wouldn't need him while he wasn't there.

Alex had provided his largest, most comfortable carriage. May was making a good recovery, but she was still delicate, and a short time in luxurious surroundings and with wholesome food would do her the world of good.

Early the next morning, an excited party clambered into the coach, eager to be on their way.

The sound of a carriage coming up the driveway had Alex striding towards the front door, and the staff gathering to welcome the guests.

Millie was first out, turning round and round, her eyes wide with wonder.

'Welcome to my home.' Alex watched her, his mouth turning up in amusement.

She spun to face him. 'Crumbs, is this all yours?'

'It is. Do you like it?'

'It's huge!' She eyed him carefully. 'You sure you ain't a lord?'

'Quite sure.'

'Hello, sir.' Fred joined them. 'Thanks for having us. This is some place you've got here. Ain't it smashing, Millie?'

'I'm glad you like it.' Alex stepped forward to greet the others now emerging from the carriage, reaching out to take the little girl from David. She was fast asleep.

'The excitement and the journey was too much for her.'

'We'll get her straight to bed, I think. How was your journey, Mrs James?'

'Oh, lovely, sir. We saw lots of sheep and other animals in the fields as we went by. May was so excited, she wore herself out.'

David smiled at Alex. 'You're going to have a lively time with all of us as guests. Fred and Millie are going to want to see every inch of the place.'

'And I shall be pleased to show them. It's time this house was filled with laughter again.'

May opened her eyes and pointed at a large tree. 'Rats!'

'No, May, that's a squirrel,' Alex told her gently, delighted to hear her speak so clearly.

'Not rats?' she asked, swivelling around in his arms so she could see the little things scampering along the branches. Then she yawned. 'Not rats. Never seen red rats.'

'Inside everyone,' Alex urged. 'Cook has a meal ready for you.'

There was a stunned silence once they were inside. The hall was very spacious and had a warm fire burning at the far end. The walls were papered in pale gold, and hung with paintings of the house and grounds. There was also a large oak hallstand just inside the door, gleaming with years of polishing, and a set of six chairs along the walls.

Fred was already running his hands over one piece of furniture after another, and his deep sigh of appreciation could be clearly heard.

'Mrs Green and Maude will show you to your rooms. Come down in an hour. The dining room is the door on the right.' He opened it to show them.

May's mother looked worried. 'Do we have to dress posh, sir? I ain't got nothing like that to wear.'

'You must do exactly as you would at home, Mrs James.'

'Oh, that's a relief.'

'Give me the little girl, sir.' The housekeeper was anxious to get the guests settled.

'Here's a chair on wheels for her,' David said, as a maid wheeled it in.

'That can stay here.' The housekeeper smiled tenderly at May. 'She's as light as a feather. We're going to have to feed you up, aren't we, young lady?'

'Custard,' May told her at the mention of food. 'Like custard.'

'Do you now? In that case I'll ask Cook to make you some.' The housekeeper glanced at Mrs James. 'If you'll

230

come with me, madam, I'll take you to your room. Maude, show the young lady and gentleman to their rooms.'

They all looked shocked and amused at being addressed in such a way, and it was too much for Millie. She giggled. 'Blimey, Fred, bet you didn't know you was a gentleman.'

'And you sure ain't no lady.'

They were all laughing as they made their way up the sweeping staircase. Even May's mother was more relaxed.

As they disappeared, Alex slapped David on the back. 'I expect you could do with a drink. Did you bring a dress suit with you?'

He followed Alex into the library. 'Yes.'

'Good. I've had an invitation to dine with the Chesters tomorrow, and you can join me. The invitation includes a guest, as well.'

'The Chesters?' David took the glass of whisky from him. 'Do you mean Lord and Lady Chester?'

Alex nodded, sipping his drink before he sat down. 'They have a house a short drive from here. Have you met them?'

'We did some business for Lord Chester once. He dabbled in shipping for a while, but he soon gave it up. He said it wasn't for him.' David frowned. 'Are you sure it will be all right for me to attend? I'm not exactly in their class, and they might object.'

'Don't put yourself down. You're as good, and better, than many I know. And you're not only my agent, but a friend as well. And –' he paused, giving a wry smile '– they have made it clear they would welcome me as a son-in-law, so I don't think they will snub my choice of guest.'

'Ah, what's the daughter like?'

'Attractive, charming, and an obedient girl.'

'Sounds like she'd make a perfect wife.'

'Hmm,' was all Alex said.

The door opened a crack and Millie peered in. 'Can we come in? There's someone who wants to see you.'

Alex nodded, the door opened wide and Fred wheeled May in, followed by Mrs James and Johnny.

The young boy couldn't contain himself as he rushed up to Alex. 'I got this huge room – all to myself. Blimey, Lord, you could get my whole street in it!'

'A slight exaggeration, I think. Do you mind being on your own?'

'Nah.' Johnny shook his head. 'It'll be nice, and Fred's next door. He said I can go in with him if I gets lonely. But I won't.'

'Good.' Alex turned his attention to May, who was staring round the room in wonder.

Mrs James knelt by her daughter, and said, 'May wants to show you what she can do now, sir.'

He waited as the little girl was helped out of the chair. Her mother held her upright, then whispered, 'Walk to the kind man, May.'

Alex crouched down and held out his hand. 'Come on, sweetheart.'

Fixing her gaze on Alex, May pushed her mother's hands away. She took a step forward, then another. There was no sign of the earlier difficulty. Although her steps were hesitant, she held herself straight, and her walk was normal.

'Good girl,' he encouraged gently. 'Just one more step.'

Little hands reached out and he caught hold of her, surging to his feet and swinging her high. She squealed with delight when everyone in the room began clapping.

'Good?' she asked.

'Very, very good,' he told her. 'You'll be running around in no time at all.'

'Hungry now.'

'Then we'd better eat.' He turned to the butler, who was standing just inside the door. 'Has Cook made the custard for May?'

'Yes, sir, and there's a splendid apple pie to go with it.'

'Ooh.' May struggled to get down. 'Walk.'

With David one side of her and Alex the other, May gripped their hands as they made their way to the dining room.

It was a lively meal and the servants had difficulty keeping their expressions neutral. But when they turned their backs it was obvious they were laughing. Johnny couldn't understand why he had so many knives and forks. Millie wanted to know what everything on the table was for, not at all subdued by the grand surroundings, and Fred was trying his utmost to make everyone behave themselves.

The servants enjoyed themselves immensely, answering the neverending questions, and instructing the guests how to use various pieces of cutlery.

By the time May had ended her meal with the promised custard, they were all having trouble keeping awake, even Millie.

The two men were soon left alone to enjoy a quiet drink. And they used the time to discuss shipping business, doubting they'd have another chance during the next few days.

Chapter Twenty-Five

The next morning it was only just getting light when Alex saw Fred wandering in the garden. He joined him. 'Good morning, Fred. Did you sleep well?'

'Morning, sir. Slept like a log in that lovely comfortable bed. It's so quiet here; didn't hear a sound until the birds woke me.'

'Does it fit your dream of living in the country?'

'Oh yes. Makes me even more determined.' He swept his arm out to encompass the open space. 'Me and Millie won't be able to have anything like this, of course, but a small place somewhere quiet will do nicely.'

'You intend to marry Millie?'

''Course. We've always been together, and don't want it no other way. Got to save up first, 'cos I ain't having my Millie slaving like our mums. No one should have to live like that. The people in streets like ours gets old before their time, and it ain't right. Most rich people don't care, and try to pretend we don't exist.' He glanced up at Alex. ''Cept you, but you're a rare gent.'

This was the longest speech he'd ever heard from the young boy, and Alex was impressed by his thoughtful intelligence. 'I agree that more should be done for the poor. What do you think the answer is?'

'Now you're asking.' He blew out a sharp breath. 'There ain't no quick answer. Education would be a big start. And those running the country need to be shown what it's really like living in the slums, often not knowing where the next meal's coming from, or if they're gonna be turned out on the street because they can't find the rent. I'll bet many haven't been further than Knightsbridge.'

'True.' Alex nodded, oblivious to the cold as they talked. 'So, apart from a good education for all, what else would you suggest?'

'Well, you could go into parliament. You've seen for yourself how we live, and you care enough to want to help. There ain't many of your class who feel like that. And you're big and tough enough to knock some sense into their heads.'

They were both laughing now as Alex shook his head. 'No, I think you're the one who should be in parliament.'

He snorted in amusement. 'What chance would I have?'

'Tell you what, Fred, I'll make you a promise. When you're twenty-five and think you might like a political career, come to me. I'll back you for election and see you damned well win.'

'That's some promise.' Fred eyed him intently. 'You serious?'

'Yes, and I never break my promises.'

'Then you got a deal.' He held out his hand. 'I might well keep you to that.'

'I hope you do. If there are going to be sweeping social reforms in the future then people like you need to make your voices heard.' He was determined to keep an eye on this bright, thoughtful boy. Given the chance, there was no telling what he could accomplish.

'Let's get some breakfast, shall we? Then I'll order the carriage and we'll make a tour of the estate.'

Falling into step beside Alex, he said, 'Carriage? How big is this place?'

'More than the eye can see.'

'Crumbs!'

'What a day.' David slumped in a chair and closed his eyes.

'Don't get too comfortable,' Alex warned. 'We're expected at the Chesters' house by eight.'

Pulling himself upright, he grimaced. Alex didn't look as if he'd done a thing all day as he stood by the fireplace, resplendent in evening clothes. 'Where do you get your energy? We've been over every inch of the house and estate. There's been a constant stream of questions from the youngsters, and I swear as soon as May's fully recovered she'll have to be put on a lead.'

'Come on.' Alex pulled him out of the chair. 'The carriage is here.'

Groaning, David stood up and rubbed his backside. 'I

shouldn't have ridden the horse. I might have to stand all evening.'

'True.' A deep chuckle echoed from Alex. 'You'd never make a cavalry soldier.'

The library door opened and the butler entered. 'You mustn't be late for your dinner engagement, sir.'

'We're on our way, Hunt.'

As soon as they entered the Chesters' house, David could see the anticipation in their eyes as they greeted Alex. Oh yes, they were definitely hoping to welcome him into their family. But he also saw genuine respect there, as well.

David was greeted warmly and he relaxed. The evening could be interesting after all. He couldn't wait to see the daughter.

They were escorted to the sitting room to meet the other guests. It was to be a select dinner party of only eight. There was a young girl standing with her mother, and when David looked at her he felt as if a horse had kicked him. She had the bluest eyes he'd ever seen, her hair shone like gold . . .

'This is our daughter, Miriam.' He heard the father's voice as if it came from a distance. 'My dear, this is Mr Gardener. He's Alexander's agent and friend.'

'I'm pleased to meet you, Mr Gardener. My father mentioned he had met you when he dabbled in shipping for a while.'

With an effort, David managed to respond. 'It's a pleasure to meet you, and yes, I remember helping your father.'

The rest of the evening was a blur. He joined in the conversation, talking politely to his dinner companions, but it was obvious Miriam Chester was interested in only one person – Alex.

Dismay was like a heavy weight on him. He'd never believed in love at first sight, but it had just happened to him. And he'd damned well better get over it. This girl was way out of his class. And how could Alex resist such a charming girl?

And there was another reason to make him feel sad. He'd known Alex would be looking for a wife, and deep down he'd hoped Gertie would have the sense to accept him. But she hadn't, and it was clear he'd now given up on her, and found a girl he would probably marry.

He groaned inwardly. What a couple of fools we are.

It was a relief when they were back in the library at Alex's house.

'Want a drink, David?'

'Thanks.' He loosened his collar and sat down. 'An interesting evening; the daughter is charming.'

'Indeed.' Alex handed him a large brandy.

'Have you known her long?'

'A while. Did you enjoy the evening?'

'Yes, they made me welcome.'

The door opened then and Fred came in carrying an armful of books. 'Oh, sorry, I didn't know you were back. Hope you don't mind, sir, but me and Millie have been reading your books.'

'That's what they're for.' Alex beckoned him in. 'What have you been reading?'

'Anything. We've just been taking the books off the shelves as they come. You've got all kinds of subjects here, and we learn something from everything we read. If we're gonna get out of the slums then we've got to know as much as possible. It's gonna be the only way. They chucked us both out of school at thirteen, you know.' He pulled a face. 'We didn't want to go, but they seemed to think we knew enough. Daft, of course. No one ever knows enough.'

They watched as the youngster put each book back in place, handling them with all reverence. When he'd finished he stood in the middle of the room, gazing at the books reaching from floor to ceiling. 'Miss would love this room. Has she got a library like this in her house, Mr Gardener?'

'Nothing like this.'

'Pity. You'd never get her out of here. Loves her books, she does.'

'She learnt to read at a very early age, and books have been her delight ever since,' David explained. 'She was so pleased with the one you and Millie gave her.'

'She came to the workshop to thank me. We're glad it gave her pleasure. It helps to know someone's thinking of you when times get rough. Night, sir. Night, Mr Gardener.'

'Goodnight, Fred.'

They watched him walk out and close the door quietly behind him. Both men sat in silence as they finished their drinks.

After a while David said, 'Those two youngsters have the most amazing outlook on life. There's a well of

240

kindness in them that puts me to shame, and yet their own lives have been ones of deprivation and hardship.'

'That's why they understand others' suffering. And Fred's a special boy. He's going far in life.'

'If he gets a chance, Alex.'

'I'll see he does.'

Chapter Twenty-Six

The weeks were slipping by, and although Florence was conscious, there was no further improvement in her condition.

Gertrude gazed out of the window at the rain. It was a deluge. Two weeks into February and it seemed to have been raining since the beginning of the month. To add to the depression, no more letters had been received from Edward. Her mother asked every day, and every day was disappointed. She could lie and pretend they'd heard from him, but that wouldn't be fair, and could lead to complications. If her mother believed Edward was contacting them regularly she might begin to question why he wasn't visiting her when she was so ill. She couldn't tell her he was in the army and miles away fighting a war. The doctor had warned them not to do or say anything that might make Florence become agitated, and if she knew where her son was she'd be frantic with worry.

Running a hand over her eyes, Gertrude stifled a sigh. The sleepless nights and continual worry were taking a toll on her health, and she didn't feel at all well this morning. She was weary beyond anything she had ever experienced before, and full of doubts. After long discussions with her father, they had decided to keep the news of where Edward was from her mother, but were they right to do so?

'Gertie, I've brought someone to see you.'

She spun round; surprised someone had entered the room without her hearing them. 'David, how . . . Millie! Don't you look smart, and it's lovely to see you again.'

'Hello, Miss.' Millie rushed up and took hold of her hands. 'Mr Gardener was coming to see you and I asked him to let me come with him. Me and Fred miss seeing you. You don't come to the office no more, and Fred said you haven't been to the workshop for ages.'

'I know, but Mother is dreadfully ill and I don't like to leave the house.'

'I've told her time and time again to go out.' Hanna came into the room. 'She deserves some time to herself, but do you think she listens to me? Hello, David . . . and you must be Millie. I've heard a lot about you.'

'You must be Aunt Hanna,' Millie said, smiling. 'I heard a lot about you, too.'

'Of course you have.' Hanna held out her hand. 'Pleased to meet you at last.'

They shook hands, then Hanna ordered them to sit down. 'I'll see tea is brought in.'

'We can't stay long.' David remained standing. 'I'm on my way to see Alex.'

'Ah yes, how is he?'

'Very well.'

'Good.' She left the room briefly to arrange for refreshments, and when she returned, she said, 'Do sit down, David. You can spare us half an hour, can't you?'

He sat.

Hanna gave a grunt of satisfaction, turning her attention back to Millie. 'And how are you getting on, young lady? Do you like your job?'

'Oh yes.' Gertrude's aunt didn't appear to intimidate Millie. 'It's a real good job, and I'm learning a lot. Fred's happy too. We're very lucky. Best thing that ever happened to us was when we met Miss.'

'I'm pleased for you.'

'What have you been doing, Millie?' Gertrude asked. 'Have you visited the bookshop lately?'

Millie smirked. 'Yes, and he don't throw us out now we've got a few coins in our pockets. We treated ourselves to a pot of tea one day in the teashop, and do you know, they remembered us. Ever so nice, they was. They asked after you.'

Gertrude laughed, remembering the happy times they'd spent together. It was only a few weeks ago, but it seemed a lifetime away. So much had happened in such a short time, and her life had changed beyond recognition.

'And we had a little holiday. We ain't never had one before. It was lovely. Sir sent his carriage for me, Fred, Johnny, May, and her mum. And Mr Gardener, of course. We stayed at Sir's house in the country.'

'Sir?' Hanna looked at David.

'Alex,' he told her.

Gertrude was astonished, not sure she'd heard correctly. 'You stayed at his house?'

'That's right.' Millie then launched into great detail about their visit. 'Little May's trotting around now, a bit slow, but steady as you like on her legs. The doc's gonna keep an eye on her while she grows, but he said she should be fine now. She loves Mr Gardener and laughs when he calls her sweetheart.'

'That's really good news, and so generous of Alex, isn't it, Gertie?' Hanna glanced pointedly at her niece.

'Very.' She nodded, even more stunned. It was hard to imagine Mr Glendale entertaining a group of children in his home.

The tea arrived then and Millie immediately took over the task of pouring. 'It looks like he's courting, don't it, Mr Gardener? Nice lady, you said.'

'She's quite lovely,' he said. 'I met her when we were staying with Alex.'

'Needs a nice wife.' Millie handed round the cups. 'Good man like that should have a family of his own.'

'Is this true, David?' Hanna asked. 'Has he settled on someone?'

'I would say so.'

'Then I'm pleased. He's wasted enough time waiting for someone else to show an interest.'

The conversation around Gertrude faded, and for the first time she saw what she had done – and why. It was the why that shook her the most. Her thoughts went back to the first time she's seen him. They'd been at a summer ball when her aunt had brought him over. She remembered watching as he walked towards them, his movements fluid and graceful for such a tall man. The shock she'd felt when he'd fixed his green eyes on her had sent a flare of panic through her. Never having experienced anything like it before, she had convinced herself she didn't like him, and wanted nothing to do with him. But that wasn't true. What she had felt was something quite different. It had been the strong pull of attraction – and perhaps more. She'd been too unworldly and inexperienced to recognise what had happened. It had taken the news of his interest in someone else to wake her up.

Her head swam as she admitted to herself how she really felt about him. She loved him, and had done so from the moment she'd seen him, and now she'd lost any chance of the happiness she might have had with him. It served her right! It was only what she deserved after the way she had treated him. She didn't blame him at all for wanting nothing else to do with her.

Gripping the arms of the chair, she bowed her head as faintness swept in.

'Gertie!' Her aunt was pushing her head between her knees. 'Come on, darling, don't faint. Deep breaths now . . . there's a good girl.'

'Take it easy, Miss, you're all right. We're all here.' Millie was kneeling in front of her.

'She's exhausted,' David said angrily. 'This has got to stop, Hanna. The burden is too much for her.'

Gertrude was aware of voices and hands holding her, but she was drained of all strength. The events of the

246

last few weeks had finally caught up with her.

'Yes, it is too much,' her father declared, as he rushed into the room. 'I've been selfish leaving her to deal with the medical bills, the business books, and staying with her mother. You're right, David, it's got to stop. And it will.'

She tried to tell her father that it was all right, but somehow the words wouldn't come.

Strong arms swept her out of the chair. 'You're going to bed for a long rest. I'm so sorry, my darling. I should never have allowed things to get so bad!'

The daylight was fading when Gertrude woke up. She sat upright, frowning. What was she doing in bed? There was so much to do.

'Oh, no you don't.' Her attempt to get out of bed was stopped. 'I've got my orders. You're staying here.'

'Millie! What on earth are you doing here?'

'Mr Gardener said I was to stay with you. You fainted.'

'I did not!'

'It's no good you arguing with me. You fainted and we're worried about you. They're all downstairs and I've got to go and tell them you're awake.' Millie wagged a finger at her. 'Don't you dare get out of bed while I'm gone.'

'I can't stay here. This is ridiculous. I'm perfectly all right.'

'The doc says you can't get up until tomorrow, and then only for a couple of hours.'

'The doctor wasn't called, surely?' She was horrified to have caused so much trouble.

'No, he came to see your mum, but he took a look at you as well. Your dad insisted. Beside himself with worry, he is, so stay in that bed,' Millie told her sternly, straightening the cover where Gertrude had tried to get up. 'I don't want to see one piece of bedding out of place.'

'Are you having trouble, Millie?' Sutton walked over to his daughter, his expression grim. 'Do as you're told, my darling.'

'Oh, Father, I'm so sorry, but I'm quite well now. I had a dizzy spell, that's all.'

'You are not all right. You've lost too much weight. I've disowned my son, my wife is seriously ill, and I will *not* watch you suffer because of my selfishness. I've been relying on my brave daughter to shoulder too much of the burden, and been too preoccupied to notice what was happening. That stops now! And I'm going to have a word with your mother. I know she's been frightening you by saying you could be left with nothing.'

'Father, you mustn't do anything to upset her.' She clasped his hand tightly. 'She probably doesn't know what she's saying.'

'There's nothing wrong with her mind, and she's got to be made to realise what she's doing to you.' He released her hand and strode out of the room.

'Oh, Millie,' she moaned. 'What a mess, and all because I had a dizzy spell.'

'And I want to know what caused it.' David came into the room, and put his hand on Millie's shoulder to make her stay where she was. 'Your father said I could see you, and I want to know why you suddenly keeled over.'

'I was overtired, that's all.'

'Don't lie to me, Gertie, I know you too well. You were perfectly fine when we arrived.'

'No I wasn't. I was trying not to show how unwell I was feeling.'

Fred's face appeared at the open door. 'Can I come in? Aunt Hanna said you needed cheering up.'

David beckoned him in. 'When did you arrive, Fred?'

'Just got here. I brought a message for Mr Melrose.'

'Well, I'm glad you're here. I'm trying to make Gertie tell us why she went all faint down there.'

'Aunt Hanna told me what you'd been talking about and it's easy to put two and two together.'

They all stared at him in amazement.

David collected chairs from around the room, placed them by the bed, then sat down with Millie and Fred on either side of him. 'Right, tell us what you think happened.'

'This is ridiculous,' Gertrude protested. 'Will you please stop this nonsense. Women faint sometimes, and I'm supposed to be resting.'

'Ignore her,' David said. 'Carry on, Fred. I want to hear your theory.'

'Yes, so do I.' Hanna joined them and sat on the end of the bed.

'I'm surrounded,' Gertrude groaned.

'Of course you are.' Hanna smiled at everyone gathered around. 'You're surrounded by people who love you, and we want to know what the devil that little episode was all about. Talk, Fred.'

'Well, you said Miss was real happy to see you all, and

there wasn't nothing wrong with her until you started talking about Sir. I reckon that's what upset her.'

All eyes fixed on her and she slid down in the bed. Fred was far too perceptive. How was she going to get out of this?

'I do believe you could be right.' David studied her closely. 'I thought you didn't like Alex?'

There was nowhere to hide, so she sat up straight. 'I can change my mind, can't I?'

'It's a bit late!' Hanna snorted inelegantly. 'Do you really think he is serious about this other girl, David?'

'It looks that way. She's the daughter of Lord Chester, and a charming girl.'

'Ah, yes, I've met her. Quite a beauty.'

'Absolutely lovely!'

'Oh, not you as well.' Catching the wistful note in David's voice, Hanna raised her hands in disgust. 'I swear the two of you need your heads banged together. I'll go and find out if dinner's ready. You'll stay and eat with us as well, Fred.'

Fred smirked as Hanna left the room. 'Everything sounds like an order from your aunt.'

'It is!' Gertrude looked at David, frowning. 'What was she talking about?'

'Your aunt doesn't miss much. She means that we've both chosen the wrong time and the wrong people to fall in love with.'

'Oh, you liked Lord Chester's daughter when you met. I'm so sorry. What a mess!' She rested back and closed her eyes. 'I had my chance and threw it away. There's no one to blame but myself, but if you're right, you'll never have a chance with the young lady.'

'I wouldn't even if Alex wasn't interested in her. I'm just an ordinary working man.'

'You're not ordinary!' she exclaimed angrily. 'You're an intelligent, loving man, and don't you dare think of yourself as unworthy!'

'There's a true friend talking.' He gave a wry smile, and then turned his attention to Fred and Millie, who had been listening with rapt attention. 'And if you tell Alex what's been said here today I'll never speak to you again! Is that understood?'

The youngsters nodded, then Millie said, 'We wouldn't do nothing to hurt either of you. We'll keep our mouths shut because we love you all.'

'That's right,' Fred declared. 'Millie's mum says no good comes from gossiping about other people. But you mustn't lose hope, as it might not work out with Sir and the lady.'

'You mean we must hold on to our dreams?' Gertrude said gently, touched by their affection.

'That's right.' Fred nodded. 'No one knows what's gonna happen in the future. Things often have a habit of working out for the best.'

'Not this time,' Gertrude murmured under her breath.

Chapter Twenty-Seven

The sea crossing had been purgatory. Edward had soon discovered he was not a good sailor, but the relief of standing once again on solid ground had been short-lived. He crouched behind a rock, listening to the officers shouting, and the men cursing. They'd run into an ambush on the way to a place called Ladysmith, which had been under siege by the Boers since early November.

Keeping low, he wriggled along, oblivious to bullets thudding around him. It was chaos, and he wondered how many of them would be alive after they got out of this. The Boers had the advantage of surprise and were making the most of the confusion. The British forces were scattered around a gully in small groups, and unless they re-formed he couldn't see how they could mount an organised attack.

Hearing an agonised scream, he turned in the direction it had come from. About thirty feet away was a group of soldiers, and one was holding his side, writhing in pain. It was Jack, who was little more than a boy. He'd been kind to Edward on the voyage and they'd become friends.

Anger flared through him. He was damned if he was going to let Jack die! He knew he was in the only relatively safe place, and the officers were doing all they could to get the men into the gully where there was some protection from the attack. Without giving it a second thought he scrambled to his knees, then in a crouched run he made for the isolated men.

'Ed, I'm hurt,' Jack gasped as Edward reached him.

'There's a medic in the gully. I'll take you there.' He gathered Jack up and put him over his shoulder, ignoring the cries of pain coming from his friend, and then he nodded to the other men. 'Follow me. You'll be picked off one by one if you stay here.'

Much to everyone's surprise they all made it back, and Jack was immediately taken from him.

'Come on men!' the sergeant bellowed. 'You saw that. These man made it safely and so can you!'

There was movement all over the hillside as men began to run, throwing themselves into the gully. It was frantic as encouragement was shouted to the running men. They lost a couple, of course, but not as many as expected. The majority came through safely.

'Well done, Melrose,' the sergeant said quietly. 'That was just the example we needed. Now perhaps we'll have a chance.'

'I wasn't going to let Jack die,' he ground out between clenched teeth.

'You could have got yourself killed, though.'

'Not a chance.' He couldn't keep the disgust out of his voice. 'I don't deserve a merciful end. I'd like to see how Jack is.'

'Go on, but don't be long.'

A first aid section had been set up just outside the firing line, and he saw Jack at once. A dressing was being applied to his side and he was grimacing in pain. Relief flooded through Edward. At least his friend was still alive. In his arrogance he'd discarded a life-long friend, David, and it was only now he realised how precious real friendship was. He wasn't going to make that mistake again.

'How is he?' he asked, sinking on to his knees beside Jack.

'He'll be all right.' The medic tied the dressing in place and patted Jack's shoulder. 'You'll do, soldier. The bullet went right through, and I don't think any permanent damage has been done.'

'It bloody hurts,' Jack complained.

'Of course it does, but you'll heal. If you'd stayed on that hill you'd have probably bled to death.'

Jack reached out to grasp Edward's arm. 'Thanks Ed, that was damned brave of you. I'm in your debt. You let me know if there's anything I can ever do for you.'

'You looked after me on the ship when I was as sick as a dog. You don't owe me a thing. Any of the men would have done the same. I got to you first, that's all.'

Jack's face clouded with worry. 'Are we going to get out of this, Ed?'

'Of course we are. The regiment's re-formed now and we'll attack. I must get back or I'll be in trouble with the sergeant.'

Over the next couple of weeks many attempts were made to break the siege, and finally, at the end of February, they were successful.

Edward was bone weary as they rode into Ladysmith. Many of the men he'd started out with had been killed, but he had the satisfaction of knowing that Jack had been moved to a safe area to recover from his wounds. Jack reminded him of David, and the thought of home jolted him. He must try and get a letter to his mother. He'd promised Glendale he would write, and he hoped to God she was still alive. The thought of what he'd done to his family was like an open wound that wouldn't heal.

The next day he was ordered to the officers' quarters. He marched in, wondering what he'd done wrong, and was surprised to see the commander there, with other officers, and the sergeant.

'At ease, Melrose.'

He did as ordered, and waited, trying to bring to mind whatever misdeed he had committed.

'Your acts of heroism have been brought to our attention and verified. Your bravery is deemed worthy of the Victoria Cross. Congratulations, Melrose, you are a credit to the regiment. There will be a presentation parade in two days' time.'

It took every ounce of Edward's control to stop himself from bursting into hysterical laughter. A medal? Bravery?

Heroism? If they only knew the truth; he didn't care if he lived or died! Only someone who didn't value his life would have taken the chances he had. He wasn't brave – he was a coward.

He snapped to attention and said the words he knew they all expected. 'Thank you, sir. It's a great honour.'

The sergeant followed him out and Edward glared at him. 'Was this your doing?'

'You deserve it for saving Jack Pendleton, not to mention all the other things you've done. Three men are still alive because of you.'

'It's a farce!' Edward shook his head. 'I was trying to get myself killed!'

'You might believe that, but I don't. Some men freeze under fire, unable to function properly. They can't help it; it's in their nature. But I've watched you closely. Your mind stays clear, and only after giving a situation careful consideration do you act. You're still alive because you made the right decisions at the right time. Not only are you a good soldier, but you also have the mark of an officer. The army is where you belong.'

'I certainly don't belong anywhere else.' Not having a place to call home had left a gaping hole in his life – an emptiness he doubted could ever be filled.

'Then make the army your life,' the sergeant suggested. 'There's a place here for you, and if you continue in the way you've started, respect and advancement could be yours. Think about it.'

Watching the sergeant march away, he thought of what the man had said. Respect was something he didn't feel he deserved, and was out of the question when he couldn't respect himself. But perhaps he could climb up the ranks? He had nowhere else to go, and much to his surprise, he did seem to fit into army life. He enjoyed the comradeship, and had taken the danger, harsh conditions and discipline in his stride. The future had never entered his head, but perhaps he did belong here. For the time being, anyway.

'Hi, Ed, I hear they're giving you a medal.'

He spun round and a smile of real pleasure spread across his face. 'Jack! I thought you'd be on your way home by now.'

'No, they've decided I'm fit enough to fight again. I hear you've been doing crazy things while trying to break the siege.' Jack slapped him on the back. 'Come on, I'll buy our hero a drink.'

'Don't call me that!' Edward snapped.

'From what I've heard it's a miracle you didn't get yourself killed. Let's get that drink. I'm gasping.'

'It's only ten in the morning.' Edward fell into step beside his friend. 'But seeing it's a celebration to mark your return, I'll have one with you.'

Others soon joined them, and it turned into quite a party.

By the time Edward settled down late that evening to write a couple of letters, he was beginning to think the sergeant was right. This was now his home, and the regiment was his family. But even accepting that, he didn't relish the thought of spending years as a soldier. What choice did he have, though?

Quite a few of the men had most of their pay sent to

someone in England, and he had decided to do the same. The money was going to David, with instructions for it to be given to his father. It was a meagre amount and would make little difference to the debt he'd left behind him, but he would feel as if he were doing something.

The first letter was to David, urging him to make his father take the money. If he refused, then he was to give it to his sister to use as she thought necessary. Gertie had a wise head and he knew he could trust her to do what was best for her family. He also asked forgiveness from David for not listening to him when he'd tried to stop him gambling. He ended by saying he would be pleased to hear from him with news of what was happening in London.

The next letter was to Alexander Glendale, telling him about the campaign to break the Ladysmith siege, knowing that as an ex-soldier he would be interested. He also thanked him for coming to the ship before they'd embarked, and hoped the short note had given his mother some comfort. He said nothing about the medal to either of them.

After sealing the letters he sat back, feeling more at peace than he'd done for some time. He could never undo the damage, or heal the distress he'd caused, but hoped they would see he was trying to reform and help.

'You still up, Ed?' Jack sat beside him and eyed the letters. 'Been writing to your girl, have you?'

'No, just keeping a promise I made before we sailed.'

Jack peered at one of the names. 'Glendale? Do you know him?'

'Yes. Why, do you?'

'No, never met him, but he was an army officer. Got a reputation for being tough, but they say his men would have walked through hell for him.'

'I can understand that.' Edward glanced at Jack. 'What have you been up to? Shouldn't you be in bed?'

'Been having a game of cards with some of the men.'

'How much did you lose?' Edward asked dryly.

'Came out about even.' Jack rattled the coins in his pocket and grinned. 'I've never seen you playing. I'll teach you if you don't know how.'

'No thanks,' Edward said firmly. 'I'm too well-acquainted with a pack of cards, and have learnt my lesson. I'll never gamble again. So you be careful, Jack.'

'Ah, lost a lot, did you?'

'Too much. It cost me my family, home, and everything I loved. I've been disowned, and that's why I've ended up here.'

'Oh, I'm sorry, Ed.'

'So am I!'

Chapter Twenty-Eight

'Good Lord!' David handed the letter back to Alex. 'I've just received a letter from Edward and he never mentioned that.'

'Sergeant Harris wanted me to know because I asked him to keep an eye on Edward. He's distinguished himself.'

'He has, and he isn't saying anything. I wonder why? The Edward I knew would have been shouting his achievements from the rooftops.'

'I doubt he's the same person now. I suspect he doesn't see himself as a hero, and doesn't feel he deserves to be given a medal. I've seen it before. Some men carry out the most courageous deeds, and then wonder what all the fuss is about when they're honoured. Harris is impressed, and as you read, considers Edward a fine soldier, and eventually officer material.'

Standing up, David began to pace, deep in thought, and

then he stopped. 'His mother would be proud of him. I think she should now be told the truth.'

'Is she well enough?'

'She's made progress over the last few weeks and is now able to sit in a chair for part of the day. Walking is still a problem, but there's more hope of a good recovery.'

'I'm pleased to hear it.'

Sitting down again, David drew in a deep breath. 'I'll discuss this when I visit Gertie and her father this evening. Edward has made arrangements for some of his pay to come to me – I received the first amount yesterday – and he's given me the task of persuading his father to accept it.'

'That won't be easy,' Alex remarked.

'No, but I've got to try and make him. Not only has Edward been honoured for bravery, but also he's trying to help with the financial situation. It isn't much, but it's all he's got, and the gesture should be respected.'

'It should, and I also agree that it's time to tell Mrs Melrose where her son is, and what he's doing. But that decision will be up to her family, of course.'

'I don't look forward to telling Sutton, but I know I'll have Gertie's support. She's the only one who could make him take the money.'

'You're quite right.' Alex handed him the sergeant's letter. 'Show him this. It might help.'

'Thanks.'

'You have young visitors, sir,' the butler announced on entering the library.

'And who might they be?' Alex asked, knowing full well who had arrived.

'It's us!' called a high-pitched voice. 'You said we could come to Sunday tea.'

David chuckled, recognising the voice.

'Ah, so I did. Show them in.'

The door swung open and in tumbled Johnny, May, Fred and Millie.

May gave a whoop of delight as soon as she spotted David and headed straight for him, arms outstretched.

'Hello, sweetheart.' He crouched down and waited for the little girl to reach him. The change in her was remarkable. Not only was she now walking freely and with hardly a trace of a limp, but also her cheeks were rosy and her speech was improving all the time.

'Davy,' she giggled. 'You have tea too?'

'Of course he will.' Alex had tucked Johnny under his arm, making the boy squeal with delight. 'I'll just take this one to Cook so he can tell her what he wants.'

Then he strode out of the room, leaving everyone else laughing. Even the butler's mouth was twitching.

'He's so strong,' Millie said admiringly, 'and quite good looking when he laughs.'

'Davy too!' May told them. 'Me marry him.'

'Now you're in trouble, Mr Gardener,' spluttered Fred as he ruffled May's hair. 'You're too young to be thinking of marriage.'

'I grow,' she told him, indignant at having her hair messed up. 'All better now.'

'You certainly are.' David sat her on a comfortable chair. 'You come and see me when you're eighteen.'

The little girl nodded and grinned triumphantly at Fred.

Johnny erupted back into the room, followed closely by Alex. 'It's all ready! You ought to see what we've got. I ain't never seen so much grub.'

It turned out to be the noisiest couple of hours David could ever remember, and he'd never seen Alex so relaxed. He hadn't mentioned how things were going with Miriam Chester, but David assumed the courtship was progressing satisfactorily. He decided he didn't really want to know, either, because the picture of that lovely girl was etched in his mind and heart.

Later that evening, David was shown into the sitting room where Gertrude was curled up in a chair, lost in a book she was reading. He was sorry he had to disturb her, because she looked so relaxed. She had completely recovered from her fainting spell and was much more her usual self. Her father had kept his word and lifted some of the burden from her, but she was still doing more than her fair share of the work. And knowing her as he did, he was certain no one could stop her. It was rare to find her relaxing, and the sight pleased him.

'Good evening, Gertie.'

She started, looked up and smiled, scrambling to her feet. 'David! I didn't hear you come in.'

He gave her a gentle hug. 'Good book?'

'You know me when I'm reading. The world could come to a stop and I wouldn't know. Sit down. Have you had anything to eat?'

'Plenty. Alex gave a tea party for May, Johnny, Fred and Millie. Then I had a quiet dinner with him so we could discuss business. He doesn't stop working for anything, not even on a Sunday.'

She turned away, but not before he'd seen the flash of sadness at the mention of Alex. He knew how she felt, but what was done couldn't be changed, and she knew that. Alex had waited, hoping she would come to like him, but he'd given up on her now and was getting on with his life. And they both had to follow his example.

'Is your father in? I've got to see him.'

'He's in his study. Has something happened? You look concerned.'

'I have some news, and I'm not sure how your father's going to take it.'

'Edward?'

'Yes, but don't be alarmed. I've heard from him and there are things your father should know.'

'But am I going to want to hear them?' Sutton walked into the room and shook David's hand.

'That's something I don't know.' He glanced backwards, and then pulled a face. 'I'll keep the door right behind me if you don't mind, in case I need to make a hasty retreat.'

'You're quite safe,' Sutton laughed. 'Today Florence did a complete circuit of her room, using only a cane for support, so I'm in a good mood.'

'Oh, I'm very relieved.'

'We all are.' He settled in an armchair, smiled at his daughter, and then turned his attention back to David. 'So, what's this news?'

'I've received a letter from Edward, and so has Alex.' He decided to give them the news about the medal before mentioning the money. He handed Sutton the letter received from the sergeant. 'Edward has distinguished himself,' he pointed out, as the silence stretched.

'What is it, Father?' Gertrude was on her feet. 'May I see the letter?'

Without a word he handed it to his daughter, his expression unreadable.

'This is wonderful!' she exclaimed, as she looked at her father with pleading eyes. 'He's trying to make something of himself, and Mother should be told.'

Her father's mouth thinned in a straight line. 'And I suppose he's told you what a great hero he is?'

'No, there's no mention of any of this in my letter or the one Alex received from him. We wouldn't have known about it if the sergeant hadn't sent that report.'

David paused. It was clear Sutton wasn't going to forgive his son even if he had won a commendation for bravery. Now for the difficult part. 'Edward has made arrangements for regular payments to be sent to me. I received the first payment yesterday. He knows he will never be forgiven for what he's done, but he urges you to accept this small amount of money. He will never be able to repay you, of course.'

'Damned right!'

David held out the envelope and Sutton ignored it. 'If you don't take it, I'm to give it to Gertie, but it would be a merciful gesture if you'd accept.'

'Please.' Gertrude reached out for his hand, pleading in her eyes. 'Think how happy this would make Mother. Her son hasn't just been awarded a medal; he's received the Victoria Cross!'

'That's the highest honour,' David pointed out, knowing they had to emphasise that. Sutton had been badly hurt, mentally and physically, by his son's disastrous gambling. And his wife's illness because of the worry must make forgiveness almost impossible. 'Edward is leaving himself very little to exist on. Please allow him to do this.'

Giving a brief nod, Sutton took the envelope from David. 'I'll accept this for six months only, after that it must stop. I don't want his money, but I'll accept it for my wife's sake. It will comfort her to know he's making this gesture.'

David breathed a silent sigh of relief. It was only a partial acceptance, but he hadn't been sure Sutton would take anything from the son who had caused his family such terrible grief and hardship.

'Thank you, Father.' Gertrude stood up and leant over to kiss his forehead. 'Can we tell Mother now?'

'Yes, I think we must.' He stood up. 'You come as well, David.'

Florence was sitting in a chair beside the bed, and David was pleased to see her smile when they entered. She was looking much better.

She held out her hand to him. 'David, how lovely to see you. Gertrude tells me you have a new job. You must tell me all about it.'

'In a moment, my dear.' Sutton sat on the edge of the bed, and cradled his wife's hand in his. 'We have good news for you.'

'Oh.' Her eyes flicked from one face to the other. 'Is it about Edward?'

'Yes, and before we start we must apologise for keeping certain details from you, but we feel you are now strong enough, so David will tell you the whole story.'

No wonder he'd been asked to come as well. Edward's father was still unwilling to talk about his son.

'Start from the beginning, and don't leave anything out,' he was urged.

After a short pause to collect his thoughts, he began with his own futile search, and then the result of Alex's help.

Florence listened to every word, her eyes never leaving his face, as the story of what had happened to her son unfolded. 'The Victoria Cross,' she gasped.

'Yes, Mother.' Gertrude held out the letter. 'Would you like to read what the sergeant says about him?'

She took the letter eagerly, reading it through twice, and then again. After that she folded it carefully. 'Do you think Alexander would mind if I kept this, David?'

'I'm sure he'd be happy for you to have it.'

'Thank him for me, and tell him I'm grateful for the help he's given our family. What our son did was a terrible thing, but he's trying to redeem himself, and that must be respected.' She looked pointedly at her husband.

When his only response was a slight nod of the head, she continued, sounding more like the woman she'd been before her illness. 'I know it will be hard for you to forgive him, my dear, but at least recognise his desire to make amends. Accept his money with good grace, and a note of acknowledgement from you would be welcomed, I'm sure.'

'Whatever you say, my dear.'

'No! Don't do it just to please me, Sutton. It must come from your heart, and if that is impossible, then don't do it. I'll write to him myself. Our wayward son is in great danger, and we might never see him again. I won't have him going to his grave believing his family hate him. I won't have it!'

Alarmed, Gertrude was on her feet. 'He won't, Mother. Please don't upset yourself. We'll all write to him. Won't we, Father?'

'Of course. I'll write, acknowledging his achievements, but you must know that I will *not* have him back in this house again ever.' He raised his hands by way of an apology to his wife. 'I promise I'll write accepting his money, but that's all I'm prepared to do.'

She nodded, giving a sad smile. 'That is enough for the moment. Now, I think we should all have a drink to mark and honour a VC valiantly won.'

Chapter Twenty-Nine

'What are we going to do?'

'We have to go.' Gertrude chewed her lip as she turned the invitation card over and over in her hands. 'Do you really think this is to announce the engagement between Alexander and Miriam?'

'Yes, it must be.' David nodded grimly. 'The Chesters are walking around with smiles on their faces. Alex is the catch of the year, and this lavish Spring Ball is the perfect way to announce a forthcoming marriage. It's going to be damned uncomfortable for both of us.'

'We'll just have to smile and offer the happy couple our congratulations.' She gave her friend a sympathetic glance. 'It's going to be worse for you. I had my chance and messed it up, but you fell in love with a girl you've never been able to get near because there was a tall, powerful man standing in the way.'

'I wouldn't have stood a chance with her, anyway, but it doesn't change the way I feel.'

'You mustn't believe that,' she said sharply. 'You're a fine man, and any girl with an ounce of sense would be honoured to become your wife.'

Suddenly he grinned. 'The way things are going we could end up marrying each other.'

'Now you're being silly,' she scolded. 'You're my substitute brother and best friend. If we tried to be romantic with each other we'd never be able to stop laughing.'

'You're right, of course.' He became serious again. 'But you still haven't come up with an idea of how we can avoid this function.'

'We can't. Mother's health is steadily improving since we told her about Edward, and she's determined to attend. This ball will be her first social outing. She's excited about attending, and Father believes the outing will do her a world of good. You know how she's always enjoyed such occasions. I have to go,' she said gently, 'and I would appreciate having your company. And anyway, it will look very strange if you're not there. It's common knowledge how well you're doing as Alexander's agent, and how close you've become. Everyone will expect you to be there.'

He nodded. 'There's no way out. It will be a glittering affair. Do you and your mother have any jewellery left?'

'Not a piece between us.' Gertrude gave a wry smile. 'Perhaps we'll start a new, unadorned, fashion.'

She was making a joke of it, but David knew their lack of jewels would be noticed. 'What about gowns?'

'We still have those we wore at New Year. Mother has

lost weight, but I've altered hers, and it fits well now.'

'You're also slimmer, Gertie.'

'I've made mine fit, as well. We don't care what others think. These last months have been a nightmare, but we've come through. Mother's almost back to full health, the business has been steadily growing. We're even making a small profit now.' She leant forward, eyes shining with triumph. 'We're winning, David. Against all the odds we're winning! Do you believe we care what other people think or say about us?'

His heart lifted in admiration for her and the family he loved. Every material possession had been sacrificed to give Florence the best medical care – even Hanna's jewellery had gone to help. But the joy of seeing Florence once again running the house, laughing, and encouraging them in their efforts, was the only reward they needed. Gertie was right – what other people thought was of no importance.

'You'll both shine brighter than any jewels.'

'We intend to. Now –' she gave an impish smile – 'your invitation is for Mr Gardener and guest, so who are you taking? You need a pretty girl on your arm.'

'I thought of asking Millie,' he joked, 'but I'm not sure Fred would allow that.'

'What a splendid idea!' She went over to the mantelpiece and picked up her own invitation. 'Mother and Father are on one card, and my invitation is the same as yours. I could invite Fred to be my escort. What do you think?'

Tipping his head back, he roared with laughter. 'What a stir that would cause!'

'Do we care?' Then her amusement faded. 'I've never met the Chesters, but I hear they are very *proper,* and I can't understand why we've been invited. You are included because of your connection with Alexander, but why us?'

'I suspect that's Alex's doing. Although the ball is being given by Lord and Lady Chester, it's to be held in Alex's London home because of the large ballroom.'

'Oh.' She studied the card. 'I didn't notice that, but I still don't understand why he should invite us. Since Edward's gambling came to light we have withdrawn from society.'

'Perhaps he thinks it's time you rejoined the social round. And he likes you, Gertie. All of you.'

'I'm aware he likes Mother and Father, but not me. I'm so ashamed every time I remember the disgraceful way I've treated him. He's done so much for us, and I haven't even had the decency to acknowledge it. I should have at least written him a note, but I didn't. I'm not a very nice person, am I?'

'Nonsense! You were uneasy about him from the moment you met, and since then you've been under enormous strain. I'm sure he understands that, and he's not the kind of man to hold a grudge,' he told her gently.

'You all talk about him as if he's perfect – some kind of saint.'

'Oh no,' he laughed. 'He has many faults, just like the rest of us, but when you get to know him you realise he is a man of high ideals, having his own standards of right and wrong. He's respected, but many are wary of him. Discipline governs his life – and that includes self-discipline.'

'It would be interesting to see him lose control just once and glimpse the hidden man.'

'You wouldn't like to see it, and if that ever happens I'll run for cover,' he joked.

'You do exaggerate,' she told him. 'Back to the subject in hand. What are we going to do about our guests?'

'Take Millie and Fred.'

'We can't, I was only joking.' She took a swipe at him, missing as he ducked. 'Be serious.'

'I am. Think how they'd enjoy the evening. I'll see they're suitably dressed. Come on, Gertie, this is going to be a difficult evening for both of us, so let's have some fun. At least Millie and Fred will make us laugh.'

'Hmm, you're right.' She thought for a moment, and then chuckled. 'All right, let's do it. They can only chuck us out.'

'They won't do that. Fred and Millie polish up quite nicely.' He leapt up and kissed her cheek. 'You're the best friend a man can have. And it's lovely to see your bright smile again.'

'You look splendid, Mother.' Gertrude checked the dress from all angles. 'And the cane Fred made you is very elegant.'

Florence ran her hand over it and smiled. 'Yes, it's quite beautiful. He's a very talented boy, and your father is impressed with his work.'

'I most certainly am.' Sutton walked into the room. 'You both look absolutely beautiful. You've done a wonderful job with the gowns, Gertie. Now, the carriage

David ordered for us has arrived, so we should be on our way.'

While her parents talked quietly, she watched the passing scenery, wondering what the evening held in store. She hadn't heard from David about their idea for escorts, so she'd assumed nothing had come of it. That was a shame really, though hardly surprising. But it would have been fun to have Fred and Millie's lively company at the ball.

Glancing at her mother, she felt a warm glow of pleasure. She still needed support when walking, and tired easily, but was much improved. The doctor was now hopeful of a full recovery, but keeping her free from worry was still their main concern. However, it was becoming obvious her mother had changed. There was a quieter, almost serene air about her at times. She talked about her son with pride as she acknowledged his heroic achievements, but his past was never mentioned, and they were happy to keep it that way. She was proud of her son, and it was the only thing that mattered. As long as her mother was happy then she would continue to improve.

'Aren't we rather early?' Florence asked her husband.

'A room has been set aside for you so you can rest before your grand entrance,' he teased affectionately. 'And you may retire there at any time during the evening should you feel overtired.'

'How very thoughtful.' She nodded at her husband and daughter. 'I do tire easily, but the doctor said I'll get stronger.'

'Of course you will, my dear. You're almost back to full health, and we're very proud of you. Ah, here we are.'

Sutton helped his wife out of the carriage, then bent his head and whispered in her ear, 'Are you ready to be congratulated by everyone on your recovery? Not only will all be pleased to see you again, but your son's exploits have been in the newspapers.'

Gertrude went to the other side of her mother, sad to hear her father referring to Edward as her son, and not theirs. Most of the reports about the breaking of the Ladysmith siege had mentioned the names of those honoured in battle. Copies of the papers were now her mother's treasured possessions.

Florence's head came up, her carriage upright as they made their way up the flight of steps to the entrance. As soon as they were inside, her parents were shown to a room on the ground floor, and with an hour to pass before the festivities began, she made her way to the library.

The level of noise hit her as she opened the door. The scene inside was unbelievable. A small boy was tearing around the room, being pursued by an even smaller girl, who was screaming at the top of her voice.

David was in the middle of the chaos, laughing, and when he saw Gertrude, he scooped up the little girl. 'Quiet Johnny!' he yelled. 'We have a visitor.'

The boy skidded to a halt, making a valuable-looking vase on a nearby table wobble dangerously. Gertrude lunged at it, managing to steady it before it crashed to the floor. 'Phew!'

'Well caught, Miss.'

She turned to face two people she hardly recognised.

'It's us,' Millie giggled, as she sketched a curtsy. She was wearing a simple white dress embroidered with blue forget-me-nots. 'Don't we look grand. We're coming to the ball.'

'You look stunning!'

'Mr Gardener got the clothes for us,' Fred told her, before spinning round. He was wearing full evening dress, and he appeared to have shot up suddenly. He was now taller than her. 'What do you think?'

'My goodness, Fred, you look quite the young gentleman.' She glanced questioningly at David.

'I put the idea to Alex and he was in full agreement. What do you think of your escort for this evening?'

She slipped her arm through Fred's. 'I'm honoured, sir.'

'Me too, Miss Melrose.'

'Oh, and this bundle of mischief is May.' David put the little girl down. 'And the noisy one's Johnny.'

'Hello,' she said, stooping down as they came to see her. 'Are you coming to the ball, as well?'

'Nah, we're too young,' Johnny told her, 'but Lord's found a place for us upstairs where we can see everything.'

'Lord?'

'He insists Alex must be a lord,' David told her.

'Ah.' Feeling a tug at her sleeve, she saw May pulling at a piece of gold satin ribbon. 'Do you like that?'

'Pretty.'

Carefully unthreading the desired piece of ribbon, she handed it to the little girl, who took it from her as if it were the most precious thing in the world.

'Ooo, ta.' May held it up to Johnny. 'Look, tie in my hair.'

'I'll do it, sweetie, come here.'

May stood patiently while a perfect bow was arranged in her fair hair. When it was done she gave Gertrude a sweet smile, and then ran over to David. 'Look!'

He made a great show of being overwhelmed by the beauty of it, making the girl shriek with glee.

'What is going on here?'

Everyone stopped talking, and turned to face the woman who had just come into the library.

'What are these children doing here, Mr Gardener?' Her mouth turned down with displeasure at the sight.

Before David had a chance to answer, Alex strode in. 'They are my friends – and my children, Lady Chester, and are here at my invitation.'

The woman was lost for words as she stared at Alex. Then she recovered and gave a girlish laugh. 'You're teasing, Alexander.'

'I assure you I'm not. Allow me to introduce you. Have you met Miss Melrose?'

'No. How do you do?'

'It's a pleasure to meet you, Lady Chester.' She was wearing so many diamonds it was hard not to blink in the glare.

'David, you already know,' Alex continued. 'This is Millie and Fred. The young boy with jam around his face is Johnny – and the delightful little girl is May.'

Alex stooped down and held out his hands. 'Show everyone how well you walk now, sweetheart.'

May fairly ran into his arms, her smile as wide as it could get. He swept her up. 'My goodness, don't you look beautiful with the gold ribbon in your hair.'

She swivelled round and pointed at Gertrude. 'Pretty lady gave me. From dress.'

'That was very kind of her. Did you thank her?' She nodded vigorously.

'Your suit will get crumpled. You should put the child down.' Lady Chester moved closer to Alex. 'Is she . . . er . . . clean?'

'Course she is.' Johnny had sharp ears and was indignant. 'We all are! Lord sent men to our street and they fum . . .' he screwed up his face in concentration. 'What's the word?'

'Fumigated,' David told him.

'That's right. They got rid of the bugs. We're as clean as you now, ain't we, Lord?'

'You most certainly are.' He rested his hand on top of the agitated boy's head. 'Daisy will be coming for you any minute now, Johnny. You and May go with her. She'll stay with you for an hour and then a carriage will take you both home. I've found a good vantage point for you on the balcony where you will be able to see the ballroom. There's food there for you, as well.'

'Lovely!'

'Jelly?' May wanted to know.

'Lots.' Alex put the child down and Johnny took hold of her hand.

'We must go, Alexander,' Lady Chester said. 'Our guests are beginning to arrive.'

As they left the room, Gertrude was calling herself every nasty name she could think of. How could she have been such a fool? He was everything she admired in a man, and she had recognised it too late.

Chapter Thirty

'Mrs Jenkins!' Alex called as he stormed along the passage. Where the devil was his housekeeper when he needed her?

'Alexander!' Lady Chester caught up with him, out of breath. 'We have to greet the guests.'

'You and your family do it, Lady Chester. It's your function. Mrs Jenkins! Where the devil are you?'

'Here, sir.' She was running as fast as her ample size would allow.

The butler and footman had also arrived, alerted by their master's raised voice.

'I only want Mrs Jenkins, not the whole damned house!' he growled, sending the men running for cover.

'I'm here, so will you tell me what you want me to do, sir?'

'Go to the library and take your workbox. Miss Melrose needs gold ribbon for the sleeve of her dress. She pulled it out and gave it to May for her hair. Be quick. I won't have her walking into the ballroom like that. And tell David Gardener to meet me in my private sitting room. Now!'

The butler had reappeared but was standing at a safe distance from his furious master. 'You are expected in the ballroom, sir.'

'I'll get there when I'm good and ready!' He spun on his heel and took the stairs three at a time.

The door of the library burst open and the housekeeper hurried in. 'Mr Gardener, the master wants to see you in his sitting room at once.'

Glancing at the clock, he frowned. 'What's he doing there? The evening is about to get under way.'

'I don't know, sir, but he's in a powerful rage. I wouldn't waste any time if I were you.' She put down her work basket and ran a hand over her hair. 'And be careful. It's rare for him to lose his temper, but when he does it's best not to question his orders.'

David left the room at a run.

Gertrude watched in amazement, wondering what on earth was going on.

'Now, Miss Melrose, I've been ordered to repair your dress.'

'Oh, it doesn't matter.' She touched the sleeve. 'No one will notice me.'

'It will only take a moment. I have some ribbon. Not the same, but I can change it in both sleeves so they will match.' The housekeeper began to work quickly, and the job was soon done.

'There, that's better.' She stood back to study her work, and then pursed her lips. 'The dress needs something at the neck.'

'I don't have anything. But I thought it looked all right.'

'I think we can improve it. We need to bring attention to your graceful long neck.' More ribbon was removed from the basket, plaited, and tied around Gertrude's neck with a bow at the side.

'That's ever so pretty.' Millie had been watching with great interest. 'You're clever, Mrs Jenkins.'

'Thank you, Millie.' She inspected her handiwork one more time, and nodded in satisfaction. 'I just hope the master feels the same way or this household is in for a stormy couple of days.'

'Has he really lost his temper?' Fred looked as if he couldn't believe it.

'I'm afraid so.'

'But he was all right when he was here,' he pointed out. 'He was laughing and joking.'

'Well he isn't now. Something has upset him.'

'Hmm, wonder what it was.' Fred pulled a face at Millie.

'You wanted to see me?' David stopped just inside the door. Alex was pacing the room, and did not look at all like the controlled man he'd come to know.

'She isn't wearing any jewellery.' His voice resonated with anger.

'Pardon?'

'Why is Gertrude wearing an old gown and not one item of jewellery?'

'The gown isn't old. I believe it's only been worn twice.' David wished Alex would stand still. It was unnerving. 'And she hasn't any jewellery left.'

'What about her mother?'

'It's all been sold to pay the medical bills.'

The language that poured forth from him was astounding.

'Alex! What's this all about?'

'I told you to bring me anything she wanted to sell. I haven't seen any since the first lot, and I assumed they were managing to keep hold of their jewels.'

'Gertie dealt with the rest of the sales herself.'

'And got less than it was worth!' Alex's fists clenched. 'That girl's too independent.'

'I wouldn't consider that a fault,' David pointed out.

Alex took a deep breath as he tried to reign in his temper. 'No, you're right.'

Relieved to see he was calming down at last, he said nothing more, as a package was handed to him.

'Give this to her.'

David knew what it was, and at the risk of making Alex erupt again, he shook his head and placed it back on the table. 'I can't.'

'I'll bloody well do it myself!' He swept up the package and headed for the door.

'Don't!'

When Alex spun round to face him, David had to gather up every piece of courage he had to face down this powerful man. 'She doesn't know you've got any of her jewellery. You'll insult her.'

'That is not my intention. I only want her to have what is rightly hers.'

'And if you do that you'll take away what little pride she has left.'

'Explain.'

'Right from a toddler, she's had to do things for herself.' David smiled, remembering the happy times they'd spent together as children. 'She would stand in front of Edward and myself, jumping up and down and saying – I'll do it! I'll do it.'

'And your point is?'

'All her life she's been cocooned within a loving family, and although intelligent in a bookish way, she's never been very worldly. Do you know what I mean?'

Alex nodded.

'When this disaster struck her family she found herself in a world she'd never experienced before. She floundered, not knowing what to do. That's why she ran to me seeking advice and help. The love she feels for her parents has kept her going, but as you know, she collapsed under the strain. This crisis has forced her to grow up quickly and face each challenge. She's done that and knows what things are important and what is of no value.' At least Alex was listening, and he had to make him understand. 'Her mother is well enough to attend this function. The fact they have to wear last season's gowns and are without jewels does not matter in the least. The Melrose family are happy tonight. Please don't spoil that for them.'

The man in front of him walked back to his desk,

dropped the package back into the drawer, then went and stared out of the window, silent.

'Gertie isn't the same person. I've always adored her – now I also respect her.'

'Thank you for explaining. I didn't understand, and I couldn't bear seeing her like that. She's so lovely and should be dressed in the finest gowns. It made me angry.'

Something in his expression shocked David. The barriers were down and it was clear to see that Alex loved Gertie. It wasn't merely affection; it was a deep and lasting love, and it had hurt him to see just how impoverished she now was. And if David was right, he was now committed to another woman.

The moment was brief, and then he was back to his usual self. 'I'd better put in an appearance.'

As Alex strode out of the room David felt sad – for all of them. They were all going to lose.

'Ah, there you are.' Sutton caught him as he walked down the stairs. 'Do you know where Gertie is? It's time to present ourselves to our hosts.'

'She's in the library with Fred and Millie. I'm on my way to collect them.'

'I might have known she'd be with the books,' he laughed.

It was a good sound, and helped lift the gloom trying to settle on David. Laughter in the Melrose family had been sadly missing lately. The whole point of this evening was to get Florence back into the social scene, and they must do everything they could to make it a success.

Hearing more laughter, he glanced round and saw Gertie

and two very smart youngsters walking towards them.

'My goodness!' Sutton exclaimed. 'You all look splendid.'

'Thank you, sir.' Fred bowed elegantly. 'Surprising what a difference the right clothes can make, ain't it?'

'No one would know where we come from until we open our mouths.' Millie smirked at the thought.

'Gertrude, that looks so pretty.' Florence joined them, leaning on the cane Fred had made for her. She never went anywhere without it now.

'The housekeeper insisted on doing it for me, and I didn't like to refuse.'

'I should think not. It's charming.' Florence smiled at everyone. 'Shall we go to the ballroom? I'm looking forward to seeing everyone again. And no hiding, Gertrude,' she scolded.

'No, Mother, I don't do things like that now.'

The six of them linked arms with their partners and made their way to greet their hosts for the evening.

'Did you find out what made Sir mad?' Millie whispered in David's ear as the walked along.

'He's got a problem.'

'Big one, is it?'

'Enormous. Hell, we've all got problems except you and Fred. Pardon my language, Millie, but it's all rather a mess.'

'Ah, I see.' She gave him a knowing glance. 'And you cuss all you want to. I've heard a lot worse.'

She probably did see, David thought wryly. He doubted much got past this bright girl.

* * *

The Chesters were greeting all the guests while Alex stayed in the background. It was their ball. He'd only offered the use of his home because of the large ballroom. It was time it was used again.

Glancing up at the balcony, he saw two little faces pressed against the bars, and hands fluttered acknowledging his smile.

When the Melrose family were announced, he turned his attention back to the entrance. He liked what he saw. Florence Melrose was frail now, but upright and smiling. The fact she wasn't wearing any jewellery was not as noticeable as it had been on her daughter, because lace filled the neckline of her gown. When Gertrude stepped into view he saw the ribbon his housekeeper had arranged around her neck. It looked charming, and he made a mental note to thank Mrs Jenkins.

When the last of the guests had been welcomed, the band played the opening dance. Lord and Lady Chester took the floor first, followed by Alex and Miriam Chester. Then other couples joined in and the room was filled with music and laughter.

Chapter Thirty-One

Much to her surprise, Gertrude was enjoying the evening. Fred and Millie had bought a book on different dances, and had obviously been learning how to do them. They were surprisingly good. It wasn't possible to hold a conversation with Fred while they were dancing because he was too busy counting under his breath in order to keep time with the music. David was an excellent dancer and guided Millie expertly round the floor. Her cheeks were flushed with excitement.

'Come and dance with me, Fred.' Millie tugged him on to the dance floor. 'I'm getting the hang of this now.'

They disappeared into the crowd and David held out his arm to Gertrude. They joined the dancers.

'I'm so pleased we brought Fred and Millie along. They're having a wonderful time.'

'Yes, it's good to see,' he agreed. 'They'll be talking

about this for days. Alex thought it was a fine idea, and that's why he's included May and Johnny. He didn't want to leave them out.'

'He's obviously fond of them, but I was surprised when he referred to them as his children.' Gertrude laughed quietly. 'Lady Chester was shocked.'

'She was lucky to get away with just that.' He pulled a face. 'Everyone else got the sharp end of his tongue, and his language would have made the roughest soldier blush.'

'As bad as that, was it?' She wished she could have seen the big man explode. It would have really been something to remember.

'Hmm.'

'What on earth made him lose his temper like that?'

'He never said,' David lied.

'Oh well, he appears to have got over it now.' She knew her friend wasn't going to say more. If he'd been told what the problem was he would never betray a confidence. 'When do you think they'll make the announcement?'

'Just before the supper interval, I expect. And I hope that gentle girl knows what she's getting into. He's a lot more volatile than I realised, and I'm not sure she's strong enough for him.' He glanced down at her. 'You would be, though. You'd fight back.'

'Now,' she scolded, 'you know that isn't going to happen. Accept it; I have.'

'I know, but it hurts.'

'Yes, it does, but many things in life are hard. We have to do the best we can, and enjoy the good times.'

'You sound like Millie,' he teased.

take that as a compliment. The last months have taught me a lot. It's been a brutal way to learn what life is all about, but I've been forced to do it.' She glanced up, a slight smile on her lips. 'Aunt Hanna told me to grow up, and I have.'

'Indeed you have.' He squeezed her hand in affection. 'And I'm proud of you.'

'Just because we can't always have what we want in life doesn't mean we have to wallow in self-pity and give up our dreams. Fred and Millie would be ashamed of us if we did.'

'And we can't have that.' The dance ended and he led her back to her parents.

Alex was there and talking to Florence. '. . . and you can be proud of your son, Mrs Melrose.'

'I am.' She smiled, her eyes shining. 'He's trying to make amends for his foolishness, and that shows he's changed.'

'It commands respect.'

Gertrude studied her mother's happy face and sent out a silent thank you to the man talking to her. She had only caught part of the conversation, but he had clearly been saying all the right things.

As if catching her thoughts, he turned. 'Will you dance with me, Gertrude?'

'I'd be pleased to,' she answered, without hesitation.

Before leading her on to the floor, he said to David, 'Why don't you ask Miriam to dance?'

'I wasn't sure if I should?'

'Of course you should. And where's Fred?'

'Right behind you, sir.'

'I shall expect you to dance with her, as well.'

'You're joking!' His eyes opened wide.

'I am not. You are my guests, and it is the polite thing to do. Millie, will you save the next dance for me?'

'Of course, sir.' She sketched a curtsy, making everyone laugh.

They joined the crush of dancers. 'You haven't run away from me this evening.'

It was time to be honest with him. She owed him that much. 'I'm not afraid of you any more.'

'Does that mean I've been forgiven?'

'It means you haven't done anything wrong. I'm the one who needs your forgiveness.'

'Shall we forget what has happened in the past and start again – as friends?'

'I'd like that.'

'So would I.' He smiled. 'I believe your friends call you Gertie.'

She nodded.

'I'm pleased to meet you, Gertie. My friends call me Alex.'

'Hello Alex.' She joined in the game. 'You dance very well.'

'So do you.'

They finished the dance in silence, both lost in their own thoughts. He was offering friendship, and she'd take it.

As they filed into supper, Gertrude and David frowned at each other, puzzled. There hadn't been an announcement!

After the interval, Florence went and rested in the room provided for her. Sutton had wanted to take her home, but n't hear of it. All she needed was a short rest and then she would stay for another hour or so. She was enjoying herself far too much to leave so soon.

The music began again, and Gertrude danced with her father, David, and Fred. The youngsters were having such an exciting time it was impossible not to get swept up in their enjoyment.

'I can't understand why I disliked these occasions in the past,' she told David.

'I knew it was a good idea to bring Fred and Millie. We can't be miserable around them.'

'That's true. I noticed you spent some time talking to Miriam and her parents before supper. Did you enjoy your dance with her?'

'Of course, she's a charming girl. Have you called a truce with Alex?' he asked, changing the subject.

She nodded. 'We've decided to be friends.'

'That's a good start,' he murmured to himself.

She heard, and when she noticed hope flare in his eyes, she said, 'I've always valued your friendship, and I'll gratefully accept Alex's. True friendship is a precious thing.'

'I agree.'

'They're leaving it rather late to make the announcement,' she said, noticing how much room there was on the dance floor now. 'People are beginning to leave.'

'Hmm.' He glanced around. It was past midnight and the room was certainly less crowded. 'They won't do it now. I was positive this was the reason for the occasion, especially as it was being held in Alex's house. It seems I was mistaken.'

'Perhaps Miriam wants a less public way of announcing the engagement. She does appear to be rather shy.'

'You're right. It will be in the papers soon, I expect.'

The letters had taken a while to reach him, and Edward found a quiet spot away from the bustling camp. It wasn't safe to venture too far on your own, but this was raised ground, and he had a good view all round.

He sat down, the three letters held tightly in his hand, almost afraid to open them. Lifting his head he watched the sun sinking slowly on the horizon, turning the sky vivid reds, oranges and gold. It was a breathtaking sight, and one he never got tired of seeing. If there wasn't a war going on he could get to love this country. He couldn't remember looking at the sky when he'd been in London. How he'd changed. He never referred to London as his home now. This was all he had, and here he'd found friendship and acceptance. He ran his fingers over the two stripes on his sleeve, sighing deeply. No one cared about his past, but the memory of what he'd done to the people who had loved him clouded his days and disturbed his nights. He'd been an arrogant fool! His father had tried hard to make him go into the business, and he'd made excuse after excuse. Why should he slave away in the workshop when he could be out enjoying himself? His selfish enjoyment had impoverished his family and cast him out. The shame was crushing. He could feel the excitement now as he'd held the cards in his hands. Didn't matter about the losses, he'd win this time . . . He groaned in despair, knowing now what a fool he'd been,

...me, the only thing driving him had been the ... the game.

The light was beginning to fade, so he had to read the letters while he could still see enough. He recognised the writing on each letter and opened his sister's first. There was no condemnation in it, only relief to know he was all right. She said nothing about the problems they were experiencing because of him. She sent her love and prayers for his safety.

The next was from his mother who assured him she was recovering from her illness. The rest of the letter was to tell him how proud she was of him, and that his award had been mentioned in the newspapers. The writing became shaky towards the end, showing how difficult it was for her to write. It did nothing to ease his distress.

The last one was from his father, and it took a while before he could bring himself to read it. It was brief and impersonal, stating that he would accept the money for a period of six months only. If he sent any after that it would be returned to him. The signature at the end was 'Sutton Melrose'. That stabbed Edward like a sabre, but what did he expect? He was no longer his son, and it was useless to dream of forgiveness. He would never see them again. His grief was too heavy for tears.

'Ed, what the devil are you doing up here alone? You could get shot, and believe me you don't want that to happen! It hurts.' Jack settled down beside him, keeping low. 'Ah, been reading your letters from home.'

'I haven't got a home,' he said bitterly. 'I've been

disowned, and it's only what I deserve.' He'd never talked much about his past, but there seemed to be a special bond between them because of shared experiences.

'I'm sorry, Ed. You want to talk about it? I'm a good listener.'

'No, not now. Perhaps I'll be able to tell you all about it one day.'

'I understand.' Jack pulled a letter out of his pocket. 'Got one myself today, and my family said you'd be welcome at our house when we get back.'

'That's kind of them.'

'Oh, they're not a bad bunch. I've got eight brothers and sisters, and the house is crowded, so they don't miss me too much. Now, let's get off this hill. There's something I want to talk to you about, and I'd rather do it without fear of a bullet whistling past my ear, or worse.'

There were men sitting around in groups, playing cards, or just talking. They found a spot where they could talk without being overheard, and sprawled on the ground.

'What's on your mind, Jack?'

'When we've done our stint out here and get sent home, do you want to stay there?'

'There's nothing in London for me, and although the sergeant said I could make the army my career, I'm not sure I want to. To tell you the truth I've become quite fascinated by this country, and once the war's over it could be a good place to settle.'

'Exactly!' Jack leant forward, his expression animated. 'There's a nice property about fifteen miles the other side of Ladysmith, and it's going cheap.'

up quickly. 'How do you know?'

...und it last week when I was on patrol. The owner, ...r Botha, lost his wife recently and wants to go to stay with his daughter in London. With all the trouble out here he can't sell the place. He's in a hurry and will take any reasonable offer. I'd have bought it there and then if I'd had the money, and I was wondering if there's a way we could buy it together.'

'I like the idea, but most of my money is going to my father for the next six months.'

'Me too.' He sighed wistfully. 'What we need is a partner with money. Got any ideas? I hate to let this chance slip by.'

'Hmm.' Edward frowned. 'No one I know would advance me so much as a penny. I was a gambler and they wouldn't trust me. I can only think of one man who might be interested in a deal like this. His reputation as a shrewd businessman is spotless. I could write to him, but it will take time for a reply to reach us.'

'What makes you think he might help us?'

'He wants to marry my sister – or at least, he did.'

'In that case write to him!' Jack was excited. 'What have we got to lose? If we don't try something we'll lose this deal. I'll take you to meet the owner and we can see if we can persuade him not to sell until we can find out if this man would be willing to help us.'

Scrambling to his feet, Edward smiled, feeling a surge of hope. Perhaps he had a future after all. 'Come on, Jack, let's get the letter written and on its way.'

* * *

It was four days later before they were able to see the land, and it took Edward's breath away. It was quite isolated, but that didn't worry either of them. 'Where's the boundary?'

Jack grinned. 'It would take me a full day to show you. The main crop is mealies, a type of corn, and pumpkins. It'll be hard work, but we could earn a decent living here.'

'Let's see if we can make a deal with Mr Botha.' He almost ran back to the ramshackle house.

With little prospect of another buyer, the owner agreed to hold the sale for them.

Now all they could do was wait.

Chapter Thirty-Two

'You're very restless today, my dear. It's a pleasant day so why don't you go to the park? The trees will look lovely now.'

Catching a warning glance from her aunt, Gertrude sat down. 'Sorry, Mother. I don't know what to do with myself now you and Father don't need me so much.'

'With the order books filling nicely, he had to employ a qualified assistant.' Florence smiled at her daughter. 'You understand, don't you?'

'Of course, and I'm pleased people are beginning to order furniture again, but I enjoyed feeling useful. I've got to do something with my life.'

'You will. You'll get married and have a family of your own one day soon. Alexander is fond of you, and you were getting along splendidly at the ball.'

'We've decided we can be friends.' Her mother mustn't

start worrying about that again, so she decided to put a stop to it right away. 'That is all there can be between us. He's going to marry Miriam Chester.'

'Is he?' Her mother frowned at Hanna. 'Is that so?'

'There's a rumour going around to that effect.'

'It's more than a rumour, Aunt. David is sure the announcement is due any moment now.'

'Ah, well, never mind, my dear, now we are attending social functions again you will soon meet someone else,' Florence said confidently. 'It's time for my nap. I promised Sutton I would sleep for two hours every afternoon. He insists, even though I've told him I am quite well now.'

'You're still not as strong as you were.' Hanna helped Florence out of the chair. 'You must do as you're told. Do you want me to come up with you?'

'No, I'm quite capable of putting myself to bed. Don't fuss.'

As soon as the door closed behind her mother, Gertrude sighed. 'I need to do something, but I can't decide. What do you think about nursing, or teaching, perhaps?'

'No, dear, you're too old to start a profession like that. You'll be twenty-one in September, and it would take some time to qualify.'

'What else is there? Don't you have any ideas?'

'Miss Melrose.' The maid came into the sitting room. 'Mr Glendale is here to see you.'

She looked up, surprised. 'Send him in, please.'

'I hope you will excuse my unexpected visit,' he said, as soon as he entered the room. Then he smiled. 'Hanna, see you again. I swear you grow more lovely every time we meet.'

'Hello, Alex. Still as charming as ever, I see.'

A deep rumble of amusement ran through him. 'I mean every word of it.'

'Of course you do. Now, what brings you here?'

'I've come to ask Gertie if she will do me a great favour.' He turned his full attention to her. 'I'm entertaining business acquaintances on Thursday evening, and I'm in need of a hostess. After dinner the men will be discussing business and the wives must be entertained. I'd be grateful if you would agree to do this for me.'

She was more than surprised by the request – she was stunned. 'Shouldn't you ask Miriam Chester?'

'No, it wouldn't be proper for her to do it, but it's quite in order for me to ask a friend to act as hostess for me. And as my agent, David will also be present.'

What he was saying made sense. It would cause much speculation if Miriam Chester did something like this before an engagement was announced. All London was buzzing with speculation, but if she and David helped Alex out it would not be thought too unusual.

He waited while she thought it over, then he said, 'Will you do this for me, Gertie? It's absolutely necessary that the ladies be looked after while the men talk. It's short notice, and I have to find someone quickly.'

He'd used her shortened name to emphasise their new friendship, and she wanted to do this, to be a part of his life, even if it was only for one evening. 'I'll be pleased to keep the ladies entertained, Alex.'

300

'Thank you.' He smiled. 'That is such a relief! Could you come to my home tomorrow afternoon? We need to make sure you know where everything is.'

'I'll be there.'

'Alex?' Hanna frowned at him. 'You appear to consider this arrangement quite acceptable. I'm not so sure.'

'As I've said, David will also be there. I would never do anything to harm Gertie's excellent reputation.' The corners of his mouth turned up in amusement. 'You wound me. Don't you think I can be trusted?'

'Of course you can't! Don't forget I remember the young man who was always in trouble.'

They both burst out laughing and Gertrude watched in fascination. It was as if layers were being peeled away from the man she'd considered stern and unfeeling. The result was enough to take her breath away.

'I shall take good care of your niece, and make sure no harm comes to her – ever.' The last word was said quietly. 'That's what friends do, and I mean what I say.'

Her aunt nodded. 'I've never known you to break your word. That's always been your code.' She studied him closely. 'I'm pleased to see you looking happy and relaxed again.'

'I've laid a few ghosts, but it took me a while.' He glanced over at Gertrude. 'Come when it suits you tomorrow. I shall be there all afternoon.'

'Will two o'clock be all right?'

'Perfect. Now, if you'll excuse me, I have another appointment.'

Gertrude saw him out, and when she returned to the

sitting room, her aunt was shaking her head.

'Watch him! There's a gleam of devilment in his eyes I haven't seen for a long time. It makes we wonder what he's up to.'

'What do you mean?'

'I can't quite work out what's happened, but the change in him is too sudden. I've seen this innocent look many times before, and when it happens, it's time to be on your guard.'

'Oh, Aunt,' Gertrude laughed, 'you're imagining things. He isn't a boy now, and I expect he's happy because he's found the woman he loves and wants to marry.'

'Hmm. Yes, I do believe he has.'

'Sorry I'm late, David.' Alex strode into the office. 'I had something urgent to arrange before I came here.'

Millie peered in through the open door. 'Hello, sir. We had a lovely time at your dance.'

'I'm pleased you enjoyed it. You and Fred looked splendid.'

'Not bad, eh?' She grinned. 'You want tea, Mr Gardener?'

'Alex?'

He shook his head. 'No time, I want you to come and have a look at something with me. It's only a short walk from here.'

It wasn't easy keeping up with the long stride of the man beside him. David was only slightly shorter than Alex, but there was an air of excitement about him, and he was moving with speed.

'I can't wait to show you this. It's a real find, but don't look too enthusiastic when we get there or they'll put up the price.'

'Another ship?'

'Yes.' Alex stopped suddenly and pointed towards a dry dock.

'You're joking!' David couldn't believe his eyes. They were in a run down part of the docks, and the ship was a wreck.

'Don't overdo the lack of enthusiasm,' Alex joked. 'Come on, let's go on board.'

'Is it safe?'

'She isn't in the water. She isn't going to sink.'

'No, but she will if you try to float her.' He grimaced in disgust.

'I agree she does need a bit of work done on her.'

'It'll take more than a bit to make her seaworthy again. She's a three mast schooner, and hardly suitable as a cargo vessel these days.'

'I don't want her for that.'

'Oh, good!'

A laugh rumbled through Alex. 'Keep up the disapproving act. Here comes Mr Stewart.'

'It's no act,' David muttered.

'Nice to see you again, Mr Glendale.'

They shook hands. 'This is my agent, Mr Gardener. I've brought him along to see *Ocean Sprite*.'

David turned a snort of amusement into a cough. What a name for a ship that looked as if a puff of wind would reduce it to dust.

'Of course. She's been neglected, but is quite sound, and it won't take much to make her a fine ship again. Really majestic she looked under full sail.'

After another glance round David was pursing his lips. He didn't believe a word the owner said. And what the blazes was Alex going to do with a sailing ship?

There wasn't much David didn't know about ships. He'd grown up following his father around the docks, and learning all he could about the construction and running of every kind of ship there was. The next hour was spent going over every inch of the crumbling wreck, and his disbelief turned to horror as he tapped and probed. True, the hull did appear to be solid enough, but the rest of the ship was in a dreadful state. The masts were still there, but the sails and all the rigging had rotted long ago. He loved all ships and it saddened him to see this one being allowed to get into such a deplorable state.

They finally went up on deck, brushing the dirt from their clothing.

'What do you think of her?' Alex asked. 'You haven't said a word. The only sounds I've heard from you have been grunts and unintelligible mutters.'

David went to lean on the rail and thought better of it. 'She'll cost a fortune to put right, but she's in a more seaworthy condition than I first thought.'

'So you believe she could sail again?'

'Yes, with a lot of work and money, but I can't understand what you want her for.'

'I'll tell you my plans later. Get her for me, and I'll see you back in the office.'

He watched in amazement as Alex made his way off the ship. No mention of the price he was willing to pay. Working as his agent was certainly not dull.

Mr Stewart came up to stand beside him, and they both watched the retreating figure.

'Does Mr Glendale still want to buy her?'

'He's left the decision to me.' David made a show of removing dust from his jacket sleeve. 'Do you have somewhere cleaner we could go to discuss business?'

'There's a hut over there I use as an office.'

It took David less than an hour to negotiate a deal with the owner. He clearly wanted to be rid of the wreck and took a ridiculously low price. But the man was no fool. He owned the dry dock and knew the ship must stay there while extensive work was carried out on her. He was tougher over the price of that, but David was well pleased with the terms in the end. At least he hadn't wasted too much of Alex's money.

He walked into his office and handed over the sale papers to Alex, who read them and grinned in approval. 'I knew you'd be better at this than me. Well done!'

'Will you now tell me what you want her for?'

'I'm going to restore her, then hire her out. There are plenty of wealthy businessmen who would enjoy a cruise on her. But for several weeks every summer children from the deprived areas can sail in her under the guidance of an experienced crew.'

'That's a wonderful idea!' David could suddenly see the old ship in a different light, but he still had reservations. 'It will cost a fortune to get her back to that standard, though.'

Alex sat back, a gleam in his eyes. 'On Thursday I'm entertaining a couple of wealthy men, and I'll offer them a share in the project.'

'What if they're not interested? You've bought her now.'

'They will be.'

David laughed. 'I wish I had your confidence.'

'You'll pull it off.' Alex stood up and slapped him on the back.

'Me?' he gasped.

'You're the most skilled negotiator I've ever met. Even better than me, and your knowledge of ships is much greater than mine.' He removed his pocket watch and flipped it open. 'Time we were on our way. We have another appointment.'

'Who with?' He was still trying to digest the remark about his skills.

'Gertie. She's going to act as hostess at our business dinner.'

This was becoming more bizarre by the minute. What on earth was the man doing? 'Have you asked her?'

'Of course.' He strode out to the waiting carriage. 'And she's agreed.'

'I don't believe this.' David climbed in after Alex. 'Why would she?'

'Because we're friends.' Alex smiled at the confusion on his companion's face.

'She agreed because you're friends?'

'Hmm.'

Chapter Thirty-Three

'You look lovely, my dear.'

'Do you think so, Father?' Gertrude smoothed the skirt of her gown, wishing she'd never agreed to do this. She had been so stunned by Alex's request she hadn't given it enough thought before answering.

Her father took her by the shoulders and turned her to face him. 'I wish we could have bought you a new gown, darling, but it just isn't possible at the moment. Business is picking up, but there isn't money to spare.'

'I know, and I'm not worried about wearing something I already have. I doubt anyone there will have seen me before. Alex knows our situation and won't be expecting me to turn up in an up-to-date creation.' She gave a hesitant smile. 'I'm regretting ever saying I'd do this. I can't think why he asked me.'

'This dinner must be important to him and he wanted

the best person by his side. You can converse on many subjects and will be able to keep the ladies amused while the men are discussing business.' Her father smiled wryly. 'These kind of meetings can take some time, you know, and Alex can trust you.'

'I do believe you're prejudiced,' she laughed.

'Of course I am. You're my daughter and I'm allowed to be proud of you. Now, your mother and Hanna are in the sitting room, so go and show them how elegant you are.'

There was only time for a brief examination before the carriage arrived, and as she drove away with their comments of approval ringing in her ears, she was determined to make a success of the evening. Alex wouldn't have asked her if he'd had any doubts about her suitability. And David would be there to support her through dinner.

She sat back and relaxed. Of course she could do this. Her mother and aunt had trained her well in etiquette. There was no need to worry.

The butler was waiting for her. 'Good evening, Miss Melrose. I'm to take you to the study before the guests arrive.'

She followed him along the passage until he opened a door at the end and announced her.

'Good evening, Gertie.'

'Good evening, Alex.' His careful scrutiny made her want to fidget, but she refused to show any discomfort. He looked splendid in his evening clothes, so she studied him in the same way, and saw his lips twitch at the corners.

'That shade of violet matches your eyes perfectly.' He nodded in approval.

'Thank you. The black you are wearing makes your eyes look like the colour of grass.'

He tipped his head back and laughed. 'Now that we have the compliments out of the way, is there anything you wish to know before everyone arrives?'

'You haven't told me who's coming.'

'David, two businessmen, their wives and one daughter.'

'Do I know them?'

'You met them at the ball.' He opened a drawer in his desk and removed an old black box. He opened it, studied the contents for a moment, then said, 'Ah, yes, this will be perfect.'

She watched him remove the contents and walk towards her.

'Turn around.'

She couldn't see what he was holding, but obeyed without question. Something cold slipped around her neck, then he turned her to face him again, stepping back so he could see properly.

'Beautiful.'

Catching a glimpse of herself in the mirror over the fireplace, she gasped when she saw the necklace. It was an exquisite amethyst and diamond pendant on a thick gold chain. 'I can't wear this!'

'Why not? It was my mother's, and it goes well with your gown. It would please me greatly if you would wear it tonight.'

There had been a note of pain in his voice, and his gaze was fixed on the necklace. He wanted her to wear it and she couldn't refuse. Touching it with her fingers, she said, 'Thank you. I'll be honoured to wear your mother's necklace.'

Smiling, he held out his arm. 'Let us join David in the lounge. Our guests will be arriving any minute now.'

Mr and Mrs Broughton were the first to arrive. She knew them only by sight, and the wife hung back nervously. Shy in company, Gertrude noted at once, so she made a point of putting her at ease.

The next arrivals shocked her. It was Lord and Lady Chester, accompanied by their daughter. She knew David had also been taken by surprise, because she heard his sharp intake of breath.

The conversation at dinner was wide ranging, covering politics, the war with the Boers, the aged Queen Victoria, and many other subjects. Gertie found she was thoroughly enjoying her role as hostess and had quickly recovered from her surprise at seeing Miriam Chester. Of course she would be here; it was only to be expected.

As soon as the meal was over, the men retired, leaving her to do the job she was here for. It was easy with such a small gathering, and even Mrs Broughton relaxed enough to join in. At one point Miriam sat next to her.

'I believe you know Mr Gardener well,' she said.

'Yes, we've been friends since we were toddlers.' She grinned. 'At least I was a toddler. I followed David and my brother around like a puppy dog. My brother was always trying to get rid of me, but David wouldn't let him. He's always been my dearest friend.'

'He seems a kind man.'

'He is one of the kindest.' It was an intriguing

conversation. For someone who was about to become engaged to another man this interest in David was strange. She spent a while longer talking about their childhood, then, aware of her duty, moved on to the other ladies.

When the men returned, the women were all laughing as she told them about the dusty old bookshop, and the grumpy owner.

It wasn't possible to tell if the business had gone well, but they all appeared to be in a good mood. That could be because of the amount of brandy they had consumed, of course. David did look stunned, though, making her wonder just what had gone on in the other room.

The guests left after another hour, and it was only when they were alone that Alex gave a satisfied smile. 'Well done, David. You put our case so expertly even I was prepared to give you money.'

'I don't believe what happened.' He shook his head as if trying to clear it. 'I need a brandy. Are you trying to make me a rich man, Alex?'

'Do you object?' Alex handed him a glass filled with a generous amount of brandy. 'You seem to be quite unaware of your talents, but I saw them early on, and am very pleased to have you working with me.'

She watched the interplay between the two men she loved, and saw how at ease they were with each other. It was clear that not only were they a good partnership, but they had become friends as well, and that made her happy. She was seething with curiosity, though, and longed to know what this was all about.

'I've received many compliments about you, Gertie,'

Alex told her. 'Mr Broughton was particularly impressed. He said he'd never seen his wife enjoying herself so much. She's often uneasy in company. You've been the perfect hostess, and I'm grateful.'

'I enjoyed myself.'

'Good. Now, I expect you'd like to know what this evening was about?'

'I'm curious, of course, but it isn't any of my business.'

'Ah, but it is because we're going to need your help, aren't we, David?'

'We're going to need all the help we can get.' He downed his drink and shuddered as the fiery liquid went down. 'It's a crazy scheme, Gertie, but if it's a success . . . you tell her Alex.'

As the story of the ship unfolded she became excited, sitting on the edge of her seat. By the time he'd finished, she could hardly contain herself. 'That's fantastic! The children would be given a chance to test their abilities, and grow in confidence. Can you do it? How would you choose the children? What age limit would you want? When would you get an experienced crew?'

'Whoa.' Alex held up his hands. 'One question at a time. Once the work is nearing completion we would advertise for a crew, and test each applicant to make sure they were suitable. It's a large ship and they will have to be the most experienced we can get. The boys will only be eligible if they come from deprived families. I think from the age of eight, but that would depend on each boy.'

'Only boys? What about the girls?'

'We can't allow girls on the cruises,' David pointed out. 'It wouldn't be safe for them.'

'I agree, but we should arrange something for the girls,' Alex said. 'What do you think they'd enjoy, Gertie?'

'Something in the country.' She gazed into space, trying to imagine what they would find exciting. 'What about somewhere they could be with animals, and perhaps learn to ride a horse?'

'A riding school! That's an excellent idea.' Alex began to pace, thinking things through. 'I already have a farm where we breed warhorses for the cavalry, but there's plenty of room, and we could buy docile horses and ponies. What do you think, David?'

'Sounds good, but the children will have to be housed and looked after.'

'There's a large, unused barn which could be turned into living quarters, but we must go and have a look at the place. Next Friday suit you, David?'

He nodded, marvelling again at Alex's energy. He certainly didn't believe in wasting time. 'One of your ships is due in, but I'm not expecting her for at least another two weeks. If she should arrive while we're away, my father will see to it for us.'

'That's excellent.' Alex spun round. 'I'd like you to come with us, Gertie. You know what the children need, and your advice will be valuable.'

'I'd love to if you think I can help.'

'Excellent! I shall, of course, ask your parents' permission for you to accompany us.'

'It might be an idea to take Millie with us as a companion for Gertie,' David suggested.

'Will your father manage without her for a few days?'

'I'm sure he will.'

Alex rang the bell for the butler, and then smiled at Gertrude. 'We've kept you up late enough. Thank you for helping the evening run smoothly. David will give you details of our journey to Kent when the arrangements are made. Ah, Hunt, Miss Melrose is leaving.'

'The carriage is ready and waiting, sir.'

'Ask Dickens to take Mr Gardener home as well, after he's delivered Miss Melrose safely to her door.'

'Yes, sir.'

She was in the hall before she remembered the necklace. Quickly unfastening it, she handed it to Alex. 'Thank you for allowing me to wear this. It's absolutely beautiful.'

He bowed his head in acknowledgement and slipped the jewels into his pocket. 'Goodnight.'

Once in the carriage, she couldn't wait to ask, 'What did you mean when you said Alex was trying to make you rich?'

'He's given me an equal share in the boat, and if the venture is successful, it could be very profitable. And if it isn't, then I'll have lost nothing. Alex, Lord Chester and Mr Broughton are to meet all the renovation costs, but Alex insisted I be listed as a partner because I have the expertise needed to see the ship is made seaworthy again.'

'And he's quite right. You know a great deal about ships. It's been your whole life, and I'm so pleased for you.

Alex wouldn't have taken this on if he didn't believe it was a sound idea, so I'm sure it will be a success.'

'And that isn't all.' He reached out for her hands. 'We're going to need carpenters for at least a year – the best in the business. Your father has those, and we're going to see him in the morning. This could change everything for you.'

'Oh, my,' was all she could say.

Her father was fast asleep in a chair by the fire when she arrived home. He looked so peaceful it was a shame to wake him, and she decided not to mention the ship. Alex would do that in the morning, and be able to explain exactly what he wanted. If she told him now he wouldn't sleep for the rest of the night. If David was right, this could be the turning point for them, but she didn't dare let her hopes rise too much. She'd learnt how quickly things could go wrong. This scheme was imaginative, but she must also remember that it was also risky. But if it was a success, it would mean a great deal to so many people, and she was so excited to have been included. She'd been looking for something to occupy her time, and this would be perfect.

'Father.' She shook him gently. When he opened his eyes, she scolded, 'You should be in bed.'

He straightened up. 'I wanted to see you safely home before I retired. How did the evening go?'

'Very well. I really quite enjoyed it, and Alex said he was pleased. I was disconcerted when Miriam Chester arrived with her parents, but she was very sweet, and I expect Alex told her I would be acting as his hostess because she didn't seem surprised to see me.' She yawned. 'But I'm tired now.'

315

'Time we were both in bed. I'm pleased everything went well. Perhaps he'll ask you again.'

'I doubt that, Father. This evening was a special dinner, and he didn't have much time to arrange for someone to help with the ladies.'

There was so much more she could have told him, but he would hear the whole story soon. Tonight they both needed their rest because it would be an exciting day tomorrow.

Chapter Thirty-Four

It was pouring with rain the next morning but Alex didn't seem to notice it. The sky was grey, the buildings were grey, and the streets were grey, and David wondered if there was any colour left in the world. This was more than April showers; it was like winter again. He shouldn't have had that other brandy last night because his head was throbbing.

'Don't look so gloomy,' Alex told him. 'It's only a drop of rain. The sun will be out by afternoon.'

'It's coming down in a solid lump,' David groaned, 'and I'm not sure I want the sun to come out. I won't be able to see if it does. You drank as much as I did last night, so how come you're so cheerful?'

'I spent ten years in the army.'

'Ah, drink a lot, do they?'

The only answer was an amused grin. 'Come on, we've got a project to get under way.'

'Where to first?' David tried to ignore the headache. There was a very busy day ahead of them.

'The Melrose workshop to see how many carpenters he can let us have.'

Sutton saw them as soon as they walked in, and so did Fred, who waved frantically at them, smiling happily as usual.

'This is a pleasant surprise.' Sutton shook hands with them. 'What can I do for you?'

David had wondered if Gertie would tell her father about the project, but it was clear he was surprised to see them.

'We're going to renovate an old sailing vessel, and we need to hire from you as many of your best carpenters as you can spare,' Alex told him. 'We'll pay you top rates for any with the right skills.'

'Wait a moment, the men must hear this.' Sutton faced the workshop. 'Stop working men, and gather around to hear what Mr Glendale has to say.'

David watched the faces as they listened to the plans for the ship. Fred's eyes were growing wider and wider, and he began to shift from one foot to the other.

'Sir,' one of the men caught Alex's attention when he'd finished talking. 'I used to sail on the *Ocean Sprite* as ship's carpenter. I know her inside out. She's a fine vessel and rides well in rough weather. I'd like to work on her again.'

'There's one for you. Anyone else interested?' Sutton smiled at the men. 'If any of you would like to do this work, then please say so.'

Three more men came forward, and Fred was practically

jumping up and down. 'Me too! Can I? Please, sir?'

'We'd be pleased to have you, Fred.' Alex placed a hand on the boy's shoulder to keep him still. 'That's if Mr Melrose can spare you. The job will take at least a year, and we can't take all his good workers away from him.'

'Of course you can work on the ship,' Sutton told him, making the boy yelp in delight. 'How many are you going to need?'

'David's the only one who can answer that.'

'Five or six who know what they're doing, and then we can employ less skilled men to work under them. The ship's a wreck, and we'll need a large workforce if we're going to get her seaworthy within a year. Which is your aim, Alex.'

'I've got a mate,' one of the men said, 'and he's a good carpenter. He's out of work and would jump at a chance for a job.'

'Ask him to see Mr Gardener. Do you know where his office is?'

'Yes, sir, everyone around the docks knows the Gardeners. It's a highly respected firm. I'll bring my mate along, and you won't have any trouble getting the workers you need. They'll be queuing outside his office as soon as word gets around.'

'Make it this evening some time,' David told him. 'I'll be there until late.'

'We'll be there, sir, and thanks.'

Fred tugged at David's sleeve. 'Plenty of men down our street are out of work. They ain't skilled carpenters but you're gonna need men to do heavy work, ain't you?'

'We've already thought of that, and Tanner Street is our next stop. We want to give them first chance, and then we'll ask around the area.'

'Thanks, most of them are desperate for jobs.'

'We know, and we're going to help as many men as we can.' David then turned to the man who had sailed on the *Ocean Sprite*. 'What's your name?'

'Harry Green, sir.'

'I'm going to put you in charge of the carpenters.'

'Thank you, sir. When do we start?'

'We've worked out that carpenters can begin their work two weeks on Monday, but we'll have to confirm that later. It all depends on how quickly the ship can be cleared,' Alex informed them. 'You'll receive your wages from Mr Melrose as usual, but while you're on this job you will all be given an increase, and a bonus when the work is finished.' He glanced round at the men. 'It's going to be hard work, and you'll earn every penny of it.'

There were smiles all round.

'I see that doesn't worry you. We're going to have an exciting time seeing this elegant lady come back to life. Mr Gardener will answer any questions you might have.' Then he turned to Sutton. 'Let's discuss terms.'

They went into the office while the men who were going to work with them gathered around David.

'I hope I'm not taking too many of your workers away from you?' Alex settled in a chair and took a notebook out of his pocket; it was already filled with facts and figures he'd spent the night working on.

'No, I can manage. Those staying are too old for the kind of work you need, and they've long years of experience with the firm.'

'Good.' He then set about outlining the deal. The terms were more than generous, and an agreement was soon reached.

'Did my daughter know about this last night?' Sutton asked.

'Yes, but I gather she didn't mention it.'

'No.' He smiled broadly. 'You just wait until I see her this evening.'

'And speaking of Gertie, I would like your permission to take her to my farm in Kent for a couple of days.'

'Oh?' Sutton frowned. 'She didn't mention that either. Explain, please.'

Sutton listened while the plan for the riding school was outlined. 'It was your daughter's idea,' Alex said. 'I'll need her advice about accommodation and care of the children. David's coming and bringing Millie as companion to Gertie.'

'Ah, well, that's all right then. It sounds like a worthwhile scheme, and I'm sure my daughter will be delighted to help.'

'Thank you.' Business concluded, he stood up, eager to get on to the next stage of the project. 'Now we must find more workers.'

'You're not wasting any time.'

'No, I've bought the ship and want the work carried out as soon as possible. I've set David a deadline of one year to complete the renovation, and every moment counts.'

'If anyone can do it, he can. He knows what he's doing.'

Alex nodded. 'That's why I want him as a partner.'

The rest of the day was hectic as they moved from place to place, hiring shipbuilders, riggers and an army of labourers. By the evening everything was in place and work was going to start immediately on clearing the ship of accumulated rubbish and debris. David had seen the joy on the men's faces as they were offered work. Fred and May's fathers were two of them, and the majority of the workforce had been found in the slum areas where there was the most need. He still had to go back to his office and see others who had been recommended and were coming to him there. But he could snatch a couple of hours to relax first.

'Where do you get your energy from?' David asked, collapsing into a comfortable leather armchair in Alex's library.

'I haven't been wandering around all day suffering from last night's indulgencies. Would you like a drink?'

'Tea?'

'If you wish.' When it was ordered, Alex also sat down, stretching his long legs out and sipping a whisky. 'That was a successful day.'

David nodded, relieved to discover the headache had gone at last. 'I suspect there's more to your enthusiasm to restore an old ship than merely a business venture.'

'There is. As a boy I used to dream about sailing the seas in a ship like this, the wind filling her sails as she surged through the waves. And when I saw her I thought she could be put to good use, and fulfil my childhood fantasy.'

'And yet you went into the army.'

'Family tradition.' Alex nodded to the maid as she brought in the tea. 'Thank you Daisy, we'll look after ourselves. Tell Cook Mr Gardener will be staying for dinner, and could she make it an hour earlier, please.'

'Yes, sir.'

'Can Gertie ride?' Alex wanted to know.

'We all learnt, but I don't think she's been on a horse for some time. She rode astride, as it was the only way she could keep up with us. She was never taught to ride like a lady.'

'What did she wear?'

'Trousers under her skirt.' He grinned. 'She borrowed a pair of Edward's.'

'Tell her to bring clothes to ride in, and Millie if she's got anything. If not, I expect there will be something suitable at the farm.'

'All right,' David agreed. 'You breed warhorses, don't you? Have you got any ordinary riding animals?'

'Don't think so, but there's a pony for Millie.'

Unable to believe what he was hearing, David's eyes opened wide. 'You're not thinking of putting us on a destrier, are you?'

'They're exquisite animals. I'm sure you'll both enjoy the challenge.'

'They're bred for fighting!'

'Hmm.' Alex's grin spread. 'I'm looking forward to going there.'

'I think I've just gone off the idea.'

'Dinner is served, sir,' the butler announced.

'Thank you, Hunt.' Alex slapped David on the back. 'Don't worry. I won't let anything happen to either of you.'

'Amen to that!'

Waiting for her father to come home was agony for Gertrude. She was bursting to know what had happened today, and would he have given his permission for her to go to the farm?

Florence closed the book she had been reading and smiled at her daughter. 'As soon as we have sufficient funds we must have a lovely gown made for you, in case Alexander needs your help again. You cannot be seen in the same one again.'

'I'm quite happy with the gowns I have,' Gertrude said gently. 'Two have hardly been worn.'

'Perhaps, but you must have at least one new gown. I'll see to it as soon as I can. Now, what is Miriam Chester like, and what was she wearing?'

'She's a pleasant young girl and she was wearing a pale lemon gown. The colour went well with her blonde hair and light blue eyes. Her hair was beautifully arranged, and swept up with a diamond comb to hold it in place. She looked lovely.'

'I've never met her, you know.' Florence looked thoughtful. 'But I expect I shall quite soon.'

'Ah, Father has just arrived.' Gertrude was glad to change the subject because her mother still seemed to have marriage on her mind. She understood it, of course, as most girls were either married or engaged by the age of twenty. She waited anxiously for her father, wanting to know what had happened.

'How have you been today, my dear?' he asked, walking straight over to his wife.

'Very well, Sutton. I'm a little stronger each day.' He kissed his wife's cheek, and then turned to his daughter. 'And who has been keeping secrets from me?'

'They came then!' There had been a spring in his step when he'd walked across the room, and years had dropped away from him, revealing the man he'd been before this disaster had hit them. 'What have they offered?'

'What is she talking about?' Florence asked, looking from one to the other.

'Our daughter had news last night and didn't tell me. When Alex and David came to the workshop this morning I was in for a surprise.' He smiled at his wife. 'I have good news, my dear.'

He then proceeded to tell her about the scheme.

'And what will that mean to us?' Florence was as excited as her daughter now.

'The renovation of the ship will take about a year, and four of our workers, including Fred, have offered to take on the task. I have agreed terms with Alex, and they are very generous. The rewards to both the men and us will be substantial.'

Gertrude jumped to her feet, unable to sit still any longer. 'David's going to benefit as well. Alex has given him an equal share in the ship in return for his expertise and knowledge. Isn't it wonderful! And I'm so pleased Fred will be involved. He'll be thrilled.'

'Oh,' her mother's hands trembled. 'I had given up hope of us ever recovering from this disaster.'

'You mustn't,' Gertrude said firmly. 'Fred and Millie told me to hold on to my dreams when things are hard. Everything's going to be all right, Mother, you'll see. I do believe the worst is behind us now.'

'We still have a way to go.' Sutton sounded a note of caution.

'Yes, but there's now hope for the future. One moment we were a happy, complete family, and the next we were torn apart. Everything went from bad to worse for us, and there seemed no way we could ever recover from the disaster, but things are turning in our favour, at last. And I am going to rejoice in this moment.'

'We owe Alexander a debt of gratitude,' Florence said.

'So many people are going to benefit from this crazy venture.' Hanna swept into the room. 'I do declare that boy is as unpredictable as ever.'

'Hello, Hanna.' Sutton greeted his sister. 'You've heard all about it, then.'

'Impossible not to. Alex and David have caused a lot of excitement. They've been sweeping round London recruiting workers, and have been besieged by men desperate for jobs. Those two men work well together, and have a mutual respect for each other. I must say they're taking a risk with this project, but if they can make it work it will be marvellous.'

'They'll make it work,' Gertrude stated, with complete confidence.

'I'm sure they'll do their best.' Sutton handed his sister a drink. 'Are you staying for dinner?'

'Please.'

'Father, did Alex mention anything else?'

'Ah, yes, I almost forgot,' he teased. 'I have given my permission for you to go with them at the end of the week, after being assured David and Millie will be accompanying you.'

'Thank you!' She was overjoyed.

'What's this all about?' Florence and Hanna demanded at the same time.

Gertrude explained the plan, and by the end, Hanna was nodding her head in approval.

'My goodness,' her mother exclaimed. 'That dear man is determined to help those children, isn't he? And he must value your opinion, Gertrude.'

'I think it's just wonderful, and I'll help in any way I can.'

Hanna looked thoughtful, and spoke almost to herself. 'This is more like the man I knew before tragedy struck his family. He's happy again.'

Chapter Thirty-Five

By the end of the week, the old ship was swarming with men, and David could hardly believe work was under way so quickly. But then he should have known Alex never wasted time once his mind was set on something. He had moved like a storm-force wind, hiring workers and suppliers, and once everything was in place he'd stepped back and let David take over, watching but never interfering.

'She's a mess, isn't she?'

David spun round to find Lord Chester standing behind him. 'We've got to tear out all the rotting wood before we can start rebuilding,' he replied. 'It looks worse than it really is at the moment.'

'I'm glad you said "rebuilding",' Lord Chester remarked dryly. 'You're the one with all the knowledge, son, so is she going to float again, or is Alex just dreaming?'

'Oh, he never takes anything on unless he's looked into it thoroughly and is sure it's a viable project. Give me a year and the *Ocean Sprite* will live up to her name.' David didn't know when he'd started to feel affection for the poor old lady, but he really believed what he'd said.

'You're right, of course, and the only reason we've gone into this is because we trust his instinct, and he has you with him. You and your father are highly thought of in the shipping world.' He gave a wry smile. 'I had you checked out before going into this scheme, and from what I've heard you're a clever young man. Alex is no fool.'

David was so surprised by this he didn't know what to say.

'Can I go on board?'

'I wouldn't at the moment, but come back in a couple of months and I'll give you a guided tour.'

'I'll do that. We're giving a small dinner party a week tomorrow. Join us.'

'Thank you, I'd be delighted to.' It was an effort to hide his surprise.

'Excellent. My wife will send you an invitation. Now I'll leave you to your work, David.'

He strode away and David watched him in amazement, rather disconcerted to know he'd been checked out. The report must have been impressive, because not only had the eminent Lord Chester invited him to dine with them, he'd called him by his Christian name.

At that moment there was the most almighty crash, which had him tearing up the gangplank. 'What's happened?' he yelled. 'Is anyone hurt?'

The man, Bentley, whom he'd put in charge of the first stage of the work, appeared through a hatchway. 'Nothing to worry about, sir. Part of the lower decking gave way, but no one's hurt. All the noise was caused by a pile of wood falling through the hole.'

'Thank God for that!'

The foreman came and stood beside him. 'Means we're going to have to replace all of that section, though.'

'Do it. This ship's going to sail with children on board, so she's got to be the safest vessel on the sea.'

'Yes, sir.' Bentley rubbed his hands together, smiling. 'She's going to be a happy ship because everyone here is working on her with love for the old vessel. I heard one man tell her he was sorry to be tearing her apart, but not to worry, she'd feel better soon.'

'I think soon is a bit optimistic.' David laughed. 'I'll be away for a couple of days, so is there anything you need to know before I go?'

'I know what's got to be done. I've been building ships like this since I was little more than a kid. You can leave it to me, sir.'

David was grateful to Alex for paying top wages. They had managed to gather together a good team, and it was already evident he wasn't going to have to watch over their every move. Which was a good thing. His workload was increasing day by day. Alex had gained more drive and purpose lately, and in this kind of mood it wasn't easy to keep up with him. David now found himself being stretched, and he loved every challenge.

* * *

Early Friday morning they were all in the coach on their way to the farm in Kent.

Millie couldn't stop smiling, she was so happy. 'We had a huge party last night,' she told them. 'The men know they've got jobs for at least a year and that means the kids will have plenty to eat. They can't stop talking about the ship and how beautiful she's gonna be when they've finished with her. Johnny said he wants to sit in the crow's nest.'

That made Alex laugh. 'You tell him I'll take him up there when we've got one.'

The journey was pleasant, and the sun even decided to show itself to brighten their way. They stopped at an inn for lunch; it was a pleasant spot and they lingered while the horses enjoyed the grass in a field adjoining the inn. Refreshed, they continued on their way. The men talked about ships, cargoes and the planned riding school, but the girls were content to sit quietly and watch the passing scenery. As the city was left behind and they began travelling through fields and open spaces, sighs of sheer bliss kept coming from Millie.

The evenings were drawing out a little by now, and it was still light when they arrived.

Millie was the first out of the coach, and she clutched at Gertrude's sleeve to urge her forward. 'Look at those, ain't they beautiful! Let's go and see that big black one. He's looking at us.'

Alex lunged and caught her as she started to run towards the animals. 'Whoa! You mustn't go near them unless I'm with you.'

'I won't hurt him,' she said, innocently.

A stocky man joined them, smiling a greeting. 'They will hurt you, though, Miss. They're warhorses and have uncertain tempers. They bite and kick.'

'That's not nice. Why do they do that?'

'They're bred as fighters,' Alex told her.

She took a step back and let out a deep breath. 'We ain't gonna ride them, are we?'

'No, I've got a gentle pony for you.' Alex then introduced the man standing beside him. 'This is Stan Brewster, he runs the place for me. Stan meet Miss Melrose, Millie, and David Gardener, my shipping agent.'

'I'm pleased to meet you all. Everything's ready for you and your guests, sir.'

They went into the house, were shown their rooms, and then enjoyed a splendid meal, cooked for them by Stan's wife. Instead of the men retiring to another room, the after dinner drinks were served in the sitting room, and with the farm manager also present, they discussed what had to be done to set up the riding school.

Alex encouraged everyone to contribute ideas, listening just as intently to the girls as he did to the men. Gertrude and Millie were being made to feel valuable members of the project, and when it came to caring for the children, they were a great help.

It was eleven o'clock before Alex called a halt. 'That will do for tonight. In the morning we'll look over the proposed site, and then we can properly assess its suitability. We have a busy day ahead of us, so I suggest we all retire.'

* * *

For a brief moment Gertrude wondered where she was, then she woke up completely. Of course, they were at the farm. Tired out by the journey and lengthy discussions after dinner, she had slept soundly. She stretched, enjoying the comfort of the impressively carved wooden bed. It was huge, and wondered if she had been given the best room in the house. It wasn't as grand as the house in London, but it was a working farm and had a lovely homely feel about it.

Telling herself she couldn't lounge around all day, however tempting that was, she jumped out of bed. The men would not be pleased if they had to waste time waiting for her. A fire was already burning in the grate, and there was fresh water on the stand. It was still hot and she couldn't believe someone had come in without her waking.

Half an hour later she was about to go down for breakfast when she heard a shout. Curious, she looked out of the window. Several men were gathered in the paddock, and her breath caught in her throat when she saw Alex vault over the fence and approach the most enormous horse she had ever seen. He was black as night, with a white star on his forehead, and he looked highly dangerous. Everyone else was keeping well out of the way.

Grabbing her coat, she ran down the stairs and out the door. 'What's going on?' she asked, skidding to a stop beside David.

It was Stan who answered, never taking his eyes off Alex and the horse. 'We haven't been able to break that beast, so Mr Glendale's going to see what he can do. We'll have to get rid of him if he can't be ridden, and that would be a great shame. He's a fine specimen.'

'They've managed to get a saddle on him,' David told her, shaking his head, 'and that was dangerous enough. That's one evil-minded horse, and I doubt if Alex will even be able to get near him, let alone mount up.'

'I wouldn't bet on that, sir. Mr Glendale's the finest horseman I've ever seen.'

'Shouldn't someone be out there with him?' she asked, frightened by what they'd told her. 'Alex could be injured – or even killed.'

'He knows what he's doing. Don't you worry, Miss.'

'This is my son, Reg, Miss Melrose. He's been working with the horse, but has had to give up.'

Reg bowed slightly, then moved towards the fence, murmuring, 'I hated giving in, but I don't think you're going to be able to intimidate the man in front of you, my beauty.'

Alex sidestepped as the animal lowered his head and charged. Then everything happened so quickly Gertrude had to grip David's arm tightly. Before the horse had turned to attack again, Alex was in the saddle. After trying every trick he knew and not being able to dislodge the man on his back, the horse stood still, not moving a muscle.

'Oh, he's decided to behave.' Gertrude breathed a sigh of relief.

'Don't you believe it,' Stan told her. 'He's just trying to make his rider believe he's won. Any minute now . . .'

Suddenly the horse went down and Alex jumped clear just as the animal rolled over, but was back in the saddle again before the animal was back on his feet.

'Did you see that?' Reg was grinning. 'Mr Glendale's got to teach me that. What you going to do now, you nasty tempered devil?' he called to the horse. 'That was your best trick. You can't get rid of him, can you?'

With fury emanating from him, the horse suddenly took off, hurdled the fence and disappeared into the distance.

'Damn!' Reg was cheering. 'He's got him, Dad. He's got the bugger!'

'Language,' his father scolded. 'There's a lady present.'

'Sorry, Miss. I forgot myself in the excitement.'

'I quite understand, but shouldn't someone go after them?' She was shaking with fright. The only horses she'd ever encountered had been fully trained and docile. She'd certainly never seen one that was still wild.

'We'll give him half an hour, but he could have gone in any direction.' Stan nodded at his son. 'Better saddle up our horses, just in case.'

'No need.' Reg pointed to a figure in the distance. 'I'll open the paddock gate and then he won't have to jump the fence.'

'Does the animal know that?' David asked, dryly.

'We'll soon see.'

They watched in silence as Alex and the horse came closer. They were still moving at a full gallop, but as they approached the fence the horse slowed to a canter, and after an obvious argument with his rider, trotted through the gate. Jumping down, Alex immediately removed the saddle, threw it across the fence, and then walked towards them.

'Well done, sir.' Reg shook his hand. 'What do you think? Will we be able to keep him?'

'Probably, but I'll leave him to think about things for a while, and I'll ride him again later in the day. We should be able to tell then if he's going to be any good, or not.' He took a blanket from Stan's hand, walked back and put it over the horse, patting him firmly and whispering something in his ear. The animal tried to bite him but he dodged, and then came back to them. He was brushing dust from his jacket and laughing. 'We're not friends yet. Now, if you will excuse me, I must change.'

'He isn't even out of breath.' David shook his head. 'Come on, Gertie, let's find Millie and have breakfast. I'm starving after all that excitement.'

He'd enjoyed that! Alex was elated as he took the stairs two at a time. It had been some time since he'd tussled with an animal like that. If he'd still been in the cavalry he would have taken the horse for himself. But he wasn't, and as much as he missed it, that part of his life was over. There were different challenges to face now.

Discouraged at one point, he'd made up his mind to dismiss all hope of winning Gertie, but then David had told him what the youngsters had written in the book they'd given her. The words had caught his attention and made him give serious thought to his hopes and dreams, and he'd decided not to give up. He'd made a mess of things from the start, and needed to embark on a different course of action. A stealthy approach was necessary – one the target was unaware of.

Once in his room he stripped off his dusty clothes and set about cleaning himself up.

Miriam was a sweet girl, but it had soon become apparent to both of them that they would not suit each other. She had readily agreed to continue the subterfuge, because she had good reasons of her own for allowing people to think they were about to become engaged. They were both in love with someone else, and believed this pretence would be an advantage to both of them.

Fully dressed again, he smiled with satisfaction. His campaign was moving along quite well, and Miriam was about to start hers.

The next few weeks should be interesting.

Chapter Thirty-Six

'Tell me all about it.' Florence patted the seat beside her. 'I know you've only just arrived back, but I can't wait to hear the news.'

Gertrude laughed and sat beside her mother. She'd only been away for three days, but the improvement in her mother was marked. She was moving easier, although she still needed to use the stick, but it was her speech where the improvement was most noticeable. The fumbling over words and hesitation had almost gone.

'We've had the most interesting time. The farm is very large, with plenty of room for a riding school well away from the warhorses.' She pulled a face. 'You should see them, Mother. Alex wouldn't let us anywhere near them.'

'I should think not, my dear. Now, what plans have been made for the riding school?'

'Well, there was this huge barn and it's going to be

turned into living quarters for the children. The manager's son has a wife and little girl, and they will run the school. The children from London won't be there all the time, of course, so it will be open to anyone who wants to learn to ride well. Their aim is to make it pay for itself in time.'

'Very sensible.' Florence smiled at her daughter's animated face. 'I can see you enjoyed yourself. Did you ride while you were there?'

'Yes.' She grimaced. 'And I'm still stiff. David can hardly walk, but he was riding quite expertly by the time we came home. He said Alex had told him we would have to ride the destriers, but he'd only been teasing. He had enough ordinary horses for us, although he rode one of the warhorses, of course.'

'Ah, well, I expect he's quite used to being in the saddle. Cavalry officers have to be expert horsemen.'

'Oh, he is.'

Something in the tone of her daughter's voice made Florence glance up quickly, speculation in her eyes, but she made no comment. 'I've kept you long enough, my dear, go and change while I order tea for us. Hanna should be here any moment, and you'll have to give her a full account of your visit to the farm.'

Standing on the dock, David watched the activity. Men were all over the ship, laughing and joking as they worked. This venture was already bringing happiness to quite a few.

'Mr Gardener!'

He looked in the direction of the call and saw Fred waving frantically. Waving back, he made his way on board. 'Hello, Fred, you're not needed already, surely?'

'I've come with Mr Green. He wants to see what's being done and find out when we might be able to start.' Fred stepped back to let a man pass with a load of rotting wood over his shoulder. He gazed around in wonder. 'We can't wait to get going. There's a lot to do.'

David pursed his lips, frowning. 'The poor old girl looks in an even worse state than last time I saw her – and it's only been three days.'

'Bound to, but once all the old stuff's been removed, and the builders start work, she'll soon show her real form.' Fred was nodding, sounding very grown-up and knowledgeable.

'The boy's right, Mr Gardener.' The foreman joined them. 'We're making good progress. The hull's been checked and it's in quite a decent state. She was well built.'

Someone yelled for the foreman. 'I'm coming! Excuse me, sir, glad to have you back. I'll give you a full report when we pack up this evening.'

They watched the foreman hurry off, and then Fred said, 'Millie told me about the farm. I'd have loved to see Sir ride that horse. She told me Miss was really worried in case he got hurt. When he rode it again she wouldn't go and watch, but Millie did, 'cos she missed the first time. She told me the bed was so soft she didn't want to get out of it. Miss had to practically drag her out, and when she heard about the horse, she was determined to watch when he rode it again.'

'He's a skilled horseman and didn't appear to be in any danger. The animal's all right now, and can be ridden.

They were all very pleased. It was a good job Alex was there, because they were afraid the horse wouldn't be any use as a cavalry mount.'

'Ah, well, stands to reason he'd be able to handle a bad-tempered animal.' Fred shoved his hands in his pockets, changing the subject abruptly. 'Is he really gonna marry that other girl?'

'That's the rumour.'

'Hmm, hope she don't stop him coming to see us. He's thought a lot of down Tanner Street.'

'I don't think he could be stopped doing what he wants to, Fred, not even by a wife. And I don't think you need worry. She's a very nice girl.'

'Nah, you're right. Will the riding school take long to get ready?' he asked, changing the subject again.

'Four or five months. Alex wants it in operation by summer, and work has already started.'

'David!' His father was on the dock. 'The *Falcon*'s coming in.'

'She's early! I've got to go, Fred.'

What a week! He'd been on the go from morning till night, and he felt more like sleeping than attending a dinner party. But he'd have a chance to see Miriam Chester again, so it would be worth it.

David studied his reflection in the mirror, and decided he looked presentable enough. The evening suit was new, fitting him well. It was the best one he'd ever bought, but with the money he was now earning, he felt he could afford it.

'Get a move on, son, or you'll be late, and that wouldn't do at all.' His father studied him 'Very elegant. The cab's here.'

'I'm on my way.' He hurried out to the waiting cab.

He arrived a few minutes before the other guests. There was no sign of Alex yet, and although David had seen very little of him during the week, he had assumed he would be here. But when dinner was announced it was obvious he wasn't coming, and David thought that was strange.

It was a pleasant meal, made all the more enjoyable because he was seated next to Miriam. As the evening progressed he knew his first reaction to meeting this lovely girl had been true. He'd loved her on sight, and the more time he spent with her, the more certain he was that the feeling wasn't going to change. How painful it would be to see her become Alex's wife.

'Miriam, why don't you show David the conservatory?' her father suggested. 'Our daughter is a wonder with plants, and has some beautiful specimens.'

'I'd like to see them.' He stood up and followed Miriam to the rear of the house. He stopped in amazement when she opened a door leading into an enormous glass room. It was filled with every kind of plant and the perfume was quite heady. As he gazed around he knew he didn't know the name of any of the plants. Ah, yes he did. 'Your orchids are lovely.'

'They're very showy, aren't they?' She ran a finger lightly over a delicate yellow bloom. 'I grow them for my mother, but I prefer the tiny violets. My father likes the ferns, he says it makes this place look like a jungle, and he keeps expecting a tiger to jump out at him instead of the family cat.' She laughed, a light musical sound that made him tingle. 'What are your favourites?'

'I don't know anything about plants,' he admitted.

'Ah, an honest man; I like that.'

'You'd soon find me out if I pretended to know what any of them are. Now, if you wanted to know about ships I could talk for hours on the subject.'

'Then we are even, for I know nothing about ships. Come with me.' She slipped her hand through his arm and guided him through the maze of plants. 'I'll show you a violet.'

They spent a lovely hour discussing, not only plants, but touching on many subjects. She was knowledgeable about politics, and he found it fascinating for a woman to be so informed on the subject. She was a quieter version of Gertie, and just as easy to talk to. He could see now why he was so attracted to her. Finally, he just had to say, 'Alex is a lucky man.'

'Is he? Why?' She picked up a can and began watering some of the plants.

'Because he's going to marry you.'

She looked up at him. 'But he isn't. We like each other, but we wouldn't suit.'

It took some moments to assimilate this information, and he wasn't at all sure he'd heard correctly. 'Would you repeat that, please?'

'I will not be marrying Alex. It would not have worked between us because both of us are set on someone else.'

The elation beginning to surge through him drained

away. 'Then they are very fortunate people. Who are they?'

'Ah, that's my secret.' A teasing smile hovered on her lips. 'And if you really want to know, you'll have to find out. It won't be any good asking Alex, as he won't talk either.'

'I see.' He propped himself up against a bench. 'Does this man you like have a title?'

'No.'

'Would your father allow you to marry someone who wasn't enormously rich?'

'I can't speak for my father. You'll have to ask him if you really want to know.' She slipped a hand through his arm again. 'It's time we returned to the others.'

Somehow he got through the evening, but his mind was in turmoil by the time he arrived back home. Miriam and Alex weren't planning to marry, so why was he still allowing everyone to believe they were? He'd been in a buoyant mood just lately, making plans, and appearing to be a man happy about his future. David had assumed, wrongly, that it was to be with Miriam Chester.

Then the reason for Alex's behaviour hit him. This was all about Gertie. Alex hadn't given up hope of winning her; he'd just changed tactics.

And what had Miriam meant with all those hints tonight? Why had she suggested he ask her father if he would allow her to marry someone who was not wealthy? Was it because she didn't want to answer the question, or was she hinting she would welcome his interest? No, it had been more than a hint. She could have been telling him to approach her father, but his mind was having difficulty believing such a thing could be possible. After all, they'd only met a few times. He shook his head. That was no argument; it had only taken one glance for him to fall in love with her, and he'd never been very good at hiding his feelings. Not like Alex. The man was a master of disinterest, when it suited him. If he really was still determined on Gertie, then he was doing a fine job of disguising his intent.

His thoughts were all over the place, and he needed to talk things through with Gertie. It might help to clear his mind, and she ought to be told what Miriam had said.

As he grabbed hold of his coat he caught sight of the clock on the mantelpiece. Not at one o'clock in the morning! He'd have to see her at a more respectable hour.

'You're up early, my dear.' Gertrude's father greeted her as she walked into the breakfast room. 'What are your plans for today?'

'I thought I'd visit the bookshop and see if I could find some suitable reading for May. I was wondering if Mrs James would allow me to teach her little girl to read. Do you think she would? I'm sure it would help with her speech.'

'That's a lovely idea, and no doubt Mrs James would be grateful.'

'I'll do that then.' She was pleased to have his approval. 'Mother's still asleep so I didn't wake her. Aunt Hanna's coming this morning to take her for morning tea and a gossip with friends.'

He nodded. 'I'm very relieved to see your mother out

and about again. Hanna's been marvellous, hasn't she?'

'I don't know what we'd have done without her.' She put scrambled egg, bacon and mushrooms on her plate, and then sat down.

Her father looked at her plate, amused. 'I see you're hungry.'

'Starving.'

Just then, David arrived. 'Good morning. I'm glad to see you're up already, Gertie.'

'My goodness!' Sutton exclaimed. 'You're early as well, David. Do you want breakfast?'

'Thanks, I haven't had time to eat this morning yet.' He filled a plate and sat next to Gertie.

'What's so urgent it couldn't wait?' Sutton had finished eating and was on his feet, ready to leave for work. 'Is it me or Gertie you want to talk to?'

'Gertie, and this is the only spare moment I've got in the day.'

'I'll leave you to it, then. I'm so short of carpenters now I'm putting my skills to work again after a long time.' He gave an almost boyish smile. 'I must say I'm enjoying myself.'

David watched him leave, and finished eating before saying what he'd come for. 'I wasn't sure I'd be able to get you on your own, but thought I'd have more chance at this time in the morning.'

'Has something happened?'

'You're not going to believe this. Alex and Miriam aren't going to marry!'

'You're right, I don't believe it.' She stared at him in

disbelief for a moment, then asked, 'Who told you that?'

'Miriam. She said they wouldn't suit, because they were both set on someone else.' He paused and took a deep breath. 'I swear those were her exact words.'

'Are you sure you hadn't had too much wine?' she joked.

'Only two glasses with dinner. I was quite sober.' He shot her an offended glance.

'All right, David. Did Miriam say who?'

'No, but Alex has been different just lately. He's been calling on you to help him. First with the dinner party, then with the riding school, and I believe he hasn't given up hope of winning you. He's changed his tactics by making you his friend – then he'll move in and conquer.'

'You make it sound like a military campaign,' she chided. 'I don't believe a word of it. You're so captivated by Miriam Chester that you're imagining all this.'

'You can scoff as much as you like, but I'm sure this is what he's doing. But you're right about my feelings for Miriam, and that's why I've come to see you. I can't think straight.' He then went into detail about what had happened the night before.

There was a tense silence when he'd finished, as she digested this information. He let her think about it for a while, then asked, 'What do you think?'

'I think the only way for you to find out if it's you she's interested in is to ask her if she'd like to go to the theatre, or for a meal at a good restaurant. If she refuses, then you'll know you were wrong.'

'You're right, of course. What are you going to do about Alex?'

'Absolutely nothing. If what you say is true, and I'm not sure it is, I'll let him continue his campaign, and see what happens. But I'm not getting my hopes up. I've had too many disappointments to cope with lately, and if I allow myself to believe he's still set on me, and then he marries someone else, it will tear me apart.'

For the rest of the day she kept to her plans, not daring to dwell too much on what David had told her. He could be mistaken. She knew he loved Miriam, and that might be clouding his judgement, but it was certainly an unexpected turn of events. However, she needed more proof before allowing herself to hope.

After finding suitable books, she went to see Mrs James, who was thrilled at the offer to help May with her reading and speech. She started immediately, and the little girl was an excellent pupil. They spent time on the alphabet, and then Gertrude read a story to her. By the time she was ready to leave, May was asking when she was going to come again. She left the books there and promised to come the next day at the same time.

It was late afternoon by the time she arrived home, and she was surprised to see her father there.

'Ah, good, you're home. Come and sit down with your mother and Hanna, my dear. I've got something to tell you.'

Wondering what this could be about, she settled next to her mother, praying it wasn't bad news. But her father didn't seem to be upset at all . . .

Her father removed some bulky papers from his inside pocket. 'I had a visit from Alex this morning, and he asked me if I would give him a shilling. It seemed a strange request, but I did so. Then he shook my hand saying it was a pleasure to do business with me, and he gave me these.'

Florence took the papers from her husband, gazed at them for a moment, then gasped, 'Oh, my goodness!'

'What is it?' Gertrude and Hanna spoke at the same time.

'I've just bought the house back from Alex for one shilling.'

Gertrude tipped her head back and laughed. She had been furious with him when he'd offered to give her the house if she married him, so he'd got around that. He'd sold it to her father for the paltry sum of one shilling. She hadn't believed David, but could he have been right?

Chapter Thirty-Seven

The boy's got some nerve, Alex thought, as he read the letter for the third time. He never invested in anything unless he could examine it carefully. His family had become wealthy by knowing what was a good investment and what was not. Instinct was telling him to walk away from this one. Edward Melrose was a gambler, and it wouldn't be wise to trust him, or his judgement of what was a good deal. Did he honestly believe he would take his word for it? How did he know he didn't want money to pay off more gambling debts? But there was also the fact that Melrose had distinguished himself in battle and been given the Victoria Cross. Perhaps he'd changed and now deserved to be given a chance?

Resting his head back and closing his eyes, Alex allowed his mind to go over every detail. Once the war with the Boers was over, it could be a fine place for Edward Melrose to settle. There was nothing here for him, for he doubted Sutton would ever acknowledge him as his son again. The suffering the boy had caused his family was too great.

On the deck of the troopship he had assured Edward he was looking after his family. A family he was hoping would be his quite soon. His campaign to win Gertie was going well. She no longer treated him with hostility, and had shown herself willing to help him out whenever he asked. She now laughed and joked with him. That was progress.

Opening his eyes again he stared into space, focussing his thoughts on the problem at hand. If this request had come from anyone but Gertie's brother he wouldn't even be considering it. He had quite enough to deal with at the moment, but the fact remained that he couldn't get involved in this unless he saw the property. There was no way he would ever buy anything unseen, but it was a long way away. That left him with two options – refuse to help, or go out there and have a look for himself. And he had to admit that the soldier in him would love to see what the situation was out there. If he'd still been in the army that's where he would be now, and he was still a soldier at heart.

Mind made up, he surged to his feet. He couldn't refuse to help Edward make a new life for himself.

'Hunt!' he yelled.

'Yes, sir.' The butler appeared immediately.

'Have the carriage made ready.'

'At once, sir.'

His first stop was David's office. 'Two of my ships are almost ready to sail again, aren't they?'

'One today, and the other in three days. The *Falcon*'s bound for Durban—'

'That's perfect.' Alex didn't give David a chance to finish what he was saying.

'When's she leaving?'

'Today. She's carrying supplies for the army.'

'Right, I'll be going with her.'

David gazed at Alex in astonishment. 'But she sails in two hours.'

'I'd better get a move on then. Look after everything here for me.'

'Tell me you haven't rejoined the army – please.'

'I haven't.'

'Thank God.' David closed his eyes in relief. 'Then what on earth's happened? Why are you doing this? It's dangerous out there.'

'I've been asked for help from someone I can't refuse. Keep an eye on the children.' He turned to leave, and then spun back. 'And if you encounter any problems with the *Ocean Sprite*, you have my permission to deal with them in any way you consider necessary. I don't want any delays on the renovation just because I won't be here. Oh, and if I should be delayed for any length of time, I've made provision for May's continued treatment.'

'Understood. Would you like me to tell the captain you'll be sailing with them?'

'Please. I'll be there as soon as I can.'

'Safe journey, Alex.'

He nodded and hurried away. There was a lot to do

if he was going to be on board before sailing time. Now his mind was made up, the prospect of the journey was exciting. He really needed to do something this crazy. In the army every day had been different, and he missed that kind of life.

David watched Alex stride out to the waiting carriage, jump in, and disappear up the road. He was stunned by this turn of events. What was Alex up to?

Millie came in carrying a cup of strong tea. 'I thought you might like this. Sir told me he's going away, but he didn't stop to tell me where.'

'South Africa.' He took the tea.

'Oh, that's bad. Has something happened to Miss's brother?'

David sat down suddenly, spilling tea in the saucer. 'I'm sure he would have told me if Edward was in trouble, so it can't be that. He said someone had asked him for help, and he couldn't refuse. It must be to do with the army, because I can't think of any other reason he would go there while a war is raging.'

'Oh, I do hope he isn't going to do anything dangerous! Did he say how long he'd be away?'

'Hard to tell, Millie, but I should think two or three months at least. It all depends on how long his business takes, where in the country he's going, and if he can get a ship back when he wants it.'

'We're gonna miss him,' she sighed.

He agreed. Alex had become a big part of their lives, and it would be strange not having him around. David stood up and grabbed his coat. 'I've got to see the captain and tell him he's going to have a passenger.'

The ship's captain took the news calmly. 'We've got an empty cabin he can use.'

While David was there he took the opportunity to discuss the values of various cargoes, and other business matters, then he left the ship.

It was less than an hour to sailing so he didn't leave the dock; he waited to make sure Alex boarded on time. He'd only just reached a small hut being used as an office when a carriage thundered up, and Alex leapt out with a kit bag thrown over his shoulder. He strode up the gangplank, and it was immediately pulled up and the ship began to move away from the dock.

Alex saw him give a brief wave, and disappeared.

'He made it on time then,' Millie said, when he reached the office again. 'I saw him go by.'

'Yes, he's on his way. Will you tell Johnny he won't see him for a while, and I'll have a word with Gertie right now.'

Gertrude was curled up in an armchair reading when he arrived, and fortunately alone.

'Hello David. I'm just preparing for my next lesson with May. She does seem to enjoy the lessons.'

'I'm pleased you're doing this for her, because I believe she's brighter than people think. All she needs is extra help.' He sat down and gave a weary sigh.

Her gaze fixed on her friend. 'What's the matter? Has Miriam refused to go out with you?'

'No, nothing like that. In fact we're having dinner

together tomorrow evening. Alex has just sailed on the *Falcon* bound for Durban.'

The book slipped out of her hand and thudded on the floor. 'Is Edward all right?'

'He would have told me if it concerned Edward, and if he had been injured, or anything, the army would deal with it. No, he just told me he'd been asked to do something, and he couldn't refuse. The army must have called on him, or else he wouldn't have gone out there.'

'Oh, dear, I don't like the sound of that.'

He leant forward, resting his hands on his knees. 'I'm dreadfully worried, Gertie. It was so sudden. He didn't have time to tell me much, and only got to the ship when she was about to pull up anchor.'

'I swear he's the most unpredictable man I've ever met.' She reached for the book on the floor, her hands trembling. 'It must have been very urgent for him to leave like that. It's bad enough worrying about the danger my wayward brother's in, and now we have someone else to worry about. Did he say how long he'll be away?'

Shrugging, David said, 'I've no idea, and neither does he. The *Falcon* will only be in Durban for a week, and if he's there longer than that, he'll have to find another way home.'

'I don't believe this!' She was looking annoyed now. 'What about the ship, the riding school and the children?'

'He's left me in charge, but I'll have to rely on you to visit the children and let me know if they need anything. I know he's been going down there at least once a week to see May and the others.'

'I'll do that, of course. We mustn't tell mother where he's gone, or she will immediately start fretting about Edward again, and we can't risk her having another seizure. All we need to say is that Alex has taken a voyage on one of his ships, picking up and selling cargoes.'

'Yes, that would be wise.'

'Oh, this isn't right.' She ran a hand through her hair. 'We should all have been there on the dock to wave him goodbye. Johnny will be very upset he wasn't able to do that.'

'We're all upset. It's going to be strange not having him around.'

'It is,' she agreed. 'He's left you with a lot of responsibility. I'll help all I can, and we'll also call on Millie and Fred. It will be up to all of us – his friends – to see everything goes smoothly while he's away.'

'Good idea.' David smiled for the first time. 'Tell you what, I'll call for you at around six o'clock this evening and we'll go to Tanner Street, explain what's happened, and enlist their help. If the children think they're doing something for him, it might stop them getting too upset.'

They all gathered in Millie's house. Children and parents were crammed in, sitting on the floor or standing. Many of the men were now working on the *Ocean Sprite* and had a lot of respect for Alex and David. Johnny's mouth trembled when he heard the news, but Gertrude put her arm around his thin shoulder, whispering in his ear that they were going to need his help. He brightened up straight away.

'What can I do?' he asked, eagerly.

'Well, I'm teaching May to read and improve her speech. What I'd like you to do is join in the lessons and encourage her to talk, so when Mr Glendale returns, he'll be able to see how much progress she's made. You know how concerned he is about her, so will you do that for him?'

He smiled round at everyone, then scrambled over to May, who was sitting on David's lap, as usual. 'I'm gonna help you talk, so Lord can see how clever you are.'

'Clever,' the little girl giggled.

'What can we do?' There was a chorus from the other children.

'Well,' May's father answered, 'the ship we're working on means a lot to him, and if we had more help we'd get it done faster.'

'It's too dangerous for the youngsters,' David pointed out quickly.

Mr James winked at him. 'We couldn't have them on board yet, but men have to leave their work to run errands, and collect drinks and food. If someone could do that for us now and again, it would be a big help.'

'We can do that,' they all agreed.

'Only after school and on Saturdays mind,' Mr James told them sternly.

David noted all the nodding heads and marvelled at the affection these people felt for Alex. All the children in the room were the ones who had followed them the first time they came here. There had been some hostility then, but there wasn't a sign of it now.

'Good.' David stood up and put May on the chair.

'Me help.'

He stooped down in front of her. 'Of course you can, sweetheart. If you can learn to read him a story from one of your books, he'd be so proud of you.'

'I do.' She beamed at Gertrude. 'She teach good.'

'You'll do it easily, May.' Gertrude gave the little girl a confident smile.

'I run too. Johnny show me.'

'And once the riding school's ready, we'll have you on a pony, as well.' David looked at everyone in the room. 'We must be on our way now.'

'Thank you for coming to talk to us,' Johnny's mother said as they were leaving. 'We'll all pray for his safety.'

Mr James caught them outside the door, frowning. 'From what you've said it sounds as if Mr Glendale's been roped in by the army for something. Let's hope it isn't too dangerous. You'll let us know if you have any news, won't you?'

'Of course.'

Gertrude slipped her hand through David's arm as they walked up the street, both silent, as they worried about the man who had become very dear to so many people.

Chapter Thirty-Eight

'Who the devil's that?' Jack punched Edward's arm and pointed to a man cantering into the camp. 'He isn't in uniform, but he looks like an officer.'

'Hmm, he's on his own so he probably thought it was safer—' Edward stopped in mid-sentence. 'It looks like . . . but it can't be!'

'Who can't it be?'

'The man I wrote to about the land.'

'Glendale? It might be, the commander's greeting him like a friend.' Jack studied the newcomer with renewed interest. 'Come on, let's get closer.'

Edward hung back, not able to believe Glendale had come all this way because he had written to him. There must be another reason. Or perhaps it wasn't him. The man dismounting was covered in dust and had several days' growth of beard. It was only his stature and demeanour that made him think it was Alexander Glendale.

'Why are you standing there, Ed?' Jack was urging him forward. 'Come on, I want to meet this man.'

Another frightening thought had come to Edward. If this was Glendale then perhaps he was bringing bad news about his family. He still thought of them as his family, even though he'd been disowned.

'Quick, before the commander whisks him away.'

As if sensing the scrutiny, the man turned and faced them. The breath caught in Edward's throat. 'Dear Lord, it is him!'

'You sure?'

'Positive, there's no mistaking those eyes. But what's he doing here?'

'He's going to help us buy that land, Ed. Why else would he be here?'

'There could be many reasons. He could have rejoined the army – or is bringing me news I don't want to hear.'

'We'll soon find out. He's coming over.' Jack was excited. 'It's been weeks, and I thought he'd ignored the letter. Impressive figure, isn't he, even under all that dirt.'

They waited while the tall, travel-stained man walked towards them. He didn't smile or shake hands.

'Edward, I want to see you and your friend when I've cleaned up and had something to eat. Two hours.' Then he turned and walked away.

Edward ran to catch him up. 'Please tell me how my mother is.'

'She's recovering. It's slow, but she's making steady progress.'

'Thank God! And my sister?'

Alex stopped walking. 'She is well, and so is your father.'

Now that he was close to Glendale he could see how weary he was. He must have ridden hard to get here. 'Thank you.'

Giving only a curt nod, Alex walked away.

'Oh, oh,' Jack grimaced. 'He don't look too friendly.'

'He isn't a friendly man, but he's the only person in London I thought might be interested in the deal.'

'Because he wants to marry your sister, and that makes him practically family?'

'I don't think there's much chance of that happening. For some strange reason, Gertie doesn't seem to like him. No, I wrote because he's the only man I know who's wealthy enough to consider buying land so far from home.' Edward sighed. 'And now we've got to wait two hours before finding out why he's here.'

'Let's go and have something to eat. He looks a typical officer, and I'd rather have a full stomach before meeting him.'

Food was the last thing Edward wanted. He wasn't sure the meal would stay down, but he did his best.

They'd only just finished eating when the sergeant found them. 'Major Glendale's waiting for you in the commander's quarters. You'd best hurry if you know what's good for you.'

'Yes, sergeant!'

As they hurried along, Jack showed the first signs of doubt. 'Damn, Ed, if he's back in the army we could be in trouble. Ordinary soldiers like us don't ask an officer for money.'

'What do you mean by ordinary?' Edward tried to joke and lighten the tension. 'You were wounded in battle, and I've earned a VC. Although I still can't understand why.'

'You saved my life, remember, and carried out other heroic deeds.'

'Heroic!' Edward snorted in disgust. 'I'm no hero, I just didn't care if I lived or died.'

'Keep on trying to convince yourself of that, my friend, but no one else believes it. You're entitled to respect, and this man knows it.'

'Let's hope you're right. Here we are – take a deep breath.'

They were marched in and stood to attention.

Alex glanced up, irritation showing on his strong features. 'For heaven's sake, sit down. I'm not in the army now.'

'Thanks, sir.' Jack nudged Edward, and winked. That answered one of their questions.

Once they were settled, Alex got straight to the point. 'Tell me about this property you want to buy.'

'We'd like to stay here when the fighting's over, and we believe we could make something of the place.' Edward then went on to describe the property, and explained that the owner wanted to go to London to live.

'There's grazing, and fields for crops,' Jack jumped in eagerly, 'and the soil's not bad. The owner, Mr Botha, showed us his records, and when the land is worked properly it makes a nice profit.'

'Any water?'

'Yes, sir, there's a well near the house, and a small lake about a mile further on. The place has been neglected lately, and the house needs a lot of work done on it. Mr

Botha just wants to get out, that's why he'd be willing to take a reasonable offer. He told us he wouldn't talk money with us because we were a couple of penniless soldiers, but when we told him about you, he said he'd discuss it with you, if you were interested.'

Alex nodded. 'Be mounted and ready to leave at eight in the morning, and don't wear uniforms, but come armed. I have permission for you to accompany me.'

'We'll be ready, and thank you.' Edward still couldn't believe Glendale was here, even though he was sitting opposite them, clean shaven now. 'I didn't expect you to take any notice of my letter, let alone come all this way.'

'I never buy anything unless I examine it first.' Alex eyed the men in front of him. 'You didn't think I would just send you money, did you?'

The implication of his words was clear, and Edward bristled. 'I don't gamble now.'

'That's right,' Jack told him. 'He won't even look at a pack of cards.'

'I'm relieved to hear it, but that isn't what I meant. I want to make sure it's a sound investment, and the only way I can do that is by seeing it for myself.'

'You'll like it, sir.'

'We'll see. Congratulations on your VC, Edward. Your mother's very proud of you, and it has helped a great deal with her recovery.'

'Without the mess I left them in she wouldn't have become ill.' His mouth was set in a grim line. 'I'm never going to be able to forgive myself for that. I've ruined three lives – four if I count my own.'

'Their situation is improving, and you are making an effort to pull your life together. Joining the army is turning out to be a wise move on your part.' Alex stood up. 'Now I must get some sleep. Write to your mother, Edward.'

He nodded.

'Thanks for helping us, sir,' Jack said.

'I haven't done anything yet. If I don't like the property I'll go straight back to London. It's too early to raise your hopes.'

'No sir, of course not.' Once outside, Jack grinned. 'I don't care what he says, there's no way he's made this journey if he doesn't intend to buy that land for us.'

'Don't be too sure. He's one of the wealthiest men in England, and he and his family didn't get that way by throwing money away on lost causes. He could take one look and just ride away.'

'Nah.' Jack shook his head. 'He's got a vulnerable spot, and that's your family. I saw it in his eyes when he talked about them. He won't walk away because it will make them happy to know you've made a future for yourself.'

'You're ever the optimist.' Edward laughed, relieved now the interview was over. 'We'll see tomorrow who's right.'

They were on their way by first light. Edward and Jack had told Alex where the farm was, but he took a detour.

'Er . . . where are we going, sir? The property's in that direction.' Jacked pointed to his right.

'I know, but we're going to do a bit of scouting for the commander first.'

'Told you he wasn't here just for us,' Edward muttered.

For the next two hours they followed Alex as he drew maps and made notes about a certain area. Fortunately they didn't run into any trouble, and Jack breathed a sigh of relief when the scouting mission was completed and they were heading for the farm.

'You sure he isn't back in the army, Ed?' Jack whispered. 'They were pretty accurate maps he's been drawing. Perhaps they're going to use him as a spy, and that's why he isn't in uniform.'

'I really don't know, and he certainly wouldn't tell us. Let's hope he isn't using the excuse to look at our land as a cover, and has no intention of buying it.'

'Oh, don't say that, Ed. I really want this place.'

'Me too.' They rode in silence for the rest of the way, both wondering what was going to happen.

Alex made no comment as they rode through the gate and up to the house.

The owner came out holding a rifle. 'Ah, it's you at last! I'd just about given up hope of seeing you again.'

'Sorry it's been so long, Mr Botha, but they moved us to another area for a while. We only returned to Ladysmith a week ago.' Edward dismounted. 'This is Major Glendale, and he'd like to inspect the property.'

'With your permission, of course, sir. And I'm no longer in the army. I don't use the rank.' Alex stepped forward and shook hands with the owner.

'Come into the house first. You must all be thirsty after your ride.'

After accepting a refreshing fruit drink made by the owner, they mounted up and all rode out to see the property. Edward and Jack were content to let Alex ask all the questions.

'He knows what he's talking about,' Jack remarked, approvingly. 'But for the life of me I can't tell if he likes the place or not.'

'Nor me, but from the thorough way he's going into everything, it looks as if he really is serious about it, and not just here to scout for the army. I hope he's impressed, because after seeing it again, I want it more than ever.'

'And me. We could make a good life here, Ed. Look at that glorious blue sky, and all this space. It's heaven compared to smoky London.'

The inspection over, they arrived back at the house and dismounted. Alex came over to them. 'Two things you need to consider before we go any further with this. You will encounter hostility if you settle here, even if the war's over. And this place is very isolated. Are you prepared to take the chance, work hard, and try your best to make this farm a viable proposition?'

'Yes, sir!' they said in unison.

He nodded to the two eager men. 'Stay here while I see what kind of a deal I can do with the owner.'

It was an anxious hour, and they rubbed down the horses, watered them, and did anything to pass the time, except talk. Eventually the door opened, and the two men came out, both smiling.

The owner turned to Alex and held out his hand. 'Thank you, Mr Glendale. I'll meet you a week from now.'

'I'll see you then.' He mounted, and without speaking to Edward and Jack, rode towards the gates.

'How did it go, sir?' Jack couldn't contain himself any longer.

'The property has potential, but you'll have to work damned hard to make it profitable. It's been sorely neglected.'

'We're not afraid of hard work, sir. Are we, Ed?'

'Does this mean you're going to help us buy it?' Edward was almost afraid to breathe, in case the hope flaring inside him was taken away.

'I've purchased the property on your behalf.'

Jack gave a yelp of delight.

'You won't be able to take over here until you've served your time with the army, and this war's over. I'm going to put a caretaker in to look after the place until then. Mr Botha knows of an elderly man who will be pleased to do that for us. Once you start working the property you'll have a year to make a profit before you need to start repaying me the purchase price. I won't charge you any interest, and as soon as you've paid half the amount, I'll deed the property over to the two of you.'

'How much did you get it for, sir?' Jack asked.

'The owner's so anxious to leave he didn't even try to negotiate a better price. I started low, and he accepted. That's all you need to know for the time being, but from what I've seen of the place you shouldn't have any difficulty paying off the loan. Once put into good, productive order, it will be worth twice the price I paid for it. I'll send you full details in writing on my return to London.'

Edward was stunned. 'That's a very generous offer. Are you prepared to wait that long for your money?'

'I'll lose nothing by waiting. It's a fine place. I've offered Mr Botha free passage to London on one of my ships, and he'll be able to bring all of his possessions with him. The *Falcon* will be returning for me in eight days. That should give us enough time to settle the caretaker in before we leave.'

'Oh, I'll bet he jumped at that offer, sir.' Jack smiled happily at his friend.

'He did. And now you two make sure you come out of this conflict alive.'

Chapter Thirty-Nine

The weather at the end of July was glorious; the sun was shining with the trees and flowers showing their full glory. It was three months since Alex had sailed away, and David was becoming more and more worried. Not knowing what was going on, or what Alex was doing in South Africa, was driving him to distraction.

'It's no use you going on like this,' Hanna told him over dinner. 'Alex is still a soldier at heart, and I've no doubt he'll want to see what's going on out there. When are you expecting the *Falcon* back?'

'Any time now. She should have been back two weeks ago, but something must have delayed her.'

'Perhaps she's been waiting for Alex. After all, he does own her and can order the captain to do anything he asks. He might be on her now.'

'Let's hope so. He should be here, not gallivanting

around the world. The *Ocean Sprite* is moving along faster than expected, and it's like pouring money down a well.'

Ah, that's what's worrying him, Gertrude recognised. 'What do the other partners think about it, David?'

He shrugged. 'They don't seem to mind.'

'Then you ought to stop worrying. Alex has put you in charge while he's away, and he's able to do that because he trusts your judgement.'

'I know, Gertie.' He gave a wry smile. 'It makes me nervous spending other people's money.'

'I would consider that a splendid thing to do,' Hanna joked, making them all laugh. 'You've all done a wonderful job, and I'm sure he'll be pleased. The difference in the ship is remarkable, and it's all due to you, David.'

'I've had lots of help, Hanna.'

'That's so,' Sutton agreed, 'but it's your expertise and management skills that have been the driving force. You should be proud of what you've achieved.'

The worry cleared from his face and he smiled. 'She does look good, doesn't she? I can't wait to see her under sail, but that's still a way off yet.'

'How is the riding school coming along?' Florence asked her daughter.

'We've received a message to say it is nearly ready, and the first children should be able to go there in August. I've already got a list of youngsters who have asked me if they can go, with May and Johnny at the top, of course.'

'And the older boys are already clamouring to sail on the *Ocean Sprite* as soon as she's ready.' David's eyes shone with amusement. 'There's a danger of fights breaking out, so I've told them Alex will decide who goes on the first voyage. His word is law, but everyone will be given a chance.'

Sutton laughed. 'You've dumped the responsibility on Alex.'

'Do you blame me?'

'I wonder if he's seen Edward while he's been out there,' Florence said, changing the subject.

'It's a big country, my dear,' Sutton pointed out gently. 'I wouldn't think it likely.'

'No, of course not.' She smiled at everyone around the table. 'I received a letter yesterday, and he's doing well in the army.'

Gertrude was pleased a letter had finally arrived. It made no mention of Alex, but she did wonder if they had met. She kept those thoughts to herself, though. Her mother was now well again, and the doctor had assured them that her recovery was quite remarkable.

'Have you asked Miriam to marry you yet, David?' Hanna asked bluntly.

He sat back, looking pleased with himself. 'As a matter of fact I have, and she's said yes. Her parents have given permission as long as we wait until next spring.'

'That's wonderful!' Gertrude was the first to congratulate her friend. 'And when were you going to tell us?'

'I was working up to it. I only asked her parents last night.' The evening turned into a celebration.

Gertrude was startled when the office door burst open and David hurtled past her, running full pelt.

'Oooh.' May watched the retreating figure of her favourite man. 'In a hurry.'

Millie tumbled out next, locking the door behind her. 'Hello, I'm glad you're here, Miss. You're just in time.'

'What's all the hurry, Millie? I'm taking May and Johnny to see the *Ocean Sprite,* and David never even stopped to say hello.'

'Someone's just brought news that the *Falcon*'s coming in.'

Jumping up and down with excitement, Johnny grabbed hold of Gertrude's sleeve. 'Can we go and see? Lord might be on it.'

'Which dock?' she asked. 'And would it be all right if we all come?'

'Course, they'll be quite a crowd. David's dad's gone to tell everyone working on the ship. If he's on board we want to give him a noisy welcome home.'

She picked up May. 'Follow me, I know where to go.'

Gertrude wasn't sure it was wise to spread the news, because there were going to be a lot of disappointed people if Alex wasn't on the *Falcon.* Including her.

The dock was already crowded with people, and the *Falcon* was moving into place by the time they arrived. It was chaos, with men running around and shouting at each other as they made the ship secure. David was right at the front, but they couldn't get near him through the milling crowd, and Gertrude felt it was safer to keep the children at the back. She held tightly to Johnny in case he tried to slip away. Millie was still holding May, so the little girl was safe.

She scanned the deck, trying to see any sign of Alex,

but with so much movement on board, it was hard to pick anyone out.

'Is he there?' Johnny was pulling on her restraining hands. 'I can't see!'

'I don't know . . .'

'There he is!' Millie yelled above the noise.

'Where? Where?'

'There, over to the right. He's home!' Millie was beside herself with excitement, and the little girl was copying her as she waved frantically.

'Oh, yes.' Gertrude's throat clogged with emotion. There was no mistaking the tall, dark-haired figure, leaning on the rail.

'I can't see! I'm too short. I wanna see him!' Johnny was doing his best to get away from her. 'We're too far back!'

She bent down and lifted the boy as high as she could. He was heavy, but she didn't mind. He was so desperate to see Alex, and she knew how much he'd waited for this day. It had seemed like a lifetime to the little boy.

'He's back!' May was still waving as hard as she could.

The workers from the *Ocean Sprite* were now streaming on to the dock, and Millie grinned. 'Look at Fred, he's got right up with David somehow. Sir's not gonna expect a welcome like this!'

It was another twenty minutes before anyone could disembark, and Alex was the first off. Everyone was waving, smiling and shouting, 'Welcome home, sir!'

Johnny fought to be put down, and Gertrude was unable to hold on to him any longer. He was off, dodging in and out of the crowd until he reached Alex. She saw him being swung up in the air, and the joy on his face brought tears to her eyes.

Millie was also moving forward with May, but Gertrude stayed where she was. She didn't want him to see the emotion and relief she felt at his return. It would take just a few moments to compose herself, she thought, dabbing her eyes with a handkerchief, then she'd go and greet him.

The crowd was clearing a little now, as everyone from the *Ocean Sprite* returned to their work. She could see as little May reached out and hugged him, then held her arms out to David. He laughingly took her from Millie. It was only then she realised there was someone else with him. He was a middle-aged man who was looking thoroughly bemused by all the excitement.

Alex began scanning the people and his gaze soon fixed on Gertrude. She smiled and waved, making no attempt to move towards him. He said something to the man with him, then to David. After putting Johnny down and talking to him for a few moments, he straightened up and strode towards her. She waited, loving the sight of him, and the easy way he moved.

'Welcome home, Alex,' she said as soon as he reached her. 'Everyone's so pleased to see you.'

'But are you pleased to see me, Gertie?'

'Pleased and relieved,' she admitted.

'In that case, you had better marry me.'

'Are you proposing?' She was so taken aback she wasn't sure she'd heard correctly. The unloading was under way, and it was still bedlam on the dock.

'Would you like me to go down on one knee?'

'No!' She caught hold of his hand when he looked as if he was going to do just that. They had far too many spectators.

Curling his long fingers around her hand, he said, 'Will you marry me, Gertie?'

'Yes!' Such a simple answer to a question she never thought he'd ask again. And that one little word was about to change her whole life. She thought she would burst with happiness.

'At last!' he laughed. 'Thank you, my darling. I'll speak to your parents this evening.'

'It will only be a formality. They'll be so happy.'

He held her briefly and kissed her cheek, sighing. 'That will have to do for the moment. I'm sorry to have to rush off, but there are things I must attend to. I'll call around seven, if that's convenient?'

'Perfect. Shall I tell my parents you will be joining us for dinner?'

'I would enjoy that, and there's much to discuss.'

All the others had joined them, and Alex turned to the man who had come with him. 'Mr Botha, I'd like you to meet my fiancée, Gertrude Melrose.'

After the introductions, Alex left at once with Mr Botha, and Gertrude faced her friends, who were grinning in delight. They pounced on her, wanting to hug and congratulate her.

'Isn't this exciting!' Millie exclaimed. 'Just wait till everyone hears the good news.'

'Don't say anything, please. Alex hasn't asked my

parents yet. It wouldn't be right for them to find out before this evening.'

'Of course,' Millie agreed. 'This must be done properly.'

They all went their separate ways then. Gertrude had promised the children a visit to the *Ocean Sprite,* so that's where they would go, even though her mind was in a whirl.

Johnny was bouncing along, as happy as he could be. 'May told Lord off for being away so long, and he promised not to do it again. He was surprised at how good she talks now, and we told him you'd been teaching her. He was ever so pleased.'

And she was ecstatic. Alex had walked off the ship and asked her to marry him. It was like a dream come true.

The welcome he had received on his return had been astonishing. After losing his family he'd felt like a piece of driftwood, floating around and alone, but now he had a larger family than he could ever have dreamt possible. He hadn't intended to ask Gertie to marry him just yet. He'd planned to do it later when all the excitement had died down, but he'd taken one look at her, and it had just seemed the right time. David had been right when he'd said she had changed. He had fallen in love with a bright, intelligent girl, but on the dock and smiling at him was a woman. The harsh struggles of the past months had made her stronger and more confident, and given her a greater understanding of the realities of life. There was so much they could accomplish together. He wanted her for his wife more than ever, and couldn't waste any more time. She'd accepted him with a simple yes, and that was the only word he'd wanted to hear. For the moment anyway. There were three more words he wanted her to say to him.

He'd been delighted to find out that David and Miriam also planned to marry. A lot had happened while he'd been away, and as Fred wisely said, things have a habit of working out for the best.

The trip to South Africa had been long and embarked upon with no more than a feeling that he needed to go. That was as close as he got to a reckless act, but it had been worth it. Edward and his friend now had the prospect of a decent future, and he was sure that would be welcomed by his family. Even Sutton, he suspected, would be relieved.

For the rest of the day, he moved from task to task. The business of the South African property was dealt with first, and Mr Botha delivered to his daughter's house. Then he went along to inspect the *Ocean Sprite* and talk to the men. The progress they had made was remarkable, and she was already beginning to show a glimpse of the majestic ship she used to be. He spent some time looking at the work going on, and praising the men, with a special word for Fred, who was working with enthusiasm, love and skill. Alex was very impressed.

After that he went to David's office, where there was work piled up for him to look through.

Before going to see Gertie's parents, he chose a ring from his mother's collection, deciding on one set with emeralds and diamonds. He was sure she would like that. It had been his mother's own engagement ring.

* * *

'What time did Alex say he'd be here?' Hanna asked her niece.

'Around seven.' Gertrude continued to fuss with the flower arrangement for the table. She couldn't say anything about the proposal until he'd spoken with her parents, but her aunt clearly suspected something was happening.

'Is David coming as well?'

'No, he's dining with the Chesters. Do you think the centre display is all right?'

'It's lovely, so do stop fiddling with it and tell me what's going on. You're far too nervous for this to be just a small dinner party.'

'I—' the sound of a carriage arriving outside put a stop to the conversation. Her aunt's continued questions were wearing her down. 'Ah, here he is.'

She rushed to greet him, and as he bent to kiss her cheek, she whispered, 'I haven't told them. Mother and Father are in the sitting room. I'll keep Aunt Hanna out here.'

'Suspicious, is she?'

'Very.'

'Then I'd better see your parents at once.' He turned and smiled. 'Hello Hanna, you look stunning, as usual.'

'And you're looking pleased with yourself.'

'I have a great deal to be happy about. Now, if you will excuse me, I have news for Gertie's parents.'

They watched him go into the sitting room and close the door firmly behind him.

'Hmm, I wonder what news that could be?'

Gertrude said nothing.

Half an hour later, Sutton called them into the sitting room. Her father was smiling broadly and her mother was dabbing at her tears.

'Well?' Hanna demanded.

'We have given our approval for Alex and Gertie to marry.'

'That's wonderful. And about time too! Congratulations.' Hanna nodded her approval.

Taking a small box from his pocket, Alex removed the ring and slipped it on Gertrude's finger. 'Ah, it fits perfectly.'

'It's beautiful.' She gazed at it for a few moments, and then smiled up at him. 'It reminds me of your eyes.'

'I'm flattered,' he laughed, slipping a hand around her shoulder and easing her closer.

'And we have more good news.' Florence's tears had dried now and she was quite composed again. 'Tell them, Alexander.'

He then told them the whole story about his visit to South Africa, and by the time he'd finished, Gertrude was stunned. He'd gone all that way to help her brother!

'You've given Edward hope for the future.' Her voice was husky with emotion. 'I do love you so much.'

At that moment the dinner gong sounded, and during the meal, Florence was intent on making plans for the wedding. 'You haven't given us a date yet.'

Before suggestions could be made, Alex said firmly, 'The second week in September. I'm going to take Gertie away somewhere special for a honeymoon. The riding school opens in August, and we must be here for that.'

'But that's less than two months away.' Florence was

horrified. 'We'll never be able to arrange it in time.'

'Yes we will.' Hanna declared. 'All we need to do is set our minds to it. Don't you agree, Gertie?'

'We'll do it easily, Mother, don't you worry.' She was in complete agreement with Alex. 'We don't want to wait any longer.'

'That's settled then.' Sutton raised his glass. 'The second week in September it is.'

They all drank to that.

'Oh dear,' Florence said, but still looked happy about the early wedding. 'Who will you ask to attend you, Gertrude?'

'I thought May, Johnny and Millie.'

Florence looked very doubtful. 'What do you think about that, Alexander?'

His mouth twitched. 'It should make for an interesting wedding. David will be my best man, so what about asking Miriam to be one of your attendants as well, darling?'

'That would be lovely. Do you think she would?'

'I'm sure she'd like that very much. That only leaves Fred. We must involve him as well, so he could help seat the guests in the church.'

'Good.' Hanna smiled encouragingly at Florence, who was still rather flustered. 'The arrangements are under way already. I told you there's nothing to worry about, Florence.'

After dinner, Alex and Gertrude left the family in deep discussion about the plans for the wedding, and slipped away for a quiet moment together. It was a beautiful evening as they wandered through the garden.

'Was going away part of your campaign?' she asked. 'Because it wasn't necessary. I knew I loved you before you left.'

'I did think it might help my cause if you missed me, but I also went to help your brother, and the soldier in me wanted to see what it was like out there.' He turned her to face him. 'But as soon as I saw you on the dock, I knew it was the right time to ask you to marry me.'

She slipped her arms around him and held tight, remembering Fred and Millie's words about holding on to your dreams. David's had come true; she didn't know what her brother wished for, but at least he now had a chance; and she knew Fred and Millie would keep their dream of living in the country alive.

And when Alex kissed her she knew they had been right, because dreams can come true.

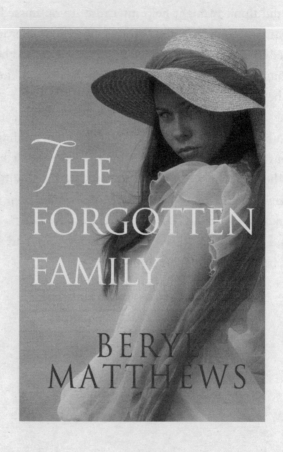

To discover more great books and to
place an order visit our website at
allisonandbusby.com

Don't forget to sign up to our free newsletter at
allisonandbusby.com/newsletter
for latest releases, events and exclusive offers

 Allison & Busby Books
 @AllisonandBusby

You can also call us on
020 7580 1080
for orders, queries
and reading recommendations

BB 6/15